C000136969

SKYTOWN

by Christine E. Ridgway

All rights reserved.
Copyright © 2017 by Christine E. Ridgway.

No part of this manuscript may be reproduced or transmitted in any form or by any means, electronic or mechanical, including photocopying, recording, or by any information storage and retrieval system, without permission in writing from the author.

ISBN 9780999430903
LCCN 2017914377

Printed by Village Books in Bellingham, WA.

v052918

For Mom and Dad

Grant and Joseph

And Loyal Friends

PROLOGUE

It was a deadly clash when the settlers moved to the South West deserts. The natives, tall athletic mice nicknamed 'Jumpers,' were feared by families moving in and settlers didn t want these savages on 'their' land. In turn, the Jumpers were being forced off their homelands they had lived on for hundreds of years. Tensions rose as the clashes became bloodier and more frequent. Finally, in the 1850 s there was an invasion of settlers that attacked a Jumper village. The bloodshed was terrible. When the smoke cleared the next morning, Jumpers who did not lie dead on the ground had vanished. Not a shadow of a Jumper has been seen since...

PART I
Attack of the Reptilian Rustlers

I

The sun had not risen fully over the hills where the Thorn Ranch was nestled, but the air was already warm, promising another hot day. The house looked quiet despite the activity inside. Alice Thorn was already up and bustling about to get breakfast ready for everyone while Buck Thorn was pulling on his boots to start the day.

Across a dusty stretch of barnyard from the house, coveys of California Quail were beginning to rise from their slumber. They shook out and fluffed up their feathers. Young ones tugged on the topknot feathers of the adults until they were rewarded with annoyed pecks on the head. Those who weren't already up and scratching testily at the ground immediately lifted their heads and stood listening to the swishing sound of someone coming down the hill from the ranch house.

A young mouse, Scott Thorn, emerged, detangling himself from the sagebrush that hooked his vest as he approached the covey's enclosed wire paddock. He swung a pail of alfalfa and grain mix for an early morning treat; he shook it as he neared the fence and stepped onto a low fence rung as the birds started to cluster excitedly.

"Whoa, hey settle down there's enough for everyone." Scott laughed, pushing away the beak of a curious youngster who tried to stick its whole head into the pail.

Scott stood up on the fence rung and started to toss several handfuls of the mix onto the ground where the quail began to scratch and peck excitedly. He twisted to throw some more to the quail on the right side when a feathery head ducked between the rungs and pushed against his stomach. Scott lost balance and wind-milled his arms before falling back and landing on his tail in the dust. There was a chorus of churring sounds from the quail as they seemed to laugh at Scott's stumble. The young mouse snorted and looked up to see his attacker before smirking.

"Cali, you great chicken!" He stood up and dusted off his pants as a feisty looking quail hen was leaning over the fence, a playful glint in her dark eyes. Scott stretched out a hand to ruffle her topknot feather, but she evaded his touch and stretched for the bucket of feed he was still holding.

Scott looked at the bucket then back at the quail with a smirk.

"Oh, so you want a treat? Then you shouldn't have pushed me down you big bully." He patted her beak and she snorted in his face. Scott coughed and wrinkled his nose.

"Nuh uh, not for you, not 'til you start acting nice." He teased and shook the bucket.

Cali fluffed out her feathers in mock annoyance then her eyes got a mischievous glint and she flicked her beak up and snatched Scott's hat off his head and dashed off further into the paddock followed by another chorus of churring from the other quail.

"Hey! Come back here!" Scott set the pail down and swung a leg over the fence but paused with a sigh and got down.

"Cali come on, be fair, you know I'm not allowed in the paddock!" he rapped his fist lightly on the fence post.

Cali ignored him, prancing around with the brim of his hat in her beak and swinging it from side to side playfully. She looked over to see he wasn't playing with her and narrowed her eyes. She tossed the hat up and caught it again, shaking it roughly.

"Cal'!" Scott groaned and stepped onto the low bar and leaned over the fence with an outstretched hand. "Give it here and I'll give you some mix you little rip."

Cali fluffed her neck feathers out extra poofy, almost comically as she slyly stalked back over with his hat.

"Good girl! Come on, bring it here!" Scott grinned and stretched further.

Cali's eyes were narrowed in play as she paused and barely extended her neck so Scott could barely touch the brim.

"Oh come on you... Haha! Got it!" Scott's fingers wrapped around the brim of the hat. At the same time Cali made a high pitch squeal of a chirp and pulled the hat sharply backwards, pulling Scott into the paddock head over tail and he landed on his side in the dust.

"Augh! Nice Cali... real mature." He snatched the hat away and hurried out between the bars of the wooden fence.

Cali snorted in disappointment and ambled up to the fence, tilting her head to the side.

"You know I'm not allowed to go in there, Cal, "Scott sighed, dusting himself off. "Pa'll take it out on my tail with a switch, you do know that."

Cali wasn't listening, having stuck her head through the middle of the fence, stretching to peck at the spilled remains of the pail of mix.

Scott smirked and knelt down, cupping some into his hands.

"But you don't care about that, do you?" he let her eat a generous helping of the treat, laughing slightly as she nibbled his fingers and sleeves for any that she might have missed. Scott ruffled her head then stood with the pail and cast the last of its contents over the fence before turning to head back up the hill towards the house.

The sun crested the hills and Scott squinted at the fierce red light, pulling down the brim of his hat to shade his eyes until he could turn away and face the house. He hurried up the steps and went inside in the middle of the early morning hustle and bustle.

Alice was setting toast out on the table and looked over her shoulder into the kitchen.

"Mitchell! Those griddlecakes are burning get the pan off that burner will you?"

Scott's older brother, Mitch, was passing by, buttoning his shirt and nodded, stepping inside the kitchen, flattening himself to the wall to avoid hitting Charlie who was helping Alice set butter and jam onto the table.

"This one's burnt to a crisp, Ma!" Mitch called over the clink of china being set out.

"Oh, great, just toss it out then, Mitchell."

"Unhand that flapjack! Burnt to a crisp is how I like them!" Came the voice of Bo, who was rapidly descending the stairs two at a time. The black-and-white ranch hand rushed up to Mitch and seized the blackened pancake.

"Good Lord, it's hot!" Bo juggled it from hand to hand as he dashed towards the table.

"Next time use a plate, Bo." Alice slapped his shoulder good naturedly. "Has anybody seen Sc—oh there you are dear, here, go set this coffee on the table –BO! Get your fingers out of there!" She rapped the tall mouse's shoulder with a wooden spoon as he stuck his finger into a hot pitcher of buttery syrup.

Scott took the pot of coffee and carried it over to the table where Charlie was setting out silverware. He bumped into the golden dormouse by accident and spilled some coffee onto his sleeve.

"Sorry, Charlie!" Scott's eyes were wide.

The dormouse flinched for a second but brushed a hand over his sleeve and slapped Scott's shoulder lightly to say no harm done. Charlie was a mouse of few words, he barely ever spoke at all, and since it never affected his duties as a ranch hand, no one thought too much of it.

Scott let out a breath of relief and set the coffee down before he turned around and bumped into Jared.

"Watch it!" the dark mouse snapped and shouldered past Scott roughly who stumbled back into Buck who caught him by the shoulders and steered him out of the way of the activity.

"Stop getting underfoot, Scott, go do something useful." He grunted.

"I was!" Scott said in exasperation as he squeezed out of the cramped kitchen and dining area and looked for something to do.

"Doesn't look like it." Jared snorted, helping himself to sitting down.

"Look who's talking, Jare-Bear." Bo cuffed the darker mouse's hat off backwards. "Get up and pull your weight."

"No, need." Mitch grunted as he staggered past Bo carrying a heavily laden platter of griddlecakes with one arm and a huge bowl of oatmeal with the other.

"Want to move it along, Bo, before we're standing in breakfast?"

"Whoops, sorry." Bo relieved Mitch of the bowl and set it down.

Buck pulled the chair back for Alice and let her sit while everyone else gathered around to start eating.

Bo hadn't even sat down all the way before he'd taken two bites of his blackened griddlecake, smothering the remnants with syrup, butter, jam, salt and pepper.

Mitch sat between Bo and Scott and raised one brow at Bo's concoction.

"That's... different." He said with a grin, searching for an appropriate word.

"That's revolting." Jared pinned his ears back.

"Can't say 'ick' 'till you've tried it Jare-Bear." Bo spoke around a mouthful of food and Alice cleared her throat.

"Don't talk with your mouth full." Buck Thorn muttered around a mouthful of pancake, which made Scott and Mitch both snort into their mugs as they took a drink of coffee.

Charlie said nothing as usual but gave a small eye-roll at Bo's antics and went on with spreading blackberry preserves across his toast.

"Scott." Buck grunted and Scott sat up a little straighter.

"Yes, sir?"

"You feed those quail in the barn-side paddock?"

"I gave them the morning mix but I'll throw some more grain out there after breakfast." Scott promised.

Buck grunted and Scott guessed that meant he was saying 'alright' so he returned to his toast and oatmeal.

"Eat something Mitchell, there's nothing on your plate." Alice said from across the table.

"I'm working on it, Ma." Mitch grinned and took some toast off the stack with a smirk to ease her mind. Mitch was watching his mother in concern. Alice had been getting thinner and more frail looking lately. He could hear her coughing down the hall at night from his and Scott's room. Glancing around he could tell everyone was a little nervous for her as well.

"Well, work faster before Bo starts eating off your plate too." Scott laughed as Bo swallowed and brushed crumbs from his whiskers.

"Cheeky kid." Bo grinned at Scott with amused gray eyes.

Scott liked Bo, he was easy to get along with.

"Seventeen, Bo, I'm hardly a kid." Scott sipped his coffee and started mixing blackberry jam into his oatmeal out of curiosity.

"I still got nine years on you, kid." Bo teased and downed his coffee in one go and set the mug back down on the table with a clunk.

"You're in a big hurry today Bo, plans for the day off?" Alice asked with a blink of pale blue eyes.

"Yes, ma'am, Charlie and I are heading into town. Gonna… visit with some old friends." He added with a glance to Scott.

Scott smirked into his mug. Bo wasn't only easy to get along with, but he was quite the lady's man and had many 'friends' in the nearby town of Redcliff.

"I'm coming too." Jared added sourly.

"If you must." Bo shrugged and started pouring himself some more coffee and dipping his toast into it experimentally.

"Oh, then could I ask you to pick up a few things while you're in town, Bo, dear?" Alice asked, perking her ears.

"Absolutely, ma'am, what did you need?" Bo asked, shaking the extra drops of coffee from his toast into his mug before taking a bite.

"Oh just some dry goods we're running low on, we also need, cream, two bolts of denim and… what else was it, dear?" she turned to Buck.

"Need a new axe." Buck scratched the scruffy beard of fur on his wide chin. "A pound of nails wouldn't do too bad either, you might need to take the wagon."

Bo looked only put out for a second, the wagon would take longer to get to Redcliff but he wanted to help out so he nodded as he dipped his toast into the coffee again.

"Sure thing, Mr. Buck, anything else?"

"We'll check the cellar after breakfast and write you up a list."

"Bo I could give you some money, could you pick up a new wing-strap harness for me? Cali found hers and must have played with it, it's pecked through." Mitch asked.

"Why not go with them and get it yourself." Buck grunted.

Mitch frowned. "I was just asking." He said in a lower tone, dropping his eyes to his coffee as he took a swig.

"Sure I can." Bo said, breaking the tension and knowing how much Mitch didn't like going into town.

"Can I come?" Scott asked hopefully.

"You've got work to do here." Buck grunted.

"But I…" Scott sighed. "Yes, sir."

"We'll bring you back something." Bo reached past Mitch and ruffled Scott's head fur.

Mitch raised his mug and drank around Bo's arm then stood up. "I'll help you guys hitch up the wagon." He offered as he bent to clear his place.

"Me too." Scott set down his empty mug.

"Dishes." Grunted Buck.

Scott sighed and turned to take Mitch's plate from him, but his brother smiled.

"I can clear and wash my own dishes; you just take care of yours."

Scott grinned and turned to take his dishes to the wash pump but Jared stacked a syrupy mess of plates on top of his and got up from the table and went outside letting the door creak shut.

Scott frowned at him and heard Bo mutter "jackass" under his breath.

Bo and Charlie were nice enough to clean their own dishes up as well, then Scott only had to clean his parents' plates plus Jared's and his own.

Bo knew Scott wanted to help so he took his time crossing the yard, much to Jared's annoyance, pausing here and there until Scott burst out of the door and raced down the porch with sleeves still rolled and wrists still soapy.

"Alright, let's get hitched up." Bo grinned and led the way to the barn.

2

"We'll just take the draft quail, Mitch, Cotton doesn't do well with the wagon reigns and besides, we can all fit in the wagon."

"Huh! That wagon driver bench only has room for two!" Jared pointed at the wagon in annoyance. "So who's gonna be bouncing around the wagon bed this whole trip? It's not gonna be me. You two ride the wagon I'm taking my own bird."

"Suit yourself, Jared." Bo rolled his eyes and turned to go fetch the wagon quail from the paddock.

Mitch took down the harnesses with Charlie and Scott and hitched the lines to the tongue while Bo brought the quail over.

Scott went to help Charlie calm one of the fussier birds when a call from outside made him turn.

"Scott! Come help me hang these linens." Alice's voice came from back near the house.

Scott sighed and Mitch shrugged apologetically.

"Go on, sorry, bud." He sighed and squashed his brother's hat down past his eyes.

Scott pushed his hat back up and headed out of the barn, running back up the hill to the house.

Alice was hanging sheets and clothes on the clothes line stretching from the porch to the scraggly dead Joshua tree a short distance away.

"Sorry, dear, I just need help get those pins down, and I… I feel a little dizzy." Alice seemed to stumble a little bit. Scott's eyes widened and he rushed over just as his mother's legs gave away and caught her before she hit the ground.

"Ma? Ma!? Are you ok?" Scott asked worriedly.

"I'm fine, Scott." She murmured but she felt so frail and weak in Scott's arms. He knelt in the course grass to let her rest back a little.

"Pa! Mitch! Someone!" He called out and waited nervously for someone to come. He heard feet thumping up the hill and sighed out in relief as Charlie showed up.

"Help me get her inside." Scott picked his mother up the best he could and carefully transferred her to Charlie, who was a lot broader in the shoulders and could carry her more easily. Charlie moved quickly and smoothly to carry Alice into the house, meeting Buck at the door.

Scott's father's eyes widened. "Alice? What's wrong, what happened?"

Scott stumbled up the steps behind them. "She called me over while she was hanging the wash. She just collapsed. Pa, what's wrong with her?" He asked worriedly.

Buck's eyes were dark with concern as he hurried over to where Charlie had helped settled her into her rocker.

"Maybe the heat." Buck thought aloud.

"It can't be, It's not even noon yet and the sun's not at its hottest." Scott twisted the brim of his hat in his hands.

"Well I don't know what it is!" Buck snapped in frustration but Scott knew he was just as worried as he was.

"She's ill, she needs a doctor. Scott, go tell Bo that we need the wagon, he and the others will have to make do with their mounts for now."

"Redcliff?" Scott asked.

"No, but Doc Evans referred us to a different doctor on our last visit in the next town over, Monty. If we leave now we'll get there by nightfall."

"Ok." Scott said and hurried out of the house to tell the others.

Within ten minutes the morning's plans had been changed. Buck was using the wagon to take Alice to Doc Evans and then on to Monty for help. Bo, Charlie and Jared were still going to Redcliff but would have to ride their own quail and disperse the food and goods amongst them to take back after the day off.

Scott was helping Mitch with some final hitching of the quail to the wagon. Scott went to adjust the breast collar where it seemed too tight and the quail started shuffling and tossing its head. Scott quickly jumped back in a panic and Mitch had to come over to calm the thrashing bird down before adjusting the strap.

"Don't be scared of them, Scott, they're just fussy today." Mitch said calmly.

"I guess." Scott brushed his hands off on his knees.

Buck Thorn peered around the corner with annoyance in his partially hooded eyes. He stalked over to Scott.

"I told you to stay away from the quail. Go do something useful and help your mother." He growled and Scott hung his head briefly before hurrying out of the barn leaving Buck and Mitch alone.

"You know the rule, he's not allowed around these birds."

"He wants to learn, if you would just teach him he wouldn't make any mistakes." Mitch folded his arms crossly.

"Don't sass me." Buck grunted at Mitch. "I make the rules around here. After that little stunt," he stepped closer and jabbed Mitch's chest with a finger. "With the Tennessee Red out here I don't want any more problems."

"That was an accident." Mitch rubbed where his father had jabbed him and with narrowed blue eyes added, "Scott's a hard worker; you don't even have to teach him yourself, I'll do it. And I'd bet a seasons wage that he'd work three times as hard as Jared."

"Enough!" Buck spread his arms wide in finality. "He's not allowed near the quail on THIS ranch and that's final! Don't you look at me that way Mitchell James Thorn, you may be willing to relive the havoc of that day but I am not!"

"You're not? Tell me what exactly happened to YOU that day!" Mitch flung his gloves into the side of the barn wall in frustration. "Nothing! You just watched an accident unfold." He pointed at himself angrily. "Bodies mend! Memories fade out, it's in the past! The only one still grudging about it is you!"

Buck Thorn seemed to swell in anger.

"If I had my hand on a switch-"

"You'd what?" Mitch said angrily and stalked out of the barn past him.

Buck whirled and grabbed his shoulder but Mitch shrugged it off roughly and continued back towards the house at a brisk pace.

"If I come back and he's roping and ridin' I'll tan both your hides!" Buck growled out from the barn entrance.

Mitch's tail flicked irritably but he didn't turn around as he crossed the porch and let the door close loudly behind him.

Scott was helping his mother pack a small basket for the trip when Mitch came into the house looking frustrated. He watched him take off his hat and run white-tipped fingers through his head fur before letting out a long sigh and coming into the room where Alice, although frail and tired was still trying to run everything from her rocker.

"Scott, dear, not the good blanket for travel, take the blue one, yes it has a hole in it. Oh Mitchell, good, there you are, is the wagon ready? Did you see the boys off? Oh, thank you, Scott, here set it next to the canteen. Did Bo get that list? I forgot to add flour!"

"Ma, it's alright, I told Bo to get flour before they left. He says he hopes you get well soon." Mitch smiled and rested a hand on her shoulder. "The wagon's ready, Pa's just bringing it around to the house."

"Oh he shouldn't fuss; I'm perfectly capable of walking." Alice said as she tried to stand and wavered unsteadily before Mitch quickly held her upright.

"I'm fine, I'm fine." Alice said rubbing her temple and pushing a strand of blonde hair from her eyes.

Mitch smiled gently at her stubbornness and looked over at Scott.

"Bring the basket and we'll meet you out front."

"Oh don't worry, Mitchell, I wanted to talk to you boys a moment." Alice patted her son's arm.

Scott shouldered the basket straps.

"What is it?" He asked as he adjusted the wicker pack.

"Well, we'll be gone a few days I should think, and in that time, Scott, I want you and your brother to get in some training."

Scott's eyes widened. "But, Pa said—"

"Never mind what Pa said, I'm saying this, Pa's got the past in his head but that doesn't mean Mitchell can't make a good rancher out of you, and given time Pa will see how wrong he's been and give you a fair shot. I know he knows you're a hard worker, you just have to show him he's got nothing to worry about."

"I… uh…" Scott wasn't sure who to listen to when his father said one thing and his mother said another. The decision was apparently made for him when Mitch grinned and shook his shoulder.

"Will do! When you come back Pa'll think we hired him a new hand!"

Alice smiled gratefully.

"Good," she sighed. "Now, you boys won't have much to eat while we're gone but you can manage, there's cornbread in a pan just resting in the cupboard and I have a whole crate of potatoes and carrots down in the cellar…"

"We'll be fine, Ma, you don't have to worry about us starving." Mitch said with a laugh as he guided her to the door as his ears picked up the sound of the wagon wheels creaking to a stop in front of the porch.

Scott settled the basket in the wagon bed and Mitch helped their mother up onto the long bench seat above the tongue.

"We should be back in two days, three tops if it takes any longer I'll send word back to Redcliff and someone can ride out and tell you." Buck said gruffly as he helped Alice onto the bench beside him.

"Mitch you're in charge while we're gone, remember what we talked about." Buck growled and a flicker of annoyance passed through Mitch's eyes and he flicked an ear, not responding.

"Listen to your brother, Scott, we'll be back soon." Alice smiled at her boys.

"Don't worry about a thing, Ma, just you concentrate on getting better, we'll be here for you with a decent spread when you come home." Mitch tipped his hat with a half-smile, though he was still worried for her.

Alice waved a farewell to her sons as Buck gave the reins to the quail a light snap and they started to trundle down the dirt path through the hills towards town. Scott and Mitch took off their hats and waved them until they were out of sight and sound.

Mitch's ears angled forward as he listened to the wheels getting further away until they were gone. He turned to Scott with a grin.

"Ready to learn some ropin'?"

"I dunno, Mitch." Scott worried the brim of his hat. "Pa said not to…"

"Well, Pa is as crabby as a skinny goshawk these days, besides, the workload's heavy and it would be great to have some hands out there actually doing something, and not just leaning against a fence like Jared, come on, it's not that hard once you know what to do." Mitch flicked him on the shoulder with his hat then headed towards the barn.

Scott gave a sigh but gave into his excited curiosity and followed his brother.

3

Several miles away the hills and scrub grew rougher with wild grass and Joshua trees and rock formations started to jut from the ground near a shallow canyon that bottomed out to a dry river bed. The canyon ledges were craggy but shaded from the harsh noon day sun. In one of the shadows a tall figure stood dark against the pale blue sky in the entrance of a fair sized cave.

Delgado was a very tall, slender lizard that was not common among the other desert reptiles. His scales were smooth, small and oddly enough black, blue and yellow. The native lizards were big, stocky and husky, with rough, pebbly skin in dusky tones of gray or brown. Five-lined skinks such as himself were not common in the desert area but Delgado served under the employment of none other than the great Gila monster, Sol Diablo himself.

Delgado's flame-orange eyes scanned the paper in his hand, a list of items Sol Diablo had sent him out to retrieve. The great Gila hardly ever left the safety of his quarters, a hidden mine set deep in the canyons beyond in the tower of a massive monument-like rock.

Delgado wasn't fond of being the Gila's errand boy but he would do what was necessary to earn his lodging and keep warm on the sometimes-chilly nights where thin-scales like him could be badly affected.

A groan of complaint from behind him caused the skink to turn his striped head slowly, his brow stripe set low in a permanent glare as he stowed the list in his vest and went to see what his companions were up to.

Three horned lizards were making a small cooking fire in the entrance to the cave, roasting several fat crickets they had caught the night before. Two of them were working hard, apparently trying to look very busy as Delgado passed them with hooded eyes and went to inspect the quail pulling their two-wheeled wagon.

Once his back was turned and he busied himself adjusting the lines he picked up the muttered conversations of the lizards by the fire. His eyes narrowed further as he eavesdropped.

"Huh, this gig is going downhill, boys, way down. Takin' orders from that skinny blue fella all day? What makes him so much better'n us? Nuthin'! Sol Diablo pays him more and I'll bet he does half the work that we do."

"Shhh! Not so loud, Larry!" A cautious sounding voice murmured.

"Yeah, Spike's right, you jus' got here, best just keep yer head down while you still got it on yer shoulders."

"You threatnin' me, Stubby?" Larry growled out resting a scaly hand on the pistol handle tucked into his holster.

"Stubs wasn' threatnin' you, Larry, he's warnin' you, so'm I, just keep yer voice down, Delgado's dang'rous."

"Huh." Larry snorted and prodded their small fire with a dry stick until the end caught fire. He raised it and extinguished the fire in his scaly fist with a hiss and a wisp of smoke. "Like he could do anythin' t'me."

"He'll shoot yer tail off'n beat you t'death with it." Stubs warned in a half whisper, glancing worriedly from Spike to the mouth of the cave where Delgado stood by the wagon.

"I'd like t'see him try!" Larry growled fiercely and snapped the stick in two.

Delgado narrowed his eyes, realizing Larry was no longer trying keeping his voice down, Larry wanted him to hear. He pulled the paper idly out of his vest pocket and leaned against the wagon, reading the already memorized list to pass the time before he heard what he was waiting for.

"Well I dunno 'bout you two ladies but I'm fed up with this working-for-Delgado crap. I'm endin' this now." Larry stood up and turned to face Delgado, his dark amber eyes narrowed. "Hey! Delgado!" he called into the cave, his voice amplifying slightly making the quail jump skittishly.

"Shut up, I'm reading." Delgado snapped the flopping paper stiff once more, his eyes unmoving as he stared into the list, one hand on his holster out of view of Larry's eyes.

"How 'bout you put down that paper and pull out yer guns like a real man." Larry snorted, putting a hand on his pistol handle.

"Put that thing away before you hurt yourself." Delgado muttered icily without looking up.

"Look at me!" Larry bellowed angrily. "I'm talkin' t'you, mister!"

"And I'm ignoring you." Delgado muttered through clenched teeth and moved his hand from his pistol to his knife hilt.

"You stinkin' blue bastard." Larry hissed in the back of his throat and pulled the pistol out of the holster, cocking it with a click as he raised it to fire.

Delgado moved like blue lightning almost the second the trigger was pulled. There was a bang! The wagon had a hole blown clean through the edge of the side board and Delgado was in the entrance to the cave. With one quick motion there was a flash of silvery steel in the air then a sickening thud.

"AUGH!" Larry dropped his pistol and staggered backwards, Delgado's knife was buried in the middle of the lizard's chest up to the hilt. He stumbled through the fire that Spike and Stubs had abandoned. They were now hiding behind a rock. Larry's mouth gaped wide in surprise as he fell backwards off the ledge and landing heavily about on a ledge far below.

Delgado strode from the cave, orange eyes narrowed as he stalked past Spike and Stubs cowering behind their rock with nervous eyes. Delgado leapt down the ledge, landing easily on his feet before crossing over to the dying horned lizard.

Larry looked shocked as blood was spreading dark and wet under his grubby green shirt. He looked up at the towering form of Delgado in terror.

"D-d-don't shoot me!" He begged.

Delgado stepped on his gut and reached down, gripping the knife handle.

"Scum like you ain't worth the wasted bullet." He wrenched the knife out and Larry shrieked his dying breath before shuddering and laying still.

Delgado wiped the blade clean on Larry's shirt then rolled the body with his foot until it fell off the ledge into the dry river bed at the bottom of the canyon with a nasty sounding crunch.

Sheathing his knife, Delgado turned and scaled the sheer wall easily like most light lizards do and pulled himself over the ledge where Stubs and Spike were nervously roasting their half-charred crickets, keeping their eyes down and swallowing a lot.

Delgado stooped and picked up Larry's cricket, dusting off some of the ash from it. He pulled out his pistol with a click and aimed it at the two remaining horned lizards who looked up in fright.

"Anyone else got something they want to get off their chests?" He asked flatly with a tone that suggested a threatening dare.

Both horned lizards shook their heads so rapidly they almost hit each other.

"No! No! No! Absolutely not! All fine here, sir!"

"Good, then pack up, we're moving out." Delgado bit the crispy cricket in half and wrinkled his nose in distaste before tossing the remainder over the cliff edge. He mounted his Gambles quail while Spike tied Larry's quail to the wagon. Stubs clambered onto his own bird bringing up the rear as they left their shady sanctuary and stepped into the hot sunlight on the west side of the canyon.

Delgado rode out ahead and looked about for the place he had scouted last month. A small quail ranch several miles outside Redcliff, it was about another ten miles but they could make it before sundown.

"Keep up!" he called over his shoulder and started them away from the dry canyon through the scrubby hills towards the flatter lands, and beyond that, Thorn Ranch.

4

Scott was sore and covered in dust from tip to tail as he followed Mitch back into the house. The sun sank low with the evening. Crickets were already chirping lazily around the paddocks and scrub, occasionally quieted with a crunch if they wandered too close to a curious quail.

Scott rubbed his rope-burned palms and shrugged to loosen his strained shoulders.

"Mind telling me what went wrong that last time?" he asked as he took off his hat and set it on the back of his chair before slumping into it and leaning against the table.

Mitch had a smile tugging the corner of his mouth as he tried not to laugh at the thought of Scott's comical attempts to throw a lasso.

"Uh, well…" He had to turn away to grin, taking off his hat and rubbing the back of his neck. "You swung the loop too hard, uh, and stepped out on the wrong foot and somehow managed to get the quail that was behind you… But I really think you're improving!"

Scott flicked an ear in static silence.

"You just make it look so easy." He sighed tiredly, brushing dust off his knees.

"Heh, that's because I have years of practice under my belt, but don't worry, bud. You'll get the hang of it after some more tries." Mitch assured him, ruffling the fur between his younger brother's ears and dodging a playful swat from Scott.

"Alright, I'll tell you what, we'll lay off roping for tomorrow, I'll teach you how to saddle up and ride a quail, how's that sound?" Mitch pulled out a chair and sat down.

Scott smirked and drummed his fingers on the table surface.

"Thanks, Mitch, heh, I hope I'm better at riding than roping."

Mitch leaned back in his chair and put his hat back on, pushing it down over his eyes.

"Ha, you and me both!" he teased.

Dinner was a simple affair. Cornbread, honey and some walnuts Mitch had found stashed in a cupboard. Mitch had made another small pot of coffee and was scraping the bottom of the green crockery jar for the last of the sugar.

"Sure hope Bo remembers the list, he tends to get scatterbrained when he stays the night in town." He headed back towards the table where Scott had opened up one of the books from the shelf nearby, a battered copy of adventurous tales from out West.

Mitch pulled out his chair and sat down.

"Whatcha reading?"

"The Battle of the Jumpers." Scott answered without looking up.

"Again? You must have read that one a hundred times over." Mitch swirled the coffee in his mug then took a swig.

"It's my favorite story!" Scott held his place with a finger and raised his head. "All those settlers coming together to protect their families from those killers. They must have been really brave." He turned the page. "Or really crazy." He added as an afterthought.

"Hmm." Mitch hummed into his mug. "Well, I don't know much about that, I doubt they were as savage as everyone makes them out to be."

"Have you ever seen a Jumper? Like while on a quail drive or something?" Scott asked, pointing to the sketch in the book of a tall and frightening looking creature with long teeth and claws.

Mitch glanced at the depiction and shook his head.

"No, I've never seen one but I hear stories about those who have, but a lot of it's probably whiskey talk around fires, mostly tall tales I guess."

"But… the battle isn't a tall tale is it? I mean, it really happened, right?" Scott asked, his ears perking in wonder.

"No, the battle really happened, but as for how it went down I think that book stretches the truth." Mitch leaned back in his chair and looked out the dark side room window to see the reflection of him and Scott at the table in the glow of the lantern. He was just settling back to rest his eyes when his ear twitched hearing a sound from outside. Mitch sat up abruptly, knocking his mug over and spilling the remnants of his coffee across the table.

Scott hurriedly picked the book off the table to avoid the coffee flood.

"What's wrong?" he asked in alarm as Mitch got to his feet.

"Shh." Mitch shushed him as his ears angled towards the front of the house where the sound was coming from outside across the yard.

Now Scott could hear it too, a startled flapping and pipping sound from the paddocks.

Mitch was already crossing the floor to the front door.

"Mitch, what's going on?" Scott stood up and took a step forward, blinking in surprise as Mitch took the rifle off its pegs from above the coat hooks on the wall and cocked it with a royal *chik-shik*!

"Something's spooking the covey, it might be owls, or it could be rustlers. I'll check it out."

"I'll come with you." Scott started forward, not liking the thought of his brother going out towards something dangerous alone but Mitch shook his head firmly.

"No, stay inside."

"But-"

"No, Scott, just stay here, I'll check it out, just stay inside." He opened the door and stepped out onto the porch.

Scott set the book on the table away from the coffee puddle distractedly and gripped the back of his chair firmly as he waited for Mitch to return. He hoped it was nothing.

5

Delgado slipped into the inky shadows that the moon cast from the barn into the caged paddock.

The quail were startled but couldn't see well in the dark. They bunched and chirped nervously. Several rowdy ones scratched the dry ground loudly and started to shuffle around with louder 'bawks?' of confusion.

Where the shadows were blackest beside the barn Delgado finally turned to address Spike and Stubs, who were each carrying a coil of rope and Spike, an unlit lantern.

"Alright, get that main gate open and get those birds up the hills towards the wagon. No funny business, no noise." Delgado ordered.

Stubs was chewing his scaly lower lip and fiddled with his rope. Delgado spotted the behavior and gave the nervous lizard an intense glare.

"You got a question?" He asked, narrowing his eyes.

Stubs gulped loudly and shook his head instinctively then paused and nodded rapidly.

"Well, spit it out." Delgado hissed in the back of his throat.

Stubs looked across the paddock and farmyard where there was a small but unmistakable light in the downstairs lower window.

"Uh, what about them? If they come out I mean."

Delgado followed his gaze dryly and straightened up.

"If there's a problem leave them to me." He answered promptly, fingering the handle of one of his guns. "If things get too out of hand we'll torch the place, that oughtta distract them. Your job is just to get the quail out of here. Is that clear?" He turned and fixed them both in a glare.

Spike nodded and started to shuffle back. "I'll go start herding them up and'll light the lantern when we're all ready." He said, raising the unlit instrument.

"Get to work." Delgado dismissed them and departed, pressing to the shadows he went towards the barn and pried open one of the large doors.

Inside the barn asleep in her stall, Cali rose her head from her wing and peered towards the entrance, an unknown figure stood in the dark doorway. She knew it wasn't her rider or the other ranchers. The hen started to raise her feathers in aggressiveness but didn't make a sound as the lizard started to go through the various crates and boxes looking for usable supplies.

Delgado stooped to pick up a grain sack and the sound of the grain rolling inside awoke the young quail in the stall next to Cali. The fledgling raised his beak over the top of the stall with a peep for food.

Cali snorted at the youngster for quiet the same time Delgado stiffened and drew his gun to point at the darkness. He holstered in once more seeing it was just more quail. Riding quail.

Delgado started to stride over towards them when a shout from outside made him turn around and head back to the door, drawing his gun once more.

Mitch was on the porch with the rifle pointed into the darkness.

"Alright, who's out there!" he demanded. His calm blue eyes were narrowed and defensive as he tried to pick shapes out in the darkness. He couldn't see into the paddocks near the barn but he knew something was amiss.

His ears perked and he couldn't hear the sounds of the startled quail anymore.

"Where's the…" he stopped and listened harder hearing hushed voices and muffled steps of quail. Rustlers were stealing their covey!

Gritting his teeth Mitch hurried off the porch towards the paddock. His eyes adjusted slightly and he could make out two burly looking horned lizards making off with the birds.

"Hey!" he snarled at them. "What do you think you're—" Mitch vaulted the paddock fence and at the same time Delgado emerged from the shadows like a phantom and punched him across the face, knocking Mitch to the ground.

Mitch lost grip of the gun when he hit the ground hard, stunned for several seconds before he looked up and realized he was in big trouble. The lizard before him towered above him at least twice his size, and he had a pistol pointed at him.

"Stay where you are." Delgado clicked the hammer back threateningly and bent to grab him but Mitch rolled and jumped for the cover of the water trough. A shot rang through the still night and Mitch scrambled behind the trough barely making it with a wince, clutching his shoulder. The bullet had grazed him and he could feel the blood welling up from under his torn sleeve.

In the house Scott heard the shot and flinched in surprise. His knuckles tightened their grip on the chair.

"Mitch?" he murmured worriedly, his eyes wide as he tensely headed towards the partially closed door.

Delgado swore and started to advance towards his unarmed adversary hiding behind the trough. Mitch could hear him coming and wriggled under the trough, pressing low to the damp earth and grass. As soon as Delgado passed his line of sight he could see the rifle on the ground, it was his only chance against the rustler. Mitch heard a crunch of boots on pebbles, the lizard was nearly upon him. He crawled rapidly out from under the trough and leapt for the gun.

Delgado leapt over the trough easily with his long legs and seized the back of the mouse's collar before his fingers touched the barrel.

"Auugh!" Mitch was momentarily choked as he was jerked backwards. The lizard had a hold of him and had picked him up off the ground by his collar, cutting off his air flow. He kicked as his boots dangled off the ground while he turned to see the face of his attacker. Gritting his teeth Mitch kicked out and struck the lizard's thigh. Delgado hissed and holstered his gun to grab the leg that kicked him. Holding Mitch by collar and leg he bodily threw the smaller creature as hard as he could into the side of the barn.

Mitch struck the side of the barn and slumped to the ground with various shovels, rakes and hoes falling onto him.

Delgado took out his weapon once more as he stalked forward where the mouse was trying to push the equipment off his legs. The mouse's startled blue eyes raised to the gun that was pointed at his face.

BAM! Ka-PING! Delgado fired and Mitch ducked behind the spade of a shovel with a flinch. Shakily he opened his eyes to see a sizable dent in the shovel but the bullet had not hit him. His ears were ringing from the shot and he tried to shuffle back as Delgado raised his gun again.

Scott heard the second shot and bolted onto the porch. He couldn't stay inside any longer, those shots didn't sound like long guns they sounded like side arms. His brother was in trouble.

"Mitch!?" he shouted out into the darkness, gripping the porch column tight as he tried to make out the paddock where the noise was coming from.

Delgado turned hearing the new voice, great, another witness to dispose of. He turned the gun away from Mitch and trained it on Scott who was standing on the porch, oblivious to the danger.

Mitch's eyes widened, this rustler was going to kill his little brother! Rage coursed through his veins like fire as he struggled to his feet. Gripping the bullet-dented shovel in both hands he swung it in a fast arch.

Delgado heard the shovels fall behind him and turned just as the lethal spade missed his neck and sliced through his cheek under his eye.

"AUGH!" The lizard cried out and stumbled back into the fence, gripping his gashed face with one hand and gripping the fence post with the other to keep from falling down.

Mitch ran forward with his shovel to hit the reptile again and looked over to see Scott standing rigid, not knowing what was going on and blind to the fight in the darkness.

"Scott! Get inside! Lock the door!" He shouted and raised the shovel to strike but Delgado had recovered and grabbed the shovel mid swing, wrenching it from the mouse's hands and throwing it to the side. His orange eyes blazed as blood from his face oozed down his neck, staining his collar.

Mitch started to back up, looking around desperately for something to use as a weapon, but his search was cut off with a savage kick to the ribs from Delgado that lifted him off his feet and sent him flying through the open barn doors to the ground. He gasped for air and tried to rise but Delgado was already upon him and grabbed him by the throat before flinging him into the tack wall shelves. With a crash he fell to the ground where all the tack supplies avalanched on top of him. Mitch didn't stir.

6

Scott heard the crashing and commotion near the barn. He knew Mitch was in trouble and he needed help! He started down the steps and froze, Mitch had told him to get inside and lock the door. His emotions battled inside him between his respect and obedience to his older brother and the urge to fight and help protect him. Mitch was trying to keep him from getting hurt, but what if he got hurt himself? What if he got killed?

Scott shook himself out of his mental state of option weighing, Mitch needed him and he was not going to hide while his brother was in danger. He flung himself off the porch and ran across the dark yard towards the barn side paddock. The noise had stopped. Where was Mitch?

Scott was almost to the fence when something grabbed him by the back of his vest.

"Ouch! Let go of me!" He thrashed and kicked out and tried to turn to hit his captor but a rough, scaly hand grabbed his neck and pulled him into a tight chokehold.

"Spike I got one!" Stubs shouted out for his companion as he tried to stop the mouse from squirming in his grip.

Scott was wriggling as hard as he could but the horned lizard was much too strong to break away from. He tried to bite the scaly arm, but flinched when he felt something cold forced under his chin. Stubs had taken out his gun and pushed the barrel into Scott's neck threateningly.

"Quit movin' or I'll blow your head off you lil' rat." The lizard snarled gruffly, tightening his grip around his prisoner.

Scott coughed, but stilled himself in fear, his eyes, however, scanned the dark paddock wildly for his brother.

"Where's my brother!" he gasped. "Mitch!" he tried to call but yelped as Stubs pushed the gun barrel into his throat more forcefully.

"Shut up!" he snapped.

In the barn, Delgado was breathing hard, his fists clenched as he glared at his handiwork. The mouse was half buried under a collapsed shelf of farm equipment and not moving. The quail in the stall nearby was snorting and shrieking at him, knocking against the stall walls trying to get out and get at him.

Delgado narrowed his eyes and started across the barn, opening the stall doors and shooing the chicks and fledglings out of the barn to be taken with the others, when he reached the stall of the fiery hen he had to step back hurriedly as she charged at the bolted door with fire in her eyes as she shrieked and clacked her beak, her feathers fluffed out in aggression.

Delgado was no fool, he knew letting this bird out was suicide. On the upside they could use the meat. He raised his gun and pointed it at the bird's head to put her down when light flooded the barn and he spun around with the gun pointed at the bearer.

Spike nearly dropped the lantern in fright.

"Don't shoot! It's me!" he squeaked and jumped behind the barn column. He peered out hearing Delgado's gun being slipped back into the leather holster of his belt. He gradually emerged and gave his report.

"I've been wavin' the lantern for several minutes, we're all ready out here, and Stubs caught a—great skies! What happened t'yer face?!" Spike's jaw dropped seeing the deep gash that was still welling blood on Delgado's left cheek.

"Never mind that! Give me that thing!" Delgado snarled at Spike and snatched the lantern away. His pent up rage at being sliced up and trying to block the pain had filled him with irrational anger, and right now he wanted to torch this place.

He headed to the side of the barn where the bedding straw for the quail stalls was stacked against the wall, dry and plentiful. He raised the lantern overhead and smashed it to pieces on the nearest bale. The dry grasses immediately went ablaze, crackling and growing as it crept and consumed the bedding then started to leap higher, lighting the sacks of dry millet feed and the ropes hanging from the straw laden hayloft. The barn was on fire.

Delgado stared at the destructive flames as the fire reflected in his orange gaze until he turned to Spike.

"Move out." He shooed the stout, horned lizard from the barn. Spike needed no second bidding as he hastily bustled out to the paddock. Delgado followed more slowly then turned to watch the fire as it began to spread to the rest of the barn. The quail was shrieking and trying to escape her stall and the mouse still wasn't stirring under the pile of shelf debris.

He gripped the two heavy barn doors and closed them hard and raised a big bolt across the two doors.

Scott swallowed with difficulty his throat being pressed with the gun. He saw another horned lizard appear from the paddock. He could hear Cali shrieking in the barn and smell smoke. Where was the smoke coming from? He tried to twist his head to see the barn and his eyes widened in shock before Stubs jerked him back into place. Scott had seen flashes of light between the cracks in the wall and the smoke billowing through the rafters and holes in the barn roof.

He jumped hearing the doors slam and he tensed in fear seeing a tall and bloody faced lizard emerging from the shadows, straightening his vest and glaring at Scott with burning orange eyes.

"What's this." Delgado snapped at Stubs.

"He was runnin' towards the paddock so I caught him. He's pretty young, reckon Sol Diablo could use him in the mines?" Stubs arched a scaly brow spine at his leader and forced Scott's face up for Delgado's inspection.

"Are there any others?" Delgado asked gruffly, undoing the bandana around his neck to stop the bleeding on his face.

Stubs shook his head.

"Ain't no one come out of the house after him."

Scott tried to look around the lizard, where was Mitch. Did they kill him? Had they captured him too?

"Where's my brother?" He gasped out at last, trying to control the trembling in his voice. He yelped as Stubs clouted his ear with the butt of his gun. Stars filled Scott's head as he tried to shake his head free. His eyes flitted nervously around the three lizards. What had happened to Mitch?

Delgado turned and looked over his shoulder at the barn, ablaze from the inside where the quail was still shrieking in terror.

"Put him in the wagon trunk. We got what we came for." Delgado ordered the others.

"What!? No! Where's Mitch!? Where's my brother! Let Cali out of the barn!" Scott thrashed in f Stub's grip as he was half-dragged and half-carried towards the hills.

"Mitchell! Mitch—AUGH!" Scott slumped against Stubs as the huge lizard pistol whipped his head with a swift blow.

Scott could barely struggle as he was dropped and latched into the wagon trunk like a sack of corn feed. He clutched his head feeling the sting and wetness of the blood. He pulled himself to the keyhole in fright as he felt the wagon start to move. Mitch was back there! And Cali! He had to help them!

"Mitchell! Mitch!" he shouted through the trunk as the roof to the barn caught fire as well, lighting the entire homestead in a destructive orange glow.

7

Cali tossed her head in panic, shrieking at the top of her lungs. She pushed at the stall door and pecked at the slide bolt trying to escape. Burning cinders of straw fell from the hayloft and rafters and singed her smoke stained feathers. She cried out and screeched more shrilly.

Under the collapsed shelf of tack Mitch stirred and pushed an old saddle off his back with a wince as he clutched his ribs and chest. The savage kick the lizard had dealt him had surely broken several ribs and badly bruised the rest of his torso. He groaned and coughed hard, flinching at how it affected him as he looked around trying to clear his head, stunned at the blurred flashing light and searing heat. He shook his head clear and coughed seeing the flames and smoke filling the barn. He heard Cali shrieking and his heart leapt into his throat remembering everything. The fight, the lizard… Scott! He gripped the wall and got to his feet, staggering over to his quail, coughing hard from the thick black smoke.

"Cal!" he croaked and felt into the stall for his panicked bird. He felt feathers and reached up, patting her shrieking beak as he undid the door clasp and lead her out of the stall. She panicked and tried to run and Mitch stumbled and fell to the ground clutching his middle. He was having so much trouble breathing and he was inhaling too much smoke.

Cali turned and rushed to her rider's side and nipped his ear. This was no time to sit! This was time to run! When her rider didn't stir she pecked his hat gently and shrieked.

Mitch flinched and reached up, grasping her halter, rising as she helped pull him up.

"Come on girl." He coughed and blinked teary smoke-filled eyes as he tried to lead his scared quail to the door. A flaming wall of bedding straw fell from the loft and blocked their path. Cali tossed her head and leapt back from the flames. Mitch blocked his face with his forearm as cinders and hot embers rained down on him. He coughed hard and looked around for the rake. He staggered to the wall and grabbed it from the hook before hastily forking the burning straw away from the door.

"C-*cough*- c'mon Cali!" he called to his bird but the hen was too distressed to move.

Mitch gritted his teeth and shed his vest, grabbing Cali's halter he covered her eyes with the vest and lead her across the flames to the door. He pushed at the wood then flinched and used his good shoulder. They didn't budge.

"No…" he croaked. The door was locked and the barn was falling apart. He squinted through the clouds of smoke and looked up. The loft window! That had to be the way out. Mitch left Cali blinded at the door with his vest as he stumbled towards the ladder leading to the loft. The ladder was on fire at the bottom already, he knew he had to hurry.

Not able to breathe, Mitch coughed and clutched at the wood, wincing at the strain from climbing. He was halfway up when the lower part of the ladder snapped and he was left swinging.

Gritting his teeth he managed to get a knee on the next rung and pull himself up into the loft. He brushed away some smoldering straw and crawled towards the loft window. It was closed, but he just had to lift the latch and push.

The loft door swung open and smoke billowed out as Mitch leaned out the entrance and gasped for air. The sooty smoke stained his face and turned his blue shirt to gray. He heard Cali shriek and he looked down, it was a long jump. He gritted his teeth and swung his legs over and dropped.

Hitting the ground almost made Mitch black out. The shock of pain to his ribs was immeasurable. He slumped onto the ground and coughed a hollow gasp like a fish on a river bank. He rolled stiffly, clutching his ribs until he caught sight of the blazing barn. He rolled to his knees and stumbled into a walk, pushing hard at the bolt until it fell to the ground. He dragged open one of the doors and put sooty fingers to his mouth, blowing a loud whistle to Cali.

The blinded quail was already at the door and Mitch pulled her through by her halter. She bolted out into the paddock, trying to shake the vest from her face. Mitch tried to run after her but couldn't make it. He stumbled to his knees and collapsed. He looked around for Scott through half-closed eyes. He couldn't see his brother; he couldn't hear anything, just the roar and crackle of the flames behind him and the shrill cry of his quail nearby. He pushed against the ground and tried to rise but his grazed shoulder gave out and he slumped to his side once more.

"Scott…" he croaked as the flames started to blur into lights and shadows. His head fell back and his eyes flickered. The last thing he saw before darkness clouded in was the west half of the barn collapsing, sending flames shooting towards the stars.

In the wagon being pulled through the hills, all Scott could see through the key hole were the towering flames and hear the screaming of Cali. He gritted his teeth as the wagon moved behind the hill and blocked the ghastly sight from view. He hung his head and slumped against the wall of the trunk. Burning tears stung his eyes as he cradled his head in his hands.

"Mitch." He choked out and folded his arms over his knees; resting his head on them as his shoulders shook, mourning for his brother.

Delgado glared over his shoulder as the distant flames with a bandana pressed to his bleeding face.

"Pick it up!" He snapped to Spike and Stubs as he spurred his quail ahead, leading them away into the darkness.

8

The next morning was warm as the sun turned the dark sky pale blue. Three figures on quailback were pushing their way through the hills on the old wagon rut trail.

"Whatever, Jared." Bo groaned, rolling his eyes as he flicked Cotton's reins, urging his scaled quail to ride ahead of his irritating companion.

"You don't believe me! I could so have taken on that letter licking pencil tail!" Jared snorted, trying to catch up to the black-and-white mouse.

"Dennis woulda creamed you, Jare-Bear. I've seen him take down rats bigger'n you so stow the gab. Come on, we should have been there by now."

Jared fumed and snorted his nose. "What idiot is burning brush this time of the year? They're gonna light this desert up like the Fourth of July!" he muttered, wanting to direct his crossness at something else since Bo kept brushing him off.

"Yeah, we've been smelling smoke for a while; reckon it's coming from the ranch?" Bo looked over at Charlie, who's ears were forward as he sniffed the air.

"Huh, probably Scott. Dumb kid, probably burned the barn do—" Jared dropped off in mid insult as they rounded the bend as saw the ranch in the distant. A column of dark smoke spiraled up from the charred wreckage of the barn.

"Dear God, I was right!" Jared's eyes were wide with a cocked brow of confusion.

Bo's gray eyes were huge. "Come on!" he urged them and spurred Cotton into a sprint as he left a trail of dust behind him.

Charlie skidded to a halt behind Bo in the main yard and quickly dismounted his bird, running after Bo to the collapsed, charred barn.

Bo stepped inside the smoky ruins and coughed as his steps sent up clouds of white ash.

"Where are Mitch and Scott?" he breathed searching the blackened debris.

"Damn! All the quail are gone! Rustlers! They made off with the whole lot!" Jared stormed into the barn and looked around with angry eyes.

"How are we supposed to earn money without those birds!"

Bo's eyes narrowed as he turned to the darker mouse.

"We've got bigger problems than missing birds right now! Go check the house for Mitch and Scott. We'll look around here."

Jared scowled, but turned and headed towards the house, grumbling under his breath about expenses and loss of pay.

Bo headed out the other side of the burnt out barn and slipped through a hole in the wall. He turned to Charlie with a worried face.

"Any sign of them?" he asked hopefully, but his silent friend shook his head and climbed out of the wreckage after him.

Outside they looked around when Charlie grabbed Bo's arm and pointed into the barn-side paddock where what looked like a pile of sooty, smoke-stained feathers were huddled on the ground.

"Hey, that can't be… that's Cali! Come on Charlie!" Bo ran down the slope and vaulted the fence with Charlie on his tail.

"Cali! Cali girl! You ok?" Bo clicked his tongue as he neared the ragged looking quail.

Cali raised her head sharply, her feathers bushed out defensively as the two ranch hands came nearer.

Bo stuttered to a halt and Charlie almost ran into him. Cali looked aggressive and scared.

"Easy, Cal, it's us, remember?" Bo put up his hands and walked slowly near the sooty hen.

Cali's dark eyes were narrowed into sharp points and one of her wings was lower than the other.

"She might have a broken wing… wait—" Bo spotted an arm sticking out from under her lowered wing.

"Charlie, Mitch is there!" he pointed and stepped closer to Cali, resting a hand on her head to calm her.

"Good girl, Cal, it's ok, good girl." He lifted her lowered wing and saw Mitch sprawled out flat on his back, smoke stained and covered in ash. His shoulder was red with dried blood and he was motionless, save for the rise and fall of his chest.

Charlie ushered Cali to her feet and led her a short ways away by the halter to let Bo get closer to Mitch.

"Mitch?? Mitchell? Come on, buddy wake up!" Bo snapped his finger in front of his friends face and patted his cheeks a few times with his hands.

Mitch's eyes flickered slightly and Bo leaned over.

"Mitch?? Can you see me? How many fingers am— "

Mitch's eyes snapped wide open see a blurry shape leaning over him he punched out and caught Bo in the nose knocking him backwards.

"OW! Sonaba—Mitch! You're okay!" Bo rubbed his nose and inspected his fingers. It was bleeding slightly but he was more concerned with Mitch. He came back and knelt next to him.

Mitch groaned and shaded his eyes from the sun with his hand to look up as who he'd hit.

"Ugh… Bo?"

"Come on, here, let's get you on your feet." Bo looped his hands under Mitch's arms and helped ease the half-dazed mouse to his feet. He swayed slightly and Charlie stretched out an arm to steady him.

"Thanks." Mitch said, wincing as he put a hand to his ribs.

"What happened?" Bo demanded and looked from the barn to Charlie and then to Mitch again.

"What… hap—?" Mitch looked behind him at the barn and blinked in shock at the black, smoking ruins. The night events came flooding back to him. The lizards, the fire…Scott!

"Where's Scott?" Mitch's eyes grew huge as he tried to pull himself out of Bo's supporting arms and nearly fell to the ground on unsteady legs.

"Scott? Isn't he in the house?" Bo asked in alarm. "Mitch what happened?"

"Rustlers—lizards! They got the quail. I told Scott to stay in the house!" Mitch stumbled over to Cali and used her as a crutch to get to the fence. He looked across the yard towards the house and shook his head.

"Is he in there?" he asked Bo with fearful eyes.

Bo looked to Charlie.

"Well, Jared's looking but, Mitch what's going on? What lizards?"

"Rustlers! They took the covey, I tried to stop them but…" he winced and grabbed his ribs and Bo hurried over to help him.

"You alright? You look a mess! What's this? Blood? Did you get shot?"

"Yeah," Mitch tried to shrug away from Bo's fussing and spotted a dark figure running down the slope towards them. For one hopeful second he thought it was Scott before his hopes deflated when he realized it was just Jared.

"Was Scott in there?" Bo asked as he came up on the other side of the fence.

"No." Jared snorted. "The house is empty. See you found Mitchy though, so what happened?"

"Rustlers, it seems." Bo waved his hand to brush away the information. "But Scott's missing, we need to find him, come on, we'll all check the house."

"Are you deaf? I already told you there's no one there." Jared rolled his eyes and shook his head.

Mitch glared at Jared. "Then we'll look again!" the injured mouse snapped. Mitch gingerly ducked under the bars of the fence.

"Stay there, Cali." He told his quail, who settled back to wait for them.

Mitch tried not to lean too heavily on Bo as they crested the hill and headed into the house. All four mice checked the house, attic to cellar and couldn't find a whisker of Mitch's younger brother.

"Mitch, did Scott try and help you fight the lizards?" Bo asked, running his fingers through his headfur anxiously. He liked Scott, he was a good kid. He hoped nothing bad had happened to him.

"No." Mitch groaned worriedly and slumped into a chair with a wince and shook his head.

"No, Scott was on the porch, I told him to get inside and bolt up but… then I got attacked and I don't remember what happened to him." Mitch cracked his knuckles tensely.

"We have to find him; maybe he's outside, hiding somewhere safe." He eased himself back up to his feet and headed towards the porch.

"Mitch you should rest, you're in bad shape, let us look and we'll come back, just sit on the porch." Bo encouraged.

Mitch shook his head. "I can't just sit around and do nothing, Bo." He narrowed his eyes at a snort from Jared but chose not to respond.

Mitch ended up searching around the woodpile and smokehouse with Charlie while Bo and Jared covered the rest of the immediate area.

"Mitch, he's gone, he's nowhere on the home site." Bo said as the two parties met up in front of the porch once more. The noon sun was hot and high in the sky, beating down on the four mice as they stood and waited in silence. The heat buzzed around them like cicadas when Mitch finally spoke.

"They must have him."

"Who?" Jared asked, crossing his arms.

"The rustlers, they must have taken Scott. They made off with the whole covey." Mitch turned around and tried to remember everything about last night. "They were heading that way, Northwest."

"You really think they took him?" Bo tilted his hat to see the place where Mitch was pointing.

"That just leads out to wild desert, they could be anywhere."

Mitch felt his gut clench in worry for his brother.

"We gotta go after him, Bo. Those lizards are killers. They tried to kill me so why would they need him alive? It can't be good."

"Hold on, 'we'"? Jared snorted in annoyance behind Bo and Mitch, making them turn.

"Last I checked, Scott was your problem, Mitchy. I got hired out here to ranch quail, not play wet-nurse to someone else's kid. If we're going after the covey then fine, that's where my paycheck comes from. But don't expect me to get shot at 'cause you couldn't protect your own kin from a few lizards."

"Jared!" Bo snapped angrily at the heartlessness of the dark mouse's outburst.

"How dare you!" Mitch's hands balled into fists as he glared at the ranch hand. "You care more about your money then my brother's life? I should dock your pay! You'll get waged in quail dung!"

"Last time I checked, Scott wasn't my brother and I work for your daddy, not you, Mitchy." Jared glared back haughtily. "So unless you make getting your dumb brother back worth my while, I don't see why it's any business of mine to help."

Charlie glared at Jared mutinously and Bo was stunned at the unmasked hostility and downright rudeness Jared was showing. Neither was expecting what happened next.

Mitch snapped and dove at Jared much to the dark mouse's surprise. He grabbed Jared around his neck as he knocked him backwards and somersaulted until he was on top, punching him in the eye.

"Ow! You dirty-!" Jared punched Mitch in the bad shoulder and rolled him to the ground but Mitch kicked Jared in the gut and sent him flying backwards.

Bo and Charlie rushed to help pull the two angry mice apart, but they had already clashed together again, each wrestling the other to the ground and rolling around trying to hurt the other as much as he could.

"Charlie come on we gotta help him!" Bo leapt aside as the fight past them so he wouldn't catch a stray fist to the middle.

Charlie shot him a confused look as if to say: Which one?

Mitch leaned back and threw his whole body into a blow that knocked Jared backwards through the porch railings with a crash. Jared yelped and clutched his nose, which was bleeding like a faucet.

Mitch stood panting hard, bleeding from his lower lip, part of his smoke-stained shirt was torn but he had won this round.

"Listen up you yellow streaked shrew. I don't care if you come with us or not. All I know is if you don't, get off my family's ranch now, because a job isn't welcome to the likes of you."

Jared groaned and glared at Mitch as he rubbed his broken nose.

Bo looked from Jared to Mitch. Both had gotten in some good blows, and Mitch was already hurt. He watched Mitch start to falter and stepped up in time to give him an arm to lean on.

"You can't chase after lizards in the desert! You're falling apart where you stand!" Jared snorted blood at Mitch as he winced and held his ribs.

"He's right," Bo said sternly and turned to Mitch.

"Mitch, I know you're worried about Scott, but you're hurt bad, you need a doctor."

"I'm fine." Mitch said stubbornly. "We're wasting time; we've got to go after them while the trail is fresh."

"We can't go anywhere with you, Mitch, your saddle and tack was in that blaze." Bo gestured to the charred remains of the barn. "Doctor or not we need to get you to Redcliff, there's tack and trail supplies there and we can look to see if your lizard rustlers have a wanted poster in the post office. It might give us a clue where they are going."

Mitch frowned in annoyance. He wanted to go right now, find his brother and get him safe. Bo's words made sense though, he needed tack and supplies, the household wares the others had brought back for Alice wouldn't do them much good on the trail.

"Fine." He sighed after a while. "Let's go now."

"Go change into something not smoky and covered in blood. We'll fetch Cali and meet you out here." Bo said and patted Mitch's good shoulder.

Mitch nodded and went inside. Jared got up and stalked away from the others in a huff.

"Where you going?" Bo asked, folding his arms.

"Where else, to get my damn quail ready to go on this wild goose chase." Jared growled back.

Bo smirked. "Awe, Jare-Bear. You do care after all." He turned away from Jared as the darker mouse made a rude gesture at him and looked to Charlie.

"Can you go fetch Cali? I'll bring the other supplies inside for Alice. There's rope in my saddle bag and the new wing harness strap should be next to it. I'll meet you out there."

Charlie tipped his hat and went to fetch Mitch's quail while Bo went inside the house once more.

Mitch was coming down the stairs buttoning a fresh shirt, he crossed to the table where Scott's book s lay next to the puddle of coffee that Bo was mopping up.

"Leave them a note for your folks in case they get back before us." Bo said as Mitch picked up his hat and donned it.

"Right…" Mitch looked around for a scrap of paper. He found one and left a note for his parents:

Dear Ma and Pa,

There was an accident with some rustlers. They got the covey, no worries, Bo and the boys are with me getting them back. We hope we are back before you. If not we headed Northwest.

— Mitch

Mitch didn't add that the rustlers had Scott, he didn't want to put his mother through any more worry than necessary.

Half an hour later, the ranch hands were headed to Redcliff in the opposite direction the rustlers went. The trail was long and quiet. Mitch rode Cali bareback with her wing strap harness. His eyes were downcast as he tried to quell the miserable feeling of guilt and worry in his chest. Scott was gone, and it was his fault.

9

Scott wasn't even aware that he had fallen asleep until he found himself waking up stiffly. The trunk was cramped and dark but at least the wagon wasn't moving anymore. Outside he could hear the sound of running water and the churrs of the stolen quail splashing and bathing in the water.

Scott sat up groggily and hit his head on the trunk with a soft thud. He winced and squinted through the keyhole.

He could smell the smoke from a nearby cooking fire and guessed they must have stopped earlier to rest the quail and make some food. A rumble in his stomach made him realize he was hungry too. This was hardly the time or place for him to be thinking about food. He ached all over and still felt miserable.

Scott felt around inside the dark box for anything useful and his hand bumped something spongy. He picked it up and gave it a tentative sniff. Stale cornbread, it would have to do for now. If he was going to get away from these reptiles, he was going to need his strength.

He ate the stale biscuit, choking down each dry swallow and set the rest aside, peering out the keyhole.

The lizards were preoccupied with the fire. He narrowed his eyes, those lizards killed his brother; they killed Cali too and destroyed their barn and possibly the whole ranch. He wished that he had a gun.

Scott put his hand on the trunk lid and tried to push it open, but it wouldn't budge. He rubbed his wrists and figured the latch must be locked on the outside. He rested with his back against the side of the trunk and tried to think of a way to escape. He could try to fight them off when they opened the door, right? No, they were too strong, and why would they even open the door?

He sighed and scrapped the plan, massaging his temple. He was trying to formulate another plan when a noise outside caught his attention. Scott shuffled over to the keyhole to check it out.

Delgado rose abruptly from where he had been wetting his bandana in the water to use for his gashed face. His orange eyes narrowed across the wide but relatively shallow stream where Spike and Stubs had gone to round up some stray quail. Suddenly he heard a loud yelp then a fierce rustling sound in the scrubby brush followed by a cry from Stubs.

"JUMPEEEEEEEEEERRR!"

There was a crash as three creatures fell from the top of a brush covered boulder into the shallows, wrestling and grappling like mad. Two of them were the large horned lizards, Spike and Stubs, but the third was a tall, tawny-colored mouse with powerful hind legs and a long tufted tail.

Delgado whipped his gun out of his holster and straightened as the fight rolled into the deeper water in the middle of the stream. The Jumper was every bit as tall as Delgado and Scott knew they were formidable fighters. This one was young, but he was fighting like mad trying to escape the lizard's claws.

In the deeper water the Jumper whirled and kicked out catching Stubs in the jaw with a loud cracking sound followed by a howl of pain from the lizard.

Scott couldn't see the fight from the direction the keyhole was facing, but he could see Delgado rush back to the camp fire and seize a coil of rope from the back of the wagon.

Scott swallowed sharply. Jumpers?? As if being kidnapped by lizards weren't bad enough! He remembered the horrible illustration of the bloodthirsty Jumpers in the book at home and his heart pounded in his throat yet he strained to see the fight through the tiny opening.

The Jumper thrashed away from Spike and ran sluggishly through the waist deep water to the other shore in line with the sights of the keyhole. Scott watched in nervous fascination as the Jumper shook out a sodden head of wild, tufty fur and tried to run along the shore on long, strong legs but Delgado barred the path with rope in one hand and gun in the other. The Jumper skidded to a halt in the pebbles.

"Stop where you are, Jumper!" Delgado hissed threateningly but shockingly the Jumper seized a fist sized rock from the ground and flung it at Delgado with surprising strength. Delgado sped to the side out of line of fire and the stone smashed into the trunk of the wagon, knocking Scott on his tail on the inside as he'd been pressed against the keyhole.

Scott gritted his teeth and massaged his eye, but scrambled to the keyhole once more using his other eye to watch the fight.

Delgado fired a gun at the Jumper's feet and the tall creature stumbled in alarm, dancing out of reach then was tackled around the middle from behind by Spike. The lizard thrashed out of the water and brought him to the ground with a crash.

The Jumper wriggled and seized another rock, smashing it into the knuckles of the lizard that held him captive. Spike yelped and let go but as the Jumper made to leap away he flung out his other hand, raking his claws down the creature's back until they snagged on rough looking brown clothing it was wearing and flung him into the bank wall out of sight of the keyhole.

Scott strained his eyes and twisted as much as he could, trying to watch. He saw Delgado throw the coil of rope to Spike and pick up another coil and throw it to Stubs as the growling and moaning lizard emerged from the shallows.

The Jumper was cornered against the bank wall in the shade of the clay and rock overhang. Delgado nodded slowly, orange eye burning. "Rope him up! He's got nowhere to g—" his words were cut off as the Jumper gave a massive spring, sailing over his head and back into the line of sight of the keyhole and camp fire.

Before Delgado could draw his gun the Jumper had seized the skillet from the fire and flung it hard, catching Stubs on his head spikes and snapping the tip of one off. The lizard howled with pain and clutched his head as the Jumper seized the end of a burning bit of firewood in one fist and a large rock in the other. He threw the rock at Delgado and missed then charged Spike with the burning branch.

Scott's eye widened, would the Jumper beat all three of them? He pressed so close to the wood he got splinters in his nose.

The Jumper was mere steps from striking Spike with the burning wood when a lasso was thrown and cinched around his waist causing him to stumble short and drop the wood as he flung his hands out to catch himself from falling to the pebbly shore. The Jumper grabbed the rope around his waist and bared his teeth at its wielder, Stubs had cast the lasso and was holding the rope tight, glaring at the tall mouse with smoldering eyes.

The Jumper rushed towards the lizard to free himself when a second rope was cast and caught him around the neck and under an arm, stopping him short once more.

Scott watched in shock as the Jumper wrapped his arms around the ropes on either side and pulled with incredible strength, almost jerking the two lizards off their feet. Scott suddenly found himself willing the Jumper's escape, but his hope faltered when a third lasso thrown from behind caught the Jumper around his neck and pulled tight, cutting off his air.

The Jumper gagged and tried to turn and loosen the rope around his neck for some slack to breathe, the other lizards used the opportunity to pull their ropes tight in opposite directions until the Jumper couldn't pull in any direction. The Jumper was gasping for air and coughing as Delgado held the final rope and pulled slowly tighter.

"No, no come on…" Scott murmured as the Jumper fell to his knees and pulled vainly at the noose around his neck. He started to slump to the side, gasping like a hooked fish. Delgado tied the rope to the saddle horn of one of the hitched riding quail and strode forward towards the defeated critter.

Scott watched, straining his ears as the blue-tailed lizard pulled out his knife. Bile rose in Scott's throat. Was he going to kill him!? The young mouse couldn't tear his eyes away. He watched as Delgado brought the flat of the blade under the Jumper's chin and forced his face up to look at him, as the soaked creature's chest heaved for air cut off by the noose. The swooshing noise of the river water and the rustling of the quail barred Scott's ears from picking up the lizard's low soft voice, but he gathered he must be asking a question because he straightened impatiently and asked again. Scott could see the Jumper's face as it glared defiantly up at the lizard with fierce, brown, wild eyes.

Delgado raised the knife and flipped it in his hand so the hilt was down then brought it crashing down across the Jumper's head, making Scott flinch as he witnessed it. The Jumper keeled over on the pebbles out cold.

The skink glared at his newest captive and turned to Spike and Stubs as he sheathed his knife.

"Tie him up and lash him to the back of the wagon. He won't fit with the rest of the supplies in the bed, but he's got legs, when he comes to he can walk. Bind his hands and arms good." He turned and headed back to the fire, stooping to pick up the skillet that had been chucked and filled it with stream water before dousing the cooking fire with a smoky hiss.

Scott swallowed and watched Stubs and Spike roughly tie up their prize, Scott held his breath as they neared the back of the wagon to tie the ropes. When they had finished, Stub's eye caught his through the keyhole.

"What're you lookin' at, boy!" he smashed a broad scaly hand into the trunk knocking Scott flat on the inside. Scott pressed into a back corner until they left. He could hear them packing and mounting their birds. The wagon shifted as Stubs took his seat on the bench and flicked the reins.

The wagon started to move and Scott edged forward watching the Jumper being dragged across the rocks.

"Hey… hey! Get up!" he called in a whisper to the still form. Scott thumped his fist against the side of the trunk trying to wake the Jumper and a loud thud on the trunk lid from Stubs' nubby tail made him jump in fright.

"Shut up back there or'll rope you up 'n drag you too!" Stubs snarled.

Scott swallowed and watched as the unconscious Jumper was dragged over rocks and clay, sand and brush. He pinned his ears flat to his head. Would the Jumper wake up and start walking? Or would Scott be the witness of watching him slowly dragged to death across the blazing desert?

The sun beat down on the trunk as It grew hotter with the day; it was stuffy and humid inside and Scott pressed close to the keyhole for air and tried not to doze off from the terrible heat that muddled his head. He was so thirsty; he watched the winding stream disappear behind the rocks as they set out to cross the open hills and flatlands, dragging their catch behind them.

"C'mon, get up…" Scott sluggishly mumbled as he wiped the sweat beading on his brow as he slumped against the wall. "Get up…"

10

Redcliff wasn't a big town, but it always had critters coming and going from all over the area and that morning was no exception as Bo led Mitch and the others down its main street. The day was bright and sunny with only a few clouds, everyone seemed so cheery, smiling and waving as they passed.

Mitch's eyes tried not to wander, his stomach was in knots and it hurt to breathe. Guilt, worry, and physical pain was making him look grim faced and unfriendly.

Bo steered towards a vacant hitching post and dismounted as the others tied up the quail without saying much. Since Cali was already makeshift tied to Cotton, Mitch didn't bother hitching her as he stepped onto the covered porch out of the harsh sun. He squinted up at the battered sign that hung above the door reading "Redcliff Post."

"We'll load up on trail supplies and meet you in the General Store." Bo said and flicked Mitch's shoulder with his hat. "You remember the face of the guy you're looking for?" he asked as he re-donned his hat and looked around at some of the pictures of the various felons posted on the post office window.

"Yeah, how could I not?" Mitch arched a brow and stepped inside the post office to cut the conversation short.

Bo watched him go with a sigh then turned to the others. "Alright, let's go get us some trail chow and gear." He clapped his gloved hands together.

Inside the post office Mitch adjusted his eyes to the dimmer light. The building was not very big, shelves of mail and stacks of parcel wrappings and twine spindles lined the rows of cases behind the rough cut wooden desk at the front.

"Hello?" Mitch looked around at the seemingly empty building. He checked over his shoulder to the door but there was no sign that said they were not open. He rested his hand on the wooden desk and let his eyes wander through the various posters that lined the corkboard on the wall. Most of these faces were rodents, he was looking for reptilian.

The sound of slithering scales in the back made Mitch turn sharply. He narrowed his eye into the back of the shelves. "Hello?" he reached into the umbrella stand near the door and slowly drew out a solidly made cane. "Who's back there?"

The slithering sound continued and Mitch knew only reptiles could make such a cold sounding movement, and not just any reptile, a snake.

Mitch edged behind the desk and started to head along the shelves toward the back where the noise was coming from, the cane raised at the ready. He rounded the corner and jumped as he nearly ran into the snake, which was carrying a stack of letters in his mouth and dropped them with a gasp of surprise seeing Mitch.

"What do you think you're doing back here!" The small grass snake demanded, stretching himself up until he swayed at eye-level with the mouse. "Only postal officials are allowed back here! Get back behind that desk at once you little snip! And put that cane up! My father's tongue! You nearly gave me a heart attack!"

Mitch sighed out in relief and hastily complied, heading back and around the desk. "I'm sorry, Lawrence, I forgot you lived here, I haven't been in Redcliff for so long... wait, you work at the Post

Office now?" Mitch asked as he put the cane back into the umbrella stand.

"Of course I work here, someone has to keep Dennis and Davey in check, the lazy—" The snake muttered under his breath as he coiled up on top of the desk. "What were you snooping around the shelves with that cane for?" the snake's cool gray eyes narrowed slightly in mild annoyance.

"I thought you were someone else, a lizard." Mitch stood behind the desk. He had no reason to be afraid of Lawrence. The grass snake was only as big around as a fence post and he wasn't a threat to mice. Though he did have a barbed tongue at times and was never short on opinion.

"Phaw! A lizard! Nasty legged vermin! At least this lot is." Lawrence tapped a stack of upturned papers on the desk with his tail tip. "These arrived on the noon coach, and not a decent scale on the hides of the lot of 'em. Murderers, thieves, assassins and vagabonds."

"Could I leaf through those?" Mitch asked eagerly, pointing to the paper stack.

"Suit yourself, they're an eyesore." Lawrence pushed the stack to the table edge. "What on earth do you know of lizards anyway, Mitchell, that's not a lot your family would get on with."

"You're right, it's not. Lizards came to the ranch last night; they burned our barn to the ground and made off with our California Covey."

"Mercy! Your family is alright I hope?" Lawrence's tongue flickered out in anticipation. He was a good friend of Mrs. Alice and hated to think she was in danger.

"Ma and Pa weren't there; they were heading to Monty yesterday afternoon. It was just Scott and me…" Mitch trailed off as he leafed through the papers, setting aside various depictions of collared lizards and whiptails. They were not what he was looking for.

"Your brother? Is he here with you? I haven't seen that boy in months! Are you both alright?"

"No…" Mitch sighed feeling a sick emptiness in his gut. "Lawrence, Scott was kidnapped, that's why I'm here." He raised worried blue eyes to the snake's startled face.

"What?!" Lawrence looked beside himself with shock. "You've got to tell the sheriff! Great scales! This is terrible! Who did it? I have half a mind to bite those dirty shrub-squatters!"

Mitch patted the snake's scales reassuringly, not used to the smooth and somewhat cold texture. "Don't worry Lawrence, I'm going after him. I'll get him back."

"By yourself? Don't be silly and you look like you've been injured." The snake's tongue flickered, his eyes stared pointedly at Mitch's shoulder, which was crudely bandaged with torn linens under his clean shirt.

Mitch raised a brow. "How do you know that?" he asked as his eyes returned to the posters in his hands.

"I'm a snake, Mitchell, we can taste the scents of the air and feel the heat sources in a room, your bruises are giving off heat and I can smell the blood on your shoulder. I'm no fool, you're hurt and you need Doc Evans."

"No," Mitch said as he reached the last poster and his eyes widened in familiarity. "It's him!" he slapped the paper on the table and Lawrence twisted his head to read it upside down.

"Delgado? A tall fellow was he? I've never seen markings like those before on a lizard."

"The colors are strange too, Lawrence, that skink was blue and yellow striped."

"You're pulling my tail, a blue lizard? Come now, Mitchell, be serious."

"I am! I know it sounds odd, but he's blue, at least his tail is, he's the one who burned down our barn, he's the one that did this to me… he's the one who has Scott. I don't need a doctor, Lawrence, I need a saddle." Mitch folded the poster in half. "Can I take this?"

"I don't suppose there's any way I can talk you out of this?" Lawrence shook his head slowly and slithered off the table with a soft thud to the floor, coiling beside Mitch.

"No, I have to get Scott back. But could you do me a favor?" Mitch asked as he stashed the paper inside his vest.

"Of course, like what?" Lawrence stretched up to eye level once more.

"If you see my folks come back through this way, tell my Pa what happened and that I'm trying to get him back." He sighed and looked away.

"Will do, but come now, let's report this to the sheriff before you leave."

"Before who leaves?" a voice from the narrow staircase to the side asked as a dusky colored mouse stepped down off the stairs and grinned broadly seeing Mitch.

"Mitchell Thorn! Hell's bells! Look who's in Redcliff! It's been months!" the broad shouldered mouse hurried over and seized Mitch in great hug, thumping him on the back. Mitch grimaced in pain from the embrace and tried to step back from the larger mouse.

"Ow! Hey, Dennis." He gasped and was relieved when Lawrence pushed his scaly face into Dennis's chest and made him release.

"You're hurting him you great lard!" Lawrence snapped and Dennis looked in bewilderment as Mitch gingerly rubbed his ribs.

"It's alright Lawrence. It's good to see you Dennis." Mitch winced as he straightened up.

"Hurt ya? Sorry about that, didn't know. What are you hurtin' from? Quail throw you into a fence again?" Dennis asked perking a torn ear.

"No, try a lizard threw me into a wall, our ranch got raided last night. They stole our covey and kidnapped my brother."

"Little Scott? What for?" Dennis looked appalled.

"The same reason rustlers do anything, because they're rotten in the head and dark in the heart." Lawrence hissed and coiled in annoyance.

"Well if I didn't know any better, Lawrence, I'd say you weren't fond of them." Dennis cocked his head at his companion and Lawrence shot him a peeved look. Dennis looked back to Mitch. "Does Davey know you're here?"

"No, no I was just leaving, I was looking for one of you so I could look through your wanted posters, but Lawrence helped me. I have to go get a saddle and some tack, mine burned when they destroyed the barn and the hands and I need to get after that lot while their trail is still fresh."

"Well Davey should be at the store now, the rest of the family alright?" Dennis asked as the three started out the door into the bright sunlight.

"My folks are in Monty, and Bo, Charlie and Jared were here last night." Mitch said as he crossed the street towards the General Store."

"I know they were, Jared tried to pick a fight with me last night, Bo smartly talked him out of it, the cheeky fuzz ball. Sorta disappointed me, that saddle buffer could use a good belt to the mouth."

Lawrence slithered behind them and up the steps to the store where the door was propped open with a broken brick of clay in hopes of welcoming the nonexistent breeze into the building.

Mitch's ears perked as he heard Bo's voice talking animatedly behind a shelf of dry goods. Turning the corner with Dennis and Lawrence he saw Bo and Charlie talking to a young mouse built very much like Dennis with broad shoulders, but he was completely white and his eyes were almost completely red but they did not make his appearance any less friendly. The white mouse turned and saw the others and smiled.

"You alright, Mitchell? Bo's just told me about your brother, any idea where they were headed?"

"No idea, Davey, but they stole the covey and those birds don't exactly tread light, they'll leave us a good trail to follow if we hurry." Mitch answered and turned to Bo who was holding several brown packages under his arm.

"I got the supplies Mitch, all you need is a saddle and some riding gear, there's one in the back, but it may be a little pricey." Bo cautioned.

"If it's a saddle I'll take it, I've got a littlesaved up." Mitch headed towards the back and spotted the saddle resting over a sawhorse. It was made from dark leather and looked more expensive than his previous one; Mitch knew he also needed to buy saddle bags, a saddle blanket, and a bridle. He wasn't sure how far his savings would stretch.

He rested a hand on the saddle as he tried to estimate how much it would cost when a deep voice startled him.

"Never expected to see you back here."

Mitch turned and saw the burly form of Mr. Brown, a large-built reddish-furred mouse with his sleeves rolled up showing beefy forearms. His girth could be seen on either side of his white clerk's apron tied in a small bow behind him. His whiskers were fashioned into a short but bushy mustache, which he twitched as he looked down at him.

"Mr. Brown, sir." Mitch took off his hat respectfully. "Yes, it has been a while." He felt his insides squirming, this man was one of the main reasons he had been avoiding Redcliff.

"Almost a year it would seem." Mr. Brown said gruffly and patted the saddle without moving his eyes from Mitch's face. "What's your business this side of town?"

"I need a new saddle, sir, my brother… was kidnapped. The boys and I are going after them. Er, could I get a price on that one?" he asked touching the dark saddle that Mr. Brown was leaning against.

"Hmm, I see, someone you love, taken away, but this time, you're going after them." Mr. Brown seemed to ignore the question of the price and Mitch winced at his words.

"Please, sir, you must understand, it's not like that…" he tried to explain.

"Not like what, I suppose my daughter never meant that much to you otherwise you'd have gone after her as well." Mr. Brown's eye bore into him and Mitch's ears flattened, feeling old wounds start to reopen at the mention of Mr. Brown's daughter.

"I…" Mitch backed up a little but his legs felt like stone. He didn't know what to say, his heart started to pound and more guilt made his chest tighten. Luckily, Bo seemed to sense Mitch's awkwardness and hurried over, smiling broadly.

"Mr. Brown! Fancy seeing you here! Well, of course, it is your store I suppose. We're headin' off on a little trail ridin' and Mitch here's lost his saddle in a fire, how much is that dandy looking one under your arm?"

Mr. Brown eyed Bo testily, determining whether or not he felt like dealing with the grinning fool. "A fair price, for what it's worth."

Mitch worked the brim of his hat. "And, what would that price be?"

Mr. Brown fingered his bushy mustache. "Hmm, I suppose I'll sell it for… twenty-five dollars." He looked at Mitch and folded his beefy arms.

"Whoa whoa whoa, Mr. Brown, I could buy a matching pair of Bobwhites for that price!" Bo said, dropping his friendly mannerisms slightly now that he knew the store clerk was taking advantage of them.

"Then go buy those Bobwhites." Mr. Brown seemed unfazed as he rubbed the saddle with the side of his hand.

Mitch looked to Bo then reach into the pocket for the money he'd brought with him. Mitch didn't have a lot of money, himself, most of it he gave back to the family to help them financially, he knew he'd never be able to afford the rest of his gear.

"Please Mr. Brown, you know I can't afford that. That's twice what it's worth I'm sure." Mitch tried to barter. He was incredibly intimidated by Mr. Brown, and not just because he was so much bigger than him.

Bo frowned as Mr. Brown eyed Mitch's money then the floor creaked as Dennis, Davey, Charlie and Lawrence stepped up alongside Bo and Mitch.

"What's the problem over here?" Dennis asked, folding his arm and raising his brow at the clerk.

"Mr. Brown is trying to sell this hunk of leather for twenty-five dollars, I's worth twelve at the most and that's with a head harnesses included." Bo said before Mitch or Mr. Brown could respond.

"Highway robbery!" Lawrence hissed and slithered up onto the saddle. "Why, the price tag is right here, and it says fifteen dollars. Mr. Brown, care to elaborate on this thievery?"

Mr. Brown looked frustrated at being called out by a reptile in front of his customers. "Twenty." He muttered.

"Fifteen like the tag says." Mitch pulled out the bills and held them forward. Mr. Brown took the bills stiffly and stuffed them into his apron pocket.

Mitch turned away and picked up a folded saddle blanket, he rested a harness, a coil of rope and two saddle bags across it. "And this should be about five." He let Mr. Brown check the tags before taking the money and giving him change reluctantly.

Dennis shook his head at Mr. Brown then turned and picked up the saddle, carrying it outside for Mitch.

Mitch let out a deep breath once he was outside and crossed the street wordlessly over to the quail. It didn't take long to saddle Cali up with the new gear. The feisty hen snorted and shifted her back side to side, listening to the creak of the new leather.

"I'm sorry it's not broken in, Cal, it'll have to do for now." Mitch stroked her facial feathers and the hen churred and nibbled his ear affectionately.

"Sorry Mr. Brown was so rude back there Mitch." Dennis said as Davey returned from where he had gone to get the sheriff.

"He's just upset…" Mitch said and dropped his gaze slightly.

"Still, it's no reason to take it out on you; it's not your fault Charlotte ran off with ol' whatsisface." Dennis paused seeing Mitch turn away and start messing with the straps to busy himself.

"Still sore about that?" Dennis pried gently. And Mitch shrugged and shook his head.

"No," he lied. "I'm worried about Scott. We need to go, where's Bo?"

"He's talking to the sheriff, er, Buxley." Dennis pointed to where Bo was returning with an old, dusky-colored rat wearing a hat with a ragged feather in the brim.

"Morning, Buxley." Mitch said to the older deputy. "Where's Dan?"

"The ol' sheriff ain't here right now, called up to Monty for summin', some sorta trial. Been quail rustlers hitting up that way, only sometime more'n quail go missing. I heard ya got bashed up by a blue lizard? Sure, you wuzzin' hittin' the whisky?"

Mitch frowned. "Of course not." He swung a leg over his saddle and steered Cali onto the main street. "Bo let's go."

"Ease up, Mitch, you need a doctor to take a look at you first." Bo tried to reason but Mitch narrowed his eyes. He didn't want to stay in Redcliff for another minute.

"I'll be fine, but we have to go before daylight's gone. Let's go!" he started to lead Cali away from them.

Dennis, Davey and Lawrence turned to the others. Dennis shrugged at Bo. "Best go with him before he kills himself doing something foolish."

"Foolish wasn't the word I was looking for." Bo muttered and patted Dennis's shoulder before climbing up onto his bird. "I'll send word when we get back." He smiled assuredly down at them, hoping they would all make it back in one piece. The lizards sounded like a tough lot.

"Give these to Mitch. He might need them." Dennis said passing up his old gun belt wrapped around two pearl handled six guns.

Bo took them with a blink of surprise and nodded. "Alright." He sighed and put them in his saddlebag.

"We'd come with you boys, we really would, but we can't leave Redcliff." Davey sighed. The white mouse hadn't been out on the trail in years after badly breaking his leg and Dennis was in charge of the post office with Lawrence. "But we'll get ahold of Buck in Monty for you. Lord knows Buck will scrape together a posse."

"I'll point him in the right direction." Dennis promised.

The grass snake slithered foreword. "Good luck, boys, bring Scott home, we'll be thinking of you."

Bo nodded appreciatively and a little further off Mitch tipped his hat in thanks before turning and spurring Cali into a run out of town, wincing at the jostle to his ribs as he went.

Bo beckoned Charlie and Jared then followed Mitch out on Cotton back towards the ranch where the trail started.

Mitch's eyes were set determinedly on the horizon. "I'm coming, Scott." He muttered as his quail thundered down the path home.

II

Delgado touched his fingers to the gash on his face. It felt sore and tight. Heat blurred the horizon line in the distance and left shimmery illusions of water where the land dipped. He spotted a dark blot in the distance and first dismissed it as a rock or a scrub patch but as he grew closer he made out that is wasn't a rock, but a rundown looking tavern with a rickety looking shaded porch.

Delgado pulled back on the reins to slow his Gambel's quail to a halt, behind him Stubs pulled the wagon up alongside him before slowing to a stop.

"What's that?" Stubs asked following his leader's gaze towards the building. "Gonna raid that pile o' sticks?"

Delgado silenced him with a glare and turned his bird to face Spike, who was approaching them from the rear of the little convoy.

"Stay here, I'll be right back." Delgado ordered then spurred his quail off in the direction of the building, leaving Spike, Stubs and the rest to stay amongst the brush and rocks out of sight.

When the wagon stopped Scott winced and rubbed his head he took off his hat to better sit up in the trunk. He felt miserably overheated and perspiration drenched his collar. He squinted his eyes to look out the keyhole, wondering what they were stopping for and spotted the Jumper on the ground, still tied to the wagon.

Scott swallowed and he shifted to better see out of the tiny opening. Was the Jumper still alive? Scott didn't know how long he'd been asleep, but the Jumper had been dragged this whole time. It couldn't be good.

Miraculously, the Jumper shifted and squinted open his dark brown eyes, rolling stiffly to the side and propping himself up on an elbow.

Scott couldn't believe it, save for a few bruises the Jumper looked ok! He let out a sigh of relief watching him sit up on his knees and look around with narrowed eyes.

Spike smirked and pushed Stub's shoulder from where they were at the front of the wagon and pointed over at the Jumper. Spike rode his quail over towards the Jumper and leered down at him.

"Rise 'n shine, Jumper." The horned lizard circled him on quailback and The Jumper shifted sharply, his eyes never leaving the lizard's face as his lip curled in a sneer.

Scott swallowed grimly as he witnessed Stubs come up behind the Jumper and tug the ropes sharply just when the Jumper made to rise to his feet. Pulling him back down to the ground.

"Heh, stay down where you belong, filthy rat." Stubs sneered at the Jumper as he tried to sit up again. The Jumper bared his teeth at Stubs and flinched as Spike flung some water from his canteen onto his head from behind.

Scott gasped as the Jumper rolled sharply on the ground and struck one of the legs on Spike's riding quail with a powerful kick. The quail stumbled with a startled squawk and the Jumper kicked out again, knocking the legs out from under the bird and sending both quail and rider crashing to the ground.

Spike yowled out in alarm then anger as the Jumper ripped the rope from Stubs' grip and used the slack to leap onto Spike. The lizard wrestled the Jumper to the ground but the sinewy Jumper ducked and rolled kicking the lizard off with powerful hind feet before grabbing the rope and wrapping it around the lizard's neck, pulling it tight as he tried to strangle him.

Scott gaped in shock then startled in fear watching Stubs come over and smash his fist into the Jumper's head, knocking him away from Spike. The Jumper recoiled and sprang but Spike untangled himself and stepped heavily onto the rope, forcing the Jumper down as the rope was looped around his neck and through his bound hands. The Jumper threw himself on his side and kicked Spike's leg knocking the lizard down again.

"Enough o' this!" Stubs pulled out his gun with a click and rushed forward kneeing the Jumper in the chest and making him fall flat on his back. He pushed his boot down onto his neck and bound wrists to hold the wriggling captive still and pointed the gun at his face.

"Yer more trouble'n yer worth!" the lizard hissed menacingly.

Scott heard the gun cock and he panicked. He banged his fist on the inside of the trunk and shouted before he could stop himself.

"NO! STOP!"

Delgado stepped inside the rickety looking tavern and squinted in the half-light. He heard sniggering and looked in the corner to see several scruffy looking mice, all clearly drunk as they sloshed drinks down their fronts and banged half full tankards on the three-legged table, roaring with laughter as if someone had just told a joke.

Upon Delgado's entrance they had turned around in their seats to see the newcomer. One drunken looking shrew belched loudly and pointed a finger at the lizard and slurred. "Bluuuuuuuuuue!" before keeling over in his chair to the floor, leaving the others laughing and spewing drinks raucously.

Delgado narrowed his eyes, disgusting creatures. He came up to the table nonetheless and glared down at them.

"Is there any aloe in this establishment?" Delgado asked with blazing eyes as the scruffy rodents continued to snicker and point at him. "Or other medicines your cretins store?"

"Hehehe! He's blue from his nose to his tail!"

"I din't know lizzids painted 'emselves!"

"And all stripy like a wasp to boot!"

Delgado was getting fed up, he reached down and grabbed the drunk shrew off the floor and before whirling and throwing the sloppy critter through the nearest window with a shatter.

The scruffy lot roared with laughter and banged the table with their fists gasping for breath.

"Oh hahaha! Yeah there's aloe here, Stripes, off in the back!" he waved off towards a cabinet with the door broken off.

Delgado shot each of them a threatening look that quelled their laughter before crossing the room to the cabinet and pulling out the container of thick aloe gel. He pulled out his knife and used its reflection to apply the pulpy concoction to the gash on his face using the mouse's shovel then set the rest of the jar back on the cabinet shelf and headed out the door without a second look at the scruffy lot who were howling with laughter.

The shrew looked in from outside the window, his rose-colored eyes crossed as he hiccupped, "Oiiiii what did I miss?"

Delgado was looking forward to getting a move on again, he hated dealing with rodents. He mounted his quail and was steering him around a large prickly pear cluster when he pulled the reins suddenly to stop short.

Pinned up by the cactus spines were several wanted posters, and one looked all too familiar. The skink reached up and ripped down the paper that held a likeness of himself sketched in black and white staring back at him.

Delgado gritted his teeth in anger and stashed the poster in his vest. The Gila and he were going to have a serious talk. He made his way back towards the others in a fast lope.

Scott thundered his fists against the inside of the trunk and Stubs turned to see what the noise was. The distraction was enough time for the Jumper to roll from under Stubs' boot and kick out at his stout legs, driving him back.

The Jumper leapt to his feet just as he was tackled from behind by Spike, who forced a burlap sack over his head, blinding the Jumper.

"Bag him good!" Stubs snarled as Spike cinched the bag tight so the mouse couldn't shake it off, nor could he see anymore, so he couldn't avoid the sucker punch to his middle by Stubs as the horned lizard approached.

Scott pounded the trunk again with gritted teeth. They were going to kill him!

A gunshot shattered the air and made Scott's heart jump, thinking Stubs had pulled the trigger on the Jumper, but for the first time he was almost relieved by Delgado's presence as the blue-tailed lizard rode his bird in view of the keyhole, holding his gun out and pointing the barrel at the sky.

"What the hell is going on!" He demanded of his two cohorts who started to shuffle their boots in the dirt like naughty children caught in a bad act.

"The Jumper, Delgado! The beast went savage an' knocked me off my quail!" Spike stammered and pointing at the Jumper now bent double from the previous blow, with his head still bagged.

Delgado glared at them each in turn. "Then teach him that's not acceptable."

"That's what we was doing!" Stubs raised a fist to hit the Jumper again but Delgado snorted, causing him to stop.

"And clearly it's not been working, use a switch, that'll break him, or break the switch." Delgado flicked his head in the direction of a stunted mesquite tree.

"Cut a green sprig off that, that'll settle him." Delgado holstered his gun and watched Spike force the Jumper against a rock, exposing his back to Stubs as the other lizard snapped off a whip-like branch from a low-hanging limb and started forward. He brought it slicing across the Jumpers shoulders and Scott flinched seeing the Jumper stiffen from the pain, but not make a sound.

"Heh, you don't like that do ya, savage, then you won't like this! Or this! Or that!" Stubs went switch-happy on the Jumper's back, cutting into his back and slicing open the tattered shirt the creature was wearing.

"Leave him alone!" Scott yelled from inside the trunk, starting to rock it from side to side. Delgado turned and rode over to the box and banged his fist on it.

"Unless you want us to use this crate as target practice you'll shut your mouth, mouse!" he hissed threateningly.

Scott swallowed nervously, seeing the lizards blazing eyes and froze until he left before inching to the keyhole again. Stubs had finished whipping the Jumper and was now hauling the creature back to his feet with Spike's help. The Jumper shrugged both of them away roughly. Scott could see blood where his shirt had been torn from the switch.

Delgado rode out ahead. "Let's get moving again, No use being stuck out here any longer."

Stubs got back into the wagon as Spike remounted his quail. Scott felt the wagon lurch to go forward then felt it stop as the Jumper grasped the rope with tied hands and strained backwards to keep the wagon from moving. His strong legs shook with tension as he dug his feet into the ground.

The quail tied to the wagon strained and peeped in confusion.

Scott watched the Jumper wide-eyed, wishing the creature could break free but also wishing he would lie low so he wouldn't be hurt by the lizards again, but it was too late. Delgado rode to the back of the wagon and kicked at the Jumper's back from his saddle mount, knocking the mouse to the ground.

"Stop it!" Scott shouted at the lizard before he could remind himself to remain quiet. He barely got out of the way as the lizard turned and threw his knife at the box. The steel stuck through the wood, the point pricking Scott's chest. Scott gasped sharply and pressed to the back of the trunk as Delgado rode back over and yanked the knife out.

"Next time that knife will be sticking out of your carcass." Delgado warned. "Not another word out of you!"

12

Thorn Ranch was already long out of sight as Mitch and the others set off on their quail through the scrubby hills following the wagon grooves in the clay and the flattened grass from the line of the covey that had gone before them.

Mitch's saddle leather creaked from newness and every now and then Cali would snort her displeasure for the sound. Mitch leaned over to pat his quail's neck reassuringly but winced and held his ribs stiffly. Mitch had broken ribs before, but this time it hurt to breathe.

Bo rode Cotton up alongside Cali and Mitch and slowed his bird to the pace Mitch was keeping. He saw Mitch's hand on his ribs before Mitch hastily moved it to the saddle horn, gripping it white knuckled and keeping his eyes fixed to the ruts in the ground that he was following.

"I wish you'd just see a doctor." Bo said, resting his reins in one hand to pull his glove tighter onto the other. "What happened to you?"

"I got in a fight, and he was too big." Mitch mumbled, laying his ears flat, he really didn't want to talk about it but Bo pressed on.

"Didn't you have the rifle? Did you get a shot at him?"

"No, he knocked me down, I didn't see him. He came from behind the fence." Mitch's eyes narrowed in obvious annoyance at the subject. All the more reminder he couldn't protect his brother, even when armed on his own property.

"I just don't see how it could have happened… he must really be something to whip you. Did you hurt your ribs? I'm just wor—"

"Bo! I don't want to talk about it! He beat me, torched the barn, stole the quail and I was unable to protect my brother or stop any of it! I don't want to talk about it anymore!" Mitch snapped, glaring at Bo with angry blue eyes.

Bo put up his hands in defense. "Mitch you need to calm down. I know you're worried about Scott. And what happened last night wasn't your fault. We'll get him back, and the covey. Those scaly brush poppers will have to keep near the streams to water those birds, we'll catch up."

Mitch laid his ears back and returned his gaze to the wagon ruts in the ground. "Sorry." He grumbled for snapping at his friend.

Bo shrugged then looked towards the west. "It'll be evening soon, we should find a town nearby to rest for the night, and get you looked over."

"No, we should stay on the trail." Mitch could think of nothing worse than losing the trail in trade for a night's rest in some inn.

"Mitch, be reasonable, you can't track in the dark, and you're hurt. I've seen you holding your ribs and favoring your left arm. You need some help."

"I'm staying on the trail; if you and the others fancy a bunk over a bedroll I won't stop you from riding on to the next town. I can't lose this trail, Bo, it's the only tie we have."

Bo sighed and flicked his eyes skyward as if summoning strength to deal with Mitch's stubbornness. "Very well, we'll stay on the trail. But we're stopping here."

Mitch looked up sharply. "We've got at least two hours before we lose the light, we could go on from here."

Bo looked over pointedly. "It'll take time to set up camp, and I'm not stumbling around in the dark for firewood in scorpion country. Dismount, Mitch, this is as far as we can make it today."

Mitch frowned and wanted to argue further but Bo seemed to sense this and turned Cotton around, riding back to Charlie and Jared to tell them to unpack for the night.

Night fell faster than expected as the sun bled beneath the horizon, staining everything red before the shadows went black and the stars took over.

The four riders were gathered around a crackling cooking fire as Charlie tended to the night's rations. Using some water from the canteens they brought, he chopped and boiled some potatoes and wild onions to go with a few biscuits that Bo passed around.

Mitch wasn't eating anything as he sat on a rock looking down at the flames unseeingly as he held a hand under his vest, pressing gently against his side trying to breathe easier. He snapped out of it when Bo took a seat on a rock beside him and offered him a tin plate of his ration.

"Eat up, rider, it'll probably help with that." Bo tried to sound cheery but Mitch just couldn't be swayed.

"No, I'm not hungry." Mitch mumbled and removed his hand from his side so Bo wouldn't bring up his injuries again.

"You gotta eat something." Bo said around a mouthful of food.

"If he won't eat it I will." Jared snorted from across the fire.

Mitch set the plate aside and stood up, barely masking a wince. "I'm going to check on the birds." He muttered and left the light of the fire in the direction of the tied mounts.

"What a moper, guess he's got reason to though, Scott's got about as much chance as a snowball in hell at this rate. Huh, I bet- YIPE THAT'S HOT!" Jared leapt back and fell into the dirt as Bo flung the contents of his tin coffee mug across the fire into Jared's lap.

"You rat! I'll throttle you! I'll—" Jared stalked over as Bo, a head taller than Jared, rose and shoved Jared's chest with one hand, easily causing the darker mouse to fall over a rock backwards and land on his tail. Bo put one foot on the rock and leaned on his knee.

"You shut up about, Scott, you hear? Or next time I'll throw you in the fire, and don't think I won't." Bo's normally cheery face was set in a hard, grim line as he glared at Jared. Jared rose up brushed himself off and returned back to his seat at the other side of the fire muttering darkly under his breath.

Charlie rolled his eyes at Jared then looked past Bo up the spur of rock and scrub above where the quail were hitched for the night.

Mitch stroked Cali's feathers then rubbed the soot from between his fingers. He raked more ash from her feathers with his hands, wishing he had a brush. Cali churred softly, resting her beak on his shoulder and Mitch patted her cheek. He looked out across the endless desert and sky strewn with stars and sighed as he clasped his hands and looked skyward.

"Please let him be ok." he whispered.

13

The sun had since set and Scott couldn't see outside the keyhole anymore as he sat hunched in the trunk with his arms around his knees. Outside he could hear the Jumper stumbling after the wagon in the dark. He'd recovered enough to walk, but still blinded by the burlap bag over his head he couldn't see and had tripped and fallen many times, always getting back up again without a word.

Scott was exhausted from the heat of the box. He was parched and hungry as well. He stiffened feeling the wagon creep to a halt. Scott rubbed his eyes to wake up and inched to the keyhole maybe they were bedding down for the night.

Delgado clutched his vest about him. He didn't like the night, despite it being a warm summer night the darkness and breeze was more noticeable for a thinscale like himself. He dismounted his bird and tied him to a Joshua tree. He surveyed their camp site, a curve in a dry riverbed that hadn't had a drop of water since the previous spring. It would shelter them from any sudden winds and keep their fire from view.

Spike was riding around the roving covey, bunching them together to rest for the night before tying off his own bird and helping Stubs with the fire.

Scott realized he must have dozed because he found himself waking up and seeing a light outside the keyhole from the crackling fire and he could hear and smell something sizzling in a skillet.

He tried to stretch out in the cramped space as he peered through his only window to the outside. He spotted the Jumper curled up on the ground, his tufted tail under his head like a pillow, still bagged as he rested. Scott could make out the cuts from the angle of his back and felt angry towards the lizards once more. He was not a fan of Jumpers, he'd had the occasional fantasy of shooting one back home on the ranch and being recognized for it. But now he and this Jumper were both prisoners, and in danger.

Scott's stomach growled hungrily and he shifted to settle on his side in a tight fetal position to rest. He curled his tail in anxiety, thinking about Mitch. He missed his brother so much, but he was dead, and nothing could bring him back. Scott's chest tightened in misery remembering the flames and Cali's shrill screeching from the burning barn. He covered his head with his hands. Hoping that Mitch and Cali didn't suffer long. He squeezed his eyes shut feeling them burn under the lids. He blinked them quickly to rid the unshed tears. The lizards, it was all their fault.

Scott wished he was brave like Mitch or Bo, or even the Jumper, to be able to face the lizards and hurt them as much as possible for killing his brother. Scott knew he couldn't though. How could he? He was trapped in a box, helpless.

Delgado returned to the campfire with a fistful of thick long green leaves. He'd discovered some aloe nearby and had set to work exposing the succulent flesh to rub onto his stinging gash. He glared at Spike and Stubs as they twisted to watch him from the fire. The two hastily turned away and began to act very busy with their fire poker sticks and trail dishes.

Delgado sat near to the fire to keep his blood warm as the night would get colder. His eyes settled on the sleeping Jumper and he blinked thoughtfully.

This time, perhaps this time, they would finally find the Jumper's little hide out. He rubbed scaly hands together as he thought. And perhaps that would be enough to get him out of the Gila's posse for good.

14

The sun was barely up over the horizon and Mitch was already cinching his new saddle in place on Cali, eager to get moving. He led her to the fire where the others were moving slowly, getting ready in the dark.

Charlie and Bo were packing the chuck supplies and bedrolls while Jared was still sitting down looking cross with one boot on and shirt unbuttoned.

"Come on guys, let's get going." Mitch asked, agitated by the slow morning pace.

"We're coming Mitch, just a little tired." Bo answered cracking his back stiffly before heading toward the quail to pack the saddlebags.

Jared snorted causing Mitch to turn and look down at him, Jared sat with folded arms on his unpacked bedroll.

"I don't see why we're waking up this early. The trail will still be there after sleeping in and getting some breakfast."

Mitch fumed. "Because, you idiot, Scott needs our help! And he won't get it if we sit on our tails spreading honey on biscuits!"

Jared rolled his eyes and muttered something darkly making Mitch stalk over challengingly.

"What was that!" he snapped at the dark mouse, who rolled his eyes before repeating.

"For all you know we're rushing after a corpse. Sleeping in or riding all night ain't gonna make him any less dead."

Mitch's fist clenched and he kicked Jared over backwards with a boot to the gut.

"Stomach that you vulture! I don't give a damn what you think, but if you're going to talk like that then you can beat feet back to Redcliff and stay there!" Mitch snarled at him.

Jared moaned and bared his teeth rising up to engage Mitch in the fight they both so badly wanted to get into again but Bo came racing down the hill and got between them, shoving them apart an arm's span.

"Fellas!" he barked. "Cut that out! You're supposed to be fighting lizards, not each other! Jared, clam up before I nail your mouth shut! Mitch, calm down, *again*!"

Mitch shrugged away from Bo and rested a hand to his ribs quickly, which started to twinge in pain from the stress of the impending fight.

"That's it, Mitch you need a doctor, we'll go to the next town and get you seen to."

"No, Bo! I'm not repeating myself anymore! We're sticking to the trail!" Mitch snapped, venting his anger from Jared's snide comments to the black-and-white mouse before him.

Bo narrowed his eyes and held his hands akimbo. "Mitch you're hurt! You aren't thinking clearly! What if Scott needs a rescue? We can't drag you around half busted and expect to make any decent time getting him back. You want to get him back then you have to go see a doctor first!"

Mitch spun around away from Bo and mounted Cali with a wince and spurred her away from Bo and Jared.

"I'm sticking to the trail. You can follow me or stay here but I'm going." Mitch kicked Cali's wing and the hen gave a feisty snort then took off running across the scrubby hilltop.

"Charlie what do I do with that guy." Bo folded his arms and looked to his companion who had arrived in time to see the dispute.

The golden dormouse shrugged his broad shoulders then jerked a thumb in Mitch's direction with raised brows.

Bo nodded slowly. "Yeah, we're going after him alright; don't want him getting himself killed." Bo swung a leg over his bird and Cotton scratched at the ground, eager to start the day.

Jared was pulling on a boot. "You're just gonna leave me out here?" he whined.

"Only if you don't get your tail up and into a saddle in the next minute!" Bo flicked an ear in irritation at Jared's slowness and spurred Cotton onward after Mitch, leaving Charlie and Jared to catch up.

The sun was still climbing into the sky a short while later and the group was together again, traveling in an awkward silence broken only by the matching strides of the quail and the occasional snort or yawn my bird and rider.

In the distance Bo could see scrub trees growing thick off to the left and the low flat roof tops of a town a mile or so away down the hill. He slowed his quail to a walk and Mitch turned to see what he was looking at.

Bo turned to the others. "We should cap off those canteens before much longer, we'll be hitting flatlands before the next river and I'm sure the birds could use a drink before then." Bo looked over at Mitch, knowing he cared very much for his quail, Cali, but Bo wasn't sure if he would go for it.

Surprisingly, though frowning, Mitch nodded slowly and turned his quail toward the direction of the town in the distance and rode on behind Bo and Charlie as they took the lead.

The town was called Hanson, and was half again as big as Redcliff with big, wood and stone buildings with large windows. Everything was well painted in light, wash colors and the town hardly seemed to have dirty window or a bench out of place. It seemed very well maintained and friendly enough.

Mitch waited at the hitching post trough with the birds, watching Cali drink her fill.

The playful hen tossed a little water at her rider with her beak, trying to get a rise out of him. Normally he would grin and splash her back but today Mitch did nothing, merely leaned heavily on the edge of the trough, holding a hand to his ribs under his vest with a strained look on his face.

Cali stuck her beak under the water and blew bubbles, no response. She raised her head and snorted water before clacking her beak trying to garner some attention from her rider.

Mitch looked over stiffly and stroked her damp, feathered face with a finger.

"Sorry Cali, No playing right now." He blinked slowly and perked his ears watching Bo, Charlie and Jared coming out of the white building in front of him.

Bo tipped his hat to the person inside then stepped out and headed across towards the quail.

"Any sign?" Mitch asked hopefully.

"No, the secretary checked word with the saloon bartender and store runner. They admitted they don't like serving lizards much but neither have even seen a blue lizard-tailed before. Sorry Mitch." Bo glanced to the side and rubbed the back of his neck.

Mitch straightened up with a wince. "Well then, let's hurry back out onto the trail and get moving. We won't find Delgado or Scott in this place. It's so spick and span they'd stick out like broken tail." He looked down the street as the native townsfolk walked about, children playing with empty barrels and their mothers scolding them from beneath brightly colored parasols.

Bo sucked in air through his teeth then let out it out slow before turning his gray eyes to Mitch's face.

"Mitch I'm not letting you leave these city limits until you see a doctor. As a friend, I want you to get patched up before doing something reckless."

Mitch's brows rose then furrowed in annoyance.

"You're not *letting* me?" He almost snorted as he grabbed Cali's reins and his quail gave a hiccuppy snort from being pulled away from the trough.

Bo reached out slowly for the reins with one hand.

"Mitch come on, be reasonable, I know you're worried about Scott, but we're worried about you, come on, don't make us drag you kicking and screaming down the town street among the women and children. It wouldn't be a pretty sight, but if that's what it takes I'll do it."

Mitch glared at Bo and tugged the reins sharply out of reach and stuck a foot into the stirrup, hopping slightly with the hen as she backed up before clambering onto the saddle with a wince.

Bo started forward and Mitch jerked the reins, backing Cali up quickly.

"Back off." Mitch glared at Bo. "I'm not getting babied by some doc while Scott's out there with those rustlers doing God-knows what to him. You can't make me stay here."

"Mitch!" Bo started as his friend spurred Cali's wing and the two set out down the street and out of the city in a cloud of dust.

"Wow, you told him." Jared snorted from the shade of the eaves.

Bo turned and glowered at him. "Shut up." He looked to Charlie who was watching Mitch's form disappear with a look of disappointment.

"He's just scared, Charlie, it's messing with his head and he's not thinking straight, he won't get far, we have his canteen, he's got no water outside this creek and this is a good mile from the trail. All the same, we better go after him, I'll try and find a doc who can look at him on the trail." Bo started walking down the street with Charlie at his side, leaving Jared to mind their birds from the luxury of his bench.

Driven by frustration Mitch rode Cali at a run all the way to the outskirts of the town and slowed her to a fast walk along the ridge of scrub trees sloping sharply down to the creek below. The ridge was lined in clay, loose rocky soil, scrub and prickly pear cactus.

Cali gave her head a shake, sending her topknot swaying and Mitch patted her neck in apology. He would normally never ride Cali out of a place so fast after letting her have a deep drink like that.

"Sorry, girl." He sighed as his thoughts battled inside his head. He knew Bo was worried about him and just trying to help, but on the other side Scott had no one to help him, and Mitch didn't want to wait around while his younger brother was in danger. If that meant avoiding a doctor's visit in order to get to Scott faster, then so be it.

Cali snorted sharply all of a sudden, her dark eyes wide as she almost stumbled to an abrupt stop. Mitch pulled the reins wondering what spooked her then heard a scream from down the steep ridge near the river, a doe's scream.

Mitch turned Cali sharply as he tried to peer through the scrub tree branches and brush that led down to the water. He could hear other voices too now, gruff male voices and the sound of splashing and quail. Shortly afterwards a mouse on quailback came into view driving a small string of bobwhites up the river. The birds looked young and confused, something didn't seem right.

Mitch heard the scream again followed by crows of laughter. He spurred Cali down the rock a bit to see better and looked down the steep face to spot three gruff looking mice cornering a doe against the rocky wall in the creek shallows. She held a dripping stick pulled from the water out at arm's length as if to fend them off but they were crowding closer. All at once the two mice on either side rushed her and ripped the branch from her grip. She leapt to the side as the center mouse advanced forward swiftly, he knocked her into the shallows near the bank. She was now facing uphill with her arms pinned back and the larger mouse straddled across her. The other two mice laughed.

Mitch's blood boiled in his veins at the sight of the attack. He remembered at a young age his father beating the tar out of someone for badmouthing his mother and now he felt the rage that his father must have felt even though he had no idea who this doe was.

"Go Cali!" He snapped his reins and the hen gave a fiery snort then raced down the steep rock face in a fast run sending pebbles and debris clattering down before them.

The mouse holding the young doe down was smirking until his ears pricked up hearing a noise from above. He looked up just as Mitch and Cali thundered down the rock almost upon him and caught Mitch's boot and stirrup full in the face, knocking him backwards off the doe and into the shallows with a squeal of pain.

Mitch and Cali splashed into the stream from the momentum, Cali's eyes were wild and fierce with aggression towards the others matching Mitch's blazing blue gaze as he turned to the other two mice who gaped momentarily stunned at the rider who had come from nowhere.

The mouse Mitch had kicked in the face lay still in the water, but submersion in the cold stream seemed to revive him and he slowly stumbled to his feet and spat out a mouthful of bloody teeth into his hands.

"YOUSHUNNUBA—!" The mouse started to splutter but Mitch swung himself off the saddle into the water and grabbed him by the collar, belting him across the nose and sending him crashing back into the shallows with a gargle of pain.

The young doe on the shore had scrambled to her feet once more, water dripping from her hair and clothes as she retrieved her stick from the ground for defense.

The two cohorts of the mouse Mitch had attacked regained their senses and rushed Mitch standing in the shallows. Mitch ducked the first two punches thrown and kicked one of them back into the other before the two split up, one rushing behind him. Mitch whirled to stop his rear attacker and the other rushed in and socked him in the back before seizing him from behind and forcing his arms back. The other Mouse leaned back and threw a heavily weighted blow into Mitch's ribs.

There was a nasty snapping sound and Mitch was blinded by pain letting out a hollow choking sound, unable to move to defend himself further. The mouse raised a fist to clobber him again but the sudden appearance of a large wet stick struck him upside the face knocking him back.

The dark-haired doe had rushed into the shallows and laid the attacker flat before whipping around and bringing the stick smashing down between the ears of Mitch's captor, causing him to release his prisoner. Mitch dropped to all fours in the water gasping for air.

The other two mice had recovered and were now rushing towards Mitch and the doe, splashing madly while the other restrained Cali by the reins. The hen shrieked loudly and tried to get back to Mitch.

Mitch felt a hand under his arm pull him up as the doe helped haul him to his feet; he stumbled backwards to the pebbly shore.

Mitch landed on his back as the other mouse dove and landed on top of him, hands closing around his throat as he tried to strangle him.

Mitch was already in considerable pain from the blow to his damaged ribs but the cut off air flow brought him into a panic. He reached up and pulled the gun from the mouse's holster all while driving his knee into his attacker's gut. An accompanying whack from a branch onto the mouse's head caused the mouse to release his stranglehold and tumble back, letting Mitch know the young gal was still up and fighting.

Mitch managed to scramble to his feet and raised the gun at the bloody-mouthed leader as he started towards them, then stopping abruptly when he saw the gun.

"Back off!" Mitch snarled out, panting raggedly. "Or I'll shoot!"

"Heh heh, you ain't got it in y—" BANG! BANG!

The mouse stood open mouthed in shock as Mitch fired two shots clean through his left ear.

"Get lost! Get out of here!" Mitch demanded and re-cocked the hammer with his thumb and started forward. "Unhand my quail! Get OUT!"

The three mice backed off and hurried to their mounts, yelling to the fourth of their party, "Leave the birds!" as they tore down the bank upriver and around the bend.

Mitch felt his vision growing hazy and as his gun hand lowered, the pistol slipped from his fingers hitting the pebbles on the bank below. He stumbled backwards, pain lancing through his body with every painful, shallow breath.

The young doe beside him turned and glared at him suspiciously then realizing he must be hurt asked, "What are you—are you alright?" She asked in confusion then yelped in surprise as Mitch passed out cold and fell to the side, collapsing onto her and knocking her to the ground.

"Oh, get off me!" she snapped in annoyance and tried to shove him off. She looked up sharply hearing the sounds of voices and quail coming down the ridge. She squirmed out from under Mitch as four mice riding scaled quail emerged onto the river bank.

"June!" the leader of the troop, a mouse with a tall white hat and reddish whiskers waxed down into a handlebar mustache. "What happened here? Rustlers!?" he spotted her trying to untangle herself from one and drew his gun.

"Let her up!" he snapped and cocked the hammer but June stood up without any trouble, brushing the grit sticking to her wet fur away.

"Sheriff! The rustlers!" she panted from the fight and was soaked through from the water. "They tried to steal the Elm's quail, I was trying to stop them but they grabbed me and—"

"You mean him!" The sheriff pointed his gun at Mitch's still form.

"What? Him? *No!* —I was—" June tried to explain but was cut off.

"Looks like we finally caught one boys! Tie him over that bird's saddle over there; Lord knows what fellow he stole it from. Damn rustlers! Did he hurt you, June?" The sheriff asked without really listening to her, his eyes alight with the glow of a hunter taking in a prize catch.

June stumbled back as two of the deputies came and seized Mitch's unconscious body from the bank as June tried to explain.

"No! He wasn't with them, he's hurt, Sheriff, it's not what you think!"

"Ms. Jordan I'm sure you've experienced something terrible down here and the ordeal has left you in a great deal of stress, nevertheless this rustler is my prisoner now and I'll take him to Doc Mosley's to get him patched enough for questioning. Then we'll find and hang the whole lot of 'em!"

"*Sheriff!*" June shouted exasperatedly as one of the deputies tied her rescuer over his saddle like a hunting trophy and led the quail over to the others, tying its reins to the saddle horn.

"You're not *listening* to me!" She rushed up to his quail but the sheriff seemed distracted and deaf to her protests but turned to her with narrowed eyes.

"Adam take Ms. Jordan back with you to Doc Mosley's as well. She's been through so much the trauma may be getting to her." The sheriff turned to lead the way up the hill. "Ms. Jordan, I've had to endure you and your family's lies long enough, I'll get to the bottom of this, your assistance is not required."

The deputy tried to pull June up onto his saddle but she jerked her wrist roughly from his hand, her green eyes blazing.

"I'm perfectly capable of walking! I'm fine! And—you've got the wrong mouse!" she pointed at the mouse slung over the saddle like a sack of feed.

"I'll be the judge of that." The sheriff called as he led the way up the hill. "Adam, just make sure she gets some help one way or another."

June was shaking in anger as the sheriff and two of the deputies leading the California hen and her rider disappeared over the lip of the ridge and headed back towards Hanson. She glowered at Adam, as the mouse still held a hand out for her to come up.

"Keep your hand! Sheriff Slaughter is going to hang an innocent man and you'll just watch!"

"The sheriff is the law, Ms. Jordan, you must recognize that." Adam tilted his hat.

"His law is wrong!"

"Ms. June are you riding back to Hanson with me or not?" he sighed.

"Ride back yourself for all I care! I'd rather eat river mud then listen to your worthless law talk!" June started to hurry up the rocky slope on foot after the others, her soaked clothes dripping from her riding chaps and dark hair.

"That trigger happy lawman won't hang another honest critter!" she panted in a growl under her breath as she broke into a run towards the top and crested the ridge, running along the path back to Hanson.

15

The lid to the wagon trunk was flung open and blinding sunlight poured in, waking Scott with a jolt from his cramped resting position. He flung up a hand to shade his squinting eyes and made out Delgado pointing his gun down at him in one hand as he rested a tin cup of water down near Scott's head before slamming the trunk lid back down leaving Scott in the dark.

Scott swallowed and tried to calm his rapid heartbeat before twisting to sit up as best he could. Then finding the tin he drank the water thirstily, trying not to waste a precious drop. He set the tin down then bent his whiskers to get at the few remaining drops he had left.

A sound outside caught his attention and he bent to look out through the keyhole.

Stubs had leaned down and whipped the bag off the sleeping Jumper's head, waking him with a start before Stubs stomped firmly on the rope binding the Jumper to the wagon to keep him grounded while he offered the Jumper a similar tin of water. The Jumper glared at it and slapped the tin away with bound hands, splashing the water all over Stubs' pant leg.

Stubs snarled in anger and raised a hand to strike the Jumper but Delgado crossed over and grabbed the horned lizard's raised fist and jerked his arm around, causing Stubs to spin awkwardly and stumble back in a sloppy pirouette.

"Leave him, if he doesn't want water he won't get any. We break from the river today, boys, he'll see the consequences of that choice when we cross the flatlands."

Scott blinked in alarm. The flatlands? He'd never been that far before, even his brother and father on quail drives always stuck close to the rivers that cut through the scrubby hills. The flatlands held nothing but searing hot ground and shimmering heat waves. What could survive out there?

The Jumper glared at Delgado in defiance until finally Stubs and he went to get ready to leave.

Scott dared not make a sound to give attention to himself but he wished he could communicate to the Jumper. He really wished he hadn't wasted his water like that, who knew when they would be offered it again? As much as Scott hated the lizards he knew better then to pass on offered water. They needed the water to survive.

The wagon gave a creak and a lurch as it started to go forward again. Scott watched the Jumper get to his feet and follow with his head twisting this way and that as if trying to see where they were or maybe where they were going.

Spike rode in the back driving the covey as they bunched together and before long they spread out, narrowing into a ragtag line to follow the wagon.

The sun was unforgiving on the harsh desert landscape as the hours dragged on. Inside the trunk it felt like an oven to Scott as the cramped space quickly heated up, soaking his collar with perspiration and blurring his senses until his head felt like mush. He had splinted his finger badly by picking apart the knife-hole in the front of the box to try and get at some fresh air, and had his face pressed against the jagged cut to breathe.

Outside the Jumper wasn't fairing much better. He was starting to stumble with his head bowed to shade his face from the sun. His steps were starting to meander as he tried to keep up with the wagon. His collar was dark with sweat and he was panting sluggishly. Every now and then he would give a half-hearted tug on the ropes, but he didn't have the energy to keep the fight up for long.

Delgado narrowed orange eyes from under the shade of his hat as he twisted in the saddle to look over his shoulder at how the wagon and covey was fairing. The birds were keeping up well enough but some of the younger fledglings looked tired and some were limping, their tender feet not used to the harsh heat under-talon and endless walking.

"Take the wagon over there in the shade of those big prickly pears." He ordered Stubs as he headed back to help round the quail to the slightly shaded area.

Scott was glad of the shade, even if it didn't make much of a difference inside the trunk. He looked out the keyhole as the wagon slowed to a halt and watched the Jumper sink to his knees to rest, looking weak and stiff.

Delgado oversaw the quail as the younger ones settled to rest and tired churrs heard among the others. He turned his head to inspect the Jumper and his eyes narrowed and his head nodded in approval. He was starting to break down. The heat would crack him into submission soon enough. Delgado turned to the prickly pear behind him and dismounted his quail. He twisted his slender body around the sharp and lethal cactus spines to get to the leaf of the succulent. Taking out his knife he carved out several chunks of plant then edged out again, careful not to let himself get snagged on the spines.

Scott flinched as the trunk lid flung open again and then small chunk of cactus was dropped down next to him with a thunk before the lid slammed shut again. Scott picked up the scrap of cactus and took a bite. It was crunchy and watery, not tasting like much with its cucumber-like flavor, but Scott was thankful for the moisture it gave him. He looked outside the keyhole to see if Delgado was giving any to the Jumper.

The Jumper barely flicked narrowed eyes up at Delgado as the lizard passed him, but he didn't bother to give the Jumper any of the prickly pear. Instead, he tossed shares to Stubs and Spike then turned and headed back towards his quail.

Scott swallowed another bite and looked to the Jumper, who had returned his gaze to the ground once more. Scott looked at the rest of the succulent plant in his hands then looked out at the Jumper.

The wagon started to lurch as Stubs climbed back into the seat. Scott dug his fingers into the cactus flesh and pried it apart. He started to break it into pieces in his hand. He peered out the knife-hole for a moment to check for the lizards then stuck the first small piece of the prickly pear out and let it fall to the ground outside. He looked over at the Jumper, who didn't raise his gaze from the ground.

Scott forced several more pieces of the prickly pear out of the hole in the trunk and he froze as the Jumper's ear twitched and he flicked his head up sharply, his eyes boring into the trunk, staring unseeingly at Scott. The Jumper's eyes dropped seeing the cactus on the ground but made no move towards it.

Scott felt the wagon lurch as it started to move. "Come on…" he murmured seeing the Jumper's ears perk at the sound of the wagon. The tall mouse rose to his feet and started forward, bending at the last second to snatch up the bits of cactus with his bound hands.

Scott let out a sigh of relief. At least he would get some sort of water now. He tried to catch the Jumper's eye for any sign of a thanks but the wild rodent was looking at the ground once more, squinting in the bright light.

The wagon left the sanctuary of the cactus shade as Delgado led the group towards the flatlands, away from the scrub hills, a land that blurred into sky on the horizon in a trembling haze of shimmering heat.

16

Mitch groaned slightly and squinted open his eyes as he woke up. He wasn't sure where he was, but he became aware he was lying on a bed. His torso felt stiff and he realized it was a little easier to breathe now, but he still hurt. He perked his ears slightly hearing voices and blinked the blurriness from his eyes. There were two figures bent over the cot looking down on him.

"He awake, Doc?" Asked a pale mouse with a reddish, whisker mustache.

Mitch flinched as he felt a hand on his forehead. A black furred mouse peered close to check on him.

"Yes, he's awake. I splinted his ribs and bandaged that graze in his shoulder, your work I presume? Were you ready to talk to him?"

Mitch was confused why they seemed to be talking over him like he wasn't there. After the doctor removed his hand from his head he shifted to try and sit up.

"Stay down!" The reddish mouse snapped the order and Mitch laid his ears back in surprise at the hostility in his tone.

"Sorry, er, excuse me. Sirs, where am I?" Mitch tried to recall what happened. There had been a fight at the river. He'd taken a painful hit to the ribs that dropped him. He frowned feeling something heavy on his wrist and turned his head to look at his right hand and blinked in surprise.

His wrist was clasped into a set of iron cuffs that were also clipped to the railing on the wooden headboard of the cot.

"What's all this?" Mitch asked, blinking in confusion.

"Quiet down, boy. You're in a heap of trouble." The red mouse stood up looking angrily down at him in a pose that suggested ultimate authority. "You're under arrest for quail thievery and assault on a young lady. In my town we don't tolerate either."

Mitch's blue eyes widened as he shook his head rapidly.

"What?? Sir, I think there's been a mistake, I'm no thief, and I was trying to help that doe—"

The red mouse wasn't even listening. "Is he well enough to move to the jail house?" he asked the doctor, turning his shoulders away from Mitch as if dismissing his words and presence entirely.

Mitch felt his heart thudding loudly in his ears at the news. He was under arrest? He hadn't done anything wrong! His eyes flicked up at the mention of the jail house and he looked to the black-furred doctor.

"He's a little sore I should think, but doubt he'll be in the jail house long." The doctor said without looking up from packing his black leather bag.

"What? What do you mean?" Mitch asked, feeling his shoulders tense as he guessed the words that the reddish mouse growled out a moment before he said them.

"Thievery and assault is punishable by hanging in my town. And of course there's being associated with the Jordan Gang." The sheriff's eyes bored into Mitch's startled face then he turned to the doctor. "Sorry you had to waste your bandages, Mosley."

"As long as you keep ridding this area of this sort of trail scum it's the least I can do." Mosley shut his bag with a snap that made Mitch frown.

"Hang on, sir!" he spotted the silver star pinned on the reddish mouse's vest. "Sheriff, you haven't been listening. I wasn't stealing birds down there. Honest, I've never heard of the Jordans. I have perfectly good riding quail of my own, as well as a covey of Californias back on my pa's ranch, what use is a gaggle of bobwhites to me? Sheriff I'm not a thief!" Mitch flinched as the sheriff pulled out his gun and spun it on his finger and then fingered the long black barrel fondly as he addressed him.

"I have no need for your useless lip, and I've heard enough lies from quail rustlers to last me ten lifetimes. You have a covey? Then where is it?"

Mitch tried to sit up again. "I don't have them on me, they were stolen by rustlers, *real* rustlers, two horned lizards and a third, a tall lizard... he had a blue tail... with... yellow... stripes." Mitch slowed his tale as the sheriff snorted and the doctor laughed in amusement.

"Blue stripy lizards? You think I'm a fool? Your lie might get you out of turning in papers to the local school house, but they won't pass me, thief. Unless you give me the names of the other riders, I can promise you'll hang before tomorrow night."

Mitch gritted his teeth. "I'm telling the truth! The lizard's wanted poster is in my vest, wherever you've put it, and my friends can tell you the truth!" His eyes widened as the doctor held up the wanted poster, blotted out from the water of the stream, reducing the image to a blotchy, ink smeared mess.

"Your friends? The other rustlers?" The sheriff looked intrigued. "Go on."

"They aren't rustlers! They're hardworking, honest ranch hands just like me! They work for my father! Buck Thorn! We own a ranch near Redcliff!"

"Steady your tone, boy." The doctor snapped at him as the sheriff snorted.

"I've never heard of anybody named, Buck Thorn. We'll send a rider to Redcliff to seek him out; in the meanwhile you'll stay in our jail house cell where we can keep an eye on you."

"But riding to Redcliff will take all day! And who knows if he's even there! My Ma's ill and he took her to Monty. I don't know when they'll be home!" Mitch tried to gesture but his chained hand prevented much movement.

"Oh boy, you just have an excuse for everything? Well, I'll send a rider to Redcliff, and if Buck Thorn isn't found in three days," the sheriff stood straight and holstered his gun, "then I'll watch you hang and enjoy every damn second of it."

Mitch shook his head in disbelief. They weren't listening to him. He could see it in the sheriff's bright, maddened eyes, his mind was set. He was going to hang him either way.

"You can't do this." He shook his head in frustration.

"I'm the law in Hanson, stranger, I can do as I please." The sheriff put his hat on and headed towards the door. "Lock the door after you, Mosley, I'll send Adam and Shaw back here to take him to the jail house soon."

The doctor nodded and faithfully followed him out of the room, closing the door and locking it with an audible click.

Mitch felt cold dread in the pit of his stomach. He couldn't afford to wait for three days. He'd be hung for sure, and even if he wasn't he might lose the trail for good, and Scott was still out there.

"I don't have time for this!" Mitch muttered darkly and shook his restrained wrist, listening to the chain clatter against the wooden headboard.

Mitch twisted his head to see the rail the second cuff was secured to and narrowed his eyes. He kicked the sheets away and pivoted gingerly on his back until he could kick at the wooden bar. After three sharp kicks the wooden rail snapped and he was able to slip the second cuff ring off.

He quickly stood up, ignoring the numb pain to his bandaged ribs.

"Boots, boots where did they put them?" He murmured as he hurried around the room quietly until he found the rest of his damp clothes and boots. He pulled his shirt and vest on without bothering to button either before cramming his hat onto his head and crossing to the door. He jiggled the handle to test it, but it was locked like he had thought.

Noise from outside the bedside window made him turn and edge towards the light coming in through the thin cotton curtains. Pulling one to the side, he looked down to see a porch roof and the street below. The activity was light this time of day when the heat was at its hottest, most creatures were inside trying to keep cool.

"I'm coming Scott." He murmured and he pulled open the window and stepped out onto the roof gingerly. He swallowed slightly not fancying the drop to the street below with his legs feeling as shaky as they were.

Mitch edged along the roof toward the far side of the building, looking for a place to climb down when suddenly the sheriff and the doctor walked out from under the very porch of the roof he was crouched on, they headed into the street talking quietly to one another then paused in the sun to carry on their conversation.

Mitch froze, totally exposed on the roof, if the two of them turned around now they would see him, no doubt about it. He held his breath and backed up slowly to one of the nearest windows and felt behind him for the glass or wood.

Suddenly a pair of hands thrust through the curtains of the next window, one arm seizing him around the waist and another clapping over his mouth to stifle his gasp of shock as he was pulled backwards through the window into the room.

The sheriff and the doctor looked up at the noise but seeing nothing they carried on with their conversation.

Mitch fell backwards onto another bed near the window, almost landing on his captor but they managed to move in time.

"Shh!" June snapped at him as Mitch sat up abruptly as if to ask something. She peered out the window, watching the sheriff and the doctor cross the street to the post office and disappear inside.

She turned and let out a long sigh then narrowed her eyes at Mitch as he jumped to his feet.

"Who are you?" He demanded.

"You're welcome!" June snapped, tossing her hair behind her shoulder and giving her tail a lash of agitation.

"What?" Mitch arched a brow and backed away from her, not sure to trust anyone in this crazy town anymore.

"Sheriff Slaughter would have killed you and Doc Mosley would have been thrilled to pronounce you dead! Why were you sneaking around on the roof like a lizard!"

Mitch's head was reeling in confusion so he blurted out his question again.

"Thanks, I suppose but WHO *are* you!"

"June Jordan!" June grabbed his hand, shaking it roughly with no sign of actual friendliness in the introduction, her sea-green eyes sparked in annoyance.

"Mitch Thorn." Mitch grunted back and withdrew his hand. "What's going on?"

"That sheriff has been obsessively hunting criminals for the past six years, he's gone a bit noose happy and I've seen him hang a young man for something so petty as stealing a pair of boots." June peered out the window then whipped around to face Mitch.

"I heard you in there, I know you did nothing wrong, but Slaughter is crazy, mad even. He's going to hang you and anyone who tries to back you up. You're a stranger in these parts and that makes you the target enemy."

"Is this whole town crazy? Why do they let that weasel run this place?" Mitch seemed shocked at the sheriff's description then frowned. Wait, June Jordan? The Jordan *Gang*? That's what he accused me of being a part of!"

"Because they're all morons who think he's keeping them safe from every possible bit of harm." June crossed the room briskly and opened the door, sneaking a glance around the stairwell before beckoning him over. "Yes, the same Jordan. And no, the gang is no more, just shut up and follow me."

Mitch followed tensely, mind reeling.

"Your quail is outside the sheriff's office next to the jail." She murmured as she stole into the hall. "Now shh, don't make a sound."

"But what about—"

"*Shh!*"

Mitch narrowed his eyes at June's snappiness, but had to trust her as she lead him downstairs into the sitting room below, no one was there.

"Doc and Sheriff like to check the post and the arrival of the mail coach when it comes in before their lunch, we haven't got long."

"Why are you helping me?" Mitch asked, his head still spinning from the accusations the sheriff made and now June's blunt delivery of assistance.

"You helped me down by the stream, consider it payback." June grabbed his sleeve and hurried him to the back of the building. They stepped out the door into the shaded alley.

"Now hush and keep close, if the sheriff catches you out here consider yourself target practice." June narrowed her eyes gravely and Mitch nodded, uneasily. What a mess he'd gotten himself into again.

17

Bo frowned as he headed down the main street with Charlie and Jared. Bo had hoped Mitch would return for his canteen by now, but then again Mitch wasn't himself lately. He was impulsive, worried, desperate and snappy. Bo wanted to help him, but Mitch didn't want to be helped so it seemed.

The black-and-white ranch hand looked over at Charlie, who had tapped his arm and was pointing across the road where Cali was tied to a hitching post in front of the sheriff's station.

"Cali? Well what do you know; he must have come back here after all. Whew, glad some sense got drilled into that thick skull of his. He must be asking the sheriff for some help. C'mon you two." Bo headed up the steps with Charlie while Jared grumbled and trailed them into the building.

A young deputy, a skinny pale gray mouse, was sitting at a beautifully carved oak desk, his boots were kicked up and resting on top of the desk and a cigar was sticking out of his mouth awkwardly, as if he wasn't sure how to hold it. Upon seeing the three newcomers the young deputy jumped and scrambled to remove his feet from the desk, knocking a jar of pencils over. He dabbed the cigar into the tin ash tray before standing abruptly, trying to pick up the pencils and put them back into the jar.

"Gentlemen, is there something I can help you with? The uh, the sheriff's not here right now…"

"Take it easy sonny," Bo grinned disarmingly and waved his hands telling him to slow down. "We were actually looking for a friend, have you seen the rider of that California hen outside? He's a fellow about this high," Bo drew a line about level with his chin with his hand. "He's got a bruised face, reddish brown fur, stubborn look in his eye?"

The young gray deputy blinked and rubbed the back of his neck. "Oh, you mean the quail thief that Sheriff Slaughter brought in about an hour ago? He's with the doc and… wait, you lot aren't with him are you? I uh…" The young mouse backed away from the desk slightly, suddenly feeling outnumbered.

"What? Quail thief? What are you talking about, sonny?" Bo cocked a brow and even Charlie and Jared looked puzzled.

"That's what the sheriff said; he's under arrest for quail rustling, and assault on a young woman by the stream. He thinks he's part of her old man's old gang come back to town."

"Hold on there, boy, your sheriff's got the wrong man there, Mitch is probably the most honest man I know. He's got no business stealing birds. He works on his father's quail ranch, he can get all the birds he needs! As for assaulting a young woman, the man's not so much as looked at another dress-clad lovely since his floozy fiancé left him high and dry last year. Avoids them like the plague."

The young gray mouse shuffled his boots, his eyes flicked to Bo then the desk papers then back. He looked as if he wanted to believe the kindly faced stranger but obey the sheriff's orders at the same time.

"Are you sure?" the young deputy asked, his eyes darting to Charlie and Jared.

Jared grudgingly nodded, looking sour and annoyed. Charlie nodded, his eyes sincere as Bo grinned.

"Of course! Mitch would never steal anything, wouldn't take an apple off a tree without asking the branch's permission first! Can you tell us where to find this sheriff? Perhaps we can talk reason with him, I'm sure this is all a big misunderstanding."

The gray mouse's mouth twitched slightly at Bo's contagious smile and he nodded. "I uh, I could take you sirs to him—oh but mind you he's probably eating and I can't leave the office, but he's probably at Rosie's Cantina. It's the little Inn and restaurant across the way by the post office. He and the Doc take lunch there every day, I'm sure you'll run into him there".

"Much obliged, kid." Bo tipped his hat, then picked up the cigar the deputy had left in the tin and struck a match on his belt, lighting the end. "Tend to work better when they're properly lit." he extended the cigar to the deputy who took it with a nod of thanks.

Bo followed the others out of the building and started to head down the street.

June lead Mitch through the back door of the general store and lead him to the front window to see out into the street.

"There's Cali." Mitch said, seeing his hen tethered next to a gaudy looking mountain quail with a long topknot feather.

June nodded. "I'll get her and bring her around to the back of the store, stay put." She left the store before Mitch could say anything. He was stuck watching her as she crossed the street and headed toward the hitching post.

Cali turned her head toward the doe that approached her, not recognizing her as her rider she huffed and turned away indifferently.

June reached up to untether her and Cali narrowed her eyes and let out a sharp clucking sound. This mouse wasn't her rider! Why was she untying her? She was a stranger!

"Cali, shh!" June cooed softly, trying to calm the aggravated hen as the bird tugged at the tether and scratched at the ground loudly.

Mitch bit his lip; Cali would never let another mouse untie her apart from him or the ranch hands. She would make noise and try to alert him or Bo about it and right now the last thing they needed was his quail drawing attention.

June untied the reins and tugged lightly at Cali's halter, reaching up she patted her cheek feathers. "Easy, girl, it's alright. I'm taking you back to your rider."

Cali snorted loudly and scuffed at the ground.

"It's alright, come on, come with me—"

"What are you doing?" The young, gray-furred deputy asked from the doorway, drawn to the sound of Cali's alarm.

"I…" June's mind whirled then she smoothly put a hand on one hip and adopted an irate expression. "What does it look like I'm doing? The sheriff comes riding in full bore with a rustler and leaves a perfectly good riding quail out in this sweltering heat in full tack with no water? I was sent over her to put her in the stables and let her have a good preen. Just because a bird's got a rotten rider doesn't mean we should abuse the poor thing."

The gray deputy blinked a few times then nodded. "Er, alright, carry on." He leaned against the doorway, showing no signs of going back in the building anytime soon.

June nodded and turned, swearing softly under her breath as she made her way away from the general store towards the stables under the deputy's watch.

Mitch watched her in confusion from the store window. Where was she going with his quail? He was beginning to have second thoughts about trusting this bossy doe.

Further down the street Bo pushed Jared in the shoulder so he would stop complaining.

"I told you he said Rosie's was this way but no—"

"Hey, what's this?" Bo cut Jared off, frowning slightly seeing a strange doe leading Cali towards them. Bo picked up his pace as he neared her.

"Excuse me miss, where are you going with this bird?" he asked.

June narrowed her eyes up at the stranger. "What business of yours is it where I take my quail?" she asked testily, not sure who these mice were.

"Um, well, for starters, that's not *your* quail." Bo gestured to Cali, who was fidgeting excitedly at the sight of the familiar faces.

"Very well, I'm taking her to the stables." June smiled sweetly at them. "Care to join me? I may not be able to handle her."

Bo grinned at the pretty young mouse. "Gladly, ma'am." He followed her with Charlie and Jared into the stables.

From the window of the store Mitch watched June and Bo's confrontation then saw them head towards the stables. He glanced down the street and decided he'd have to get over there somehow himself. He eyed the deputy and waited for him to go back inside.

Once inside the stables June's false sugariness dissolved as she grabbed a pitchfork and pointed it at Bo's chest, forcing him and the others back towards the wall.

"Who are you and how do you know this quail?" She demanded.

"Whoa, easy there miss, don't go poking holes in people." Bo grinned sheepishly, holding his hands up.

"Augh! Put that thing down you crazy —" Jared was smacked by Bo and Charlie on either side, who were both trying to remain calm.

"Answer the question." June narrowed her eyes.

"I'm impressed at your cunning, young miss, I'm Bo, Bo Jensen, this here's Charlie Nickels, and that annoying one cowering behind me is Jared Pierce. We're friends of that quail's rider, Mitch Thorn? Something tells me you two are already acquainted? I must say, you're quite pretty, must have had him pretty tongue tied."

June arched a brow, the black-and-white one talked too much. She raised the pitchfork slightly higher.

"June!" Mitch slipped into the stable, having just dashed across the street, and seized the pitchfork, forcing the tips down. "June they're alright, they're my friends."

"Hmph," June snorted slightly and looked at Bo who was still grinning as he adjusted his hat.

"Glad to see you again, Mitch." Bo said crossing over to him. "Looks like you got patched up a bit, I heard you got arrested?"

"I *am* under arrest, I broke out, Bo, that crazy sheriff's gonna hang me." Mitch stumbled slightly as Cali hurried over and pushed her head into his shoulder with a soft churr of delight at seeing her rider again. Mitch smiled gently and patted her head. "It's ok, Cali."

June folded her arms as she came back from checking outside. "Well, great we've missed our chance, Slaughter and Mosley have left Rosie's and now they're going to have tea on the porch. There's no way to leave without being seen."

"You mean, we're stuck here?" Mitch asked in exasperation.

"Well, *you're* stuck here." Jared pointed out dryly and Charlie glared at him.

June looked at Jared then to Mitch and finally to Cali. She twisted a finger in her hair then looked up. "You three *can* leave… that's it! I have an idea." She beckoned them over to reveal her plan.

18

The trek across the flatlands had been long and hot, especially in the trunk, but now as Scott looked out the keyhole he could see large reddish rocks spiking up from the ground. They had reached a monolithic rock formation that cast a huge shadow shading them from the sun. It was an entrance to a canyon.

The wagon gave a sharp jostle and Scott felt himself leaning forward. Were they going up? From outside he saw the Jumper still tied to the wagon following up a rough looking rock ledge that served as a crude path.

Scott shifted and tried to see if he knew where they were, but all the keyhole revealed was the enormous rock formations. He could not remember ever being in this area before, then again, he had never traveled too far outside of Redcliff.

In the lead, Delgado signaled to Stubs to stop the wagon with his hand. They had gone as far up the rock face as they wagon wheels could handle.

"Park it under that ledge, bind up that mouse and bring him out here. Spike, mind those birds and make sure they don't spook off the trail."

Scott barely heard Delgado's muffled words, but the next thing he knew the trunk lid was flung open and he was looking into the ugly, scaly face of Stubs. The horned lizard reached in and grabbed the front of his shirt, hauling him up and out with one fist as if he was a sack of cornmeal. Scott's feet dangled off the ground for just a moment before he was dropped and had a noose around his throat before he could even think about bolting. The Jumper saw the creature inside the box for the first time but his expression barely changed from angry and exhausted. Stubs severed the tie to the wagon after throwing another rope around the Jumper's neck and tying it to the end of Scott's rope so he could lead them both at the same time as they continued up the cliff face. The ledge trail disappeared almost completely leaving rough, rocky jumbles to be climbed.

Scott swallowed slightly as he was led by the lizard; he glanced sidelong at the Jumper who was a little further behind him. The Jumper was gazing over Scott's head with narrowed eyes at the back of Delgado, who lead from atop his quail.

When they rounded a sharp bend the rock face opened up to a wide crescent ledge with a fair sized nook in the rock face.

Looking down below Scott saw a river threading lazily along a mostly dry bed. He stiffened realizing how high up they were. Where could they possibly be going? Were these rustlers going to pitch them over the side?

Scott's questions were cut off by a grating, rumbling sound. He looked over his shoulder in shock to see thick, scaly coils wrapping around the edges of a rock that Scott had originally thought was part of the wall.

The massive diamond-patterned coils gripped the huge rock and started to slide it to the side, revealing a great black hole in the cliff face.

Scott was pulled to the ground as the Jumper leapt backwards in alarm, eyes wide as the massive triangular head of a rattlesnake appeared from the entrance. The long, forked, black tongue flickered in and out to taste the air before it gave a cruel smirk and slithered the rest of the way out onto the crescent ledge.

Scott's heart leapt into his throat. The great snake was big enough to wrap itself around his *house*! Stubs jerked at the thrashing Jumper's rope to still him, but the wild mouse kept pulling and straining to get away from the direction of the serpent.

More noises from the hole caught Scott's attention as several dozen critters made their way out; Banded geckos, fence lizards, collared lizards, horned lizards, beaded lizards, desert toads and a few patchy-furred mice and rats all armed to the teeth with pistols, ammunition belts and sharp looking knives. Several even held coils of rope as they spread out on the ledge past where the great snake was coiling to give them room.

Now there seemed to only be one lizard left in the hole. Scott could hear the heavy steps and the clink of spurs. His mouth dropped open slightly as a massive Gila monster swaggered out of the tunnel, easily doubled in height over most of the lizards there and at least four times as broad. His giant, blunt head was masked in bumpy, black scales and laced with fiery orange patterns from the crown of his head down his back. His thick, muscular tail was banded orange and black, dragging on the ground from beneath a long, leathery overcoat as he made his way past the others, patting the under scales of the rattlesnake before standing before Delgado.

Even on quailback Delgado was shorter than the giant lizard, and by the look in his flame-colored eyes he was less than enthused to see him.

The Gila laughed richly in a gravely deep voice. "Nice face, Delgado, you get my birds?"

Delgado snorted. "Spike's got 'em, also picked up a mouse and a Jumper. Figured you'd find use for them too."

"A Jumper?" the Gila sounded much more interested and turned toward Stubs who was trying to pull the struggling wild mouse into view.

"He's kinda a strong one, boss!" Stubs puffed.

"They all are in the beginning." The Gila smiled cruelly and beckoned his other lizards forward with a curved white claw. "Bring him over."

The collared lizards with the rope coils hastened to obey, casting their lassos around the Jumper and pulling him forward. Stubs kicked the backs of the Jumper's knees and he stumbled to the ground. Rough, scaly hands grabbed his shoulders and forced him to stay down.

The Jumper panted from the struggle and glared up at the Gila as he came over. The huge lizard took a knee smirking down at the Jumper he grabbed a fistful of his golden head fur and pulled his head back exposing his throat and chest.

Scott panicked from the ground; the Gila was going to kill him! His heart pounded in his throat as he got tensely to his feet.

The smile on the Gila's face vanished as he turned to Delgado.

"Where is it!" he bellowed.

"Where's what!" Delgado snapped, his patience already dangerously thin.

"The stone! You idiot! What did you do with it?"

"I never saw it, Sol Diablo, ask Spike and Stubs." Delgado hissed through gritted teeth.

The Gila made a loud hissing sound in the back of his throat then turned to the Jumper.

"Where's the stone!" he demanded. The Jumper's eyes narrowed coldly up at him and didn't respond. "Where is it you wild rat!" Sol Diablo pulled out a massive pistol, at least five times bigger than any rodent gun Scott had ever seen, it looked like a small cannon to him. The monstrous reptile pushed it into the Jumper's chest, cocking back the hammer with a loud click. When the Jumper made no move to respond Scott panicked and before he could stop himself he called out.

"He can't understand you!" he blurted, having no idea what sort of stone they were talking about. He quailed as every set of cruel eyes on the ledge turned to him and his heart rate raced as the Gila rose and lumbered slowly over to him. The Jumper's eyes flicked from Scott to the Gila then back as the Gila crouched down, still looming over Scott. Behind the Gila, the rattlesnake uncoiled and slithered up alongside him and the mouse.

"Look here, Morgan. A new worker for the mines no doubt, doesn't seem to know his place just yet."

"Give it time, Sol Diablo, I'll soon have him working until his bones crack."

The Gila smirked and rested a wickedly curved white claw under Scott's chin. "You be a good little slave, mouse, or I'll feed you to my friend Morgan here."

Scott stiffened feeling the forked tongue tickle the back of his neck.

"I do love the taste of young mouse flesh." Morgan laughed cruelly. "Especially when it's still alive."

A pebble bounced from the top of the Gila's head and he turned to see the Jumper, struggling to his feet despite the three lizards trying to force him down, his eyes practically giving off sparks from his livid glare, lips curled back as he bared his teeth.

Sol Diablo snorted a laugh and turned to the others. "Take them to the tunnel!" he snapped and the other lizards came forward, seizing their ropes and leading them towards the dark, gaping hole. Scott was practically running to avoid being dragged along the ground. He entered the cave with the others and discovered they had entered a long cavernous tunnel lit with lanterns along the walls. The world grew darker and cooler and Scott strained to look behind him in horror seeing Morgan coiling around the big rock and sliding it closed once more. There was a last sliver of light and then it was gone.

Scott was bodily picked up and thrown to the right, down a sloping tunnel cavern. He shuffled to sit up and scrambled back as four lizards wrestled with the Jumper to pin him to the wall. They were tying his wrists to the iron rings studded into the rock.

Stubs smirked as he oversaw them struggling. "Make sure to tie those arms back good and tight, we don't want him throwin' any punches." The Jumper snorted and lifted both long feet and shot them out in a powerful kick, launching Stubs across the cavern into the opposite wall with a heavy thud. Stubs grumbled and swore as he stood up. "You idiots!" he snapped at the others who had finished securing the Jumper back and quickly cleared the way to avoid being kicked as well.

"Let's go." Stubs growled out and left the tunnel with the others. There was a loud grating sound as a second slab door was rolled shut over the tunnel and then silence.

Scott squinted in the dim light cast by a single lantern on the floor one of the lizards had left in their haste to get out. He pushed himself onto his knees and looked over to see the Jumper struggling without success to get free. Finally he paused, slumping slightly and panting to regain some energy.

Scott loosened the rope around his own neck and let it fall to the floor. The others had been so occupied with the Jumper they had failed to bother securing him further or perhaps they just didn't care since he wasn't much of a threat. There was no way he could open the door to escape.

He rubbed the raw spots on his neck where the rope had rubbed before standing up and brushing off his knees. Here he was, alone in a cave somewhere, with a Jumper. He was a prisoner. He jumped slightly as the Jumper started to struggle again, rattling the iron rings loudly.

The Jumper pulled at the rings and stomped at the ground trying to get free but soon gave up for a moment to catch his breath once more with his head down. Scott swallowed and slowly started to step closer towards the wild mouse. The Jumper was easily twice his height if not taller, and he'd seen what a powerful kick could do to a big lizard like Stubs, a kick to a mouse his size could be fatal. He pried his tense gaze from the Jumper to the rings on the walls; he could untie them… but then what? Would the Jumper kill him? Scott wasn't sure, but as he was contemplating the Jumper's head snapped back up and glared fiercely at him, baring his teeth and laying his ears back in aggression. Scott stumbled back and fell, scrambling to put distance between them until he remembered the Jumper was tied fast.

"I… I'm not gonna hurt you." Scott said nervously, putting his hands up slowly. The Jumper ceased teeth-baring, but still eyed him with hostility and suspicion.

Scott kept his hands up slightly and he slowly got to his feet. "I… I can, untie those… if you want? But… you're not gonna hurt me either… r-right?" he asked as he took a few tense steps forward, trying to keep out of range of the Jumper's kick zone.

The Jumper blinked steadily at him but didn't answer, finally he looked away and flicked an ear.

Scott guessed that meant he wouldn't hurt him as he dared get closer. The Jumper made no move to struggle or be aggressive and he returned slowly.

Scott stretched up and gripped the rope tired to the nearest ring. His eyes flashed to the Jumper in time to see him glance at Scott then back to the wall.

Scott let out a nervous sigh and started to pry the knots apart.

"This is crazy." He muttered to himself, his voice resounding softly in the spacious tunnel. "I can't believe I'm doing this…" He looked up at the Jumper who was still looking away from him. Scott sighed as the knot loosened enough to be undone.

"I just wish you could understand me." As he unbound the Jumper's wrist, the Jumper let out a sigh of relief, flexing his hand to circulate the blood once more before turning to Scott with an arched brow.

"And what makes you think I can't?"

PART II

Escape from the Mines

19

June led a jaunty looking bobwhite into the stable. The bobwhite looked over at the others and tilted its head curiously, letting out a friendly '*chup*' sound of hello. Cali gave the other quail a dismissive clicking sound and turned back to watch her rider who was changing shirts with Charlie.

Mitch winced and moved stiffly due to the tight bandaging around his ribs as he buttoned up Charlie's red shirt which was several sizes too big for him. Charlie's broad shoulders barely fit into Mitch's blue shirt as the golden dormouse buttoned it up only in a few places before looking back at June questioningly.

"You really think this will work?" Bo asked, cocking a brow as he leaned against the nearest stall holding Cali's reins. "The sheriff's got a thicker skull than I thought if he can't recognize Mitch with a different shirt."

"Maybe, but on a different quail, Slaughter won't think twice about it. He'll be more suspicious of strangers riding Gambel's and Californias than bobwhites. Besides, Mosley's near sighted." June led her quail over as Mitch tucked in his shirt.

"This is Bowie, He's not the brightest, but he'll get you out of here." She handed Mitch the reins and Cali gave a cluck of dislike from across the stable.

"Cal, I can't ride you out of town, calm down." Mitch waved a hand at Cali and the hen scratched at the ground moodily.

"Just take him up over the ridge and out near the brush. I'll ride Charlie's quail out there and meet up with you."

Mitch nodded distractedly, unsure if he liked this plan or not, so many things could go wrong.

"Just wait until you hear the signal." June said as she donned her hat and stepped out into the sunlight carrying a small paper sack with her.

"What exactly is the signal?" Jared muttered to Bo, but loud enough for June to hear.

"You'll know." June answered without turning around as she headed out and down the street. They watched as she hesitated outside Doc's office and then went inside.

Mitch held his breath as he clambered stiffly onto the saddle of the bobwhite and waited next to Bo who was already atop of Cotton.

Bo looked over at Mitch and gave a reassuring smile. "Don't sweat it, Mitch." He thumped his shoulder lightly.

"I'll quit sweating it when we've left this town in the dust." Mitch muttered back dryly then jumped inwardly as a loud banging sound erupted down the street like gun fire followed by several screams and yells.

"I'm gonna take a wild guess and say that's the signal!" Bo had to raise his voice slightly over the loud pops and bangs sounding from down the street.

Bowie gave several squawks of confusion at the loud sounds and Bo leaned over, slapping the quail's wing.

"Come on Mitch let's go! You two go around the back and meet us over the ridge!" Bo instructed Charlie and Jared before spurring Cotton out of the stables in a fast run with Mitch and Bowie right on his tail.

June had her back flat to the side of the building as she grinned in spite of herself. She'd dropped the paper bag filled with fire crackers along with a lit match into the bronze spittoon outside the door of the doctor's office and went inside before screaming about a gun. When the crackers went off she watched from the window as both the sheriff and Doc Mosley threw themselves to the ground thinking they were under fire and crawled under the porch like a pair of spiders. June had slipped out the side door in time to see Charlie and Jared leave the stables before she darted back across the street to the stables herself to get Charlie's quail.

Just outside of Hanson, Bo led the way to a brushy part of the ridge before slowing Cotton to a brisk walk so he could turn and check on Mitch who wasn't far behind.

Mitch pulled up alongside Cotton on Bowie and tugged the reins, but the bobwhite cheeped and tossed his head spiritedly. Mitch frowned and tried to control his mount while the bobwhite gave a few hops and scratched at the ground.

"There's bobwhites for you." Bo pushed the brim of his hat up and rested his hands on the saddle horn.

Cotton gave a snort of irritation at the other quail's antics and seemed to straighten up as if to show how well-mannered quails behaved.

Mitch finally managed to control Bowie and rolled his eyes. "No wonder Pa never took an interest in bobwhites, I tell it to do one thing and it goes off and does what it wants! Probably not fully saddle broke."

Bowie clacked his beak and ruffled his reddish neck feathers before looking behind them with a peep of confusion.

Bo shifted to hear the others coming and looked back to Mitch. "So… you got *arrested*?" He smirked.

"Oh shut up." Mitch groaned as he undid Charlie's shirt. "I got arrested by a psychotic sheriff."

"What did you get arrested for, *bandito*?" Bo grinned teasingly and Cotton snorted.

"Helping June, she was getting roughed up and robbed." Mitch waved his hands trying to dismiss the subject as Charlie and Jared pushed through the brush into the cover. Mitch dismounted Bowie and handed Charlie his shirt back and waited to receive his once more. Cali churred and pecked at Mitch's tail affectionately until he swatted her topknot playfully.

Finally the sound of a quail riding through the brush reached their ears as June rode up on Charlie's Gambel's quail and slid down to return the dormouse his bird.

"Everyone alright?" she asked as she turned and pulled down a bag and roll she had tied to the back of the saddle before crossing over to Bowie and cinching it up again.

"Yeah, what's the gear for?" Mitch asked, slipping into his vest.

June patted Bowie's cheek and he tugged at the brim of her hat. She looked back to Mitch. "Well, I was thinking I'd come with you boys." She said brushing her hair off her shoulders and putting her boot in the stirrup to climb up.

"What? No. Absolutely not!" Mitch spread his hand wide in finality and narrowed his eyes. "Thanks for getting us out of there, June, but you aren't coming with us."

"Says who, bucko? Any reason I can't come along?" June replied sassily, her green eyes blazing in challenge.

"Because!" Mitch threw out as he tried to sum up a concrete reason. "Because it's too dangerous". He folded his arms. "And you'd slow us down."

"Excuse me?" June glared down from her saddle mount at Mitch. "Who had to get your tails out of town? You'd be in jail right now! I don't see any reason why I can't come along."

"Quiet down, lovebirds, you'll wake the baby." Bo teased beside Charlie.

"Oh shut up!" Mitch and June snapped at Bo at the same time, making the black-and-white ranch hand smirk.

"You have no business telling me where I can and can't go." June said haughtily to Mitch.

"I'm not responsible for you out there." Mitch glared back pointing into the desert.

"Of course not, I can take care of myself, now are you lot going to picnic here in the shade all day until the sheriff starts sniffing around or are you going to mount up and get back on your trail?"

Mitch looked like he'd been force-fed lemons as he turned sharply and climbed into Cali's saddle stiffly.

Jared rolled his eyes. "You just gonna roll belly-up to this girl and let her tag along? This is a buck's journey!"

"Then what the hell are you doing out here, Jare-Bear?" Bo rolled his eyes and glanced to Charlie.

"Girl yourself, saddle-trash. Don't make me find another pitchfork." June snorted at Jared then spurred Bowie out of the brush into the sunlight.

Mitch rode out ahead on Cali and broke her into a run to get back to the trail. They had already wasted enough time here, and now they had a tagalong. "Just what we needed," he grumbled.

20

Scott flinched in surprise and almost tumbled back again. "You can *talk*? I didn't know Jumpers could talk! Like us I mean…" he stammered looking up at the wild face of the Jumper still partially tied to the wall. The Jumper glanced at the ropes then back to Scott and raised a brow for him to continue untying him.

"Oh, uh, sorry," Scott crossed to the other side and stretched up to untie him from the other ring. "It's just, I can't believe it…"

"What's so hard to believe? That I can talk? Get over it, all of us can talk." The Jumper rubbed his freed wrists and set to work untying his neck and middle until he could stand freely. "Whether we can talk like you or not is different."

Scott tilted his head up as the Jumper stood. "Who taught you how? Settlers?" he took a few hasty steps back as the Jumper glared at him.

"No, settlers would rather kill us then bother *listening*." He growled out slightly. "No, my mother taught me, and she learned it from Father Willy. He was a mouse, I guess, a bit like you."

"Father who? Like a priest?" Scott asked in surprise.

"I guess," the Jumper shrugged. "From what I've heard." He took a few steps away from the wall and gave the place a good look around. When he turned, Scott could make out the rips in the back of his shirt from the switch lashes Stubs had given him.

Scott got up gingerly from the wall and watched the Jumper go towards the door and shove it. He frowned and thrust his shoulder into it and strained, but the slab didn't budge. Scott stepped over tensely.

"I think it only opens from the outside." He suggested gently as the Jumper glared at the slab with blazing eyes.

"This is useless, what is this place? Do you know?" The Jumper turned to Scott and looked down at him, lessening his glare.

Scott shook his head. "I don't know, they stole our covey, you know, quail? And... they killed my brother and took me. I'm as... in the dark as you." Scott swallowed slightly then backed up and sat down slowly on a rock, after being cramped in the wagon trunk for so long it felt better to sit up. He still missed Mitch so much; the memory was like a kick in the gut.

The Jumper's tufted tail swished across the ground. "They *killed* him?" he seemed surprised.

"Yeah," Scott said with a shake of his head. "I don't know what they wanted the quail or me for, but it can't be good. I've never seen a real rattler before, and the one out there scares the fur off me."

The Jumper nodded and backed up a little ways before sitting down, keeping the lantern between them.

Scott glanced up at the tired looking Jumper. He was covered in scrapes and bruises and his clothing looked ragged and torn. Scott sat up a little. "My name's Scott... Scott Thorn." He introduced, not knowing what to call the wild mouse.

The Jumper pricked his ears. "Scott?" he repeated then blinked as if deciding whether or not to give out his name before shifting slightly to get more comfortable. "Well, I'm Bright Storm, but they gave me another name when I was younger, Samuel, or Sam Bright Storm. Either name is good, both names are mine."

Scott listened interestedly as he wondered where he was from and how he had two names. Of course, he thought; he had two names, three if he counted his middle name. But he didn't press it.

"Bright Storm? And Sam?" he echoed. It made him think of lightning, the element seemed to match the Jumper's rapid fighting style and aggressiveness.

Sam nodded and continued to cast his gaze around the cavernous tunnel when he stiffened and stood up abruptly making Scott flinch in surprise.

"What's wrong?"

"We aren't alone." Sam muttered back so his voice wouldn't echo as loud.

Scott strained his hearing and heard a shuffling sound from the blackness beyond the lantern light. "Who's there?" he called out.

"Shh!" Sam hissed, flattening his ears at Scott.

"My question exactly, who's there?" a voice responded from the shadows.

Scott arched a brow, this voice didn't sound threatening like the lizards, it sounded almost shy, and an Irish brogue coated the few words spoken.

"Uh, I'm Scott Thorn." Scott looked up at Sam, who looked tense and defensive against the unseen speaker. "And Sam Bright Storm. Are you... a *slave*?" Scott asked remembering the Gila having called him his new slave, surely that meant there were others?

"Well, I guess you could call me that... if you're one of them. But you don't sound like one of them."

Scott looked and Sam then shrugged and pricked his ears to the next response.

"I can't see you from in here, but you can bring your light over this way. I won't hurt you."

Sam looked uneasy about it, but nodded stiffly as Scott picked up the lantern and headed further back into the tunnel. Scott was surprised that the tunnel abruptly ended at a wall of rocks and rubble, it looked like a cave-in had occurred recently.

"Over here." The voice spoke and Scott turned rapidly, shining the light into a huge crack in the wall, barred off with a cage-like door fashioned from bound sticks.

"Aye! Watch the light, please!" the voice sounded from inside the crack and shuffling was heard as Scott lowered the light.

"Who are you?" Sam demanded, taking a step closer to the crack in the rock and peering through the bars to see a huddle looking figure looking back with large green eyes.

"Er, well, they called me 'Pipsqueak' here when I started, I suppose you can too. Name's don't mean much anymore in this rotten place I guess. The others called me Pip, before…" The figure shifted in the dim light and Scott stepped back slightly seeing the strangest creature he had ever seen. He was bigger than Scott, but not by very much, and at first he thought he was a mouse. But then two enormous ears raised up and as Pip grew closer to the bars the light revealed a blunt muzzle and two sharp pointed teeth sticking out slightly and what looked like two folded wings bound tight to his sides with cord, causing him to shuffle awkwardly.

"You're a *bat*!" Sam said looking in at him and arching a brow. "But I've never a seen a bat like you before."

"Yes, well, so I've been told, my *kind* isn't from here." Pip settled against the cage bars and shifted to be able to see both of them. "I'm from Ireland."

"Ireland?" Sam cocked a brow in confusion and Scott nodded in understanding. "So you came over here… but how did you get in *here*, exactly?" he gestured to the dark cavern they now all shared.

"Long story short, I got caught and they threw me in here. They told me to cooperate or they'd cut off my wings or feed me to Morgan." Pip shuddered.

"Morgan?" Scott realized that the name sounded familiar. "You mean the –"

"—Snake, yes, the rattler. He's always coming in here lately, sticking that great tongue between the bars." Pip shivered. "He's been coming in less since the collapse; he can't find easy pickings anymore." Pip's eyes shifted downward and darkened.

"The collapse, you mean that?" Sam pointed to the pile of rubble that blocked off the tunnel. "What happened?"

Pip nodded and sighed. "There were others, mice, rats, some shrews, even some other lizards. They were forced to dig this tunnel. We were supposed to dig out to the other side, so we could follow this opal vein. The tunnel was supposed to break out to the other side, for dumping backfill and makin' a new entrance. My job was to listen for cave-ins... I told them not to... but they kept goin' and then..." Pip winced involuntarily. "The tunnel collapsed and killed almost all of them... those who didn't die were hurt, screamin' in the tunnels, half-buried, noise everywhere, then Morgan came and... and finished them off."

Sam balled his hands into fists at the story, his heart pounded and his stomach was hot with fury and icy with dread at the same time.

"That's horrible!" Scott was appalled.

"Yes, and they haven't got any new slaves since, the cave-in happened last month or so, but I can't remember. It's impossible to tell day from night in this pit."

Scott looked over at the mound of rubble as Sam went up and pulled at some of the loose stone.

"How close was the tunnel to being finished?" he asked as he turned around.

"Nearly there, we had another crew make a small tunnel to connect the two chambers, and then they were going to blast it open from the outside to make a big openin'."

"So, there's a tunnel on the other side of this one?" Scott felt hope rising in his chest.

"If it hasn't caved in with this one then it should be there, yes."
Pip nodded, narrowing his eyes slightly seeing their faces. "Wait,
what? Are you two thinkin'... no it's suicide!" He shook his head
nervously. "Morgan'll kill any who try to escape, I know, I've heard
their screams."

Scott bit his lip. The snake scared him, yes, but they needed to
get out. And if there was a way to escape then they should try.

"It's better to die trying to escape then live in this miserable hole."
Sam said darkly, resting his hand on the rubble pile. "I'm getting out."

"Gettin' out? You mean escapin'? Weren't you just *listenin'*?" Pip
said worriedly.

Scott blinked in surprise. "Wait, can we escape with you?" he
asked. "It would be faster if we worked together."

"*We?*" Pip looked nervous.

"Come on, Pip, you can't want to live in this hole for the rest of
your life. How long will that even be? You have to try."

"I..." Pip looked around the cave and laid his huge ears back. "I
don't know." He was afraid, Scott could tell, he had no idea how long
he'd been down here.

"We can do it Pip, but we need your help." Scott encouraged.

"You really think it would work?" Pip seemed skeptical.

"It has to." Sam came back over.

"Well, I suppose it's better to risk my life tryin' to get free, than
wait for it to end in here..." Pip's shaking voice didn't sound as
confident as his words.

Sam nodded and sat down on a rubble boulder. "We're getting
out of here." He nodded, "All three of us."

21

Late afternoon sun was beating down on the backs of Mitch and the others as they followed the wagon ruts through the brush. Mitch was still feeling sour about taking June along with them, after all, she had nothing to gain by coming along and she barely knew any of them. He couldn't imagine her being of any help to him or the others.

Bo, however, had dropped back and had been talking non-stop to June for the past two hours. Trying to charm her with a grin and a daring story until even Charlie was rolling his eyes and riding ahead next to Mitch to avoid the malarkey.

"Yeah, he was a big fella, huge mouse, did I say mouse? Nah, he was at least a rat. Meanest brush popper I'd ever seen, 'course I wasn't scared."

June groaned and looked over at Jared. "Does he ever stop talking?"

"No." Jared rolled his eyes and spurred his mount further ahead to avoid being roped into the next conversation.

Mitch straightened up in the saddle seeing a building not too far off near a cluster of prickly pear. "Hey hold up." He called back to the others, silencing Bo in the middle of his latest fight story.

"...so I jumped on his shoulders and reached back—What?" Bo glanced up at Mitch and June mouthed something that looking suspiciously like 'Thank God' before pulling alongside with Bowie.

"There's a building over there, I'm going to go check it out. Wait here on the trail."

"What? No way, who knows what sort of varmints live in there, nuh uh, I'm coming too." Bo said.

"Bo just stay here," Mitch rolled his eyes, not putting up much of an argument.

"I'm coming too." June rode past on Bowie and Mitch narrowed his eyes.

"Fine, Jared and Charlie stay here." He pointed at Charlie.

"What? What if I want to come!" Jared snorted.

"Stay!" Bo and Mitch said in unison before nudging their birds forward.

The rickety old shack looked like a building that was one good gust of wind away from collapse. Several scruffy looking mice and a shrew were sitting on upturned buckets and other makeshift furniture on the porch as Mitch, Bo and June rode up. Mitch eyed the rough looking characters before tilting his hat up.

"Afternoon."

"Effernon." A few of the porch dwellers muttered, squinting up at them with thick-lidded eyes. One of the brown, scruffy mice started to pick something out of his teeth with a pocket knife while the shrew pulled crusty debris from his whiskers.

Mitch straightened up a little. "Have any of you seen some lizards pass through here, particularly a blue-tailed one with yellow stripes?"

All the scruffy lot looked at each other and sniggered before the shrew gave a squeaky hiccup and fell off his bucket.

"Bluuuue lizzids!"

"Hurr, git up Jake you drunken beetle." The gray scruffy mouse with mustache-like whiskers snorted. "Yeah, we seen the blue lizzid."

Mitch's brows rose and even Bo looked surprised.

"When? Did you see which way he went?" Mitch asked, hope coursing through him. What if they were nearby?

The gray mustached mouse scratched the side of his neck with a smirk. "What's it to yeh where he went, boy?"

Mitch frowned. "It's just very important and we need to find him. Now can you tell us when he was here and where he went?"

"I dunno, fellas, should we tell him?" the gray mouse leaned back and asked the others snidely.

Bo frowned. "Look, mister, that blue lizard is a rustler and kidnapper and we aim to catch him, so tell us where he went. We're in a bit of a hurry."

The porch mice burst out laughing at Bo.

"Oh hee, hee, hee, he called Darnell '*mister*!'"

"In a *hurry* he says!"

"Catch a rustler with a *giiiiirrrrl*!"

June glared at them heatedly, but said nothing as Mitch moved closer to his companions with Cali.

"Look, it's obvious they aren't going to be much help unless we give them something." He muttered to Bo and her.

"Give them something? Like what?" Bo arched a brow. "We don't exactly have much, Mitch, what do you propose we give them?"

"How about a kick in the pants," June muttered icily. Mitch frowned at her, but was cut off from responding when the porch lot trailed off from laughing.

"Why you guys in a hurry, must be pretty important." The gray mouse, Darnell stood up and swaggered off the porch. "Infermation must be purty valuable."

Mitch clenched his jaw slightly. "Yes, it's very important, now will you just tell us what we need to know?"

"Tell you what, boy, that's a mighty fine hen you're ridin', I'll swap you the information for the hen." Darnell smirked up at him, behind him the others were getting up and coming down off the porch.

Mitch's eyes blazed and Cali made a chuffing noise, sounding almost as disgusted as he felt.

"Listen up you chiseler, this hen is worth more than a dozen of your run-down shacks and the lot of you thrown in together. I'm getting tired of asking you, so tell me where he went!"

"Chiseler? Amos, see how many holes you can put in that boy!" Darnell snorted and the brown mouse drew his gun and was greeted with sharp metallic sound a click from either side of Mitch.

"Drop 'em!" June barked from behind the sight of her rifle pointed at Darnell's chest while on Mitch's other side Bo had one pistol trained on the gun-wielding Amos and the other at the drunken shrew, who was trying to load his pistol and kept dropping the bullets.

"Nice and easy," Bo smirked at them. "Put 'em down."

"Now tell me where he went." Mitch demanded coldly, his icy gaze still having not left Darnell's smirking face.

"Huh, stupid boy, go after him, git yourselves killed and save us the trouble. Headed West's far as I know."

"When was he here," Bo growled out.

"Yesterday, noonish, or the day before, can't remember." Darnell shrugged. "You gonna shoot me, patches, or git lost?" Darnell snorted at Bo.

"We're going." Mitch glared at them and tugged the reins to turn Cali around. Bo kept one gun drawn and followed behind June and Mitch as they headed back towards Charlie and Jared.

"Whatcha find?" Jared asked as they met up and started back along the trail.

"Not a whole lot of solid information, but we know he came through here alright." Bo rolled his eyes as he tucked his gun back into his holster. "Let's get away from here, those mice looked like a rough bunch and I wouldn't want to be in their range after dark."

"Me neither." June snorted irritably. "I hope that lot meets up with a group of Harris hawks."

Mitch looked over his shoulder at the lengthening shadows he and Cali were casting on the dusty ground. He still couldn't believe that they wouldn't give them more information. He couldn't believe that they were so close, but still knew so little. Delgado had been there though, and they were going to find him.

"Mitch lets ride a ways up near the scrub hills and camp there for the night, by the time we get there it'll be nearly dark and that way we won't have to camp in the open." June suggested and glanced at Bo who nodded.

"Fine, but let's hurry, it's gonna get dark soon." Mitch flicked the reins and Cali picked up the pace.

A few hours later the sky was inky black and studded with a million stars as the travelers sat around a rough ringed campfire. Charlie had found the charred wood remains of a fire on the edge of the dry creek bed and Mitch hoped they were on the right trail, but it was getting too late to explore in detail.

Dinner was eaten in near silence as everyone munched their cornbread biscuits and drank from canteens. Even Bo seemed too tired for much conversation as the black-and-white ranch hand leaned back against a rock and unbuckled his holster to set aside for the night.

June had ended up sitting next to Mitch and the two mice ate tensely, trying not to glance at each other. Mitch finished first, almost hurriedly, and rose to his feet. "I'll go check on the quail and take first watch." He offered as he headed away from the light of the fire.

June watched him go with narrowed eyes then brushed crumbs off her chaps into the fire. "What's his problem with me anyways?" She muttered crossly to no one in particular then looked up at the remaining three ranch hands. "Well?"

Bo arched a brow and looked at Charlie. "It's not you, June, Mitch doesn't like any does!" he grinned with a shrug and Charlie elbowed Bo sharply with a cross look.

"Sorry, let me rephrase, Mitch doesn't *trust* does." Bo rubbed his shoulder and glanced at Charlie. "Happy?"

Charlie rolled his eyes and went back to consulting his canteen, letting June narrow her eyes and sit up in annoyance. "And why is that? What's a doe ever done to him? And even if they did why should he punish all does for it?"

"He might not like you 'cause you're annoying." Jared muttered from where he was rolling out his bedroll on the other side of the fire.

Bo glared at him and interlocked his fingers, stretching his arms over his head. "Well, it's kinda a long story." He started to explain.

"Well? What's the story?" June asked curiously. Why exactly did Mitch resent her so much in the first place? He barely even looked at her! Not that June wanted his attention, but she found it a little odd that he was so much colder than the others.

"Er... well—" Bo shrugged and Charlie elbowed him sharply again and shot him a look through narrowed eyes.

"Sorry, June, it's not really our story to tell." Bo said and rubbed his arm giving Charlie a cross look. "Besides, Charlie'll probably elbow a hole in me if I did tell you, so I'm gonna save myself a bruise and not get into it."

June sighed in mild frustration. "Fine, maybe I'll just ask him myself later." She rose and picked up her bedroll, crossing around the fire to roll it out.

"It'll be warmer over here." Jared snickered from inside his bedroll. "We could share body heat."

June found a fist –sized rock and hefted it at Jared's bedroll, catching him in the midriff.

"Ugh! Why'd'ja do that?" Jared rolled into a ball gasping.

"G'night Jared." She snapped and wrapped up in her bedroll, boots and all.

The night wore on and the fire started to burn down into small glowing embers. Charlie had taken over the watch for Mitch and was sitting on a rock near where the quail were resting, heads tucked under their wings or lolling down with beaks against their breasts.

The silent dormouse shifted to stretch out his back from his position when rough hands grabbed him from behind. A thick calloused hand clapped over his mouth and the cold barrel of a gun wedged against the side of his head.

"Stay quiet or I'll blow your ear out the other side of your skull." A gritty voice muttered.

Four others slunk into the camp towards the figures around the fire and drew their weapons. Jared was tackled in his bedroll and tied inside of it like a sack of feed. Mitch bolted awake hearing the commotion and was shoved to the ground before he could stand, his face shoved into the reddish soil and a boot planted between his shoulder blades.

Bo snapped awake and seeing his friends being attacked and quickly whirled around to see if someone was behind him. He came face to face with the drunken shrew from the rickety inn. The creature still only looked half sober and was holding a length of rope. He looked shocked that Bo had caught him in the act then proceeded to try and tie him up anyway.

Bo frowned and shoved the shrew backwards then turned to grab his gun belt when another mouse grabbed him from behind by the shoulders and flung him into Mitch.

"You son of a—", Bo tried to get up, but at that moment Darnell came into the weak firelight holding Charlie as his hostage.

"Settle down, patches." Darnell smirked and Bo glared at him and backed up, fists balled and shaking in quiet rage.

Darnell flung Charlie into his friends, knocking them down like ninepins as the four scruffy mice and the drunken shrew grew nearer to them.

Darnell laughed grittily. "Shoulda given us the quail, boys, woulda saved us the ride out here... hey, wasn't there a doe with you?" Darnell frowned.

"Yeah there was—" *WHAM! BONK! BONK! BONK! BONK!* All five armed mice and the shrew fell as they were attacked from behind. June stood behind them, having just swung her rifle butt across the backs of all their heads. She spun the rifle and cocked it with a loud click before surging forward and kicking Darnell over. She jammed the rifle so hard into Darnell's face that his nose went up the barrel.

"*That's* for calling me *girl*." June glared at him and rested her finger on the trigger. "Let them go, drop the guns and let them go!"

Darnell glared at the gun, but glancing into June's eyes he only saw fury so he flicked his ragged ears at the others and they dropped their guns.

Bo grabbed his guns and pointed them at the others. "Tie 'em up," Mitch told Bo. "Jared see if you can find their quail." Bo nodded, beckoning Charlie and the three mice untied Jared from his bedroll allowing him to go search for the rough bunch's quail. Then Bo and Charlie bound the hands of the three mice and shrew, leaving Darnell for last.

"Found their quail." Jared snorted, leading the five Gambel's quail into the firelight, several minutes later.

"They bound their feet in sheets, no wonder no one heard them stealing up." Bo looked to Charlie, who frowned seeing the bird's feet wrapped in dirty cloth and bailing twine.

"Tie their hands to the saddle horns." June said prodding Darnell sharply in the kidney with her gun as the others tied the ends of the ropes to each rider's bird.

"Follow us again and you'll regret it." Mitch glared at the other others. "If I even see your shadows out of the corner of my eye I'll put a hole though you."

"Like Swiss cheese." Bo snorted and spun his pistol in his hand testily.

"Get them out of here." June nodded to Bo and Mitch then all five trail riders smacked the bird's wings and fired shots into the air. The panicked quail bolted into the night, dragging their squealing and shouting riders behind them.

Bo fastened his holster about him once more then turned to June with a broad grin. "That was brilliant!"

"Good work I guess… for a *doe*, but we coulda handled it." Jared mumbled.

"Thanks June, that was great." Mitch said distractedly as he straightened up slightly. If it weren't for June they might have been killed.

June smiled at Bo then blinked at Mitch. "Well, next time maybe you guys will be more help, but alright."

Mitch suppressed an eye-roll of annoyance, "Yeah, ok. I'm gonna go check the quail. Er… nice work, again." He passed her and headed towards their birds and Bo ran up and thumped June's shoulder lightly.

"I'm still blown away by that, you were great! How did you hear them?"

"Truth is I… just got up for some water… it was nothing." June shrugged him off turned to Charlie to see if he was alright. "You ok?"

Charlie shrugged and nodded, dusting off his sleeves. June tilted her head in slight puzzlement then turned around to see Mitch with his quail, patting her beak and calming her down.

Behind him the sun was starting to lighten the horizon with a thin gray line, the night was drawing to a close and it had been anything but restful.

22

Inside the heated rock caverns of Sol Diablo's cave Delgado stirred in his chambers where he was resting on his firerock, stone furniture heated by a small fire that crackled in a grate below. It lit the room faintly with a dim red light that cast long shadows. The blue-tailed lizard had a bandana pressed to his cut face as he rested, but now, despite being surrounded by walls of rock, his internal clock was telling him morning was here, and it was time to get up.

Delgado sat up stiffly and swung his legs over the side of the rock, glaring at nothing in particular due to the stinging and swelling from the left side of his face where it had met the mouse's shovel. He stood and crossed the cave-like room. Delgado had few possessions that he didn't keep on him at all times. The cave room he occupied was mostly barren rock save for a long, leather overcoat thrown over a rock in the corner beside a few coils of rope, a whetstone, boxes of bullets and a few half empty sacks of dry goods.

Delgado buttoned up his shirt and pulled on his vest before donning his hat and leaving his chambers. He stepped out onto a ledge that looked down on the main cavern, the Red Dome, named for the dozens of flat, firerocks below in its center that kept the cave lit with a dim red glow and the hot, welcoming smell of warm stone.

Several lizards were still lounging on the rocks below, some sleeping, others grumbling back and forth with each other. All went silent as Delgado came down from his ledge and passed through them.

None of them wanted to get in his way this morning. He looked angry.

In his fist, Delgado clutched the folded wanted poster of himself as he headed towards the darker tunnels that branched out from the Red Dome, leading towards Sol Diablo's chambers. The warmth of the Red Dome lessened and the light grew dimmer as Delgado passed through the winding tunnel. The light faded to complete blackness until finally rounding the next bend, a light poured out from the chamber entrance into the tunnel again.

Delgado's boots made little sound as he headed closer, picking up the voices of Sol Diablo and Morgan from within. He couldn't help but grind his teeth; he'd hoped to confront Sol Diablo alone. He hated Morgan, but the great snake and the Gila were seldom far apart. Nevertheless, Delgado stepped into the doorway, fully illuminated by the light from the large crackling fire in the hearth behind Sol Diablo's enormous stone desk, set up by supporting a slab of stone across four stout rocks.

Sol Diablo was sitting at the desk while Morgan was coiled around the perimeter of the spacious room, his front half raised near the desk to look at the pile of colored gemstones the Gila was handling.

"Yes, yes, I know we need more slaves to finish the tunnels, all I'm saying is we've dug here for years, there just isn't enough here to keep going anymore." The Gila sounded frustrated as he gestured to one side of the desk, where only a Gila-sized handful of the colorful stones lay in a pitiful pile.

"But, look at the ones we've pulled from those savages." Sol Diablo pointed to a much larger pile of bigger stones on the left side of the desk. "Look at them, look at the *size* of them! Those Jumpers *know* where to find these stones."

"Yes, but how? Our opals have been no picnic to dig up and I doubt the Jumpers slave among themselves to find it." Morgan said in a gravely tone, shifting to prod the pile with his bulbous rattle. The snake glanced to the side and smirked. "Delgado is waiting for you." He muttered to the Gila and Sol Diablo glanced to the entrance of the room.

"Ah, Delgado, come in." The Gila sat up slightly and pushed back from the table, resting his huge boots on top of it. "What do you want?"

"It's what I don't want." Delgado flicked the folded paper onto the stone table and the Gila picked it up to unfold it as Morgan shifted to hover over his shoulder.

"Heh-heh ha! This ain't you." The Gila slammed the paper onto the table. "Take a look in the mirror Delgado."

"Yes, this critter doesn't have an ugly scar on his face, how's that going for you by the way?" Morgan leered, his black, forked tongue flickering.

Delgado ignored Morgan's jive and pulled out his knife, slitting the cheek on the left side of the drawing. "This drawing is my face alright, and I'm tired of doing the dirty work for you while you hide up here in your little hole." Delgado half hissed as he glared up at the Gila.

"So what do you want?" The Gila groaned, unfazed by Delgado's threatening tone, but giving him a warning glare of his own through dark eyes.

"I'm tired of pulling all the weight around here, either get the others to work or get them out of my way, and this poster is going to cost you double." Delgado sheathed his knife in his belt as the Gila slid his boots off the desk in anger. "I didn't take this job for its 'popularity.'"

"What!" The Gila hissed grabbing the front of Delgado's vest and shirt and practically pulling the smaller lizard over the desk towards him.

"You ain't worth that much." The Gila hissed and Morgan narrowed his amber eyes at Delgado.

"You've killed several of my workers and now you demand a raise in pay after you got yourself slashed and posted up all over the jurisdiction!" Sol Diablo bared pointed teeth.

"Those slopheads weren't doing their jobs. They were trying to take mine. If you didn't want them dead you shoulda kept them clear," Delgado glared up at the Gila defiantly.

The Gila let go of his vest and shoved him back away from the desk in front of Morgan. Delgado stumbled slightly, but quickly recovered and stood up straight once more.

"You'll get the same pay you've always got, and if you mess things up again," the Gila picked up the wanted poster and jabbed the reward price at the bottom with a claw. "I could do a lot with this money, and that's bringing you in dead *or* alive."

"I'm not much good to your operation dead now am I?" Delgado snorted.

The Gila frowned in irritation and crumpled the poster in his hands. "Get out of my chamber, Delgado. You get the same pay for the same job, and that's final."

Delgado's eyes narrowed to slits and his fists clenched, but Morgan shoved him with his blunt head, pushing him out the doorway before he could say anything else.

Morgan turned back to Sol Diablo, "Why do you bother to keep him here?" The snake frowned moodily. "You should have let me kill him ages ago. He's killed four of our lizards in the last month."

"He's the best there is and he damn well knows it." The Gila growled deep in his throat. "And he's starting to get a little too big for his boots. I underestimated him when I hired him two winters ago, but now things are getting clearer. He's got to go."

"Go?" Morgan smirked, bunching his steely coils together in faint excitement. "Would you consider letting me tend to that?"

"Not yet, I've got one last job for him before it comes to that." Sol Diablo turned back to the pile of opal stones on his desk and picked up one in particular, a yellow one, flaked white and transparent.

"The opals?" Morgan asked, leaning in slightly.

"Yes, the Jumpers know where these stones are better than anyone. Do you know what these opals are worth, Morgan? Not as precious as gold or silver, no, but still a fair amount to the right buyers. If the Jumpers know where a good vein is, then why don't we share?" he smirked, dragging his wickedly sharp white claws down the table surface, scratching into the stone.

"So, you want Delgado to help you find the Jumpers for you?" Morgan tried to piece it together.

"He's the best tracker I've got since he killed Larry. Your job comes later."

"Sounds interesting." Morgan's rattle quivered slightly in approval. "But how will we find the Jumpers? No one knows where they went, few believe they still exist."

"Well, we've got one in our claws right now, what do you say we pay our newest Jumper a little visit? We'll get the whereabouts from him and be on our way."

"Might not be so easy." Morgan slithered back to allow the Gila to pass in front of the desk.

"They all break in the end, Morgan. You'll see. We'll come out of this with a good reward. No more Jumpers, a vast supply of opals, Delgado dead, and reward money to split." He slapped the snake's belly scales as he passed and Morgan snorted a laugh, his rattle buzzing in approval. "If I may pose a suggestion to you, Sol, tracking is easiest when the trail is fresh. What if the Jumper was set free? I bet he would high-tail it home to his little friends, and we could follow him right to it."

Sol Diablo frowned thoughtfully. "Perhaps, if my way doesn't work we can try that."

"Don't rough him up too much then, hard to run home on broken legs." Morgan cackled with a hiss.

Outside in the tunnel, carefully wedged in a cleft in the ceiling, a slender figure watched the two reptiles leave the cave and head towards the Red Dome.

Delgado's eyes narrowed spitefully, having heard every word.

23

Scott hadn't known he'd fallen asleep and wasn't sure how long he had been out. He blinked tiredly and groaned as he stretched out his arms in the inky black. He felt around for the lantern, dimmed to preserve the oil, and turned it up. He had been resting against the wooden bars of Pip's cage. Looking around he spotted Sam, curled on the floor with his head resting on his tufted tail like a pillow. Scott watched him a few moments, but let him sleep. He looked exhausted and he was sure he could use the rest. He heard a sigh and looked around for a moment in surprise then spotted Pip settled against the wall in the rock cleft, his green eyes staring up at the ceiling.

"Pip?" Scott asked quietly and the bat looked over. "Why are you awake?" Scott asked, Pip didn't look tired at all, his ears were perked and his eyes were alert.

"I never sleep at night, I'm a bat. Nocturnal?" Pip explained, shifting slightly to see Scott better.

"What? So you sleep during the day? But what about when you were working in here?" Scott asked curiously.

"Well, I had to stay awake durin' the day to work, but it was hard." Pip sighed. "My whole colony always went to sleep at dawn and woke at dusk."

Scott moved over closer to sit on a rock. "What was your colony like?"

Pip looked reminiscent for a moment then opened his mouth to speak when his huge ears perked up and his body stiffened.

"Someone's comin'." He murmured.

Scott arched a brow and was about to ask who, but then a grating sound resounded in the tunnel. Sam's eyes snapped open and he pushed himself up to look over where the rock slab was being pushed aside. Firelight from the lanterns outside filled the tunnel with a yellow and red light before the forms of the Gila and rattlesnake could be seen.

Sam leapt to his feet, standing in front of Scott and Pip's cage as Morgan slithered into the room with a smirk.

"Guess he wasn't tied very well. Bring me the Jumper." The Gila ordered.

Morgan smiled cruelly. "With pleasure."

"Sam…" Scott breathed in shock as the snake lunged foreword, but Sam sprang away.

"Don't run! He'll kill you!" Pip shouted, clinging to the bars of his cage with his thumbs as Morgan let out a hiss of frustration from the chase. Sam leapt over Morgan's coils and turned to face the snake, but Morgan hissed loudly and slammed his thick coils heavily into Sam's torso, pinning him to the wall with a loud *thud* sound.

Sam coughed as the air was driven from his lungs. The snake moved closer, winding his coils around the Jumper.

"No!" Scott ran forward and kicked the snake in the coils; it felt like he'd kicked a boulder. Morgan whirled and rammed his blunt head into Scott, sending him sprawling.

"You little interfering brat!", he hissed, mouth open, fangs bared as he loomed over Scott.

Scott's heart leapt into his throat and he couldn't move for fear as Morgan drew closer.

"Morgan! Leave the mouse, he's nothing; we're here for the Jumper." Sol Diablo barked out and Morgan snorted, batting Scott into the wall with the side of his head before winding back to the Sol Diablo.

Scott, shaking madly, backed away until his back touched the cage where Pip was trapped. Pip watched the scene with horror as the Gila ambled over to where Morgan was constricting Sam.

"Ease up a little, Morgan; he needs to breathe to talk."

Morgan relaxed his coils a fraction and Sam coughed hard for air, taking deep breaths. He glared up as the Gila leaned over on a knee and smirked at him.

"Hello, Jumper, welcome to the caves of Sol Diablo." He pointed at himself with a long, white claw, speaking slowly as if to a small child. The Gila grabbed ahold of Sam's shoulder with a viselike grip and wrestled his arms free. There was a clink of metal as Sol Diablo produced a pair of iron shackles from his belt and roughly chained Sam's wrists behind his back before returning him to Morgan's grip. Sam tried to struggle, but he could barely move as it was.

"Now, when you came to be here, you were not wearing a necklace with a stone on it. Where is your stone?" the Gila demanded and with a single claw he ripped open the front of Sam's ragged shirt, exposing his neck and chest. "All Jumpers have them."

Sam snorted and spat in the Gila's face. Pip gasped and flinched, Scott's eyes widened as the Gila hissed deafeningly loud then brought his claw ripping across Sam's collarbone, flecking the stones with blood. Sam winced and continued glaring at the Gila.

"Where is it! Where do all these come from!" The Gila roared and reached into his vest, grabbing a fistful of the large opals he had taken from his desk and shoving them in Sam's face, hanging them from their strings.

Sam's face morphed from angry then shocked, then finally anguish as his eyes wandered from stone to stone.

"Heh heh, someone he knows?" Sol Diablo muttered to Morgan and looked back at the necklaces.

Sam shook his head in disbelief he was shaking all over, he tried to lunge towards the necklaces, but the coils held him too tight, and the fight was leaving him quickly.

The Gila watched him breaking down and smirked, with a snap of his claws Morgan released the Jumper from his coils and Sam fell to his knees, all signs of rebellion gone. He looked torn apart.

"Stones? What stones?" Scott whispered in scared confusion to Pip, who hastily explained;

" Sol Diablo's got us diggin' for these gemstones, Jumpers called them spider bite, but I think they're really called opals. All Jumpers wear them that I've seen, I'm not sure why, but Sam's the first I've heard who hasn't got one… and I think Sam knows who those stones belonged to. Like a name label."

"What happened to *those* Jumpers?" Scott hissed back in alarm.

"Morgan…" Pip murmured and turned his attention back to Sam as Sol Diablo turned towards the entrance where Delgado was standing, attracted by the noise.

"Delgado, get in here." The Gila growled out and the five-lined skink entered with narrowed eyes.

"I'm going to ask you one last time, Jumper, where do the Jumpers get their spider bite, the opals, and where is yours?" Sol Diablo glared at Delgado and the blue lizard came up behind the Jumper and unsheathed his knife, pulling Sam's head back by his head fur he rested the knife blade on his throat.

Scott's brows shot up and he shakily stood up, Pip's thumbclaw rested on his shoulder. "Scott no…" he murmured fearfully, but Scott could see a thin line of blood forming on Delgado's blade.

"It… it broke!" he yelled out. All reptilian eyes turned towards him and Scott swallowed the bile in his throat from fear, his heart hammering loud in his ears. "His... his broke when they got him, in the river."

The Gila glared at the mouse and turned back to the Jumper. "Is this true?" he asked in a gravely tone. Sam didn't answer as Delgado let his head free and removed the knife.

"Answer!" The Gila snarled, patience wearing thin. Finally The Gila hissed aggressively and backhanded Sam with his massive hand, throwing him into the wall.

"Tie him back to the wall, don't give the Jumper food or water for three days. That should be enough to wear him out." The Gila turned and stalked from the slave tunnel, leaving Morgan and Delgado to chain the Jumper back to the rings.

Sam didn't put up any fight; he stood placidly as they cinched the chains and bindings tight.

Delgado left the tunnel stiffly, leaving Morgan to slide the stone in place.

Scott watched them leave and his blood boiled. "*Bastards*!" he snapped as the rock slid shut. He seized a rock and threw it at the door, it hit and broke apart. Scott stood seething for a moment then turned back to the others.

"You alright Sam? ...*Sam*?" Scott's ears laid back seeing Sam, the Jumper he'd known to be so strong, so wild, was now slumped in his chains, head bowed and shoulders shaking with tears streaking his face.

24

June headed up the little slope as the morning sky grew bluer and brighter. She spotted Mitch, partially slumped against his quail's wing, sound asleep. She glanced at the quail, Cali, who was eyeing June suspiciously as she approached.

"I'm not gonna hurt him, Cali." June murmured to the quail reaching out to stroke the bird's crown feathers. Cali narrowed her eyes then churred softly, arousing Bowie beside her with a soft peeping sound.

The noise reached Mitch and he shifted in his sleep slightly, starting to wake up. June turned back towards him and stepped back across the rocks as he blinked awake.

"Morning." She said, sitting on one of the rocks.

"Morning." Mitch mumbled, stretching and squinting around. "We should be on the trail. The sun's already up…"

"We thought you could use the rest after that raid, here, Bo made coffee." She passed him a tin and Mitch took it with a curt thanks.

June stood up and dusted off her chaps. "Well, we're just cleaning up to go now; Charlie left a biscuit out for you."

"Guess I should get packing." Mitch sighed and got up, cracking his back. Behind him Cali got to her feet and perked slightly when Bowie nudged her with his wing, offering her a dead cricket in his beak. Cali narrowed her eyes slightly at the cricket, then to Bowie, before accepting the cricket and devouring it with a few crunchy bites.

Bowie trilled and fluffed out his breast feathers flirtatiously, but Cali rolled her eyes and turned away from the flirty bobwhite.

As Mitch followed June back to the main camp Jared and Bo were smothering the campfire, kicking earth and river clay over the remains while Charlie was packing up their supplies.

Mitch drained the last of his coffee and let Charlie take the tin to pack, accepting his biscuit in return, which he ate in a few famished bites as he crouched to roll up his bedroll.

"Ready to ride?" Bo asked as he finished up with the fire and started tying down his gear on the back of Cotton, who scratched restlessly at the ground as he waited.

"Yeah, just gotta tie down." Mitch said and he headed back towards the other quail to tie his gear in place.

Within ten minutes everyone was on quailback and heading out towards the flatlands to follow the wagon trail once more. The land started to dip as the sun grew higher, dropping into a lower, stonier part of the flatlands. The grasses thinned as the clay and dirt turned to rock that sloped smoothly into a winding dip. The trail was gone but from the direction of the wagon ruts Mitch figured they had gone to the right along the bottom of the sloping embankment. Mitch spurred Cali onward and Bo followed on Cotton.

"Wait!" June called from up above on the higher ground.

"What?" Mitch called, back over his shoulder, not wanting to stop.

"We shouldn't go this way it's too dangerous… look over there." June pointed towards the northeast where a thick band of purple-gray storm clouds was bubbling up on the horizon.

"So?" Mitch called back. "It's sunny here, we'll be fine, besides, we have to beat the rain across the flatlands or it'll wipe out the trail." Mitch said, pulling Cali's reins to stop her.

"Mitch haven't you ever heard of *flash floods*? Look at the stripes on the rocks, water carves through here all the time or these wouldn't be here, it's not safe!"

"Then stay here." Mitch groaned and started to spur Cali onward. Bo and Charlie looked uneasily at one another as June narrowed her eyes and spurred Bowie down the rock slope, riding aggressively in front of Mitch, barring his path.

"Will you just *listen* to me, I know what I'm talking about, I'm trying to help!"

"Well, you're not helping! The trail went this way, we'll be fine! If you're too scared to come along then stay here! No one's making you come." Mitch argued back and tried to steer his quail around hers before spurring ahead with Cali.

June watched him go, her eyes angry and narrowed. Bo rode up alongside her as Charlie and Jared followed Mitch hesitantly, glancing at June as they passed.

"June maybe it would be better if you stayed, it'll be safer." Bo suggested warily as he rode up alongside her.

"What? No! I'm going." June snorted and kicked Bowie's side sending her bobwhite running after Mitch leaving Bo and Cotton in the dust.

"I hope you're wrong, June." Bo muttered uneasily, looking at the storm clouds in the distance before nudging Cotton onwards to catch up with the others at the bottom.

The clouds moved faster than any of them had expected. Soon low, grumbling sounds of thunder reverberated all around them as dark clouds stretched overhead making shadows disappear beneath them. Mitch eyed the sky warily but tried to keep his gaze fixed on the tumble of rocky cliffs and spires in the distance, the end point of this winding gully he assumed. They were close to the edge of the flatlands after that, just another hour, maybe two. Mitch flinched as Cali gave a tense stumble and started to pip and scratch worriedly.

"Shh, calm down, easy Cal, it's alright." He tried to correct his quail, looking over at the others to see they were having similar issues.

"You think the thunder is spooking them?" Bo asked as he patted the neck of his scaled quail. The black-and-white mouse stretched out his hand feeling fat drops of rain starting to spatter.

"*Mitch...*" June trailed, nervousness etched in her voice as the rain started to pick up.

"The thunder's getting louder!" Jared called as the rain started to pour like a bath faucet.

Bowie let out a shrill chirp of fear and Bo started to look around with brows knitted in concern.

"That's not thunder!" He called over the noise.

"What?" Mitch called and struggled to control his jumpy and fidgety bird.

Suddenly a wall of brown, muddy water surged across the shallow valley. Mitch hardly had time to blink let alone yell before the roaring flood crashed into them. Cali was swept off her feet with a squawk that turned into a gurgle as they submerged, tumbling and rolling in the wake.

Mitch clung to the saddle horn as dark water filled his nose and ears. He could feel Cali pulling him down deeper until finally the thrashing quail gave a massive kick off a submerged rock bottom and both their heads broke free into the torrential downpour. Mitch coughed, water streaming down the brim of his hat, which by some miracle was still on his head. Nearby he saw Charlie, desperately trying to keep his chin above the churning waves while his quail snorted and squawked in panic.

In front of Charlie, Bo was trying to wrangle Cotton, but the scaled quail was uncontrollable, bucking and splashing, shrieking at the top of his lungs. Bo fell off the back of the saddle with a yell and got swept under the wake.

"BO!" Mitch cried out in shock, but Charlie was ahead of him, urging his quail onward clumsily through the waves. The dormouse thrust his head underwater and reappeared seizing the front of Bo's shirt, pulling the gasping ranch hand onto his quail while Cotton thrashed ahead rider-less and screeching.

Mitch and Cali were spinning in the water as the flood swept them all along at a dangerous speed. Up ahead like a dark smear rising from the depths Mitch spotted a scrubby hill just high enough to make an island that forked the two directions of the flood path.

"Head for that hill!" he shouted to Charlie and Bo. Jared was way ahead of them, kicking his floundering bird to kick faster until he scrambled out and claimed the highest part of the hill. Cotton was smart enough to follow Jared onto the island while Mitch trailed behind Charlie as the flood pushed them right into the land instead of sweeping them around.

Cali scrambled up out of the water with Mitch still on board, the hen was wild-eyed with fear and shook out her doused feathers making shrill chirruping sounds of alarm as walls of water rushed past them. Her shrill calls were answered by a terrified shriek of another bird being swept passed the fork. Mitch twisted in the saddle to see the black-and-white striped head of Bowie, fighting fruitlessly against the waves as the slipstream towed the frightened bobwhite around the rock, rider-less.

"June..." Mitch's eyes widened as he fumbled to uncoil his rope on the saddle and he spurred Cali along the strip of land from above and flung out his lasso, thanking the heavens his aim was true as he roped the bird's neck and around the saddle horn.

Cali's feet dug in as he strained to pull June's quail onto dry land. Bowie clambered up the steep hill with a lot of help from the tow, and huddled against Cali looking terrified. Mitch dropped the rope and whipped around.

"JUNE??" he shouted. "June's gone!"

Bo and Charlie's eyes seemed to bulge and they began screaming her name into the rain, Charlie lending his seldom used voice to the search. They jumped off the quail and ran over the rock top calling her name and searching the steep banks.

Heart pounding in his throat Mitch raced around the edge of the flood and spotted the scrubby top of some sagebrush sticking out of the water by the next partially submerged knoll. Grasping it vice-like to keep from being swept away, was June, the water flooding over her head rendering her deaf to their calls, every few second she fought to break the surface and suck a lungful of air down before being forced under again.

Mitch slapped Cali's reins to spur her towards the water. The hen snorted and gave him a wild-eyed 'are you mad!?' look before sliding down near the swift shallows racing towards the next outcrop. Mitch had no rope now and June was too far to reach. He leapt off Cali and wound her reins around his hand. He waded in up to his waist and was immediately knocked down by the current that ripped at his body. The reins held as Cali dug her feet in on the bank. Mitch thrashed towards June and grabbed a hold of the sagebrush.

"June! Give me your hand!" he coughed as waves tried to silence him.

"No! I can't let go!" June coughed the water streaming into her mouth and nose.

"You'll drown! Give me your hand!"

"I can't reach! You can't reach me, I'll wash away!" she choked.

"TRUST ME! I won't let you" Mitch bellowed hoarsely reaching as far as he could.

June looked petrified as she tensely let go of the branch to reach for his hand when the branch snapped under the strain and she plunged into the water with a scream just as Mitch lunged and grabbed her vest, the current felt like it was going to rip him in half as he strained to pull her close and pull to shore at the same time. His ribs felt the strain and he gritted his teeth against the pain.

Cali thrashed on the shore trying to pull backwards against the strain, moving them bit by bit onto the shore.

Mitch's boots found purchase below the water on the striated rock and he pushed against the ground, pulling June close they both fell onto steep bank. Mitch fell flat on his back with exhaustion and June collapsed onto his chest, her fingers fixed into his vest and arm in a death grip.

She was shaking uncontrollably and sobbing for breath. "You-you-you STUPID *yokel*!" she snarled pounding his chest weakly. "We could have all been ki-killed! You wouldn't li-listen to me!" she broke down shaking from the perils of the flood waters and sobbed into his ribs.

Mitch flattened his ears. She was right. He'd gotten them into this mess. It was his fault. He realized his arms were still wrapped around June protectively and could hear her trying to control her terrified sobs.

"I'm sorry June… I'm sorry, you were right… it's ok." He edged to his knees and stood up, helping her to her feet. She stayed close a few more moments then gently pushed away from him, her arms wrapped tightly around herself as her wet hair hung in her face.

Mitch watched her go then turned and patted Cali's beak. "Good girl." He panted in exhaustion. He turned to June and tapped her shoulder. She looked over at him as he mounted the bird and offered her his hand.

"Let's get back to the others."

"My quail is gone…" June's voice shook slightly.

"No, Bowie's, alright, he's back with the others, come on, the water is going down." Mitch assured her.

June's brows rose in surprise. "He-he's ok?" she took his hand hesitantly as he pulled her up.

"Yes, he's fine." Mitch sighed as he urged his reluctant back along the edge of the water; Cali coughed and sneezed a few times before ascending the rock up to the top again.

June slipped from the saddle and rushed towards her quail. Bowie trilled happily and pushed his head into her middle as June hugged him around the neck and rubbed his drenched feathers in relief.

"June!" Bo and Charlie rushed over, followed by Jared.

"June you're ok!" Bo looked ready to collapse with relief.

"I'm fine." She murmured and looked around, still holding onto Bowie's halter, looking afraid to lose him again. "Where's…" she spotted Mitch down by the edge of the receding water. He was staring around the area of windy canyon land they now faced. She watched him take off his hat and run his finger through his head fur.

"He's lost the trail now." Bo murmured to the others.

The water swirled lower and lower, leaving smooth stretches of clay, flattened grass and rock. The trail he had hope to find at the end of this rocky maze had been completely erased.

25

Scott swallowed, unnerved by Sam's tears. "Sam, are you alright?" he repeated as he neared the chained Jumper.

"Go away!" he snapped and turned away from Scott, his voice cracking and heavy with grief.

Scott stepped back in alarm and stood there a moment, watching Sam slumped over, sniffling quietly with his head bowed.

Scott edged backwards and sat close to Pip. He glanced at the bat questioningly, but Pip shook his head in confusion. Scott scuffed his boots in the dirt, his insides twisting. He hated seeing others upset. He was worried for Sam.

Suddenly, Sam threw back his head and shouted something in a language Scott didn't understand, but it sounded outraged and mournful. Sam took a few shaky breaths then yelled again. "You'll pay for what you did!" before slumping down again, emotionally exhausting himself.

Scott stood up once more and started to head towards Sam, feeling tense as he neared the restrained wild mouse.

"Sam." Scott asked and he grew closer. "Sam what's wrong? What did those stone things mean?"

Sam continued to stare at the ground, shoulder trembling from silent sobs and exhaustion.

Scott moved in front of Sam and cleared his throat, trying to get his attention. "Sam, please tell us what's going on, what's wrong?"

Sam glared at Scott through bright eyes, swimming with unshed tears before looking away.

"*Sam!*" Scott said in exasperation.

"What! Why would you care!" Sam snarled making Scott jump back slightly, but then he stood his ground.

"Because I want to help you! And I can't help if you don't talk!" Scott lashed his tail, feeling like his mother back home.

Sam glared at Scott as if analyzing him from the outside. Scott remained where he was, his eyes searching the Jumper's face as if the explanation might be written there.

At long last Sam looked away, eyes closed and brows knitted in remorse. "Those... stones, are very special to us." He muttered, his voice echoing faintly in the tunnel. Pip's ears perked as he leaned towards the bars of the cage to listen.

"They... they're given to us when we're young, when we become old enough to learn to contribute to our community... they're all different, no two are the same..." Sam sniffed and shook his head. "I knew them all, all those he was showing... I *knew* them." His eyes misted slightly and he shut them tight, tears slipping out. "One of them belonged to my mother... I was looking for her and her group when the lizards and you found me."

Scott's eyes widened. "What? Are you sure?" he asked in astonishment. In the cage, Pip's ears laid back in shock and he shook his head in sympathy.

"Yes. She and the others... they went out to find the killer of my friend's father... he had been found in the desert, alone, without his stone. Murdered and robbed." Sam's eyes hardened. "These... these lizards must have done it... they must have..." he sniffled loud and looked to Pip. "Have you ever seen any Jumpers they brought in?" he asked, his eyes begged for answers.

Pip swallowed feeling on the spot. "I... I have but, Sam I'm so sorry... they weren't alive when I saw them..."

Sam winced and looked away, "I was looking for her... when they caught me." He muttered to Scott. "When you first saw me... I had to find her, I had to protect her! I was too late... I failed to save her, the others..." he shut his eyes tight again.

"Why weren't you with the group?" Scott asked in confusion, he felt terrible for Sam's loss, but he had to learn more.

"I wasn't allowed, I got in a fight, and I was told I couldn't go with them as punishment. I should have been with them... gone after them sooner."

"Then you'd be dead too!" Scott was shocked.

"Maybe... but I might have been able to save her." Sam couldn't be swayed; guilt clawed him from the inside and showed on his face.

Scott sat on the rocks and looked up at Sam. "Sam... what about your stone? What happened to it if all the Jumpers have them?"

Sam shook his head. "It doesn't matter, I don't have one, I haven't had one since I was little..." Sam seemed reluctant to share anymore, his eyes clouded with pain and loss.

Scott sat down on a rock next to Sam and sighed. "They came to my house, it was just me and my brother... they killed him, burned him in our barn... My mother's very sick; when she comes back... she'll think both her boys are dead." He sighed shakily.

Sam looked over at him and blinked slowly. Pip swallowed and looked back and forth between the two of them.

"I'm so sorry for your losses... both of you." Pip settled back. "I guess, I guess this means the escape is off, what chance did we ever have anyway..." he asked gently. He didn't feel a lot of hope left in this cavern, he turned away and settled glumly against the wall.

Sam's deadened eyes closed then reopened, a fierce fire re-ignited in their dark brown depths as he straightened up slightly. "No, we're getting out of here, all of us." He vowed, strength returning to his raw-sounding voice.

Scott smiled slightly; this sounded more like the Jumper he knew from earlier.

"How will we get out, then?" Pip shrugged weakly, holding onto the bars of his cage with his thumb claws.

"Tell us more about the tunnels, Pip." Scott asked as he stepped closer to Sam to help clean the blood off his bleeding collarbone with a handkerchief from his pocket.

Sam nodded, accepting the help. "Yes, that's the way we'll get out."

"I'll tell you what I know, it won't be easy though." Pip began.

"Nothing ever is." Sam said somberly but nodded for Pip to go on. In the dimming lantern light, they began to hatch their plan.

26

Cali's feathers were soaked through, making the hen look small and scraggly as she and the others trekked across the flood-sodden ground to the shelter of the rocks and canyons in front of them.

Mitch was devastated, for a moment they had been close, now their last sign of hope seemed gone forever. Washed away like the wagon ruts in the wake of the flash flood. Behind him, Bo was patting Cotton's wet feathers as the scaled quail walked with a slight limp, probably twisted his foot in the flood. Charlie followed Bo, head bowed in exhaustion. Jared and June brought up the rear, both looking equally tired.

Everyone was soaked to the skin and in low spirits as they reached a rocky alcove in the side of a canyon wall and dismounted onto the hard packed clay ground slick with rain water.

Bo promptly sat on a nearby rock and pulled off his boot, tipping it to pour some water out. Charlie gave himself a good shake to rid most of the water from his thick, golden fur, leaving it looking spiky and mussed before he sat on the rock next to Bo.

Mitch slid off Cali and stroked her wing, looking over his shoulders at the miserable bunch as Jared and June dismounted and went to try and find drier places to sit and rest. Mitch let out a long sigh and turned around slowly, walking over to them, the water in his boots squelched in every step.

"I'm sorry you guys. I could have gotten everyone killed out there. I just wanted to find Scott; I should have listened to June. She was right about the flash floods, but I didn't, and it nearly got us all drowned. I'm sorry June… sorry everyone." Mitch took off his hat and raked his fingers through his head fur, still devastated by the loss of the trail.

Jared snorted. "You should be! This whole damn trip is your fault!" he snarled, unbuttoning his shirt to wring it out.

"Shut up, Jared! He can't control the weather." Bo snapped back at the darker mouse before shrugging at Mitch. "It's fine, Mitch, we're all here and we'll dry out alright."

June shivered in her soaked clothes and nodded slowly to what Bo said, she could see how miserable Mitch looked and didn't want to make anything worse. "Well, we're alright now," she murmured. "Maybe next time you'll listen…" she muttered under her breath.

Mitch donned his hat again. "I'll try to find us some fire wood." He muttered and stalked past Jared.

"Yeah, and then what, we'll follow the trail? Oh wait! It's *gone*!" Jared shook his head and stared after him as he disappeared around the spur of rock.

Charlie picked up a rock and tossed it at Jared, catching him in the shoulder. Jared yelped and glared at the dormouse, eyes blazing. Charlie stared back grimly, daring Jared to make another comment but the dark mouse just grumbled under his breath and took off his shirt, wringing the water out and standing to hang it on an out crop of rock.

Bo shrugged out of his shirt and vest and did the same, followed by Charlie. June watched them with narrowed eyes, arms hugged around herself trying to get warm.

"Heh, you shouldn't wear wet clothes, June, might catch something. Better take them off." Jared smirked at her, but before she could snap a retort at him both Charlie and Bo punched him in each shoulder.

"Ouch! Geez!" Jared grumbled.

June stood and grabbed Bowie's halter, leading her Bobwhite away from the others. "Come on Bowie." She growled irritably and rounded the rock spur to an opening in the other side to shed her drenched clothes after removing Bowie's saddle. Her quail settled in at the entrance, shielding her until she could wrap up in the saddle blanket. It was damp as well, but better than nothing. She settled back against Bowie's wing. The quail lazily rested his beak on her shoulder with a soft churr.

Awkward silence hovered over the small group of mice around an hour later as Mitch crouched over a small, sputtering fire that coughed and sparked as it tried to engulf the damp grasses he'd found to burn. June had rejoined the others, wrapped up in her saddle blanket. The sky was getting darker and was still heavy with passing clouds, thunder rumbled past them as the storm headed southwest away from them.

Bo watched Mitch work from where he was seated on a rock, his chin rested on clasped hands with his elbows on his knees. The black-and-white ranch hand straightened up as Mitch sat back to feed the fire bits of damp kindling.

"Mitch." Bo spoke, causing everyone to look over.

Mitch glanced over at his friend, dreading the question he was sure was about to be asked.

"What do we do now? The trail's gone, and I want to find Scott as much as you." He spoke sincerely. "But you've gotta be rational. It's been three days. We don't know where we're going. We're in unsettled wild-land right now with barely any supplies or any idea which general direction to go from here." Bo stood up, dusting grit off his chaps. "So what's the plan now?" there was no challenge in the ranch hand's tone, just genuine puzzlement.

Mitch stared into the flames a moment, a piece of kindling held viselike in his hand, as if he could crush a decent answer from it. He sighed and dropped the wood into the fire with a clatter and stood up.

"I'm still going after him. I don't know where he is, and I don't know how long it will take. I'm not stopping until I find him or a body. In that case, I'll bring him home to be buried at the ranch." He answered quietly.

June gathered her blanket more snuggly around her. He was so devoted to this most likely lost cause, but she admired him for it.

"I'm not asking the rest of you to come with me, Bo, you should take Charlie and Jared back to the ranch, Pa'll need help rebuilding the barn. June should go with you; I don't want anything else to happen to her either." Mitch scuffed some dust with his boot sole. "You can tell Pa what happened, and tell him I'm not coming home until I have him. Dead or alive, I'm not gonna leave Scott out here away from his family."

Bo nodded slowly. "Well, you're dumber'n prairie weeds if you think I'm letting you search alone," Bo said hands akimbo.

"What? Bo I don't want to risk anyone else getting hurt. It'll be easier to travel alone."

"There's safety in numbers." June stood up, holding the blanket about her like a cloak she blinked green eyes understandingly at him. "These are wild-lands Mitch, it'll be safer for us all to stick together." Charlie stood up beside June, nodding silently.

"You're all insane." Jared grumbled.

"You wanna ride back past those pleasant gentlemen and Darnell on your lonesome, Jare-Bear or will you ride with us?" Bo asked with a smirk.

Jared snorted and grumbled moodily. "Seeing as I ain't got much of a choice I'm following you, but once we hit any matter of civilization I'm getting off this hellish goose-chase and you're on your own, Mitchy. I wouldn't go half this distance for Scott even if he was *my* brother!"

"I'm not asking for you to come and I don't want your help or sass, Jared, I'd be happy to shove you in a direction of a town if I knew where the hell we were in the first place." Mitch glared at him, blue eyes flashing. "But until we find a town just stay close and shut up. The good Lord only granted me a limited amount of patience a year to deal with you, and I used it all up about two days ago."

Jared frowned and stalked off towards the drying supplies to check the state of his bedroll and jacket.

Mitch turned back to the others. "I'm glad you guys want to help, I just don't want to lead you into something dangerous."

"We don't know where we are, anything's dangerous." Bo shrugged. "Besides, we'll take turns leading, that way we can each give tracking a try."

"What exactly are we looking for besides this wagon?" June asked, brushing hair from her face.

"Lizards," Mitch answered before Bo could respond. "Lizard signs, quail tracks, wagon ruts. There was about three lizards and a wagon, and about fifty California quail stolen from our ranch. These rocks and boulders of the canyon must be crawling with lizards."

Charlie made a face of dislike and Bo looked down at him. "They might not be the friendliest of sorts either. This isn't exactly the setting for a rodent-friendly welcome party. We should try and stay away from the open areas as much as possible."

"Might be Jumpers out here too," Jared muttered, crossing back over to roll out his nearly dry bedroll.

"*Jumpers?*" June's brows rose slightly in surprise. "I thought they were all gone?"

"Don't think so, those wretched vermin are still out there." Jared snorted at June. "They hide up in the rocks waiting for riders to come by…"

"Jared." Bo groaned but the darker mouse continued.

"Then they leap down! And slam their savage spears through your chest! Then they rip off your—OW!" Charlie slapped Jared upside the head, his ears pinned back.

"Thanks for the lovely image." June rolled her eyes.

"Yeah, I love going to sleep with the thought of an enormous wild mouse ripping me to pieces." Bo muttered and settled down against a boulder, resting his arms behind his head after tipping the brim past his eyes. "I volunteer Jared for first watch."

"What??" Jared protested, tail lashing.

"What, you afraid the big, bad Jumpers are gonna get you?" Mitch scoffed; Charlie grinned and went to fetch his own bedroll, leaving Mitch and June beside the fire.

Mitch scuffed his boot sole on the ground. "Well, I think your clothes should be dry now. You should get some rest." He shrugged. "If you're tired." He added, not wanting to sound like he was ordering her around.

June nodded, "Yeah, you too."

"I'm gonna go tend to the birds. They've had a rough day too." Mitch gestured towards their small, drowsy covey.

"Alright, night then," June said, edging towards the branch where her clothes were hung, holding the blanket securely about her.

"Night…" Mitch turned and headed towards the birds.

"And Mitch?" June turned around. The ranch mouse stopped short and looked over his shoulder.

"Thanks… for earlier." June sighed, brushing hair from her face.

"You're welcome." Mitch replied in slight confusion before tipping his hat and heading into the shadows away from the light of the fire, the night air smelled fresh after being soaked in the day's rain, it felt cool on his face as he reached the tethered birds and made sure they were all dried off.

A playful nip rid him of his hat and Mitch twisted to see Cali holding his hat by the brim.

"No playing tonight, girl. Rest up, ok?" he patted her feathery cheek, retrieving his hat. He glanced up at the cloudy sky. Breaks in the clouds showed cracks of indigo sky and flecks of stars before being smothered by clouds again. "I'm not giving up on you, Scott." He sighed as Cali churred in his ear. "Neither is anyone else."

27

In his chambers, Delgado sharpened his knife slowly with a whet stone; its grating sound pinged around the stone walls quietly until he paused, hearing a booming voice outside in the Red Dome.

"Come on out you lot I got jobs for you!" Sol Diablo bellowed, his voice resounding with the acoustics of the cavern, washing into every crack in the rocks.

Delgado felt a hiss of annoyance in the back of his throat but stifled it as he sheathed his knife and headed out into the dome. Sol Diablo and Morgan were perched on one of the massive slabs of heated firerocks as the reptilian crew assembled.

"Well, you know what time it is fellas. We've run out of workers to mine the tunnels, and I'll need yer generous assistance in getting' us some more." The Gila's dark eyes glinted wickedly. In the crowd below several lizards elbowed each other's ribs with snickers. Others fingered their guns and rope coils in anticipation.

"Get yer birds we're heading out! Hit up the railroads, the rivers, the settlements in the hills!" The Gila roared above their chatter. His followers called back in raucous agreement and bustled in every which way to fetch their gear. Finally only three reptiles remained in the dome; Sol Diablo, Morgan and Delgado.

"Ah, there you are, Delgado, thought you might have slept through this meeting like the last one." The Gila snickered.

Delgado's eyes narrowed. Being a thinscale, his body shut down into an almost hibernate-like state when he got too cold. The Gila's last raid was in mid-winter, when Delgado had been weakened by cold, barely able to move.

"I guess you called louder this time." Delgado said icily.

"Maybe, in any case I don't want you on this raid. You, Morgan and a skeleton crew will stay here in the cave. I want information from that Jumper when I get back." The Gila's dark eyes glittered maliciously. "Do what you have to do to get it. If nothing works tell Morgan to go ahead with his plan."

Delgado's knuckled clenched tightly. Being practically alone in a cave with Morgan was a deadly accident waiting to happen. His eyes flicked to the great snake, who was smirking cruelly back.

"We should be back in two days; we're leaving at dawn tomorrow." The Gila explained.

"Fine," Delgado stepped back as Sol Diablo stepped off the fire rock and headed towards the tunnel leading to his personal chambers.

"If I were you, I'd get cracking." He called back to them.

Morgan slithered off the rock, his massive head lowered close to Delgado. "Come on," he hissed, flicking his black, forked tongue.

Delgado ground his teeth and headed towards the slave tunnels.

Back in the tunnels, Pip had finished telling Sam and Scott all he knew about the tunnels a few minutes earlier. Scott was now sitting close to Pip's gated rock cleft, stacking pebbles with the dim light of the lantern. "So you think the debris is thinnest here, near the top, where the next cavern leads straight to the back of the canyon wall. That shouldn't be too hard to break through if it's as close to the outside as you say it is." Scott said, tracing his finger through the stacked stones.

"Yes, it's a thin wall I could hear the wind outside in some places." Pip nodded then froze, "Someone's comin'."

"Who," Sam straightened up and glared at the stone slab?

"Morgan!" Pip's huge ears pinned back in alarm as steely coils started to roll the stone back and Delgado and Morgan entered the tunnel.

"Everyone seems chummy in here," Morgan snickered. He loomed in front of Sam, letting his forked tongue tickle the Jumper's throat. "An odd mix I should say."

Sam turned his head away from Morgan and glared down at the floor.

"Not very friendly today either, are we." Morgan huffed. "No matter, we'll have you talking by tomorrow, or I'll enjoy a meal of Jumper, it's delicious raw, from what I've experienced." He taunted, making Sam tense angrily.

Delgado cleared his throat irritably and Morgan snorted, slithering out of the tunnels with a shake of his rattle before rolling the stone into place.

"You alright, Sam?" Scott asked.

"I'm fine, but that monster…" Sam muttered something darkly in his native tongue.

Scott sighed and clapped his hands together carefully. "No more waiting, we've got to escape now."

"Escape now? How? We need more time to break free," Sam argued.

"Sam, it's the only way, you heard Morgan. They will be coming here tomorrow to interrogate you again, Morgan didn't sound patient…" Scott explained quietly. "If we don't get out of here now, I don't think he'll let you live."

Sam's eyes narrowed and he looked at the floor. Everything seemed so bleak.

Scott looked over his shoulder around the rubble where a pile and broken shovels and pick-axes lay in a messy heap. He rose and hurried over, prying a heavy pick-axe free.

"What are you doing?" Sam asked hearing the wood from the other tools shift as the mouse rummaged around.

Scott heaved the axe over his shoulder and walked towards the tumbled of caved in rocks. "What does it look like? I'm tunneling!"

Pip grinned. "Aye, I'd help you, Scott if I could swing one of those axes, my wings can't hold those up, but I'll pull those other ones up there near the top, come here and untie me." The bat's eyes flickered to the rocks near the ceiling, where dark cracks promised more unstable rocks.

"It's alright. You can help shift the rocks we move out of the way too." Scott said turning around towards the wooden gate containing Pip, "Back up." He advised, swinging the pick and splintering the edge of the gate enough to pull it down.

"*We?*" Sam said, looking at his chained wrists pointedly.

"Yes *we*, close your eyes!" Scott hefted the axe back. Sam's eyes widened a moment in realization then tensed, grimacing as he waited for the blow.

Pang! CLANG! *CLINK*! Scott had to strike three times, but finally the chain was severed.

Sam let his arm fall to his side then rolled his wrist to get the feeling back. He nodded to Scott. "Hurry! Get the other free!"

"Ok hold on." Scott promised, panting from the weight of the pick-axe, made for at least a rat, not a mouse his size.

Pip nodded, as he hopped out of the crack in the wall, falling onto his side clumsily, he waited as Scott untied him then fluttered up to the top of the rubble pile. "Come on, let's get to work!" he looked down at them.

Sam's second chain clattered against the stone wall as it was broken. "Yes." He nodded to Scott and bent to relieve the mouse of his oversized tool. "It's now or never." He bounded over to the wall and started to ascend the rocky precipice.

28

Mitch poured some of the water from his canteen into his hand and splashed it onto his face, rubbing his hand back over his head and under his collar to cool off. The morning sun already promised a hot day at it rose over the canyon walls the group was weaving through.

Bo yawned from behind Mitch where he was riding in the line. The black-and-white mouse had received the last watch of the night and hadn't been able to sleep much before that, trying to think of where they were, he'd never been this far north in this part of the wildlands before.

Charlie glanced sympathetically at his friend before letting his eyes wander about the canyon that rose up all around them, boxing them in with walls of layered orange and white rock.

"Is anyone thirsty?" June asked after a bit, her voice echoing slightly from the acoustics of the bend they were rounding. "I took the opportunity to fill up my other canteen last night before those pools dried up."

"I'll take some." Bo reached out, pulling back on the reins to drop back beside June and Bowie.

Mitch capped his own canteen, it was half empty, they would need to find some more water soon. Cali gave a jump under him and he wobbled to avoid falling off.

"Whoa, Cal'," he frowned. Cali never acted jumpy like this before. He glanced down and followed the quail's line of sight. "Hold up!" he told the others, his eyes narrowed against the sun to see.

"What is it?" Jared asked in annoyance from atop his quail, the tired mouse's bloodshot eyes showing his lack of sleep.

"Hopefully nothing," Mitch dismounted and tossed his reins to Charlie to hold before he headed towards a scrubby looking grass patch and squinted at something in the sandy soil. It was a track, but not just any track; it was a bird's track, four times as large as a quail's print, with deeper talon marks.

"What did you find?" Bo called over; capping June's canteen and handing it back to her before riding over to where Mitch was kneeling in the grass.

"Chaparral…" Mitch murmured, exposing the track.

"A what?" June asked as she neared them.

"Roadrunner," Bo translated grimly, his ears tilting back slightly. "This track is old, about two or three days, this bush sheltered it from the worst of yesterday's rain." Bo explained.

"Fresh or not, it's bad news." Mitch stood up. "We've got to be twice as careful and stay together. Roadrunners'll pick us off like lizards over a line of ants if we don't see them first."

"You think they live in this canyon?" June asked worriedly.

"Seems like their sort of place, lots of rocks, paths to run, perfect lizard spot, they probably snatch them up when—" Bo gestured with his hands.

"Bo, that's enough, they're a danger to everyone, lizards, mice, quail, everyone." Mitch waved his hand in finality.

"You led us to some roadrunner-filled deathtrap of a canyon?" Jared snarled; his eyes wide with alarm.

"Not if we keep moving, there's got to be a place around here for lizards to hide from them." Mitch glanced around warily.

"Oh and what, you're going to knock on their door and beg them to hide us? Another brilliant plan," Jared snorted. "You're going to get us all shot."

"Then let's hear one from you." June shot back scathingly, the darker mouse glared back but didn't reply, merely looking away and muttering something that sounded suspiciously like '*does.*'

"We don't have a lot of choice." Bo remarked and fingered his pistol handle before glancing at Mitch. "Dennis left me some guns for you Mitch; I suggest you hold onto them now." Bo fished about in his saddlebag and handed the wrapped gun belt and pistols down to him gently.

"Thanks." Mitch buckled the holster on and remounted his quail. "Let's get moving again, keep close and keep looking around, remember, they're fast and they like to ambush."

Charlie nodded warily and the group tightened up its ranks, continuing to head forward in a more united group.

A short distance later Bo's torn ear gave a flick, "I hear something," he murmured, causing the group to tighten again and slow drastically.

"Where?" Jared asked nervously looking all around.

"Over there by those rocks. It sounds like—"

"Water!" June grinned, hearing the melodic bubbling sound.

"We can follow that trickle to its source and navigate from there." Mitch felt a small smile on his face. Water was everything, if there was life in these wretched canyons, it would be by the water. And if those lizards took his brother in here, they would need water to survive.

29

Scott slumped against the edge of the cramped hole they had crudely created through the loose rocks at the top of the cavern. His sleeves were torn and dirty, rolled up past his elbows. His hands were throbbing from blisters, and several fingers were bleeding. After a few breaths of rest he hauled himself to his feet and started to shove and pull rocks from his path again, rolling them past the ever dimming lantern and behind him to Pip, who pushed them back to Sam to dispose of.

The golden-furred Jumper coughed from some rock dust as he started to set the rocks aside, not chucking them to the ground so they wouldn't alert any lizards, or worse, Morgan. He peered into the tunnel, the soft light in the back greeted his vision, but it wasn't enough light to able to see more than a few feet, though he could hear Scott prying a new rock loose from the opening.

"How much farther?" Sam asked, backing out as Pip rolled a new rock to him, the bat's head poked out of the small tunnel.

"Very close, we've broke through, but there's not enough room for your shoulders to get through yet. I think we'll have to make the tunnel wider," he explained.

"Can't," Scott gasped from inside the tunnel, grappling with a rock. "This one's stuck fast and the other side's holding up a big rock above our heads. It'll cave in if we try to move it. And the lantern…" Scott's voice trailed as the sputtering lantern's light dimmed lower and lower before it finally extinguished altogether, out of fuel.

Sam seemed to deflate slightly. "Let me go back there, maybe I can slip through anyway."

"I'll be back here to pull you out if you get stuck." Pip nodded and flapped past Sam into the main chamber, letting the Jumper drop on all fours and then to his belly, sliding forward on his elbows, his shoulders scraping the tunnel walls slightly as he neared Scott.

"Sam that you?" Scott asked feeling his tail brush the Jumper's forearm.

"Yeah, slip through that exit and I'll see if I'll fit."

"Alright, hold on, it's a real tight squeeze…" Scott turned around and wriggled backwards, feeling the space widen around him. Suddenly, he dropped down slightly and landed on solid ground. He flailed in the inky darkness before standing and feeling his way back to the wall.

"Ok, I'm out, there's a drop but it's not far, can you fit?" Scott asked, his voice echoing eerily, even his breathing sounded raspy and amplified. He heard Sam grunt as he hauled himself partially through the small exit.

"I've got one shoulder through." He gasped out. "Pip, give me a shove, my other shoulder's stuck."

"Won't that hurt?" Pip's muffled response came from behind him.

"My shoulder's stuck fast." Sam explained in frustration, trying to wriggle.

"Here, I'll pull, you push, Pip." Scott grabbed onto Sam's arm. "Go!" he said and strained backwards, for a few seconds Sam seemed jammed tight then all at once he came through, plowing Scott into the ground, Pip managed to stop himself from adding to the critterpile by gripping the lip of the hole with his thumb claws.

"You fellas alright?" Pip asked. He let out a shaky chuckle as he scuttled down towards them.

"Ugh, yeah, just slightly flattened." Scott wriggled up to a sitting position as Sam rose onto his knees, looking around at the pitch blackness of the cavern.

"I can't see a thing…" Sam stood up, arms out trying to touch his surroundings.

"Use your ears." Pip said in a matter-of-fact tone and helped Scott to his feet.

"Our *ears*?" Scott frowned as he waved his arms for balance, unable to see the uneven ground below his boots.

"Yeah… don't mice use sonar too sometimes?" Pip asked in puzzlement.

"So-nar?" Sam repeated the word, as if it were alien and didn't make sense.

"Oh, well, you make a noise, and listen for when it comes back, er, it bounces off things, it makes a picture I can see lots of things, this room is huge, it slopes down… there's the wall!" Pip exclaimed and started to shuffle away.

"What? Wall? Hey! Come back we can't see anything!" Scott called out and flung an arm out, hitting Sam's leg.

"Watch it!" Sam snapped, wavering on the sloped ground.

"Sorry." Pip scuttled back and wrapped his thumb claw around Scott's wrist. "Sam, hold onto Scott's shoulder, I'll lead you there, just watch your step, there's a bit of dip there, step over, there, that's right, now come on." Pip slowly navigated the two down the slope with painstaking care until they reached level ground.

"It curves to the right here… look!"

"Look at what? Wait… is that?" Sam squinted in the dark.

"That's *light*!" Scott grinned, his heart pounding in excitement.

"Come on the ground's more level." Pip let go of Scott's wrist and hurriedly crawled over towards a small white crack between two rocks.

"We just have a little ways to bust out of here." Pip grinned, his face dimly lit through the tiny aperture.

"Are there any more tools down here? Like from before." Scott asked as Sam braced his shoulder against the rocks to test the stability.

"Er, there should be, let me have a listen." Pip swiveled his huge ears around to follow his sonar, the noises he made almost too high for the others to hear. "Yes! There's a broken pick-axe over there."

"How broken," Sam asked?

"Missin' half the handle, but it'll work, come on." Pip scrambled off to fetch the tool and hurried back, dragging it to Scott with some difficulty.

Scott squinted and saw something that looked like a square in the faint light beam. "What's that? A box?"

Pip crawled over. "Aye, dynamite."

"That would make getting through this wall easier, we'd be out in no time if we could find some matches!" Scott said excitedly.

"Hmm, or bring the whole tunnel down of top of us and alert everyone in the posse where we are." Pip said gravely. "Let's keep to the picks."

"This would go faster if we had the other axe." Sam pointed out.

"We left it in the other chamber," Scott gestured over his shoulder.

"I'll go get it; I can find my way there and back faster than either of you." Pip offered.

"Alright, in the meantime, we'll start on the wall." Scott hefted the axe and swung at the crack. Clangs and blunt '*tung*' sounds resounded with each strike as he swung. Blood started to seep through his fingers from the blisters and sores from working with the heavy hand tools.

Sam shoved and pulled at rocks in the wall, pushing them through, widening the crack.

"I can fit my hand through now." The Jumper panted in excitement.

Pip grinned, revealing pointed teeth before half-crawling, half-flapping back to the tunnel to retrieve the pick axe they had left behind.

30

Morgan moved slowly though the cool, dark tunnels outside of the Red Dome. His belly scales picking up the vibrations of the quail and their lizard riders near the entrance of the caves as they headed out on their raid. He'd slid the door open, but Sol Diablo was large enough to budge the door back into place from the outside. Besides, the great snake was preoccupied.

Today was the day he and Delgado were going to give the Jumper a final interrogation. Morgan was infamous throughout Sol Diablo's caves for coming up with cruel tortures. Jumpers were tough nuts to crack, but Morgan would find a way. Jumpers were loyal to one another, and although there were two other critters in the tunnel that weren't Jumpers he seemed to have bonded with them, and perhaps he would cave to guarantee their safety. If not, as Sol Diablo has said earlier, the mouse was nothing, the raiding parties would bring back more.

Morgan paused, nearing the slave tunnels. The pit censors between the snake's eyes and nostrils checked the dark area for heat. Oddly enough he couldn't sense any body heat nearby. The snake's amber eyes narrowed and he frowned. The reptiles in Sol Diablo's ranks were cold-blooded; body heat from warm-blooded mammals was usually easily detectable for the snake. He stilled himself outside the tunnel entrance, listening hard and using his scales to feel soft vibrations. There was nothing.

Maybe they were asleep. The snake snorted and raised himself, wrapping his steely coils around the rock slab door and pushing it aside just big enough for him.

"Good morning," he hissed threateningly. The giant snake made his entrance into the blackness. He cast around, his pit censors picked up nothing. He flickered his tongue, tasting the air. He could smell them in the cool, damp air. They *were* here! But where are they now? He couldn't see, taste *or* hear them.

Morgan hissed in frustration and shot forward towards the wall where the Jumper had been bound. The wall was bare. The chains lay broken on the ground. The great snake started to shake with rage. He swung his head towards the cleft where the bat had been kept. The bat was gone, the gate broken open and the ropes that had bound its wings lay in a heap. Morgan swelled in anger. Where had they gone? Had they escaped? Impossible! They couldn't open that door! And the tunnel was collapsed, there was no way out!

Just as the snake was about to alert the others to the situation at hand with the prisoners, he heard a scuffing sound. It was a barely audible sound and it seemed far away.

Morgan froze as still as stone after raising himself in a tense, muscular 'S' shape. Glaring at the spot in the dark toward the caved in rocks, the noise was coming from over *there*. The snake's vertical cat-like pupils dilated to see better, he started to sense heat. And then he sensed him.

Pip thrust himself out of the small tunnel and wiped perspiration from his brow, walking around on all fours was hard work. It was unusual for a bat to crawl along the ground instead of fly and climb. He jumped out onto the ledge below and reached for the pick-axe where Sam had left it then stiffened. The door was slid open.

Pip's heart hammered loud and his acute ears cast out to their full range. He could hear him. The slow heartbeat, the raspy, almost silent breathing, he could taste the musky serpent odor in the room. Morgan! Pip's eyes locked at the snake before him in the shadows, made visible by his sonar just as Morgan lunged to strike. Only by a lucky miracle did the bat lash out his wings to the side and escape the deadly fangs as Morgan's face smashed into the rocks, causing a miniature rockslide.

Pip took to the air out of panic for a few rapid wing beats while Morgan screeched and hissed in rage and.

His eyes dropped below the snake. The pick-axe was inches from the great snake's armor-like belly scales. To go after it was suicide!

Morgan hissed, the snake reared up almost two thirds his impressive body length and took a flying snap at the hovering bat.

Pip saw his chance and dove under Morgan's jaws as they snapped shut and shot down towards the axe. He wrapped his feet around the handle and tugged the heavy instrument into the air with him, his wings pumping madly as he tried not to lose his grip on the handle. He needed to keep aloft and keep out of strike range at the same time.

Morgan recoiled and swung his head around, his heat-sensitive pits casting around until it found the bat's body heat.

"You flying rat! You'll die slow!" He lunged and Pip trimmed his wings to his sides and dropped like a stone, he bee-lined into the small tunnel, crashing into the ground. He coughed, air driven from him by the crash landing. He grasped the axe with his thumbs and tugged with great difficulty, he pulled the heavy instrument backwards through the tunnel as quickly as he could.

Morgan gave a bellow of a hiss and smashed his blunt head into the tunnel entrance, blasting away some smaller boulders in his savage attempt to get at the bat.

Pip cried out in alarm and grabbed the pick-axe after dropping it in fright and hauled it back again. He was almost to the end!

Morgan slammed into the tunnel again causing rocks to shudder, the tunnel ceiling bowed dangerously low and several small rocks fell.

Pip laid his ears back as rubble rained on his head. His heart leapt in his throat as a rock fell onto the axe, pinning it down. He strained, but he lacked the grip to pull the tool free. He looked wild-eyed as Morgan battered the tunnel entrance for a third time, his bloodied muzzle stopping right at the rock that pinned the axe, pushing it slightly away.

Pip's heart felt like it was going to explode seeing the outraged snake so close, but then he felt the axe loosen as the snake tried to worm his bulbous head further back into the tunnel.

The snake was so close now his breath steamed the bat's facial fur. Pip suddenly let his eyes narrow and unfurled his wings, baring his teeth he screeched and jabbed a thumb claw into Morgan's eye.

The snake screamed in pain and slammed his head into the tunnel ceiling and withdrew, showering the bat with earth and rocks. Pip grabbed the axe and practically threw himself out of the exit, tumbling out partially onto the slope where he slammed into something big and softer than rock, knocking them both down.

"Pip! What's going on? What's all that noise?" questioned the demanding yet worried voice of Sam as the Jumper helped the flailing bat to his feet.

Pip thrust the axe into the Jumper's hands. He could now see Sam's silhouette against the fair-size hole in the wall to the outside. The room was lit with a harsh white light coming in from the bottom of the slope where Sam and Scott had been working. Sam had run back up after hearing the commotion in the tunnels.

"Morgan! He was there! He knows about the tunnel!" Pip panted, shaking violently from the close encounter. "He's comin'!"

Sam leapt back in alarm. "Come on!" he grabbed the bat by his scruff, practically lifting him off the ground as he bounded down the rocky hill towards the light.

"Morgan's coming!?" Scott asked half-yelping in terror.

"Yes!" Sam started to smash at the hole with the axe, breaking away chunks and making it bigger. Light filtered in and rock chips sprayed everywhere with each strike.

Pip turned to look towards the tunnel, his large ears perfectly erect as he gasped hearing Morgan in the other chamber bellow out into the hall.

"THE SLAVES ARE ESCAPING!"

31

Delgado had been in the Red Dome, having just exited his chambers to fetch water. Sol Diablo's past slaves had carved out huge basins to hold water in the stone floor of the lower caves where the water trickled in naturally through dark caverns underground.

The blue-tail lizard halted, hearing Morgan's bellow from further up the tunnels and hissed in the back of his throat. So the serpent had let them escape? No doubt the rattler would blame him if he didn't do something about it. Looking to the six lizards perking up on the fire rocks he narrowed his orange eyes and turned to face them.

"You heard him!" he snapped, bearing his pointed teeth. "Get your tails after them before I snap them off!" He rested his hand on his knife handle and the six lizards scrambled to their feet and ran toward the tunnels. Delgado followed them, snatching up a lantern as he went.

Sam shoved rocks through with his hands and went back to hammering wildly at the stone wall. Scott's bleeding hands throbbed and stung, but he dared not stop or slow his pace with the axe.

"It's big enough for you, Scott." Sam panted, perspiration misting his brow as the Jumper tried to widen the hole on the sides.

"Yeah, but not big enough for you yet," Scott gasped out between swings.

Sam looked at the mouse and gave a small nod, not stopping. Scott had made it clear. He wasn't leaving until they were *all* able to get out.

Delgado rushed into the cave behind the others, holding the lantern up to see further. Morgan thrust his bloodied, scaly muzzle at the bluish lizard.

"You let them escape!" he snarled, baring his fangs dangerously close to Delgado's outstretched lantern arm.

"*I* let them escape? I left this cave before you last night you idiot!" Delgado snapped back.

Morgan seemed on the verge of exploding as his enormous sinewy body swelled in rage.

"Morgan!" a collared lizard called to the snake, preventing what would surely have been quite the collection of colorful swearing.

"What!" the snake snapped, raising his front half and slithering over to him.

"There's a tunnel that leads through! Awfully small though, Spike and Stubs barely make the fit."

"I know there's a tunnel you insolate worm!" Morgan bared his fangs, his rattle buzzed in frustration, echoing around the room.

"Sorry!" The collared lizard shrank back. "But, h-hey! Delgado might fit?"

Delgado shot the speaker a venomous glare. The five-lined skink was much smaller in build than most of the lizards there, but tall and slender.

"Delgado! Get in there!" Morgan commanded, buffeting him from behind with his rattle-tipped tail.

Delgado stumbled forward, almost dropping the lantern and hissed in the back of his throat at the snake, but grudgingly got on all fours and crawled up to the hole, holding the lantern out in front after shoving the collared lizard aside. Delgado pushed away debris and crawled forward, letting the lantern rest as he pulled himself along. Ahead he could see the tunnel exit and could hear the frantic sounds of the axes clanging against the stone wall.

Pip gasped, making Scott turn around in time to see a fiery yellow light from a lantern leave the tunnel before Delgado's black-and-yellow striped head emerged from the tunnel.

"Don't stop!" Scott panted and kept hammering away at the wall. They were so close!

"Scott, keep going." Sam gripped the axe in his hand tightly as Delgado leapt out of the tunnel and raised his lantern to see them.

Delgado grabbed his gun out of his right holster with his free hand and aimed it with a click at the escapees. "Drop the axes!" He called out.

CRACK! Sam picked up a rock and threw it as hard as he could at Delgado, but missed. The clay stone hit the wall and exploded in a shower of grit.

"Dirty Jumper," Delgado muttered and started to advance down the sloping grade. "You idiots coming!" he shouted to the lizards listening on the other side of the tunnel, grunting as they tried to wriggle through.

Sam picked up the axe again and looked to Pip and Scott. Scott had slowed his pace out of distraction and Pip looked expectantly up at the Jumper.

"You two get out of here. I'll hold him off." Sam muttered gravely, tightening his grip on the axe handle.

"Sam no!" Pip murmured in fear. "He'll kill you!" The bat stretched out his wing to grasp the Jumper's sleeve with his thumb claw, but he couldn't hold the larger mouse back as Sam tensed his powerful legs and then bounded towards Delgado, raising the pick with a shout that filled the whole cavern, chilling Scott's blood.

"Sam!" Pip wanted to rush after him but turned to Scott. "Come on! Keep diggin'!" Pip started to scrabble and pull at the rocks to aid the mouse.

"But what about Sam?" Scott panted.

"Just do as he says!" Pip shouted.

Delgado saw the Jumper bounding up the slope towards him and fired his gun at him, missing when Sam skidded to a halt and leapt to the left to avoid getting shot straight on.

Two other lizards were wriggling out of the tunnel now; the two collared lizards spotted the Jumper and started to rush towards him, following the light of Delgado's lantern.

Scott looked over his shoulder to see the lizards advancing on Sam, but he sailed easily over them with a powerful jump, landing on the skittering sloping stones and facing Delgado again with the axe raised he flung it like a weapon. Delgado ducked low to the ground and a screech rang out as the axe buried itself in the neck of the next lizard that was trying to get out of the tunnel. Its dying body slumped forward and crashed to the rocky floor.

Delgado hissed in fury and fired two shots at the Jumper but as he did so the rocks under his boots shifted and he flung out his arm to keep from sliding to the bottom.

Sam jumped as the two rounds pinged off the wall close to his face and was thrown to the ground when the second collared lizard tackled him from behind.

"The hole's big enough!" Scott panted and looked up to see Sam get taken down. "No!" he cried out. From beside him Pip spread his wings and launched himself into the air, buffeting Scott's fur flat with the wind from his down stroke.

Sam fought and wrestled to get the lizard off of him, but the last several days of being beaten and malnourished had left him without a lot of fighting strength. The lizard's cold, scaly hands wrapped around his throat and started to strangle him, but before he could do so there was a loud screech and the lizard was tackled from above.

"Pip?" Sam gasped seeing the bat roll the lizard off him, his pointed teeth driven deep in the base of the lizard's thick, scaly neck.

His wings wrapped around the lizard's body, pinning his arms inside like a cloak.

Sam didn't waste another second. He looked up to see Delgado taking aim with his gun between Pip's shoulder blades. Sam bared his teeth and launched forward, barreling into Delgado's middle and knocking him down. The lantern fell on its side, but didn't extinguish as the two rolled down the sloped ground. Sam kicked forward, driving Delgado away as he hit the bottom and scrambled to his feet. Delgado swore and stood to shoot Sam, who was fully lit with the light coming in from the outside hole.

The light suddenly dimmed dramatically and Delgado looked to the source. Scott had blocked the hole with his body. "Move!" he shouted.

Delgado turned and aimed the gun at Scott, but Pip had wrestled free of the screeching collared lizard and flew down the grade, crashing into Delgado from behind. "Get out!" he shouted hearing the clicks of pistol hammers behind them.

Sam lunged forward and shoved Scott out of the hole then leapt out himself into the blinding white light of day before turning and thrusting his arms back through to pull Pip out. He threw the bat into the sky to be safely airborne.

"Scott! Hold on!" Sam grabbed the smaller mouse's wrist.

"Hold onto wha-" Scott was cut short as Sam hauled him off his feet and swung him around onto his back where Scott grabbed onto his shoulders and struggled to keep from falling off as Sam turned away and looked down the tumble of stone that made a very steep graded canyon slope.

"Sam??" Scott yelped as the Jumper gave a massive leap and started to run down the slope at breakneck speed.

"Sam! Follow me!" Pip called from above as he winged his way over the tumble of rocks.

Inside the cavern Spike and Stub had widened the tunnel wide enough to fit through. Behind them, Morgan shoved his bloodied muzzle through the rocks, halfway through the tight tunnel. "After them you fools!" he snarled.

The horned lizards stepped over the dying lizard with the pick-axe in his neck, kicking the lantern by accident, sending it tumbling down the slope to the bottom. Delgado picked himself up watching the glass shatter and the oil spill; the flame chased the oil trickle towards a dusty stack of what looked like a bundle of candlesticks. There was a sharp snap and a hiss and Delgado's eyes widened slightly.

"GET OUT!" he snapped and threw himself out of the wall hole into the bright outside. Spike and Stubs followed with unquestioning obedience, too used to Delgado's vicious temper to hesitate. The two remaining collared lizards and Morgan looked at each other stupidly before realizing too late the danger they were in. The fuse of the dynamite was nearly gone.

32

Bubbles gurgled up from Mitch's canteen as he crouched at the edge of the babbling stream that threaded its way around the canyon floor. Standing behind him with guns at the ready and keeping a look out was Bo and June.

Charlie was kneeling beside Mitch and capping off his own canteen before he splashed some water onto his face to cool off.

"Everyone get enough?" Bo asked. Mitch was the last to rise with his canteen. Nearby Jared held the reigns of all their quail as the birds drank their fill tipping their heads back to swallow since they lacked lips to hold water in their beaks.

"Yeah, that should be it." Mitch lashed the canteen to the loop in his saddlebag and stepped into the stirrup, swinging a leg over the saddle as Bo did the same.

"Hey, its Sunday isn't it?" the black-and-white mouse pointed out as the others mounted up.

"No…why," June asked, arching a brow for him to explain his point.

"I think its Wednesday." Mitch stretched his back with a satisfying pop, careful not to hurt his healing ribs.

"Just seems like a good a day as any to ask for a sign." Bo pointed a gloved finger up at the pale blue sky over head.

"Well then, *Father Bo*, would you lead this sermon?" Jared snorted, giving his whiskers a twitch of irritation. "Not like it helps."

"You don't know that." Bo said in mock-haughtiness, partially arguing to annoy Jared and mostly to keep Mitch from feeling discouraged. "And in any case I will lead this sermon, so take off your hats lady and gentlemen." He swept his off with a flourish. The others glanced at him, not sure if he was joking or not before they took off their hats and held them over their hearts, waiting to see what Bo was up to next.

"Oh mighty Creator, thanks for the refreshing swim yesterday, the ground needed a good soaking I'm sure, however, my friend Mitch here is on the trail to get his brother back safe and sound, which I'm sure you're doing a fine job of keeping him alive and well. Though, to be frank, it would be dandy to say, point us in the right general direction? And perhaps give us a clue to where we are?" Bo glanced around to the others, the casualness of his prayer had got him a raised brow from June, but Charlie, Jared and Mitch knew better.

"Er, help guide us safely through these canyons?" June ventured and then dropped her voice, feeling a little embarrassed and on the spot, she cast a glance at Mitch.

"And keep Scott safe, wherever he is." Mitch sighed out.

"And give us some sort of damn signal that we're going in the right direction." Jared muttered.

All eyes flicked to Charlie. The silent dormouse raised his head quite calmly to the sky and gave one word to the scorching heavens: "Please."

Not five seconds after Charlie had spoken a thunderous blast sounded through the canyons and looking down the stream bed the five travelers saw a mushroom-like plume of dust and rubble blow up into the air from the side of a canyon wall further downstream.

Mitch and Jared's jaw dropped in alarm and gripped the reins of their birds tight as they gave a jolt from the noise.

"Amen!" Bo donned his hat and looked at the direction of the explosion. "That enough of a sign for you, Mitch?" he called as Mitch kicked Cali's side to spur her along the pebbly streambed.

"Come on!" Mitch called and started to race towards the disappearing cloud of dust.

The others didn't waste long before rushing after him, their birds running through the brush, splashing through puddles and clattering pebbles as they went.

33

Delgado crashed into the rocks outside the tunnel and barely had time to scramble behind a large boulder before the canyon wall exploded in a thunderous burst of dust, rubble and chunks of flying rock. He put his arms over his head as debris rained down on him.

Across from him, Spike and Stubs had hunkered down in a space between two rocks and were clinging to each other as the stones blasted past them.

Delgado stood as the dust cleared; the canyon wall had been blown wide open. The explosion had caused the last cave wall to crumble as well, joining the two rooms. The two collared lizards had been crushed under the rock fall. Dust coated everything, including the dead, gaping-mouthed head of Morgan, crushed under the rocks that divided the two chambers originally.

"What happened!" Spike squeaked.

"Dynamite," Delgado muttered, fanning the air with his hat to clear some of the dust.

"Did they escape?" Stubs huffed, looking around.

"What do you think!" Delgado shouted, hands spread wide to show the expanse of the damage. "Get my quail ready and hurry back here! We've got to go after them!" he snarled. He watched them scrambled into the cavern and clamber squeamishly passed Morgan's flattened body. A fence lizard and a few others were scrambling over the top on the other side.

"You!" Delgado pointed. "Get on the fastest bird and go tell Sol Diablo the Jumper's escaped. He might be able to cut them off if he's still in the area.

The lizard blanched at the thought of being the bearer of such bad news. Delgado snorted dust from his nose. "GO!" he snarled, sending him scurrying.

The rocks from the blast clattered down the canyon side, crashing into other rocks and loosening them to join the rush. Near the head of the rockslide, Sam was running, bounding and leaping at breakneck speeds towards the level canyon floor. Scott was nearly flung off as Sam crashed onto the canyon bottom. He flung out an arm and stumbled, forward, never stopping. He wanted to put as much space between them and the lizards as possible.

Up above, Pip wheeled high above the canyon to see if he could spot a way out of the maze of monolithic rocks. Sam was still running out of range of the rocks from the blast and turned to cut down a fork in the path, a deep opening between two huge walls of rock. Pip lost sight of the two for a moment and panicked, but then spotted Sam coming out of the other side of the wall into a more open section of the canyon and had ceased running, instead, he moved forward in long, double footed leaps and bounds, covering the ground faster and faster. Trimming in his wings, Pip dove to get closer.

Scott clung to Sam's neck and shoulder for dear life, too petrified to loosen his grip for fear of falling off. A shadow passed over them and Scott looked up to see Pip flying over them, eclipsing the sun before the bat moved to the side and dropped lower.

"Sam! This place is huge! I can't get my bearin's down here, where are we going?" Pip called.

"Away!" Sam panted raggedly between bounds, his eyes narrowed and set ahead around every twist and turn of the canyon path.

Pip tried to follow, but the canyon walls made him feel closed in and claustrophobic. He soared up and out to follow Sam and Scott from the skies. He continued to look around, keeping an ear on Sam below, hearing him running.

Suddenly a new sight caught his eye, on the other side of the narrow plateau, barring the path Sam was running, was a cluster of three riders on quailback. They were picking up speed and gaining fast. Pip squinted to see down into the darkened canyon shadows and saw the blue tail of the lead rider streaming behind and he gasped. Delgado was after them.

Delgado's group was riding ahead now and Pip could see ahead that the paths would merge and Sam and Scott would be trapped. Up ahead there was a large gap between the two canyons with a pillar of red stone in the center like a long, thin hourglass rising up from the canyon floor. Pip dove down to warn Sam but the Jumper was moving too fast, he'd be at the intersection any second.

"Sam!" Pip shouted as Delgado's quail tore around the bend and hurtled straight for the Jumper.

Scott saw the quail and then recognized Delgado, Spike and Stubs as the riders, terror leapt into his throat. They were done for.

"Sam!" he cried out as the Jumper didn't slow, but sped up, sprinting as fast as his powerful legs could carry them.

"*Sam*!" Scott tightened his grip, they were going to crash!

Sam's breathing was ragged from bounding; they were almost upon the riders now. They could see the scar on Delgado's face.

Quail shrieked, Spike and Stubs cried out and Scott yelled out in surprise as Sam gave a massive leap, clearing the quail and their riders with plenty of distance and crashed to the ground with several stumbles before hurrying ahead once more. Sam rushed the edge of the cliff, no time to stop himself, he bunched his muscles and sprang. Scott screamed as they soared through empty space before crashing on top of the pillar stretching up out of the void. Sam went down hard and Scott was thrown off his shoulders, rolling to the far end of the pillar. He scrambled away from the edge and crawled back to where Sam was collapsed and gagging for air.

Delgado had twisted in the saddle to watch the jump, shocked and furious at the evasion. He grabbed the reins and pulled back sharply, driving his quail into a sliding stop.

"Move it, Bird!" he snapped and wheeled around, spurring the Gamble's quail into a sprint after them again as Spike and Stubs fumbled to turn their mounts.

Scott gripped Sam's collar, white knuckled and looked down to see how far the drop was and clung to Sam's shoulder tighter. The rocky pillar stretched up like a stone tree out of a dark green river that wound through the bottom of the canyon, frothing and boiling with violent, white-capped waves between half-submerged rocks.

Pip hovered nearby the best he could and looked worriedly between his trapped, exhausted friends and the ledge that Delgado had just arrived at; Spike and Stub's weren't far behind on quailback.

Delgado pulled a sawed-off shotgun from its resting place in the saddle holster and cocked it with a loud *chik-shik!*

"Sam, *Sam* we gotta get out of here." Scott urged, but winced as Sam gave a horrible cough and pushed himself to his knees, still gasping for air. He'd run too hard, too fast, too long. He was exhausted and he couldn't go anymore.

Scott could feel Sam's rapid heartbeat and the rattle in his shallow breathing as he tried to help him to his feet. He quickly looked to Pip. "We need more time, he can't move."

"What should I do??" Pip looked around wildly, they were trapped on the flat top of the pillar, the other side looked like a far jump even for Sam and the running space was undesirably short.

"Pip!" Scott yelped, seeing Delgado raise the gun to shoot. Pip dove down out of range and Scott shoved Sam flat to the ground as the shot rang out overhead.

Pip bared pointed teeth and swooped back up landing on the edge of the cliff. He spread his wings wide to look bigger and let out a shriek. The quail screeched and bucked, rushing backwards to get away from the bat as he advanced and snapped at them, large ears flared out menacingly.

Delgado turned to aim at Pip, but his quail started to get jumpy and rough and he nearly got thrown off.

"Shoot it!" he snarled at the others as he seized a fistful of Bird's topknot and tried to control him as he spun in a circle.

"I dropped my gun!" Spike's pistol had been knocked from his grip when his bird slammed him against the side of the rock wall.

Pip darted towards the gun in the dust and fumbled to pick it up with his thumbs. He had to keep them at bay; Sam and Scott were sitting targets!

Scott watched Pip, his heart racing, he shook Sam's shoulder. "Sam we gotta get out of here! Now!" He ran to the end of the pillar top and looked over the edge; it was a long way down, the distance made the fur on his spine stand on end. He swallowed and looked across at the far edge. It looked impossibly far for any normal mouse to jump... but a Jumper, a Jumper might make it.

"Sam we gotta jump the gap." Scott hurried back as Sam was getting to his feet, still breathing hard.

"Pip?" Sam looked around in confusion, but Scott grabbed his forearm.

"He's buying us time to cross! We have to go!" he pointed across the next gap, his whiskers shook with tension.

Sam looked over his shoulder and tensed before shoving Scott down, there was a large booming sound from the shotgun as Delgado tried to shoot from his anxious, fidgety mount.

Scott hit the ground, but felt something sting his shoulder before he saw a chunk of rock on the far ledge chip off in a cloud of dust.

Pip fumbled with the gun, he could barely hold it properly, and his long thumb was having a hard time reaching the trigger. He looked up; Stubs had a bead on him with his own pistol. Pip held up the gun and pulled the trigger the best he could. There was a *BANG!* and a cry of pain as Stubs grabbed his shoulder. Fuming, the ugly lizard turned on Pip and rolled his eyes back in his head before there was a sickening splurging sound and two streams of blood shot from his eyes and hit Pip full in the face and chest. Pip cried out in alarm and fell back, rubbing at his face to get the blood off. Stubs squirted the blood stream from his eyes again and Pip flung out a wing to block it, terrified by the lizard's revolting defense method.

Scott looked over and saw Pip covered in blood spatters and gasped in shock.

"Pip! No!" he shouted and scrambled to his feet, a rough hand grabbed him by his collar and hauled him up back onto Sam's shoulders.

"Sam! They hurt Pip!" Scott stammered.

"Don't look back!" Sam shouted and tore himself away from the scene, thinking that if Pip had indeed died for them, Sam would make sure it wasn't in vain.

The Jumper rushed forward towards the end of the pillar top.

"Sam..." Scott said in fear as they rocketed forward, suddenly thinking that this was too crazy, they would never make this! Scott cried out in fear as the Jumper gave a huge bound to hurtle the gap. For one glorious moment they were airborne, soaring across the divide and into the shadow of the next canyon. Then the moment ended, all too abruptly.

Sam heart leapt into his throat in a terrorized panic as they started to drop and the ledge was still an arm's length away. Sam flailed in vain; wind milling to reach it but it was too late his fingertips just barely grazed the stone ledge before they plummeted. They were falling.

34

Mitch hurried away from the small stream up a shallow slope towards where they had heard the explosion. As he rounded the corner he had to pull back sharply to avoid running Cali straight into a large boulder pile.

Bo nearly crashed into him from behind and looked up towards the top of the steep canyon.

"Looks like the work of black powder up there, these rocks must have only just fallen." He spurred Cotton to hop up onto one of the big stones.

June urged Bowie forward to look around the rubble and debris when Jared made a choking sound and she twisted in the saddle to see what.

A huge posse of lizards on quailback rode out of the passage they had just entered from and started to storm up the steep canyon wall towards the hole above. Leading the charge was an enormous orange and black Gila monster riding an equally large roadrunner to bear his mass while his supporters all rode various quails.

"*Bo, get down!*" Mitch hissed, reaching up and grabbing his boot, tugging him behind the rocks. June herded the others behind with him and peered around the edges.

"What the…" Mitch breathed watched them rush the hill and disappear into the gaping hole.

"Was that the posse you were looking for?" June asked her voice barely in a whisper. There must have been just over a hundred rough, barbaric looking critters in that group.

"I.. think it is, but I didn't see the blue tailed one, I didn't think there would be so many." Mitch murmured as the last of them disappeared into the black mouth of the blown-open cave.

"This is suicide! You lead us to an army of bandits! And one rides a Chaparral Bird! A *roadrunner* you idiot! He probably fed Scott to that thing like a sugar cube!" Jared whispered hysterically from behind Charlie and Bo.

"Shh!" Mitch hissed hearing another set of hobbling steps coming towards their spot from the passage. "Someone's coming…"

Mitch and the others held their breath as the shadow of a worn looking mountain quail rode stiffly into view, his rider, a fence lizard, was partially slumped over the saddle, and as he passed the rock he slid and fell from the saddle to the ground with a thud.

"Mitch!" June snapped as Mitch stepped towards the lizard, but stayed hidden in the shadow of the boulder.

Mitch flicked an ear and rested one hand on his pistol as he neared the lizard. He had rolled stiffly onto his back and was holding his arm as if in pain. The lizard was at least twice Mitch's size, but he looked hurt, hearing clicks behind himself, Mitch knew he had backup in case the bandit tried anything.

Taking one last swallow, Mitch stood beside the lizard and pointed his gun down at his face. The fence lizard groaned and looked up at the mouse with blurry eyes.

"Shoot me sonny, you'd be doin' me a favor…" he croaked.

Mitch looked at the arm the lizard was nursing. The dusty black cotton was soaked and torn, as if he had been bitten, and shaken violently. There was no doubt in Mitch's mind it was broken and bleeding badly. He knelt beside the lizard, gun still out. "What happened? Who were those lizards?" he demanded.

The fence lizard coughed and looked at his mangled arm. "S-Sol Diablo and his lizards… the Gila." He coughed. "He b-bit my arm, real b-bad he did. He… he was real mad when I told… told him what happened." He groaned.

"Gila…" Mitch remembered the huge Gila monster riding the roadrunner in the lead of the posse. Gila monsters were venomous lizards, and Mitch knew that the lizard before him was dying from the Gila's terrible bite. "What was he mad about? What happened? The explosion?" Mitch pressed, not knowing how much time they had. He could sense the others coming closer and flicked his tail to keep them back.

"Explosion… ac—accident. The p-prisoners escaped." The lizard slurred.

"Prisoners? What prisoners?" Mitch's heart beat faster. Was Scott a prisoner? Had he escaped?

"Ugh… A Jumper, and mouse and a bat… dug out, escaped. S-sent Delgado, Sp-Spike and Stubs after… 'tell Sol Diablo' he says… don't argue with that one… had to tell the p-posse before they left… S-Sol Diablo was f-furious. He said I d-deserved death fer lettin' them escape. Lettin' the *Jumper* escape…"

"A mouse??" Mitch listened, and looked at the lizard's eyes, growing cloudy and dim. "No, stay with us. Where did they go? When did they escape?" he shook the lizard's shoulder slightly.

"Jumper…*cough*… goes where the Jumpers go… gonna disappear… gonna die out… Sol Diablo gonna… he's gonna…" The lizard rasped weakly then let out along rattling breath and lay his head down, still as the stone he rested on.

Mitch flinched feeling a hand on his shoulder and looked up to see June standing beside him.

"He told you everything he knew I think." She murmured, looking at the corpse with a mixture of pity and disdain.

"I think so… but come on, we've got to get out of here. They would have run out of the canyons and tried to get away." Mitch stood up and sheathed his gun into his holster.

"Which is where?" Bo asked, looking around. "We don't even know how to get out."

"Check his saddlebags for a map or something useful." Mitch pointed to the run down looking Mountain Quail.

Bo nodded and went over, rooting about in the bags, "Uh, not much here, a few hunks of stale looking corn bread and a little flask of whiskey. Sorry Mitch, no map."

"Well, come on then, we're wasting time waiting to get caught out here." Mitch got onto Cali, his heart still pounding loud in his ears. A mouse had escaped. It might be Scott! They must have missed him by minutes! Scott could be alive and within a mile!

35

The vanishing cries from Sam and Scott reached Pip's ear and he looked over just in time to see them plummet towards the rocky river below. The bat gasped and scrambling to flip around he leapt off the cliff face. A shot rang out and he felt a sting through his wing membrane before he dove down after them, shooting down towards his falling friends.

Sam and Scott twisted as they fell, the river seemed to be rising up to meet them rapidly, and directly below them was a large rock sticking out of the water. Scott cried out and Sam shut his eyes tight, preparing to smash into the rock, but something else crashed into them from the side, knocking them off course and sending them splashing into the center of the river.

Pip veered wildly off course, unable to correct his flight pattern at this speed, after knocking Sam and Scott out of harm's way he slammed his furled wing and shoulder into the edge of the great rock before plunging into the swift moving river, the water silencing his yelp of pain.

Scott hit the surface of the river with force. Water engulfed him. He was torn from his grip on Sam's shoulders as the world spun him rapidly until he didn't know which way was up. He had no air left in his lungs to hold on much longer. He hit something hard and kicked away from it. Blindly he thrashed and broke the surface coughing and sputtering as he was swept down the frothing green water at an alarming rate. Where was Sam? Scott struggled to keep his head above the water and he made a quick scan of the canyon walls on either side. Where was Pip? He heard a strangulated yelp and cough and looked over to see Pip's ears poking up just above the surface. His wings beat the current as the bat tried to keep afloat. "Hel—!" The water dragged at his wings and pulled him under. Scott panicked and kicked hard to get over to his friend. He ducked below the surface and seized one of Pip's flailing wings, but they were dragging them both down by the current both creatures were buffeted into fierce underwater tumbling. Pip was being dragged down and Scott was being pulled with him. Where was Sam?

Sam had flipped around wildly after hitting the water. Heart in his throat, he broke the surface of the waves and hit something hard. Looking up he saw it was a boulder. He grappled with it and clawed with his fingers, kicking the slick base until he found a hold and clambered onto it coughing and panting for breath. A gunshot sounded and a chip of the boulder blew off near Sam's shoulder. He twisted to look over his shoulder with wide eyes to see that Delgado had recovered control of his bird and was standing on the ledge of the canyon wall, above him, Spike and Stubs were also aiming pistols in the Jumper's direction.

Sam had no time to hide so he gave a massive leap and threw himself back into the cool waters. Sam stayed under as long as he could. He didn't know where Scott or Pip were as he came up for air in time to see Scott disappear under the surface. Giving massive kicks, Sam dove under the surface once more and squinted into the blurry depths. He spotted the fuzzy form of Scott's yellow shirt and reached out to him and Pip.

Scott had lost all his air again. He tugged weakly at Pip, who had stopped moving and felt darkness clouding his head when something grabbed his collar and jerked him upwards.

Sam grasped Scott and Pip tight and kicked back towards the surface, bubbles busting from his mouth and nose as his lungs screamed for air. One last kick and he was up.

Scott coughed and gagged for air and Pip stirred weakly as Sam puffed hard to drag the two of them towards a gravely shore. His feet found purchase and he heaved the two of them forward. Letting them drop onto the bank. Sam staggered only about three steps then collapsed on his side, rolling onto his back in exhaustion as his chest heaved for air.

Scott coughed and dragged himself further up the bank. He looked from Sam, who looked like he'd passed out from exhaustion and then to Pip, who was doubled up and panting, gripping his shoulder with the single claw of his free wing in pain.

Scott glanced around for any sign of Delgado or the others, but didn't see them; maybe the ride in the river had helped get them to a safer area. The young mouse tried to stand, but his legs felt like rubber and he sank to his knees and then to all fours. He dug his fingers into the red sand and gravel and coughed as the water dripped from his whiskers. How had he gotten into such a mess?

Summoning some strength he stood on shaky legs and stumbled over to where Pip was gripping his left wing and shoulder with a pained look on his face. Scott squinted in the sunlight. His hat had been washed off in the river. He knelt close to Pip to see what was wrong.

"What happened to your wing?" he asked worriedly then froze. "And all that blood on you…"

"Got shot in the membrane… doesn't hurt so bad, but my shoulder,… I hit that rock." Pip sucked air through his teeth. "It hurts like all hell." He bit his lip. "The bloods not mine, that demon shot it through his eyes!"

Scott flattened his ears, remembering that horned lizards had a nasty habit of squirting their own blood at an enemy in a fight. Hearing a cough he looked over at Sam, who was still catching his breath. Then he looked back at Pip's wing. "Can you move it?"

"I'll try…" Pip mumbled and slowly extended his wing partway then winced and let it drop.

"Is it broken?" Scott asked nervously, not knowing anything about wings, especially bats.

"I'm not sure, I can't raise it. I can't be grounded again, I *can t*!" Pip looked at the wing worriedly.

"Wait, your shoulder, let me see." Scott shuffled closer. "One time back home, Charlie, one of our ranch hands, did something to his shoulder to hurt it while helping raise part of the barn. Pa said it was dislocated."

"Dis-*what*-ed?" Pip gasped looking at his shoulder.

"Like, it popped out of place. We just have to pop it back in, it'll be sore for a day or so, but Charlie was back to work after taking things light." Scott noticed the dent and bulge in Pip's shoulder and remembered seeing something similar with Charlie.

Scott stood up on slightly wobbly legs and looked over at Sam, who was shielding his eyes from the sun with his forearm while he continued to rest on his back and recover.

"Sam?" Scott took a few wobbly steps before he found his ground. "Sam are you alright?"

"Yes… tired…" Sam muttered between two deep breaths, squinting up at him behind his hand. "You?"

"Ok I think, Pip's hurt his shoulder, can you help me?" Scott raised his arm to jerk his thumb over his shoulder when a burning pain from his own shoulder made him gasp and drop to a knee, clutching his own shoulder.

"Scott?" Sam sat up abruptly and came forward on his knees to inspect his shoulder, moving Scott's hand aside to see spots of crimson around the torn golden-colored fabric.

"Looks like shot from Delgado's shotgun." Pip gasped as he wobbled unsteadily on his feet and good wrist.

"I can't remember getting hit, but it hurts when I move my shoulder." Scott winced as Sam pressed the wound gently with his thumb.

"Well, unless we go digging around your shoulder with sticks we won't be able to get those out." Sam sat back on the ground, his tufted tail coiling across his ankles.

"We need a doctor, I'm no good with medicine things, and Pip's shoulder, I think it's dislocated." Scott stood slowly.

"Do you know how to put it back?" Sam asked quizzically.

"Well, I saw my Pa do it once when our ranch hand hurt himself, but I've never done—"

"Well, try now." Sam interrupted, massaging red, painful looking wrists showing through his tawny fur where the ropes and cuffs had rubbed. "We've got a long way to go."

"Go where?" Scott blinked. "Back to Redcliff?" he asked hopefully.

"I know of red *cliffs*, but I doubt we're talking about the same thing, besides, you belong to a settler village, I can't go there. Settlers will kill me as soon as look at me." The Jumper's eyes darkened.

"Not all settlers—" Scott tried to explain.

"I hate to interrupt, but this is very painful." Pip gritted his teeth and tried to support his bad wing with the other.

"Alright, let's reset Pip's wing and get out of here." Sam stood up. Before Scott could ask Sam lashed his tufted tail, flicking them with water droplets. "As far from these canyons as we can get before nightfall, northward towards the mountains until I can get my bearings." He turned away from Scott and gave himself a shake to rid himself of excess water.

Scott turned back to Pip and sighed out slow. "Alright, settle against that rock, this might hurt your wing a bit…"

36

Mitch looked down over the edge of the canyon where the river threaded below like an angry, green snake. He looked back to the others, who had spread out and were looking high and low for any clues, but the rocky surface was unforgiving, bearing no prints or signs of any life.

"We should get out of here. We don't want to be wandering around in lizard country after dark." June rode up alongside him.

"Just a little longer," Mitch muttered, not looking up from the river below until she tapped his shoulder.

"Mitch it's been hours. He's probably running from these hellish canyons as fast as he can. He's probably trying to get home."

"He doesn't know where home is." Mitch looked back, worry and frustration plain on his face. "*We* don't even know where home is." He took off his hat and ran his fingers through his head fur.

"Well, think about the lizard's words, Mitch." Bo came over on foot and looked up at him. "He said a mouse, a bat and a Jumper escaped. Don't you think it might be possible that they escaped together?"

Mitch blinked thoughtfully. The idea had occurred to him, but Scott and a Jumper? Scott was fascinated by books of western heroes who hunted Jumpers down like trophies, why would he team up with one? Escape... escape seemed the only logical explanation.

"Maybe they did escape together, but where would they go?" Mitch shrugged. The frustration of knowing they had been so close was draining him of energy and patience.

"'To the place the Jumpers go.'" Bo recited.

"That's not helping." Mitch growled out.

"It's obvious! The Jumper'll go back to the other Jumpers; Scott's probably going with them." Bo tipped his hat back matter-of-factly.

"Oh that's great, Bo, let's go look for a city of wild mice that's been hidden for the past fifty years and not once seen by civilization. That sounds insanely simple. Maybe while I'm at it I'll fly to the sun on a roadrunner and slay a rattlesnake." Mitch crammed his hat back on his head, flattening his ears and breathing hard.

"Mitch, calm down." Bo crossed his arms. "I'm frustrated too, but this is the only clue we've got," Bo said stiffly, trying to keep his own head level.

"Boys, we're lost, tired, frustrated and hungry. We need to get down from these cliffs to the river. From there we can camp more safely and plot our next move." June spoke up, feeling the tension thickening in the air like smoke.

"Jumper'll probably eat Scott before nightfall anyway." Jared muttered to Charlie, who shot him a silencing glare.

Mitch shut his eyes and nodded stiffly at June's words.

"Come on, its nearly sundown." Bo grunted as he climbed into his saddle. "That only gives us a few hours to get down, make camp and find something to eat."

"Something raw, let's not have any fires out here to attract trouble." Mitch nodded, speaking more civilly as he glanced at Bo almost apologetically.

Bo nodded silently and turned towards the crumbling downward slope to lead the way to the winding river below.

Further up the cliffs, the setting sun painted a blazing orange and bloody red sunset across the sky, staining the rocks outside the gaping hole of Sol Diablo's prison mine a fiery color. The huge Gila stood in the long shaft of light that poured in from outside with his hands folded behind his back. His thick, pebble-scaled tail dragged slowly side to side across the debris-littered floor facing the remains of Morgan and the two collared lizards from the cave-in.

Hearing a squawk, he straightened up slightly. All other heads from the lizards standing in the cavern shadows turned quickly to the source at the mouth of the cave.

Delgado rode in on his quail, leading Spike and Stubs behind him. Spotting the Gila, Delgado could only guess how this whole ordeal was going to go. He dismounted slowly, hand resting on his gun handle as he hit the floor and sent his quail away into the shadows to recover with a flick of the reins.

"You let them escape." The Gila's gravelly voice was soft and furious, like steam escaping from a volcano about to blow its top.

"The fault doesn't rest with me." Delgado replied stiffly. "There was more than one of us here when they were tunneling out." His gaze flickered to Morgan's body.

The Gila seemed to swell with rage, but didn't turn around. "They destroyed my mine."

"There was nothing in this mine, you've dug here for years and have barely struck a vein."

The Gila let out a dangerous hissing that reverberated around the cavern, causing the others to step back cautiously.

"You didn't receive any information from the Jumper before you let him escape."

Delgado remained silent, his orange eyes smoldering as brilliantly as the sky behind him.

Without warning, the Gila spun around with speeds astonishing for a lizard of his size and girth. He was upon Delgado before he could pull his gun out all the way.

One massive, clawed hand shoved Delgado to the ground, knocking the freed gun from his grip, it clattered across the floor. He whipped out his left gun as the Gila lifted him off the ground with one hand over his head, baring the poisonous, black jaws like he was apart to tear him to pieces then paused and tossed Delgado into the wall, causing the lizards lingering there to scatter like roaches.

Delgado slumped to the ground, the wind driven from him, but before he could recover Sol Diablo rushed forward and grabbed him by the neck and slammed him flat on his back on top of a stone slab, ripping the knife he was pulling out from of his hand and letting it fall with a clatter.

"YOU LET THEM ESCAPE!" his extreme grip tightened, cutting off Delgado's air, making him writhe fruitlessly. "Your explosion *killed Morgan!*" He spat around huge, wickedly curved teeth.

Delgado gasped with a slight gurgle, but didn't try to talk and he glared in defiance at the lizard who now held his life in his claws, again.

"You've got one. Last. Choice." Sol Diablo growled, his voice echoing for all the other lizards to hear as they tentatively peered around rocks and out from the shadows.

"You can lay here and die from a nasty bite." He leaned close to the smaller lizard's exposed neck, Delgado thrashed and tried to push him back. "Or," the Gila sneered cruelly. "You can track down those prisoners, find the Jumpers and their hidden city and I'll let you live." He relaxed his grip slightly on Delgado's throat, letting him gasp for air, eyes blazing with hatred.

"Hell, I might even consider *letting you go*." The Gila taunted, the other lizards murmured quietly. It was no real secret that Delgado despised working for the Gila, and although he was paid for his work, he was there for the most part against his will. Delgado couldn't leave or he would risk getting tracked down, hunted by Morgan or worse. But Morgan was dead now, the only one standing between Delgado and freedom was Sol Diablo.

"You've got ten seconds to decide or we go with option 'A.'" Sol Diablo loomed over him.

Delgado glared at him. Death would not be instant; he'd seen the pain the Gila's bite inflicted. And although he didn't think the Gila would really let him go, the alternative choice meant he could live, for now, and perhaps plan his revenge on the Gila.

The sun sank lower, reflecting scarlet light off Delgado's smooth blue-black scales as he responded through gritted teeth: "Alright, I'll find them." He stood up and dusted off his shirt. "Let's get going then."

37

"Sorry!" Scott winced as Pip cried out after a sharp *click!* The bat recoiled, away from him, tense and muttering fast under his breath. He squinted open his eyes.

"Good glory, that feels much better." He slumped back against the rock.

"Really?" Scott asked in relief that he'd done something right.

"It's sore, but nothin' like before." Pip slowly raised and unfurled his wing experimentally.

"Can you fly?" Sam asked from where he was wringing out his shirt near the bank with his back to them. Scrapes and scars from the switch and being dragged showed clearly through his tawny-golden fur.

"Too sore to try right now, but I think I can travel." Pip eased forward, supporting himself on his wrists.

"Good, it's nearly dark." Sam looked up, the river-cut canyon was deep in shadow, and the sky was darkening overhead.

"Where to?" Scott pushed his sleeves up to his elbows. His clothes were still wet, but there was no time to try and dry them.

"Let's get out of these canyons and into some brush." Sam looked around. "Keep an eye out for some cactus."

"Cactus, what for, to eat?" Scott arched a brow.

"I guess you could eat them, but I'd feel a whole lot safer near some cactus in the night." Sam shrugged and pulled his ripped up shirt back on. "Let's head back this way through those rocks, it's a tight fit but it looks like the ground slopes down…" Sam jumped up onto the rocks and peered over, sighing with relief. " It goes down a little ways then rises. I can see some brush and… prickly pear!" Sam lashed his tufted tail. "Let's get going." He turned and crouched to help pull them up.

The hike down to the little rise out of the canyon was easy at first, the dying light showed easy places to pause and good holds to rest on, but as they reached the base of the hill the sky began to darken drastically. When they finally reached the prickly pear cluster Sam had spotted from the rocks the sunset was a pale yellow streak on the horizon behind the cliffs and stars were starting to stud the deep purple sky.

"What's so good about cactus?" Pip puffed exhaustedly, limping as he hobbled on all fours up to the bizarrely shaped succulent. "Looks like a dirty great, spiny nuisance." He stopped to rest as Sam circled the outside of the cluster.

"Cactus are more important to me and my people than you'll ever know." Sam muttered, dropping to his hands and knees to peer between two needle-covered leaves. "Alright I found a way in, be careful not to get snagged up." Sam inched forward and crawled up behind another thick cactus leaf before reaching the woody base.

Scott looked uneasily at Pip then dropped own and crawled forward until he spotted Sam in the gloom and inched back to rest against the woody base, glad it was free of spines.

Pip entered last, glancing around he gave the area a quick sweep with his sonar. It was small, but enough space for the three of them to rest.

"We should be safe in here for the night." Sam muttered as he eased himself to the ground, curling up and resting his head pillow-like on his tufted tail.

Pip settled back against the base beside Scott. "It's going to take some getting used to, going back to being nocturnal again, but I suppose I should grab the rest while I can." He yawned, showing pointed teeth and blinking drowsy, green eyes.

Scott hugged his knees close and glanced at his shoulder, it was sore and stiff but now that he wasn't moving the pain was quieting. He raised his head and looked up through the crisscrossed spines and cactus leaves that covered them from above. He could just barely make out some stars.

"Sam?" he murmured, not sure if he was asleep or not.

"Mm." Sam grunted drowsily, not raising his head.

"Where exactly *are* we going? I... I gotta get back home. My folks must think I'm *dead*..."

Sam sighed and stayed quiet for a long time, Scott was about to repeat himself when Sam finally responded. "Skytown."

"Where?" Pip asked, rubbing the back of his neck sorely.

"Skytown is where we're headed, home of the Jumpers. From there I can try to get you home."

"Really?" Scott felt hope bubble up inside him, as well as a little bit of excitement. Skytown? They were going to the hidden village of the Jumpers?

"How far away is it from here? Do you know?" Pip asked, turning his large ears forward to listen.

"About a day or two, I think, if we travel fast. I don't know where we are for certain right now, but I think I can find the way back." Sam murmured, sounding like he was drifting off to sleep.

Scott nodded. "Thanks, Sam." He settled back down against the woody base, "For everything." he added. Scott closed his eyes and fell asleep, leaving Pip to sit up awake a while longer before he too succumbed to exhaustion.

PART III
The Secret City

38

The sounds of the river were both calming an eerie in the black shadows of the canyon near the shore of the water. There was a brief orange glow as Bo took a drag on his cigarette from where he was sitting with his back against a rock.

Mitch was awake too, with no fire to light up their camp there seemed to be no reason to talk. Seeing the reddish glow again Mitch could smell the tobacco now. He felt bad for snapping at Bo, and seeing the cigarette only made it worse. Bo only smoked when he was nervous or when things were tense. He hadn't seen Bo smoke in a long time.

Mitch stood up, feeling slightly off balance in the darkness as he picked his way over the uneven ground towards the glow. There was a sound of a match being struck against a rock and for a few moments Bo's face with lit up as he lit another roll before shaking the flame out.

Mitch sat on a rock across from him. "You alright?" he asked, shifting to pop his back.

"Fine, just awake." Bo turned and blew out a cloud of smoke to the side so it wouldn't hit Mitch's face. "Why're you still up?"

Mitch sighed. "Guilt I guess. I shouldn't have snapped at you earlier, especially after the sort of day it's been."

"You were just frustrated, we all are." Bo settled back against the rock and set the cigarette down on the rock next to him to let it smolder.

"We were just so *close*." Mitch sighed, remembering hearing the explosion. Had Scott been hurt in that blast? Where had he run to?

"He'll be ok Mitch." Bo flicked the smoldering stub to the ground and flattened it with his boot. "He's made it this far, and he's gotten out. He's gonna try to get home no matter what."

Mitch shrugged and nodded. He was still nervous, it was several days to get to Redcliff from here, and that was on quailback. Scott didn't have a quail, or food or water. He was just …wandering.

"I just pray he finds a town soon and can catch a coach home." Mitch sighed.

"Hey, the kid'll be ok, he's not stupid, *naïve* maybe, but not stupid. He's headin' for a safe place. And maybe right now the safest place to him is with that Jumper he's run off with." Bo took off his hat and set it down on the ground. "Hopefully we can catch up to them and get Scott back before they get to that Jumper-city-place."

Mitch nodded. "Thanks, Bo. I don't like to think of him getting dragged to some place like that. I just hope you're right."

Bo nodded. "Get some rest. We've got a lost civilization to find in the morning." He slid to the ground and rested his hands on his stomach.

"Yeah, I guess so." Mitch sighed. "'Night, Bo." Mitch turned and headed back to his spot, on the way he was careful to step quietly between Charlie and Jared, who were already asleep.

He settled back down against the rock and shut his eyes to rest.

June blinked open her eyes and glanced over at Mitch before resting her head back down again. It tore her up that they had been so close, and now Scott seemed as far away as ever.

39

It was late in the night as Delgado stood alone in his chambers, wide awake as he pondered the impossibility of the task he'd been assigned to. Track down the Jumpers and find their city? It was madness. Impossible. No one had ever seen the city of the Jumpers, it was like chasing a myth.

Delgado cracked his knuckles in frustration before heading over to his flat fire-rock. The fire under the slab was fading to smoldering embers, casting and eerie red glow and harsh black shadows around the room.

Laid out on the slab were two ammunition belts, a canteen, his knife, both pistols and his long, leather overcoat. That was all he was bringing.

Delgado knew it was still night out, despite the enclosed walls of stone. He wrapped his gear into the coat like a pack and stepped into the cavern hall.

Sol Diablo was awake too, in the Red Dome, pacing between the fire rocks, most of which were extinguished by now with dying coals, making the light dim and difficult to see.

"You all packed for this goose chase." The Gila grunted without turning around.

"Yes." Delgado muttered crossly. His bedroll and ropes were with his saddle gear were near his quail in the next cavern over.

"Then I guess we can move out." The Gila turned and stumped over to the skink heavily and grabbed his shoulder, steering him roughly in front. "You will ride point, just in front of me." His claws tightened their grip into his shoulder. "My gun will be fixed on your back, so no funny business. You get me to the Jumpers. I'll let you walk free."

Delgado's grip tightened on his knife hilt, but he said nothing as they walked down the dark tunnel towards the quail.

40

Scott woke up groggily and winced at the pain in his abdomen. It took him a minute to realize that this pain was hunger, and a cruel reminder of the last real meal he'd had was that night with his brother, and that small bit of cactus flesh since. He was starving.

Sitting up, he rubbed his eyes and looked to his right to see Pip was fast asleep, wings furled close about him like a leathery bedroll.

Scott was relieved that he no longer looked in pain. As he turned to his left his felt his insides grow icy. Sam was gone. The Jumper had woken them after a short rest last night so they could travel under the coolness of dark and they had stop again and collapsed to rest under a new prickly pear just hours ago, where was he now?

Scott stumbled to his feet and looked around nervously. Where was he? He looked up through the crisscross of cactus needles then crouched and stepped outside.

"Sam?" he called, surprised at how croaky his voice sounded. His throat was dry and for a moment he was scared Sam might have left them, but then there was a soft thud behind him and he turned to see that Sam had jumped down from the top of the prickly pear with an armful of long cactus spines. He set them on the ground and blinked down at Scott.

"What?"

"I was just… wondering where you went." Scott winced as a ripple of pain went through his stomach as a gurgle of hunger became audible.

"I was looking for some food; the fruits aren't ready on this cactus though." Sam pointed at the greenish buds topped with un-opened yellow blooms on the higher prickly pear leaves.

"They still need to flower first." Sam picked up a long spine from the ground and tested the tip with his finger. "I figured we needed something a little more filling." The Jumper's ear flickered and he looked past Scott where a fat, black cricket was scuttling over a rock.

"I wish I had my bow, but I guess I'll have to catch this the hard way." Sam sprang before Scott could question him. The cricket jumped and Sam tore after it. When the cricket landed Sam was right behind it and stabbed the cactus spine down through its thorax, pinning it to the ground. With a few short, violent moves the insect was headless, and dead. He slid it from the cactus spine and carried it back to Scott. "Eat up." He dropped it on the ground and sat down in front of it.

"Eat...*that?*" Scott couldn't help but wrinkle his nose slightly. Crickets were quail food, crawly insects. He'd never eaten one before. He'd never really had to. Though he knew his father liked them roasted during a long quail drive.

"Unless you see something else to eat." Sam shrugged, pulling off a hind leg and taking a crunchy bite. "Not too good raw, but better than being hungry."

Scott knelt down and pulled off the other leg with a brittle snap that made his ears curl back. He gave it a sniff as Sam ate the last of his piece.

"Uh, you should go see if Pip wants some, I'll bet he's hungry." Scott pointed out.

Sam nodded and went to go rouse the long-eared bat. As soon as he was gone Scott took a bite of the leg, gagged and spat it into his hand, spitting any leftover bits onto the ground. "*Ew...*" he muttered. His belly gnawed and roiled for food. Shutting his eyes tight he popped the bite back into his mouth and muscled it down. Flicking his tongue in distaste, he took another unsavory bite.

Pip stumbled out after Sam, limping slightly on his scraped and bruised wrists.

"Cricket? Great, I'm starved!" Pip said in relief and ripped a hunk of the thorax off and swallowed it whole. "I've missed good food like this, not as good as moths but better than cactus anyway."

Scott was now looking at the ripped open cricket as the yellowed juices dribbled onto the sand and he felt a little nauseous.

"You alright? Here, eat some more." Sam pushed the cricket over to Scott. "Eat some of the meaty part, the juices'll settle your stomach."

"The juices will make me vomit." Scott leaned away from it.

"Just try it Scott, you need it." Sam tore a drippy hunk off and took Scott's hand, slapping it onto it. Sam licked his fingers then pulled off a piece for himself.

Scott looked at the mess on his hand then screwed his eyes shut and shoved it into his mouth. It was sour and squishy, the crunchy shell reminded him of French bread or brittle. He muscled it down and shuddered. "Ugh... not bad." He smiled weakly. His stomach seemed to calm as it welcomed the food, no matter what it was.

Sam caught another cricket and divided it amongst them before the sky started to get brighter.

"We should get moving, we have a lot of ground to cover."

"Walkin'?" Pip seemed to deflate.

"You can fly if you need to." Sam looked down at him as he stood up. "*Can* you fly?"

"Shoulder's still a bit sore but walkin's not so easy either, I'll try to keep up though." Pip leaned forward on his wrists again, ready to go.

"We won't leave you behind." Scott promised as he kicked earth over the shells of the cricket and looked up to Sam. "How far away do you think this Skytown place is from here?" he asked curiously.

"A day or so, I should think, maybe two or three at this pace." Sam glanced at Pip.

Pip hung his head. "I'm sorry. I really will try to keep up; I don't want to slow you down."

"No, don't be sorry, you're hurt, that's not your fault. We'll get there if it takes one day or three." Sam lashed his tufted tail.

Pip looked up gratefully. "Hopefully soon I'll be able to fly again, and we can move faster."

"Yeah." Scott said as he looked out over the rolling, scrubby hills around them. "I hope so too."

41

The sky was a pale, peach pink above the canyons with the early morning light. Charlie was the only one awake so far, having woken up earlier to find no one was keeping watch.

Feeling a little groggy, the silent dormouse stood and stretched out his back, rolling his shoulders before climbing over the rocks that framed the makeshift camp and headed towards the water for a drink.

The water flowed smooth and dark before him as Charlie knelt, his knee getting soaked in the wet sand as he splashed water onto his face and whiskers.

A scraggly shape caught his eye and Charlie looked to his right downriver to see a dead branch hanging out into the water from the bank where it was half submerged at one end and hanging like a hinge from a broken base up on the bank. The branch hadn't been what had caught the golden dormouse's eye, rather what was on it, caught in the branches. A hat.

Charlie stood and headed over to the branch, he was surprised the hat wasn't being washed away, the twigs were holding it just so as the current pressed it against the matted branches.

Charlie couldn't reach the hat from the bank of the river, and he couldn't tell the depth of the water below the hat from the shore. Charlie took a handful of sand and threw it into the water, watching it get whisked away. The current was strong and swift. He frowned and stepped into the water, holding onto the branch with one hand and easing further and further towards the hat. The current tugged at his steps and soon the water reached past his waist, lapping at his chest. The bank dropped away beneath him and Charlie bobbed under the water for a moment, the current pulling at him but his grip held and he managed to pull himself up for air, but jogged the branch, the hat slipped and the current started to reclaim it but he let go of the branch and seized the hat, his tail looping around the branch last second before he was carried off. Doubling back over himself Charlie pulled himself to shore, dripping wet and clutching the soaking hat by the brim in one hand.

Letting out a breath of relief Charlie flipped the hat over to peer into the bowl and his brows rose slightly. Looking back over his shoulder towards the sandy expanse of bank that wound around the river He quickly climbed over the rocks and started to jog down the bank, his eyes sweeping across the sands and clay and back into the shallows with every step. He rounded a bend in the river and stopped to catch his breath. Looking around the space in front of him was blocked by a spur of rock too high to see over but easy enough to climb.

The dormouse scaled it easily and dropped down onto the other side. A short stretch of red-sand beach covered a small distance before dropping off into the river, the was no more bank or beach after that, just sheer cliff and canyon dipping into the river that had carved it.

Charlie's eyes widened as he rushed forward seeing imprints in the sand, unusual prints he couldn't recognize. One set seemed almost spidery, but with drag marks, like their owner had been dragging a heavy cloak, their print had claw points too. The others were like mouse prints, but much larger, and the weight was set forward onto the front of the foot. Charlie frowned then his heart pounded excitedly finding what he was looking for. Boot prints, with a wedged heel.

Tracks were all over but these were the golden find. Looking at the hat Charlie dropped to his knees beside the tracks and felt them gently. They were pretty fresh, probably yesterday afternoon or evening.

Charlie sighed out in relief. Scott was alive. He was alive and these tracks proved it.

The golden dormouse leapt up and climbed the rocks, dropping back to the other side and started to run back to the others as fast as he could.

Mitch and the others were awake and passing around the few supplies they had left for breakfast when Charlie dropped down over the side of the boulder into their midst.

"Where have you been?" Bo asked, standing up and hurrying over. "I was worried! I thought one of those lizards might have gotten a hold of you!" He frowned and arched a brow. "Why are you all wet?"

Charlie waved him off and rushed over to Mitch who was sitting across from June on a rock finishing a crumbly cornbread biscuit.

"What's wrong, Charlie?" Mitch asked as Charlie thrust something into his hands. For a moment Mitch didn't recognized the soaked felt to be a hat then he stood up abruptly in realization.

"What is it?" June asked, getting up and looking at Charlie for answers, but the golden dormouse was bent with his hands on his knees, catching his breath from the run.

"It's his! This is Scott's hat!" Mitch grinned in disbelief.

"Really?" Bo hurried over.

"How can you tell?" Jared arched a brow, detangling himself from his bedroll to see for himself.

"The initials. M.J.T."

"Those aren't Scott's initials, Mitch." Bo arched a brow.

"No! They're mine!" Mitch pointed to the marks in the hat. "This hat used to be mine, I gave it to Scott when I got my new one, it still had my initials in it." Mitch tossed the hat to Bo. "See for yourself!" He went over to Charlie giving his soaked shoulder a hearty slap.

"Way to go, Charlie! Where'ja find that? Did you find anything else?" he asked anxiously.

Charlie straightened up and pointed down the river and breathed heavily.

Mitch grinned broadly, and stood straighter, as if hoping to see Scott himself.

"Anything else?" Bo called over, repeating Mitch. "Traces or tracks? Something? Anything?"

Charlie nodded, and gave a lash of his tail.

"Hallelujah! Tracks! You hear that Mitch? That boy's alive!" Bo twirled the hat on his finger, spinning excess water onto everyone within arm's length.

"He's alive. He's *alive* and he can't be far!" Mitch thumped Bo's shoulder and looked to June who was grinning stunningly.

"That's wonderful! Come on, boys! Let's saddle up and see if we can catch up! We could have Scott back before high noon!"

Mitch smiled thankfully at her confidence, then nodded and rushed over to the quail.

Cali was standing on one side of Cotton, using the scaled quail as a body shield between her and Bowie. The eccentric young bobwhite kept peering sneakily around and under Cotton to look at Cali, who paid him no mind, looking slightly irritated.

"Cali!" Mitch ruffled her head feathers, making her churr in delight. "He's close!" he hugged her tight around the neck, accepting an affectionate nibble on his ear in return. "Hope you're ready for a good run!"

42

Scott's tongue felt like it was devoid of all moisture as he walked in Sam's shadow, head down and ears flopped low from the heat. He wished he still had his hat but he realized the river yesterday must have claimed it.

A shadow flitted over both walkers and Scott shielded his eyes too look up and see Pip looping around above them. After several clumsy attempts to take off from the ground the bat had managed to take flight. He had flown ahead and back several time reporting to Sam the lay of the land to see if Sam recognized it. With Pip's help Sam managed to steer them on track and now in the distance of scrubby hills and patches of woods leading towards a large box canyon bubbling out of the ground on the heat-blurred horizon.

"We're nearly there, just a day away." Sam called to Pip. "Come down we need to rest." He looked down at Scott, the smaller mouse was stumbling in his shadow and almost bumped into him when Sam stopped.

"Scott could use a break." Sam watched Pip half crash-land clumsily on a large sage cluster nearby and clamber down to them.

"I'm fine, I can keep going." Scott said stubbornly, not wanting him to be the reason they had to stop, even though his head was pounding from thirst and his feet ached from walking so much.

Pip crawled over on his wrists. "No it's alright, I could use a short break too." He nodded, slightly out of breath from flying.

Sam led them under the shelter of the sage Pip had landed on before and they sat down in the shade.

Scott stretched out on his back and sighed out, glad for the rest, even if the shade was still hot, at least it was out of the sun's glare.

"How much further?" Pip asked, scratching behind his ear with a long thumb-claw.

Sam frowned slightly and looked at the two of them. "Not much further, but I need you two to listen."

Scott sat up and brushed the reddish dirt from his sleeves. "What is it?"

"You both need to *swear*, that you'll never tell *anyone* else where Skytown is. If word got out…" he shook his head darkly. "I'm breaking every rule just taking you this far."

"We won't." Pip shook his head. "We don't want to cause any harm to you, Sam."

"Not me, my people though." Sam raised his eyes to see them. "They'll be furious, but I'll make them see you're both trustworthy."

Scott nodded. "I promise I won't say."

Sam sighed, taking their words. "Alright, those rocks, that canyon over there to the west. We'll make it there by day's end, and we'll be in Skytown by dawn if we can manage."

"That close?" Pip blinked at the canyon, knowing he could fly there faster than they could walk. "Should I fly ahead and tell them you're comin'?"

"No." Sam said firmly. "I won't risk them thinking you're an intruder. They'd shoot you out of the sky and you would be dead before you hit the ground."

"Gruesome…" Pip's ears tilted back. "Would they do that to us? Kill us I mean, if we go back with you?"

Scott's ears flattened nervously and he looked at Sam.

"No, I won't let them." Sam shook his head. "I'll make them see you both as friends. Friends to me and friends to them."

"I just hope after all this I can find my way home." Scott hung his head.

"I'll make sure you get home." Sam assured him. "Even if I have to take you there myself."

Delgado knelt down and picked up the shriveled remains of several hand rolled cigarettes. "Mice were here." He commented, seeing the Gila's shadow overtake him from behind. "But not the ones we lost."

"Why were mice here?" The Gila grunted. "This far out into the flat lands, probably rustlers, vagabonds."

"Perhaps…" Delgado trailed, standing and looking towards the river, seeing the tracks in the sand. "Five mice and five quail." He checked the prints. "These tracks are from this morning. We're on their heels."

"Well I'm not after whoever these mice are, but if we catch up to them we can use them, so don't kill them." The Gila snorted and eyed the tracks as they went further downstream. "Where do those lead?"

"I'm *trying* to find out." Delgado hissed under his breath, passing a branch that jutted into the water and climbed over a tumble of rocks, dropping onto the other side. He spotted new tracks. Yes, these were their escapees. The spidery wing traces from the bat, the heeled boots of the mouse, the Jumper's long imprints. He saw knee prints in the saw by the boot tracks. The mice he was following had stopped and knelt here, inspecting the tracks.

Delgado's flame-colored eyes narrowed and he noted the difference in age of the two track sets, hours apart at most.

"Delgado!" Sol Diablo barked from the bank on the other side of the rocks. There was a scrabble and the Gila, riding his roadrunner, leapt on top of the tumble of boulders and stared down at him from his mount. "Are you going to take all day about it! What have you found!"

Delgado muscled down a retort and stood up. "These mice are tracking our friends, and they leave a much clearer trail, thanks to their birds."

Sol Diablo narrowed his eyes. "You suggest we follow the mice's quail tracks then?" he snorted.

"Only if I find another sign that they are tracking them. Then yes. We track them, and get them all at once."

The Gila made a rattling hiss of satisfaction in the back of his throat. "Good!" he snorted. "Then mount up again and get tracking!"

Delgado frowned after him as he jumped down and looked at the tracks himself. He climbed back over the rocks and signaled the rest of their horde over, whistling for his quail, who rode up alongside Stubs.

He climbed up into the saddle and spurred the bird over the rocks and up the rocky trail that wound out of the canyon to the open desert beyond.

Scott tipped his head back to look up at the monumental entrance of the box canyon as they reached it. To say there was an entrance was an overstatement. The whole thing seem to be made up of tumbles of eroding boulders, held together by hardy, twisted trees and brush that braced sheer cliff walls, stretching straight up from the ground to the sky. But if Sam said this was the entrance, he believed him.

The sun wasn't even down behind the distant hills as they approached the first rocks at the base of the cliffs. They trio had moved more quickly now that their goal seemed so close in sight, but now standing at the base of such an impassable looking wall of rock Scott felt like deflating.

"Stay close." Sam gestured to both to stand behind him, no sooner had he said it than a whistling hiss and thud sound whisked through the air and a cactus spine, fletched with trimmed, ruddy colored feathers, drove into the ground just in front of Sam's foot.

The Jumper spread his arms wide, as if shielding the bat and mouse that crowded behind him with gasps.

"Back up! He won't miss twice on purpose." Sam said quickly then cupped his hands around his mouth. "First Tail! Second Tail! Hold your fire!" he paused, ears perked and listening intently.

"Sam? Bright Storm! Is that you?"

"Yes! Now stop trying to shoot me and my friends! Come down here!"

Scott gasped as he followed Sam's line of sight and saw two figures seem to detach themselves from the canyon wall itself. They were Jumpers, older than Sam by several years. Their tawny fur was rubbed down red with streaks of white clay painted stripes on their faces. Both bounded nimbly down the rocks from cleft to cleft as sure-footed as if they were on solid ground. After a few moments they landed in front of them.

"Sam Bright Storm, the whole village thinks you're dead!" one stepped forward grinning. "It's a relief to see you aren't!" he clapped Sam heartily on the shoulder. This Jumper was muscled and broad shouldered, a glittering green opal hoop hung from his right ear and his right shoulder bore a jagged series of pink scars that parted his fur. In one hand he held a long staff sharpened to a spear point on the top.

"It's nice to see you too, Second." Sam smiled at them.

"Who are they!" The other demanded, not smiling yet, eyeing Pip and Scott suspiciously. "Why have you brought settlers this close to the village, Sam." He wasn't built as broadly as the other, two scars stretched across the bridge of his nose. He had a fully loaded quiver of fletched cactus spine arrows on his back and he held his bow and a loosely nocked spine in both hands out front.

"Firsty, they're friends, I told you. I'll explain everything later but I was caught—"

"Caught?" Second frowned. "Like the disappearances?"

"Yes." Sam nodded gravely. "And they're dead, Second, all of them." His eyes clouded and the two painted Jumpers' ears drooped sadly, brows raised.

"I'm sorry to hear, were they involved?" Second looked at Scott.

"No." Sam said firmly. "They were captured as well, the disappearances aren't just our people, the settlers are losing numbers too. It's a Gila monster, I'll explain more later, but these two are friends. Without them none of us would have gotten out of there alive."

Second looked down at them and smiled more warmly. "Then I say we stop talking over their heads like they aren't here. What are your names?" Second crouched down to Scott and Pip's eye-level.

Scott thought he was going to faint from the shock of both fully painted Jumper warriors in front of him addressing him so casually. He let out a stutter sound before Sam nudged his shoulder, snapping him out of it.

"S-Scott. Scott Thorn." He extended his hand and Second looked at it quizzically reaching out his larger hand in return. "Second Tail, and this is my brother, First Tail." He flicked the other guard with his tufted tail and First Tail shot him a look.

"They're twins." Sam told them. "If you couldn't tell. And this is Pip."

Pip nodded. "My real name's Jarlath O'Ryan, but Pip is… either goes." He smiled toothily at the guards. "And we don't mean any harm."

"We would have stopped you if you had." Second nodded, straightening back up. "Firsty lets take them back, it'll be dark soon and you can't have these clumsy-footed types falling off the edges."

First nodded and tucked the arrow back into his quiver. "Let's go."

43

Mitch rode back to the others with a frown. "Any sign at all?" They had been searching this hilly patch of sage, cholla and prickly pears for hours after the trail was lost atop slabs of bare rock and although the shade was a nice relief from riding in the hot sun, Mitch was desperate to continue. He spotted Bo and his quail under a twisted, stunted broadleaf tree and slowed Cali to a halt.

"Sorry Mitch, the ground here doesn't hold a decent track to follow. Rock and clay." Bo shook his head and lead Cotton out of the shade towards him as the others rode back, faces showing they had similar fruitless results.

June stroked the feathers on Bowie's head. The bird's beak was wide open as he panted to cool down. Even in the lateness of the day it was hot and hard on them all.

"Mitch, we've been looking for hours, we're nearly out of water and the birds need to rest. We can leave a marker here and go try and find it again after they cool."

Mitch sighed and patted Cali's neck feathers, feeling her panting from the heat as well. "Alright, but let's be quick. With all these plants around here there should be some water nearb—" he froze hearing a slight rustle up ahead and turned in the saddle to see where it had come from.

Bowie's eyes widened and the bobwhite wilfed his feathers in tightly, letting out harsh peeps of stress. The bobwhite's anxiety crept through the quail like a fog and in moments they were all restless and jumpy.

"Shhh! Bowie!" June hissed and looked at Mitch then up the hill at pillar of reddish stone. A dark silhouette appeared against the sky on top of the rock. A huge bird, beak open wide in defense against the heat, tail raised as its harsh, silver eyes pierced through the screen of leaf cover down onto the mice below. It hunched down slightly, taking them in, a fully-grown male roadrunner.

Charlie and Jared's jaws dropped and they slowly backed their birds up.

"Everyone stay quiet…" Bo hissed, but Bowie spotted the roadrunner and let out a shrill shriek of fear and bucked, June gasped and was almost thrown from the saddle.

"Scatter!" Bo shouted as the roadrunner sprang, smashing through branches and leaves and landing in the middle of the startled posse.

Charlie and Bo shot away into the brush and Jared tore off down the slope away from the havoc. The massive bird cut off Mitch and Cali's path and he struggled to turn her around, urging her away. The roadrunner dove after Cali and lunged out with his strong beak and missed her by a fraction but caused Cali to stumble and the quail rolled, Mitch stayed in the saddle as the frantic hen squawked and kicked to get up. The roadrunner rushed in to attack once more but a rusty blur shot in front of Mitch, a loud crack sounded as June rode past and slammed her rifle butt into the bird's beak.

The roadrunner stumbled back, its crest raised in confusion before barking out a harsh caw and taking off after June, who turned and led the chase through the brush.

"June!" Mitch breathed and yanked Cali's reins to get her up. "Go!" he kicked her wing, snapping the reins, he bolted after the monstrous bird.

June looked over her shoulder and to her horror the bird was gaining. She cried out as Bowie lurched down a surprise drop into a dry riverbed, stumbling down the steep embankment and slamming to the crackled base, her rifle was knocked away and stuck down halfway between two deep mud cracks.

June was thrown from the saddle and Bowie stumbled forward and bolted to the other side of the bank wall, trapped.

The roadrunner leapt down after them, beak wide and wings slightly unfurled, it took a snap at Bowie but the bird dashed down the streambed.

June stumbled to her feet and ran to the dry bank wall, jumping and clambering at it trying to climb out. Her struggling movements caught the Roadrunner's eye and he abandoned the bobwhite for easier prey.

Mitch skidded Cali to the edge of the drop off and saw June climbing the steep wall with the roadrunner hopping up to her level with one leap.

"JUNE!" he cried out and drove Cali down into the streambed as June reached a tangle of roots on the wall and started to use them as ropes to climb higher.

The roadrunner reached out, his huge beak clamping around her leg like a trap and ripping her off the wall like a burr on a saddle blanket. He jumped off the wall carrying the screaming doe upside-down.

Mitch skidded Cali to a stop and pulled out his pistols, shooting three rounds into the roadrunner's left thigh. The bird cried out, bellowing in pain, dropping June onto the cracked ground below with a heavy thud. The angry bird stumbled back, its leg starting to give out.

Mitch leapt off the saddle seeing June's gun sticking out of the ground. He ripped it out and braced it against his shoulder, narrowing his eyes to aim as the maddened roadrunner thrust closer, beak open to kill its assailant.

He fired the first shot and clipped the side of the bird's head, the second shot slammed through above the bird's left eye. He leapt back as the bird dropped to the ground, snorting and bleeding.

Mitch kept his distance and raised the gun to his shoulder one final time. The last shot right between the eyes put it down for good.

June winced, gasping in pain as she tried to get up; she slumped back to the ground and looked down at her leg. Her chaps were torn and her leg was twisted painfully.

Mitch rushed to her side and knelt next to her, helping her sit up. "June! Are you alright?" he asked, even though he could tell her leg was far from it.

"My leg…" June gasped and cringed slightly, rolling up the pant leg to check on it. Mitch glanced away at first, not meaning to stare at a doe's leg but when she sucked in another tight gasp he turned back and helped her see it. There wasn't much blood, but her leg had been pinched and twisted by the large, heavy beak.

"Is it broken?" Mitch asked her worriedly.

"I d-don't know." June felt it with shaking hands. "It just hurts."

Mitch raised his hand and looked at her leg then back at her for permission. She nodded and he carefully felt around her knee and shin. "It's not broken, but it looks like a bad sprain. Here." He rolled her chaps down again and looped her arm around her shoulder. "Let's get out of here." He stood up and she winced rising with him but gasped and almost fell again. "I can't walk." She said shakily. "I'm sorry."

"Don't be, you're hurt." Mitch said and looked around before raising his fingers to his mouth, whistling out.

Cali bounded over, followed a bit more cautiously by a trembling Bowie.

"Can you ride? You think?" Mitch asked.

"I just need to rest, please, just for a few moments it hurts so bad." June's ears were flat from pain and her face was pinched, muscling back tears.

Mitch nodded. "It's alright. We can rest until you think you can ride." He assured her and looked around.

"Here, let's get out of the open though." He stooped and picked June up, carrying her in his arms over the deep cracks towards the far side back wall, where the water had scooped a shallow overhang out. He eased under and set her down.

June's tail curled closer to herself as she tried to stretch her leg out to rest.

Mitch knelt next to her, pushing some rocks and pebbles aside, moving one forward, to rest her leg on it.

"Are the quail alright?" June pushed her hair back to see them outside. Cali was preening Bowie's neck reassuringly and the young Bobwhite was still trembling.

"They seem to be, I'll go check and then tie them next to us." Mitch nodded and went outside.

Stars were starting to prick through the darkening sky and when Mitch came back to the little overhang he was carrying their bedrolls and saddle blankets.

"I thought we were going to ride back?" June asked, still in pain but less so after having a while to rest.

"It's getting dark, the others are smart and they'll settle for the night, we can meet up in the morning. Besides you're hurt, a night of rest would be easier on your leg then trying to ride out of this ditch bed."

June nodded and folded her arms as he unfurled his bedroll then folded both saddle blankets and replaced the rock from under her leg gingerly with them.

"That should be more comfortable." He nodded and unrolled her roll, handing it to her to cover up with.

"Thank you." June murmured, gathering her blanket close.

"I should thank you. You saved my neck back there. You could have gotten yourself killed."

June smiled weakly. "You're so close to finding your brother, I want to make sure you do."

Mitch blinked in surprise and sat up. "You seem to understand this whole situation a lot better than I thought."

June shrugged. "I lost all three of my brothers and my father. They were the Jordan Gang, rustled a lot off the Texas panhandle and up through Colorado and Utah Territory for years, then moved out here before they were finally caught… and hung."

Mitch winced. "I'm sorry."

"Yeah, me too, they had put all that behind them, but the law is cold." She frowned. "My first brother died in the civil war, when father came home he was changed from his death, vengeful. Mother took to caring after me when he and the others took to rustling, then after their deaths mother just lost the will to go on."

"That's terrible." Mitch looked down. "I suppose I misjudged you."

"Seems to be a lot of that going around." June glanced back at him. "Here I thought you hated me, but you're not showing it."

"I don't hate you." Mitch frowned. "What did Bo say?"

"More like what he didn't say I guess, Charlie wouldn't let him. I just gathered you had a messy experience."

"Not so messy." Mitch sighed and looked outside. It was almost completely dark and they had to fuel to make a fire down in the streambed. "I had a fiancé, she grew tired of waiting for me in town, I live out on my ranch some fifteen miles away." He sighed. "She took off with some gold digger bound for California and left me a letter. After that, her father blamed her character on me and my influences."

"Sounds like a charming man." June snorted.

"He's just upset." Mitch shook his head. "I guess I started to believe him after a while."

"She sounds like a trollop, Mitch, no offense. She was crazy to leave. But honestly, if that's what she's like, you're better off without her."

"I've heard that a lot." Mitch set his hat aside. "It's not really something I like to talk about."

"Sorry." June looked down at her leg. After several minutes of silence she raised her head. "Tell me about Scott then."

Mitch smiled slightly. "He's my younger brother. He's a little quiet, but a hard worker. Pa won't let him work with quail. Won't let him work much at all, really… when he was born, he was very sick. He had the fever, and Doc didn't think he'd pull through. Pa was so worried, and my Ma… well. She was beside herself. We've never really told him about it. He got better, slowly, but then there was an accident a few years back on the ranch, Scott sorta caused it by accident and nearly got me and him killed. Ever since he's been forbidden to work with them. He mostly helps my Ma around the house. I take him out now and again, behind Pa's back. He's a sweet kid. Heart of gold, never hurt anybody." His eyes dimmed. "He likes reading about adventures and heroes, but now he's been kidnapped and everything he's probably lost and afraid." He pushed his hands through his headfur. "I just hope it won't change him from the brother I used to have, I couldn't stand to lose him."

"It might, but change doesn't have to be bad. Some change is for the better." June settled back. "You've changed, at least, to me you have."

Mitch looked over at her. Yes, he supposed he had changed since the start of this wild chase. Before what was a rushed, manic chase of rescue and revenge was subsiding to hope and persistence. Maybe he had changed, or maybe just the situation. Either way, Mitch was glad for it. He settled down and curled up. "Well, we should get some sleep. Good night, June. Thanks for today."

"Thanks to you too." June smiled and turned away from him. "'night."

44

Delgado tested the blade of his knife against his thumb claw before sliding the whetstone down it again. Sol Diablo had forbidden any fires be built in case it alerted their quarry in the night. Any food brought along would have to be eaten cold and raw.

The sound of a striking match and the spark of a flame caught Delgado's eye and he glanced sidelong at the Gila sitting on a rock across from him, lighting a fat cigar. Sol Diablo shook the match out and tossed it aside. Delgado snorted as the match, still smoldering, caught some of the dry, feathery grasses and started to crackle.

"You're gonna light the whole damn world up." Delgado hissed, getting up and crossing over to stomp the little flame out.

Sol Diablo hissed and blew a thick cloud of smoke. "I don't need your lip."

Delgado looked up from the scorched grass and held back a retort. He headed back to his own spot and sat back down, back to the warm rocks. He sheathed his knife and tucked the whetstone away for the evening.

He watched the Gila's cigar glowing in the dark for a long while, knowing the Gila was smart enough not to drop asleep in his company. The thought was both unnerving and interesting to Delgado, that such a powerfully large and venomous lizard would consider him a threat.

He pushed his hat down past his eyes and folded his arms. It was no use trying to stay up and intimidating each other in the dark. He needed his rest.

Delgado's hand rested on the handle of his gun as he drifted off. He might be resting in the Gila's presence, but he still didn't trust him as far as he could throw him.

Further ahead in the box canyon, the dim light made following the narrow cliff edge paths perilous, and with Scott stumbling from tiredness it soon became obvious they needed to stop and rest once the reached a deep crevice near the top.

Sam had been concerned about Scott as they ascended. More than twice he had needed to grab the back of Scott's collar to keep him from stumbling off the crumbling paths. Scott had grown quiet too, his eyes nearly closed from exhaustion. Once they reached the safety of the crevice, Scott dropped down to his knees and stretched out on the ground with a groan.

Sam crouched next to him. "Scott?" he nudged his shoulder. "Scott you alright?"

Scott's head was pounding and all his senses felt blurry. He frowned as Sam jostled him and tried to push his hand away to let him rest.

"He doesn't look too good." Pip clambered over, large ears titled forward in concern. "Maybe dehydrated?"

"Then he'll need water." First Tail looked down at them. "When was that last time you all drank?"

"Yesterday I think." Pip said. "I wouldn't mind a drink too if there's any place to get some." He asked hopefully.

"Sam, he's not like *us*, he *needs* water, without it he'll die." First Tail gestured to Scott.

Sam frowned. "Die? He's not dying." he said quickly. "He's fine. Isn't he?"

"Sam he's right, we need to get him some water, no wonder he was stumbling around like that." Second Tail stopped next to him and glanced at Scott. "Scott, we're going to get you some water." He assured him. He patted his shoulder and looked to First Tail. "Anything left in the skin?"

"It's empty, has been since this morning." First unsling a long water skin from his shoulder and held it up.

"Is there water nearby?" Pip asked. "I could fly out and get some."

Sam, First and Second looked at each other then back to the bat.

"Yes, there's a river down the other side of this canyon. It's part of our watch cycle so there shouldn't be any others out there, but just in case-" First Tail reached down his shirt collar and pulled off a glittering triangular green stone necklace and went over to Pip. "Wear this, and if you encounter any trouble just show them this and tell them you're with us."

Pip nodded and ducked his ears for First to slip the necklace on his head along with the water skin.

"Fill the skin then bring it back." First Tail ordered and went up to check the canyon top to see if the coast was clear.

"Bossy furball." Second twitched his whiskers. "Thanks for doing this, you'll be must faster than either of us in this light."

Pip nodded and clambered up the crevice wall after First Tail, at the sentry's nod of approval, he took flight.

Pip heard the water long before he saw it, and after finding a stretch of sand to make a rough landing he made it to the water, uncorking the skin and letting it glug away as it filled while he stooped and drank his own fill.

He managed to filter out the sounds of the water with his special ears as he tried to keep alert but the quiet steps in the soft sand behind him still eluded them until a sharp blow to his bad shoulder knocked him down. He yelped as he was tackled to the side and flapped out a wing, catching his attacker and swatting them away. Pip scrambled back to all fours and saw his attacker bound to their feet in the dark shadows. A quick blast of sonar gave Pip a mental image of a fierce, young Jumper doe carrying what appeared to be some sort of hooked stick, he didn't have time to analyze much else as she threw herself at him again.

"Wait!" Pip jumped back, flaring both wings out defensively. "Wait I'm a friend! A friend of First and Second Tail!" he cringed as she skidded to a halt it front of him, panting with her stick raised to smash him again. Her dark eyes narrowed. "Who are you, bat. What are you doing here on *Yàkin* land!"

"Put your bleedin' stick down and I'll tell you!" Pip pointed with his thumb claw at her weapon.

The doe hesitated, then lowered her stick and stepped back from him. "I don't trust you." She growled out.

Pip let out a breath of relief and fumbled with the necklace. "W-wait, First Tail said to show you this, if I ran into any of you." He stretched the cord so she could see the charm in the silvery light.

She blinked and came forward tensely to inspect it. "Firsty said that?" she squinted. "He must trust you then. Well, what are you doing here, where's First and Second? Who are you?"

"I will answer everything, my name is Jarlath, the others call me Pip, First and Second are up on the cliffs helping me, Sam and Scott…"

"Sam!? Sam who?" the doe interrupted.

"Sam… oh what did he call himself… Sam Storm? Bright, Bright Storm?"

"Bright Storm!?" she gasped, face splitting into a huge smile. "He's alive!?"

"I, yes? He's alive, but our friend's not doing so well, they sent me to get water for him."

"Where is he at? I mean where are they all at?" The Jumper pressed.

"Up on the cliff in a big rock cleft, eh… who were you again?" Pip relaxed slightly when he was sure she wasn't going to attack again.

"Swift Stream, sometimes called Carol. A bit like Bright Storm's other name." she nodded in greeting. "I'll go back with you to them."

"I have to get this water up there quickly, I can't wait." Pip gestured to the direction he'd flown in from.

"Alright, I think I know where you're talking about, I'll meet you all there when I can." She nodded and waded into the shallows, retrieving and capping the full water skin. "Here." She slipped it over his head.

"Thanks, and I'll tell them you're coming." He flapped his wings hard, stumbling across the sand before he was clumsily able to take off into the air once more.

It didn't take long for Pip to make it back to the crevice. Scott was asleep on the ground and Sam was sitting next to him while First and Second manned both crevice entrances.

It took some coaxing to get Scott to wake up and have a drink but after a few minutes he had guzzled down almost half the skin. He coughed slightly and brushed the water off his whiskers.

"You scared us back there." Second said, turning partially from the entrance to check up on him.

"Sorry." Scott rubbed his throbbing head. "I just felt real sluggish."

"Speak up next time." Sam prodded his shoulder. "Honestly!" he rolled his eyes and glanced back at him with a smirk. "What sort of story is that? Scott Thorn escapes enslavement, Gilas, guns, snakes and survives and hundred foot fall only to die the next day from thirst?"

Scott grinned and shook his head. "Sounds like a bad read." He took another drink. "Does anyone else want some?" he held it out.

"No thanks." Second Tail shook his head. "We already had our fill today. We don't drink a lot of water like you other mice, Yàkin get our water from our food back home."

"You don't *drink*?" Scott arched a brow. "At all? That's odd… oh sorry I didn't mean—"

"It's alright." Sam shook his head. "I'm sure it seems odd." He looked to Pip. "Maybe Pip wants some?"

"Oh no thanks I had some on the shore—Oh Sam! I met another Jumper… er Yàkin? She knew you. Said her name was Carol? Carol Swift Stream?"

"You saw Carol?" Sam grinned. "She didn't hurt you did she?"

"Not… badly." Pip rolled his shoulder with a playful smile. "But she seemed surprised to hear you were back, or even alive."

Sam winced slightly but his response was cut off. "It's like we said." First Tail looked down at them. "The whole village thinks Sam is dead, another victim of the disappearances. "

"Well, we'll show them he's alive, and we'll tell everyone about the Gila and the mines." Scott took another drink. "Now that you know what's going on, maybe you could all fight back?"

"Fight back?" First Tail snorted angrily. "We don't fight anymore. Your ancestors nearly wiped our whole nation out the first time, we're all that's left and you want to fight against this monster?"

"Brother," Second Tail hopped over. "Calm down. He's just a boy, he didn't mean anything bad by it."

"Well I don't understand. You're supposed to be fighters." Scott looked between them. "You're all scarred up. Don't tell me you don't fight."

Sam rested a hand on his shoulder. "Scott…" he winced.

"We *defena*. We protect this our last home front. We're not going out to seek a battle. The council would never allow it. And if they think your sole purpose here is to drag us all out of safety to fight a battle then they would throw you right out of the Crest!" First Tail said angrily.

"Fellas." Pip crept between them. "Please. No one wants to hurt anyone. We don't know a lot about each other's ways or habits, we're making do with what we know."

"I just know settlers are bloodthirsty, greedy land grabbers with no respect and would kill a Yàkin on sight even if the Yàkin was unarmed." First Tail ground, curling his lip.

Scott frowned and laid his ears flat as Sam bristled and glared back at First Tail.

"Scott's not like that. He'd never hurt any one of us." He sat up in a crouch.

Scott glared at the ground. "And I used to think the same, First Tail. I used to think Jumpers were savages. Wild and unruly, that only wanted to kill us and *eat* us. It's just what I knew growing up. It doesn't make it true." He looked up. "If I could change what happened back then I would, but I can't. No one can."

First Tail narrowed his eyes suspiciously as Scott spoke and Second Tail nodded in agreement to Scott's words.

"But I'm here now and I want to help. Look, Jumpers... I mean, Yàkin, they aren't the only targets. The Gila's lizards attack my home, a settler home, and they caught Pip, countless others. Settlers and Yàkin may not be friends, but we have the same enemy. My Pa used to say 'the enemy of my enemy is my friend.'"

First Tail frowned. "A common enemy doesn't seem just enough to throw ourselves into a fight we aren't prepared for. We live out here in secrecy and in peace. I plan on helping it stay that way." The sentry turned and went back to the entrance while Second Tail watched him go. He turned back to the others and sat down. "We'll talk to the council, make sure they know all the facts. I don't want that Gila to take anyone else, from either side." He nodded.

Scott, Sam and Pip nodded in agreement.

"But get some rest. In the morning we'll take you to the village." Second Tail stood up.

"Skytown?" Scott perked his ears excitedly.

Second grinned. "So it's been called." He turned to join his brother at the entrance. "Hope you aren't afraid of heights." He teased.

Scott blinked, puzzled, and looked at Sam.

Sam snorted a laugh. "You'll see soon enough. Get some rest." He took a small swig from the skin then capped it and curled up with his tail tuft under his head.

Scott rested back against the rock and looked around in the dark with tired eyes. First Tail's words buzzed in his head like an angry wasp. Would the council still hold a grudge against the settlers and refuse to help? Or would there be more Yàkin willing to listen like Sam and Second Tail?

Worry gnawed at his stomach as his eyes closed and he slipped off into a troubled sleep.

45

Mitch woke groggily to a tugging on his ankle. He frowned, not opening his eyes. "Cali go 'way." He grumbled, trying to get more comfortable again. The tugging turn into a pinch and he winced as he was pulled back slightly. "Cal-!" he grunted and sat up, his words were cut off with a gasp seeing a pale, bristly scorpion had a pincher wrapped around his boot and was trying to drag him out from under the overhang.

June heard the commotion and startled, seeing the creature raise the venomous sting on its tail. She grabbed one of her boots and chucked it hard at the top of its head, trying to hit some of its several beady eyes.

Knocked off kilter, the scorpion's tail jabbed into the ground instead of Mitch. He kicked at it savagely, trying to thrash out of its hold, but it was no easy task, this scorpion was just over half his size and determined to keep its prey. Mitch reached out and grabbed the end of the tail, trying to keep the barb forced down into the ground so it couldn't use it on him.

A loud squawk sounded and June looked out to see Cali tugging hard at the reins that bound her to the roots outside.

June reached behind Mitch and grabbed the rifle, turning it over she smashed the butt of the gun into the scorpion's head.

The scorpion let go of Mitch and twisted this way and that, scuttling backwards out from under the overhang. Mitch took the rifle from June and followed it outside, taking aim and shooting it down just as it was starting to creep closer once more.

Cali and Bowie jumped back, feather's wilfed from the noise, then huffed, picking the limp scorpion up by the fatty part of the barb. She pranced in place outside with the dead attacker dangling from her beak by its tail.

Mitch breathed out shakily and shook his head. "Cali drop it, you big chicken." He set June's gun down and went over to help June up to stand on her good leg. "Smart move." He nodded.

June smirked and watched Cali shake her new toy roughly. "She seems pleased with herself."

"Yeah but she should leave it alone so she doesn't hurt herself. Cali! Drop it!" Mitch tried to sound gruff, muscling back a smile.

Cali made a *churr* of disappointment and dropped the scorpion, ambling back to Mitch and pushing her beak into his chest.

Mitch smiled and rubbed her head feathers. "Good girl." He flicked her topknot and turned back to June. "Sun's nearly up, let get packed. How's your leg holding up?"

"Stiff." June frowned, stroking Bowie's cheek feathers. "But I think I can ride."

Mitch nodded and helped her sit down while he packed up for them both.

On the other side of the scrub hills Delgado tilted his hat up after hearing a gun shot in the distance.

"Hear that?" Sol Diablo growled out, looking unrested and irritable as he stood up. "Mount up and check it out." He snorted at Delgado.

Delgado frowned and got up, heading over to the covey of mismatched riding quail to find Bird.

"Take these two idjets with you." Delgado heard a thud and a yelp as the Gila had grabbed the sleeping forms of Stubs and Spike by their tails and tossed them over to him as easily as sacks of cornmeal.

Delgado grumbled under his breath and got up into his saddle. "Hurry up!" He snapped.

Delgado regretted letting either of the two horned lizards come along the further they got into the trees and brush of the hills. The sun was barely up and both were tired and fussing over how hungry they felt. Delgado knew their careless chatter would give them away so he stopped short and twisted in the saddle. "You both shut it!" he hissed. He swung a leg off his saddle and slid to the ground, walking Bird over to them. "Watch the birds and stay here." He flung the reins at Spike making him flinch.

"But Sol Diablo told us to stay wi—"

"You can stay here or you can end up like *Larry!*" Delgado lashed his brilliant blue tail and both lizards nodded in tense silence, their eyes settled on Delgado's dark claws resting on his knife hilt.

Delgado stalked away from them then slipped into the network of grass and brush, walking more steadily and silently with one pistol drawn and ready.

"Mitch!" a voice called through the grass. Delgado stopped and flattened himself down into a deep boulder cleft and saw a mouse-figure come out of the grass riding a scaled quail. Delgado tensed his finger on the trigger but waited. The name he was calling sounded vaguely familiar. He decided to follow him after the mouse turned his quail and rode off again.

Bo frowned worriedly. He'd heard the gunshots last night, but Mitch and June hadn't returned. He and Charlie managed to find Jared just after dark and settled down to wait but they never heard a thing. Now it the morning light, Bo was preparing himself for what might be the worst. What if the roadrunner had gotten them both?

"June! Mitch!" Bo called again, feeling his voice starting to get hoarse from yelling. He stopped and removed his hat to run his fingers through his headfur then heard a call back.

"Bo?"

Bo perked his ears and snapped his reins. "Mitch!" he called and pulled up abruptly after nearly driving Cotton over to edge of the dry riverbank.

"Mitch! June! Oh thank goodness." Bo seemed to deflate. "I thought you two were goners."

"You thought that?" June adjusted her hat with a slight smirk. "Glad to know your faith in us is strong."

Mitch was cinching June's saddle tight and helped up into it. "We nearly were." He called up to Bo. "June got a hurt leg." He jerked his thumb to the roadrunner's body. "It was swinging her around like a rag doll."

Delgado had altered his shadowed-course and come to the edge of the bank, hunkered down in the thick of the grass as he observed the exchanges. He blinked in surprise seeing the mouse down below. That was the mouse he'd locked in the burning barn, the one who had given him the scar on his face! He was alive? Slowly, Delgado put the pieces together. Those two were *brothers*; this mouse was looking for the one he'd taken, the mouse that had escaped the mines with the bat and the Jumper. Delgado pondered on putting a bullet through each of their heads from where he was but then smirked slightly. This could be easier than he thought. The mice had a lead on the trail supposedly. They could continue to lead the Gila's forces to the end. Then he would be scot-free.

Delgado waited as the mice talked and discussed how to get out of the riverbed. Eventually they were able to urge their quail to clamber out and they rode on.

Delgado waited until their voices disappeared before standing and heading back to Spike and Stubs.

"Are the others alright?" Mitch asked Bo as they threaded their way through the brush back to the more open ground under the trees.

"Yeah, Charlie and Jared are fine, we were worried about you lot though." Bo said as he steered Cotton towards the broadleaf tree towering over the spot where Charlie and Jared were sitting on its roots, their quail scratching at the earth nearby.

"Found 'em!" Bo called cheerily.

Charlie jumped up and grinned, running over to them and looking them up and down anxiously.

"We were worried about you too." June smiled at him, getting used to Charlie's silent behavior.

"Well if you're both finished being bird bait can we just *please* get the hell out of here!" Jared grumbled sourly where he remained sitting.

"I hate to agree with him, but he's right, no use hanging around here, this is prime roadrunner hunting grounds. We should get moving as soon as possible. Does everyone have enough water?" Mitch looked around.

"Enough for now, but we need to refill soon. If anyone hears or sees a stream they should holler." Bo nodded.

"Alright, let's move out... er, we need to find the trail again." Mitch looked around anxiously.

Jared stood up and walked out into the sun towards a clump of brush and looked under it before crouching and checking the imprints in the earth. "I found these this morning." He stood up crossly. "You're welcome." He tossed a dry look at Mitch.

Mitch grinned. "We're right on track!" he grinned. "Let's move out!"

46

The sky was still pricked with stars even as the rosy dawn light lit its edges. Scott was already awake and standing towards the back of the rocky cleft, looking out with Pip, who was also having a hard time staying asleep this morning.

"What d'you think it's like?" Pip asked at long last. "This city of theirs."

Scott shrugged. "All I've ever heard is stories legends." Scott watched the sky brighten. "I hear things like, they live in the clouds, or under the ground. But that sounds silly."

"You can't live in clouds." Pip yawned. "They're nothin' but mist. Maybe they live near clouds? Like up high? These cliffs stretch pretty tall."

"I suppose, I've never met anyone who's been here in person. I thought they were wiped out, all we have back home are our stories." Scott turned hearing First Tail up above, standing above the cleft talking to Second Tail in their native tongue.

"I don't think they're happy we're here." Pip strained his hearing. "But I don't understand them."

"I don't think *First Tail* likes that we're here." Scott corrected. "Second doesn't seem so bad, I hope there's more like him."

"There should be." Sam appeared between them. "Others will listen, they have to, if we have a chance against the Gila."

"You mean fight?" Scott asked.

"We'll see if it comes to that." Sam frowned. "That monster took my mother. Carol's father, dozens of other Yàkin, and who knows how many of yours. I think it's time he was stopped by someone."

"You all awake down there?" Second Tail crouched to peer down at them. "If so get your tails up here and we'll get going."

Excitement surged through Scott. They were going. *He* was going to see Skytown.

The trek was still difficult for Scott, but much easier than the day before. They made their way around the curve of the box canyon interior following a rough-worn trail that appeared as though the Yàkin had used it for decades. When they reached the edge, Scott had looked down to see a winding, dark green river that curved out of sight around a bend

"Are we crossing that?" he asked First Tail, who was bringing up the rear behind him.

The Jumper grunted in reply with a curt nod. Scott turned away and continued to follow Sam and Second, not wanting to disgruntle him with the hundreds of questions he itched to ask.

Sam looked down at him. "Yes, but don't worry, we'll stay dry, we have a bridge."

"A bridge?" Scott murmured as they ascended a rise in the trail. "How did you build—" he trailed, jaw dropping as Second swept back a shaggy clump of grasses with his spear that Scott had taken for part of the wall beside them. Behind the plants was a wind-sculpted hole that lead down to a craggy stone arch supported by rocky pillars stretched out of the river far below. The natural bridge connected their section of the canyon to large cylindrical canyon plateau, rising like a grand island furred green and lush with trees and brush on the rock that seemed to sprout from the river that wreathed around it far below.

Pip landed beside them all, eyes stretched wide in awe. "Oasis…" he whispered.

"The river has carved at these walls for years and years. Someday, it will carve away the bridge's supports, and we will be isolated in safety." First Tail said proudly, looking down at the river with what Scott thought could be affection or pride.

Sam nodded. "Until then, we have canyon guards like these two keeping us safe from the outside." He walked through the tunnel to stand out on the wide ledge that sloped gently up and over the hidden hole and on top of the canyon wall.

Scott followed him numbly, still taking the scene in. "It's like a fortress." He murmured.

Pip crawled down on his wrists beside them. "I see trees up on top, wait, those aren't trees what… what're those? They're huge!"

Second and First bounded down beside them. "Ah, that's the edge of our village."

"Skytown?" Scott turned so fast he cricked his neck. "Skytown is a… cactus?"

"Saguaros." First Tail looked past them up at them far above. "We should keep moving."

"Don't look down." Second Tail advised as he took the lead.

Scott followed them out across the bridge of rock. It was wide enough for a wagon to cross, but the light breeze that tugged at his sleeves and whiskers still made him uneasy. He did chance a peek over the side and immediately wished he hadn't.

"Come on." Sam tapped his shoulder, urging him along again.

"You're nearly there." Pip flew below them, passing back and forth under the bridge until they reached the other shade, shaded from the sun by the trees.

The hike up through the rocks and brush was easier for Scott, the paths were smooth, earthen, and easy to navigate. When they finally reached the top Scott was amazed on just how tall the saguaro cactus were. And how many there were as well. He had to tilt his head all the way back to see the tops of any of them. They rose like spires straight up into the clear sky above, bristling with white needles in patterned clumps along their deeply ridged trunks. Some were straight and tall, other had budded long arms that jutted from the trunks and continued towards the sky. Some arms dipped towards the ground in arching curves.

"No one lives in these." Sam told Pip and Scott. "We live near the Crest over there." He pointed across the plateau top on the other side and Scott squinted against the sun to see a larger cluster of saguaros around what looked like a slightly shorter and lumpy looking cactus shape.

"Is that thing the Crest?" Pip voiced Scott's question. "It's very odd lookin'."

First Tail frowned, looking deeply offended. "The Crest is very important. It is the only such saguaro in our entire land, it is large enough to house all the Yàkin if need be."

Pip shied back. "Sorry."

"It's fine, he just means it's different than the others." Sam told First, who snorted and perked his ears. "Someone's calling you."

Sam turned hearing the faint voice.

"Oh that's her!" Pip grinned seeing Carol bounding along the trail towards them, followed closely by a large cluster of young looking Yàkin all shouting Sam's name eagerly.

Sam grinned and bolted down the path towards them, meeting Carol in the middle with an embrace. Carol hugged him excitedly then shook his ears roughly. "I thought you were dead!"

"I nearly was!" Sam winced, tugging away and rubbing his pinched ears before he was tackled to the ground by the youngsters.

"Where have you been!"

"We missed you!"

"Did you *die*?"

"Did the settlers get you??"

Sam laughed and tried to get up from their chittery mouse-pile. He ruffled them between their ears and tried to answer their questions as he stood and dusted off. "I'll tell everyone later, but we need to speak to the elders."

"Intruders!" One child pointed at Pip and Scott.

"Firsty and Second captured a settler and a bat!" another shouted and all of them bounded over.

"What? Children no, don't say that." Sam followed them over to the others. "This is Scott and Pip, they're our friends."

"How come he's so small." One youngster poked at Scott, he was already taller than him by half a head. "He's the same size as my baby sister!"

Scott frowned. "I'm not small, I'm nearly full grown."

The children erupted with laughter. "He's so *tiny*!"

"Be nice." Sam growled in warning, the children fell silent and looked at the ground.

Sam shrugged apologetically at Scott and Pip then turned to Carol. "Carol, this is Scott and Pip, without them both, I would probably be dead."

Carol smiled at them both. "Thank you for keeping him safe."

Scott blushed slightly. "We kept each other safe." He clarified.

"Looks like it." A new voice sounded and Scott looked down to see a young doe mouse like himself beside Carol. She had been mostly hidden from view by the smaller children.

"There's settlers here?" Scott asked in surprise.

"I'm not a *settler*." The mouse shook her head with a smile. "We've lived here for years, we're honorary Yàkin. But it's not often I get to see another mouse here that isn't toting a gun and looking for a fight." She stepped forward. She was small and gray-furred with darker hair. Her red and white calico dress was slightly ragged and faded pale by the sun. Her face was young, maybe Scott's age, and kind.

"I'm Sonya." She nodded in greeting. "My father and I were rescued by the Yàkin in a storm many years ago. He's a surgeon. We live here now."

"Nice t'meet you, marm." Pip smiled and dipped his head.

"Oh! I almost didn't see you." Sonya jumped slightly then headed over to Pip in fascination. "I've never seen a bat this close before, and I've never seen one like you!" she looked at his ears and teeth in wonder. "Your ears are so large!"

Scott smiled, watching her walk around Pip, amused by the confused look on his friend's face.

"Er, thanks?" Pip tilted his head.

Carol and Sam chuckled and beckoned the children over. "Let's go into the village." Sam told the others.

"When can we have lessons again?" A young girl asked Sam.

"Target practice!" Another piped.

Scott looked up at Sam quizzically.

"I'm their teacher, well, sort of, my mother was, I helped out when she was busy." Sam told him. "We'll practice later, we have important things to tell the others."

"Like what?" one groaned.

"The disappearances." First told them sternly, making the children gasp, their tufted tails bushed out and they shrank back as they walked, whispering fearfully among themselves.

Scott looked at Sam then ahead towards the Crest. Everyone seemed shaken by the disappearances. He only hoped these elders, whoever they were, would agree that the Gila needed to be stopped once and for all.

47

Mitch slowed Cali down as he looked over his shoulder at the others. June's face was tight as she sat up stiffly on the saddle. Her mount wasn't looking much better. The crash down into the riverbed looked like it had hurt his foot. Bowie was limping heavily and starting to lag behind. Even Bo and Charlie were slowing down to ride alongside her. Jared finally stopped his quail and shook his head.

"This is ridiculous. I can walk on my own two feet faster than this." He looked at Bowie. "That quail is walking on a bum foot. If we keep it up it could get worse and then he could become useless altogether."

"Calm down Jared, maybe it's just sore." Bo slid off his saddle and knelt to inspect Bowie's leg. "Swollen and warm, might have torn some ligaments." He rubbed the scaly surface gently. "Jared's right though. Bowie can't keep trekking along in this state. He needs a rest."

The tired bobwhite tugged at Bo's hat half-heartedly then hung his head.

Mitch turned Cali around. "Well, alright, lets rest up for a while then we can keep moving." He looked along the horizon. "There's a canyon over there, could offer better shelter for the night."

"No Mitch." June said with a heavy sigh. "You boys keep going. I'll stay back with Bowie."

"What? By yourself? No, that, I don't like that plan. We can all rest." Mitch shook his head, even though he ached to pick up the pace.

"Mitch my quail and I are deadweight to you all, you were right not to have me come along. I'm slowing you down. You could lose the trail for good. I can't let that happen, you're too close to wait around for me and risk losing him. Go." She patted Bowies neck, letting him lower himself down to the shady ground. With a wince she dismounted and sank down next to him, resting her back against his wing. "I'll be fine, just keep going. I'm sorry to have slowed you down this much already."

"I don't like it, June." Bo shifted in the saddle and looked to Charlie, who shook his head uneasily. "You out here on your own."

"If she gets to stay back then I'm staying back." Jared folded his arms. "I'm not anxious to run along headfirst into a savage ambush."

"Shut it, Jared." Bo growled and looked to Mitch. "This isn't a good idea, splitting up out here." He gestured around them. The vast open hills between the wooded scrub hill they were on and the next patch near the canyons seemed empty.

Mitch sighed. "We're not splitting up. We've come this far together; we're staying together, but not here. If you think Bowie can make it, we'll cross these hills to the trees on the other side and rest there. There should be some water over there, it looks pretty green."

"Are you sure?" June asked, "I don't want to hold you back."

"Well we're not leaving you out here, saddle up, we'll take it slow so he doesn't stress it more." Mitch said with finality in his tone.

June paused then nodded. "Alright." She accepted Bo's hand as he helped her to her feet and back onto her saddle.

"Looks like Bowie's gams aren't the only ones hurting." Bo gestured to her raggedly bandaged leg where the roadrunner had ripped up her chaps.

"I'll be fine." June said more determinedly. "I'm ready."

If Scott thought Skytown had awed him from a distance he wasn't prepared for the shock he felt the moment they arrived in the thick of the group of saguaros. He could barely see the tops of them; they towered upwards like bristled castles. Great arms branched out created huge bars of shade. Scott could see the holes in the walls of the green exterior. Some had lengths of rope working like clothing lines with garments pinned up. Other ropes carried other things, Scott saw baskets and as he squinted he even saw a line of fish drying by their tails. The networks of ropes and pulleys from below gave a dizzying almost spider web-like appearance.

"What are those?" Pip asked, seeing a cluster of Yàkin high up on a roughly assembled wooden platform between two cactus arms pushing something as large as a barrel and bulbous looking into a woven net-like structure and started to bring it down with a system of ropes and cranks.

"Fruit harvest." Second smiled. "These next two weeks or so at least. The blooms are almost all dropped, time to cut the fruit and bring it down to the tunnels." He pointed at the descending fruit with his spear. "We'll cut and dry some of it, juice a great deal of it too."

"Don't forget the seeds." Sonya bobbed up beside Second. "They help nursing mothers produce milk."

"All that from one fruit. Is that all you eat?" Pip looked at them as Sonya and Second chuckled.

"Of course not, the Yàkin are great fishers and hunters, we get meat when we need it, and grow a lot of our own grains too, but the cactus fruits are special, they can be made into wine and dye and medicine. So we try and take extra care of our homes." She saw the fruit finally reached the ground to another team of four or so Yakin, who proceeded to roll it away towards the mouth of a dark tunnel leading down into the earth.

"How deep do those tunnels run?" Scott asked.

"Enough questions." First Tail shook his head and stalked foreword. "We need to get these two to the Crest before more Yàkin see them and it stirs up a panic."

"Firsty calm down." Carol reached out and touched his shoulder. "Scott and Pip are not a threat, we can stop treating them like one?"

"I'm just doing my job." First Tail muttered as Second gave a slight bound ahead.

"Job well done, so let's get them up there." Second pointed straight up at the huge, fan-crested saguaro high above them.

"But how will we get up there?" Scott looked around the base for some sort of doorway and jumped as Second and First let out sharp whistles at the same time. From a notch in the crested arms several long hoops of rope started to drop in a long unraveling coil.

"Step in." Sam hurried over to a loop of the rope and reached out a hand to Scott. "Pip, we'll meet you up there." He looked to the bat, who nodded and stumbled into flight in a cloud of dust.

"Are we climbing up there?" Scott swallowed at the great height. "Or..." he looked at First and Second as they each stepped onto a loop of the rope, holding firmly to both ropes they each tugged hard twice then with a loud *whoosh* the roped pulled tight and whisked both Jumpers off the ground, shooting them upwards. Scott's eyes grew wide and he jumped back from Sam's hand.

"What!? No way am I getting on that catapulting death trap are you kidding me!?" he stammered.

"Scott it will be fine." Sam promised. "You trust me right?" Sam extended his hand again.

"What's the hold up!" Second called from high above.

"Hold on!" Sam called back. "Scott, just step on the rope with your foot, and hold the line, as long you hold on you'll be fine." Sam tried to ease him.

Scott looked up shakily then at the rope "What if I fall?"

"I won't *let* you fall, ok?" Sam promised. "Now get on here, we have a meeting."

Scott stared tensely at the rope then walked stiff-legged over and stepped up next to Sam, whiskers trembling and ears pinned flat in worry. He gripped the rope so tight the knuckles beneath his fur turned white.

"Ok…" he murmured and tensed as Sam held a fistful on the back of his collar in one hand and gave two sharp tugs on the rope with the other.

The jerk sensation of the rope was so sudden it stole Scott's breath away and he felt his stomach drop into his boots as he gripped the rope for dear life. They zipped through the air like a bullet.

"I HATE THIS!" Scott yelled out as they shot between two cactus arms, climbing higher and higher until he felt the rope slow and he squinted his eyes open, chancing a look down he let out a yelp of fear. He had never dangled this high above the ground in his life! He remembered the horrible sensation of falling the day they had dropped into the river and shut his eyes tight. "Get me off this thing!"

Second and First chuckled and pulled their rope onto a rough-planked platform, prying Scott from the rope and setting him down on the deck. Scott's legs felt like jelly and he took enough wobbly steps to avoid the edge before leaning heavily against a bare wall of the cactus.

"Have fun?" Pip chided teasingly from where he was hanging nearby.

"Shut up." Scott frowned and stood up, brushing himself off as Sam walked up, ruffling his ears with a grin. All banter stopped as several older Yàkin suddenly appeared in the hollowed out entryway where Scott had been leading. Their eyes sparked seeing Scott and Pip. "Intruders!" one hissed and drew a stone dagger.

Scott and Pip gasped but Sam, Carol, First and Second hurried foreword. "Not intruders!" Carol said hurriedly. "Refugees! Friends! Like the Baranovs! Like Father Willy!" She quickly looked at Sam and dragged him foreword by his shirt collar, nearly pulling over. "They brought Sam Bright Storm home!"

"Sam is alive?" The dagger-wielding Jumper blinked in surprised then sheathed his blade.

"Yes, Wind's, it's good to see you." Sam smiled and bounded over to embrace him. The older Jumper seemed startled then hugged him in return before stepping back. "We thought you were dead, you disappeared. The others?" he craned around them. "Where are they?"

Sam sighed heavily. "No other Yàkin survived." He said gently. "But my friends and I need to speak with all of you. We know who's behind the disappearances. And it's not just the Yàkin who are suffering, they are taking settlers too."

"Ha! Serves them right! Let them take all the settlers they want!" a frail, ancient looking Yàkin doe leaned heavily on a carved staff and glared at Scott. "They deserve what they get!"

"Would you say the same of Sonya if she were caught!" Carol snapped back.

"Sonya is no settler." The old woman showed crooked, angry teeth. "And hold your tongue, you aren't a speaker here."

Carol seemed to fume visibly but said nothing more, eyes dropping to the floor.

Scott looked at her then to Sam, but he was too nervous to speak, he could feel the elder's eyes boring into him, he could feel her hate like the heat of the sun through a magnifying glass.

"We will talk." The Jumper Sam had called Wind's said at long last. "But not here, let us go inside." He beckoned them in, the old doe glared at them all before hobbling ahead back into the Crest.

Scott turned to Sam, his huge eyes betraying all the questions he was biting back.

"That was Owl Fear. She's the oldest of the Yàkin, she hates settlers, but Wind's Howl is a good man, he's also her grandson. He'll help us if we can convince him."

"Sam you won't be able to talk!" Carol stalked up next to him, haven't you forgotten only the heads of the family are allowed a voice in the Crest?"

Sam sighed. "Carol, I *am* the head of my family now, it's just me." He saw the shock and realization on her face and she nodded slowly in agreement.

"What d'you mean can't talk?" Pip looked between them all.

"Neither of you talk unless asked a direct question." Second explained. "You're in the Crest, you have to obey our laws and rules. Tradition is, only the heads of the families can speak. Mothers and fathers, or another family guardian."

Scott nodded. "Ok, I promise I won't talk, but Sam, what if we can't convince her?"

Sam sighed. "Then I'll keep my promise, I'll get you home, and hopefully your own law can protect you and yours from the Gila." He steered Scott into the darkness of the Crest.

48

Inside the Crest the light was dim and Scott had to use his sensitive ears and whiskers to guide him through the narrow halls and passages until they reached an opening to a large cavernous hollow lit by thin shafts of light that beamed down into the din through small holes bored into the roof and sides of the cactus walls.

Notches constructed out of the walls appeared to form little scoop-like balconies where two or three elders each were clustered in small murmuring huddles. Their voices hushed as they entered the room.

Sam stayed close to Pip and Scott as they proceeded down into a small dip in the room and sat on the ground, looking up at the balconies seats of the elders that were assembling.

"Bright Storm, tell us your story." Wind's Howl finally spoke.

Scott looked up as Sam stood and told the elders everything he knew; from the time he left Skytown in pursuit of his mother's search party, to his capture by Delgado and the Gila. And how the great lizard killed the Yàkin for their opals. He put great emphasis on Scott and Pip's efforts to help escape the mines. Scott felt slightly uncomfortable with all the elders staring at him while Sam made everything he had done sound so heroic. He knew he was doing it to paint him in a good light, but he felt far from heroic. He felt exhausted, homesick, and at the moment, starving. He winced as a loud grumble from his stomach caught the attention of Owl Fear. He made the mistake of glancing up at her eyes. They bored into his head like barbs and it was difficult to look away. She did not break her stare, and Scott was snapped out of his trance when Sam nudged him.

"Scott, Wind's asked you a question."

"Er, yes?" Scott said weakly, wondering how he should respond.

"Stand when you speak." Wind's Howl instructed gently.

Scott stood on weak legs as Sam sat down; he felt more on spot than ever now. When silence greeted him his heart pounded when he realized he never heard the question in the first place.

"He asked why you didn't leave the mine without Sam when you had the chance." Pip hissed, though his whisper in the silent room was scarcely missed.

"Oh!" Scott said and looked up nervously. "Well I… I couldn't just leave him there."

"Why not." Owl Fear hissed scathingly. "You were trying to flee. What is the use of a Yàkin's life to a settler?"

Scott swallowed slightly and looked over at Sam, but Sam was glaring at Owl Fear, and didn't notice. Finally he spoke.

"The Gila… took my brother from me. He burned down our barn, maybe even our home. And when I was taken, I felt like I lost everything." He said, his faltering voice getting stronger. "And I admit, when I first saw Sam, I was afraid. He fought like a lion against those lizards and still got captured. I was shocked something… some*one* so wild and fearless could ever be caught." He corrected himself after a slight pause. He could see Sam turning and looking over at him out of the corner of his eye.

"He was captured just like me, but he had so much *fight* left in him, even when things looked impossible. Sam reminds me of my brother."

Wind's Howl listened patiently and turned to look at Owl Fear, who was still smoldering in her seat.

Scott breathed shakily and stood straighter. "And I would never leave my brother behind."

Wind's Howl smiled slightly. "You are friends, I believe this. I do not think you are a threat to us." There was some loud murmuring in the other elder's seats and Owl Fear slammed her short staff against the ground to quiet them.

"Sam, Scott and Pip. I must ask you if what you have said is true. Then many creatures are in danger from the Gila."

Scott nodded. "Yes, sir, but I think we can stop him."

"How so?" Owl Fear curled her lip. "The little runt wants the Yàkin to fight does he!"

Loud and angry outbursts echoed in the Crest and Scott shrank back slightly against Pip and Sam until it died down.

"He's still bloodthirsty!" One snapped from above.

"He wants us to go after this monster and die!" another growled.

"Scott wants to keep us safe!" Sam raised his voice angrily, pinning his ears back. The quiet that followed was broken by Wind's Howl.

"We cannot resolve everything by rushing blindly in for the kill. I have heard your words, and I understand your worries but this is not your world." He pointed to Scott. "The elders and family heads will speak further about this amongst ourselves. Until then, I want no further talk of battles or war with this Gila."

Scott nodded and looked down, heart racing and nerves frayed from this meeting.

"Now, is there anything else that needs to be discussed?" another elder beside Wind's asked.

Scott nodded and half raised his hand, not sure exactly on how to ask questions here. Apparently not by raising his hand, as he received some very confused looks before Wind's nodded at him to speak. "Yes?"

Scott lowered his hand. "Sirs and Ma'ams, I'm sorry if anything I said seems, well, hasty. It's been a very rough last few days." He looked at Wind's face, finding him the easiest elder to talk to in the room. "I have parents back home, coming home to an awful sight, they must think I'm dead. Please, is there any town nearby I can go to, I need to get home."

"Send you home to tell your settler friends our whereabouts! They'll murder us in our sleep!" Owl Fear snapped, standing up from her seat. "Why should we let him leave!"

"Why would we want him to stay? Another soft mouth to feed."

"He's seen too much, they both have."

Sam was bristling with anger but First Tail was the one who spoke before he got the chance.

"So what do you propose? We kill them both?" he lowered his brows. His brother nodded. "Yes, why not kill them simply because they are not Yàkin? That seems like an appropriate response, they did it to us. Let's stoop that low as well. We can be *just* like them."

Scott's heart pounded hard in his chest. What were they doing?

Owl Fear glared at Second then snorted. "They will live. We will see if they will *leave*." She turned away and Wind's Howl stretched his arms wide.

"The meeting is over." Second Tail told Scott. "It's alright." He looked towards the dark tunnel in the wall that led out of the room. "Come outside now."

Scott followed them with rubbery legs, trying to cope with what they had said. He may not be let free? Would he be kept here as a prisoner forever? He chanced a look at Pip, but his green gaze was focused nervously ahead, ears back tensely as they were ushered out.

"Scott, Pip!" Sonya caught up to them in the dark halls. "Don't be afraid of what the elders said, things will be ok." She tried to ease their minds.

"Be ok? They hate us!" Scott said in exasperation. "They might never let me go!"

Sam looked down and sighed. "They're worried Scott, they'll have to let you go. Wind's is fair, he'll talk to the others."

"He's *one* Yàkin out of dozens, Sam!" Pip shook his head. "How can he convince them all?"

"We just have to hope he can." Second Tail squinted as they reached the light of day outside. It was afternoon, the meeting had taken up a large part of the morning and Scott had hardly noticed.

"Well, you should probably stay close to us, word will get around that you're not a threat soon enough." Carol huffed. "Until then, we'll keep near."

"I wouldn't worry, boys." Sonya smiled encouragingly. "My father and I went through this too, and they were very suspicious of us at first, but now we're all a big family."

"I *have* a family." Scott said hollowly. "And I need to get back to them as soon as possible. If they ever let me go."

"You'll get there." Sam promised with a firm nod. He saw Scott still looking wilted and smiled slightly. "Want to see the rest of Skytown?"

Scott looked up at him. "…Can we?"

The rest of the afternoon Scott, Pip, Sam, Carol, First, Second and Sonya explored all over the Skytown plateau and barely scratched the surface. There were so many places to see and Scott and Pip wanted to linger at every new spot. Sonya took them up into a squat, stunted saguaro with steps hollowed out from the inside to the top where she and her father lived. Mr. Baranov was a stout, silvering gray-furred mouse with a bushy whiskered moustache and thick, round spectacles. He spoke in very broken, thickly accented phrases that made him difficult to understand, but he seemed to like Scott and Pip, and they two left feeling slightly better about their situation.

Afterwards Sam and Carol showed them the circle decks between three of the tallest saguaros in the center of the village where many Yàkin were out and about drying fish and fruits in the sun or sitting with one another in the shade of the cactus arms.

"You have to try this." Second grinned and pulled a handful of dark, red fruit and squashed into Scott's hand before sucking the juice from his fingers.

"Saguaro fruit?" Scott asked. Second nodded and Scott sniffed at oozing clump that was seeping down into his sleeves. He tried a bite and smile, nodding eagerly. "This tastes sort of like raspberries." He took another bite and offered some to Pip. Along the decks, after a few hasty explanations, they met some friendly faces and Scott and Pip had their fill of roasted cricket, seed bread, fish and even some roasted roadrunner meat.

It was great to finally have a full stomach for Sam, Pip and Scott as they walked with the others down one of the canyon paths near the midway point down the plateau a few hours later.

"Now where are we going?" Pip hovered nearby as they descended the winding path.

"Some place special." Sam grinned over his shoulder. "The Painted Wall." He gestured as they rounded the last bend and the path opened to a large hollowed out overhang covered from floor to ceiling with hundreds of hand-painted Yàkin figures and symbols.

"Whoa!" Scott grinned and walked up to the wall. "Hey, these look like Jumpers fishing, I mean, Yàkin fishing." He shook his head to correct himself.

"They're stories." Second Tail laughed.

"Stories?" Pip looked over after he landed. "What about?"

"All sorts of things." First Tail spoke for the first time in hours as he walked up to the wall. "Some are about our ancestors, legends and great stories, others are about us." He reached out to one painting, a crude picture of a Yàkin attacked by a smaller looking mouse-like creature with large teeth while another Yàkin figure wielding a spear attacked the creature from behind.

"You think they painted me well?" Second Tail beamed and gestured to the spear-carrying figure.

Scott squinted at the wall then back at First Tail, the scars that stretched across his nose and the large notch in his hear. He could make out the edges of scars hidden under his shirt as well.

"Is that what happened?" Scott asked after a while walking over hesitantly.

First Tail's eyes didn't stray from the painted rock wall for a long time. "We were searching for missing scouts." He beckoned Scott to another part of the painting, a moon. "It was dark, they had been missing a long while. We heard a screech." He pointed at another depiction of the fierce-toothed mouse. "It was a Screamer. It attacked us from the side. It attacked me at least." He glanced back at the fight painting. "Second Tail saved my life."

Scott listened intently. "What's a Screamer?" he asked First Tail. "It looks awful."

"They are." First Tail frowned. "They're savage, brutish rodents. They live alone; they hunt and kill other mice. Including Yàkin and settlers."

"That sort of sounds like the stories they tell about Jumpers back home, but... Yàkin don't eat mice... do they?" he blinked worriedly.

"Of course not." First snorted and frowned at him. "Its barbaric."

Scott nodded and looked back at the wall. "So we have our monsters figured out all wrong."

"Monster is a good word for Screamers." Second nodded. "Though we haven't seen many since that night."

"What about this one?" Pip was perched on the wall near a large mural, older looking than the one with First and Second in it.

"That's the battle of the first settlers." Sam murmured. Scott walked over and tried to read the pictures. Fire, crude looking bodies on the ground, quail mounted mice with strange looking hats and the same sharp teeth that the Screamers had been painted with. The settlers were in charcoal black, the Yàkin with it a sandy white as many fought and other fled.

"My mother told me that Owl Fear painted that a long time ago." Carol shuddered looking up at that. "She was there."

"Owl Fear was there? At the battle?" Scott blinked in surprise.

"Right there." First drew an arrow and used it to point to a tiny smudge depiction of a young mouse. "She was a child. She saw so much death that day, she lost everyone accept her brother. He led the survivors into the desert, eventually we arrived here, and we've been here ever since. Owl Fear's brother died long before any of us were born, but his death only made her hate settlers more."

"But the settlers didn't kill him, did they?" Pip asked, puzzled.

"No, but he did lose an arm in the battle." Second shook his head somberly.

Scott swallowed and looked at the scene on the wall and thought back to the illustrations in his book back home. The battle had seemed so valiant, good conquering evil. But here on the wall all he saw was pain and terror. And in that moment, Scott understood Owl Fear's hate-laden glares at him and guilt gnawed at his insides.

The sun was already below the canyon ridge by the time they reached Skytown's saguaros once more. Sonya had left for her own home before when they reached the village and First and Second had gone back on duty on the other side of the canyon, leaving Carol with Sam, Scott and Pip.

Scott could feel tiredness tugging at his limbs as they walked through the cool shadows under the purpling sky. Sam stopped and gestured upwards from the base of an astonishingly tall saguaro cactus. "This is my home, but it's near the top." He explained.

"Of course it is." Scott mumbled and looked up. "I don't think I could use those ropes again…"

"Oh my cactus doesn't have ropes. We have to go inside, but we have to get to the first deck before that." Sam crouched down. "Hope on my back, I'll get you up there."

Scott clung to Sam's shoulders as the Jumper gave several bounds foreword before launching himself up and landing on a small thatched platform jutting from a dark hole in the cactus wall.

Scott was relieved for steps on the inside of the cactus that wound their way up through its hollowed core. Sam explained that they were passing the lodging of other Yàkin along the way but they had their own entrances. It took several minutes to climb to the top and Scott felt as tired as ever when they stumbled into a loft like hollow as big as the kitchen of Scott's home. A large hole in the wall led out to a small skydeck where Pip was settled, having been waiting for them to get to the top. The light revealed the room was relatively bare. A few bows hung on the wall; a few clay containers and woven mats and shelves were pushed against the circular edges of the wall. Paintings like those on the Painted Wall were visible on the inner ribbing of the wall; Scott could make out birds, moons and countless stars and suns. Near the farthest wall hung a hammock-looking structure tied through a hole in the sloped ribbing above.

"This was my room, my mother lived in the area below mine, I helped hollow this out with her a few summers ago." Sam rested his hand on one of the painted birds then looked outside as the last rays of sun peeked above the ridge. He walked out onto the deck. "Come out and see the view Scott, you can almost see the entire village from here."

Carol smiled and gave Scott a nudge to follow him. He peered outside and held tight to the woven ropes that helped support the skydeck to the cactus. He shakily looked down and shut his eyes tight. "This is *way* too high." He looked at Pip, who was completely at ease as he rested on the deck and watched the sun sinking.

"Don't look down, Scott, look up." Pip smiled toothily. "It's a better view." He gestured to the sky, painted with streaks of pink, purple and orange.

Scott chanced a look up and breathed out slow. The cacti bristled black against the stunning colors of the ending day. Everything seemed to glow and he felt his grip lessen slightly on the rope.

"Skytown is the perfect name for this place." Pip said at long last.

"You're right." Sam smiled and sat down, letting his legs swing carelessly over the precipice. "It is."

49

"What do you mean they've stopped!" Sol Diablo snarled at Delgado as the skink dismounted his quail and turned stiffly towards him.

"What it means is what I said, they stopped riding around noon. I thought they were taking a break but they've already set up camp. They aren't going any further today. Its nearly nightfall anyhow." Delgado muttered and stooped and cleared a speck of gravel from between his mount's talons.

Sol Diablo fumed silently. "Well I'm sick of this waitin'. Ride on and report back. We're gettin' close. I can feel it."

"Ride on to *what*!" Delgado glared at him. "We can't see any traces in the dark! And the shadow the moon will cast from that canyon with make it twice as black!"

"Ride on, Delgado, or I'll replace you with someone who will!"

"I'm tempted to see the fool you choose." Delgado hissed, knowing very well he was treading in dangerous waters but he was tired and growing ever impatient with the Gila's childlike demands.

Sol Diablo showed his teeth then turned around. "Rudy! Spikes! Stubs! Gear up and ride with Delgado. Check out that canyon just ahead and report back!"

"I thought we were followin' mice." Stubs grumbled, getting up from where he had been sitting on a slab of sun-warmed rock. It was turning cool with the coming night anyhow.

"The mice are stopped and I'm not waitin' for them to get movin' again."

"Want us to dispose of them then?" a broad-headed skink rode up alongside Sol Diablo, tilting the brim of his hat up to see him better.

"Not yet, Rudy." Sol Diablo growled softly. "We'll see how much use they still have to me come the dawn."

"Brilliant plan." Rudy nodded with a smirk and turned to the two horned lizards. "Mount up boys, let's get a move on."

Delgado glared at the other skink. The bootlicker was trying to get as close to the Gila as possible. Fine by him, but if Rudy thought he was going to be in charge of this little ride he had better think otherwise. Delgado climbed back up in the saddle and snapped the reins to ride ahead, making it obvious he wasn't up for chatter along the way.

The notion was apparently lost on Rudy, who hung back talking to Spike as Stubs as the entered the rich shadow the canyon cast in the darkness. They had gone the open route to avoid the trees when Delgado knew the mice had stopped to camp. They were just reaching the first crumbling boulders at the base of the canyon when Rudy snorted and pulled something from his vest pocket.

"I'm not sure why you lot even follow Sol Diablo anyhow. He's lost his edge." He held out a gleaming silvery yellow opal dangling from a string. "Stole this off him while he was sleeping, a *real* bandit could have stopped me."

Spike gasped and pulled up sharply on the reins, casing his bird to squawk. "Y-You *stole* that from the Gila!?"

"Yes sir, and I believe, with your assistance, we could rob that monster blind, and take control of this posse ourselves." Rudy smirked and looked up as Delgado twisted in the saddle to glare at him.

"Oh don't tell me you're going to start being Sol's loyal dog now, Delgado. We both know you hate him as much as the next person. But think about it, think of the riches in store."

"I think what's in store for you is a scavenger's feast." Delgado snorted.

"He's right." Stubs blustered. "The Gila, he, he'll, *no one* steals from him! He'll kill you!"

"And he'll kill *us* for knowin' about it too!" Spikes shook his horned head and looked up at Rudy, who's smirk was being replaced by a frown.

"You're all lily livered. I thought horned lizards had more guts. I've met moths gutsier than you three."

"I'm not being dragged down with you, Rudy. So cut the charm, I don't have a problem turning you over and watching Sol Diablo rip you apart like a ragdoll. Saves my ear holes the pain of listening to you trying to wheedle your way to the top of this rotten pile." Delgado turned Bird around to stare the skink down.

Rudy glowered at him. "You don't intimidate me, Delgado. You may be scared of the Gila, but I'm not. I don't have five streaks of yellah trailing down my back." He smirked.

Delgado's eye blazed and Rudy drew his gun but Delgado was faster and squeezed of a shot before the broad-head had even raised his gun. But the same time the Delgado's shot hit Rudy in the chest, an arrow thudded into the broad-head's neck. He toppled off his mount, who squawked and dashed to the side, dragging the dead lizard by his boot caught in the stirrup.

"Jumpers!" Spike yelped in panic as another arrow hissed through the air, missing Delgado by a hair's breadth as the skink flattened himself against the back of his quail. "Get out of range!" Delgado snapped. Spike and Stubs needed no further order, both raced their birds out of the shadows, only Delgado hung back long enough to ride the short distance with Rudy's quail and free it from the trailing body. He glanced down at the opal in the Lizard's hand and leapt down, snatching it up before he remounted and streaked after the trail of dust left by both horned lizards.

"Well, we found them." He growled under his breath as they left the inky shadows behind and shot towards the hills.

The gunshot echoed loudly through the air and Charlie turned his head sharply from where he had heard the sound. He had been sitting up in the crook of a tree branch above their little camp, keeping watch while the others passed out the remains of their provisions.

"You hear that?" Bo, stood and looked up at Charlie. "You see anything?"

Charlie stood up on the branch but couldn't see from this height. He motioned for Bo to hold on and he quickly scaled the tree to the uppermost branches and stared out across the hills and scrub to where he had heard the shot. It hadn't been far from here, near the base of the canyon that cast the scrub woods in such pitch-black shadow.

"That sounded close." June frowned from across the fire. She looked over where Mitch had been tending to Bowie's leg.

"We should check it out." Mitch stood up as Charlie climbed back down and jumped the last little ways to the ground and shrugged, shaking his head at Bo.

"Charlie didn't see anything." Bo turned back to them.

"Thanks for your interpretation, but I think we all got that." Jared snorted and looked at Mitch. "What? Investigate a gun shot in the dead of the night in the wilds out here are you mad! I'm not going. We should just forget about it."

"Do you listen to yourself!" June scolded and winced as she tried to stand up. "I'll go with you, Mitch." She offered.

"No, you should stay here, you're hurt. I'll take Bo, Charlie and Jared can stay here with you." When June frowned at him he couldn't help but smirk. "Not because I think you need the protection, I know you can handle yourself." He adjusted his hat and went to untie Cali and Cotton from their post, a loop of tree root.

"Be careful." June sighed as she eased back to the ground near the fire.

"We will." Bo smiled at her brightly and turned to Charlie, who looked less than enthused about Bo riding off in the dark. "I'll be fine, keep Jared in check for me." Bo grinned at his friend as he climbed up into the saddle and checked his guns for ammunition. "We'll be back as soon as we can."

Mitch nodded and checked his own guns, and double-checked the rifle he had brought from home. Feeling as ready as he would ever be, he nodded to the others before riding out of the light of the camp into the shadows.

"Sam! *Saaaam.*" Pip whisper called from the skydeck doorway. The Jumper was sound asleep in his hammock and showed no signs of hearing him. Frowning, Pip stumbled inside, navigating easily in the dark until he saw Scott asleep in another makeshift hammock that hung lower and easier to reach. He shook it until Scott jolted awake.

"Wha—! Pip! You scared me!" Scott hissed and sat up, resulting in him falling out of the hammock backwards and landing with a thud on the floor.

Sam winced and groaned. "What are you both doing?" He stretched and got up, looking down at them both.

Scott rubbed the back of his head and looked at Pip, waiting for an explanation.

"Sorry, I was out for a fly and I heard a shot, like a gunshot."

Scott sat up straighter and frowned in concern. "Did you find out more?"

"Tha's just it, I flew out towards the cliffs and I met up with Second Tail, he and First said there were lizards at the base!"

Scott scrambled to his feet. "Are they alright? First and Second?"

"Yes they're fine, but they managed t' kill one lizard. I think they might be from the Gila's forces!"

"They followed us here…" Sam breathed, icy shock evident in his eyes.

"We don't know that for sure. We should go see if we recognize the one they killed." Pip nodded. "We have to prepare if it is them."

"Where are First and Second now?" Sam reached up on the wall and fitted himself with a full quiver of arrows and started to string himself a bow.

"They told me they were off to the Crest to report it to the elders. I'll meet you there." Pip turned and flew out the doorway once more.

Scott turned to Sam in the darkness, the contrast of shadows deepened to look of unease on both their faces. "Let's go." Sam said at long last.

Getting to the Crest was easier along the upper levels of cactus in Skytown. Many branching arms of the succulents were bridged with decks, plank bridges, rope bridges, ropes, lifts and pulleys. Before long, they were on the deck of the Crest, lit by a smoldering fire in the clay pit in the center. Scott spotted First Tail and Second Tail conversing with the elders, their faces concerned under their camouflaging war paint. Carol and Sonya were there too; perhaps Pip had awoken them as well along the way there. Scott crossed over as the elders turned grimly to face them.

"There were outsiders at the base of the cliffs. First Tail says they were lizards. Hostile ones." Wind's Howl told the assembled group. "I fear there may be more. Until we know more, no one is to leave the village. All light must be extinguished, and we can hope that they will leave us."

"But they know you're here." Scott couldn't help but speak, receiving a venomous look from Owl Fear, but before she could silence him he continued. "First Tail, you got a lizard with an arrow right?"

First Tail frowned in realization. "Yes… Yes, and the arrow is still down there." He turned to the others. "If we are going to pretend we are not here we need to erase the evidence."

"I could get it." Pip offered.

"You're forbidden to leave the village; did you not forget." An elder glared at the bat. "How do we know if we let you beyond the cliffs that you will ever return!"

"You don't." Pip frowned slightly. "You'll have to trust me."

The silence that followed was unnerving to Scott but at long last, Wind's Howl nodded. "You would get there the fastest. You must retrieve the arrow, before it's too late. Now go." He spread his arms in finality and the other elders filed after him back inside the Crest while the rope handlers began to douse the fire with a smoky hiss.

Sam turned to Pip. "We're going with you." He muttered.

"You can't keep up." Pip frowned. "I'll be fast."

"What if they're still out there? What if they shoot you down? We're going," Scott nodded fiercely.

Pip sighed but didn't argue further.

"You'll need some guides," Second stepped up, "to show you the way."

"We'll all go." Carol nodded.

"No." First Tail frowned. "You and Sonya should stay here,"

"We can help." Carol frowned.

"I know, but a large group will attract attention. You should stay here, and make sure the village stays safe and knows what's going on.

Douse all the fires, no smoke, no sound." First explained. "Keep them safe for us."

Carol sighed, wanting to be on the front lines rather than back behind the walls but she nodded and beckoned Sonya to cling to her shoulders before she dashed off to the other decks to spread the word.

"Let's hurry." Pip insisted and spread his wings for flight.

50

Despite Bo's joking demeanor, Mitch could tell he was nervous, and as they reached the base of the cliffs their hushed talk ended altogether in the inky black shadow. Bo pointed ahead and whispered. "There." He could make out something lying on the ground at the base of the ground boulders. Drawing their guns in precaution, the two rode over quietly until they reached the skink's body.

"Look in his neck." Bo murmured tensely, Mitch nodded seeing the long arrow. "His chest though, this Lizard was shot with an arrow and a gun."

"Guess he wasn't liked too much by either party." Bo said grimly and dismounted. "Mitch, this is a skink." He squinted in the light. Mitch blinked in surprise and dismounted to crouch beside him.

"Is it him?" Bo asked eagerly.

"No." Mitch's hope died slightly. "I don't know this one."

"What was that." Bo said suddenly and straightened up, both guns out and at the ready. Mitch jumped up, fear crawling through his skin as he watched Bo look around tensely. "I heard something. I *swear* I heard something." He looked up at the ominous wall of black shadowed rock before them.

Mitch swallowed hard. "Let's get out of here." He stepped back and his boot cracked a twig, making Cotton spook slightly, the movement scared Bo and he fired off a shot into the dark.

"*Bo!*" Mitch hissed with wide eyes, heart pounding.

"I'm *sorry!*" Bo hissed back and yelped as an arrow hissed past his face. "RUN!" he shouted at Mitch and turned to clamber back onto Cotton.

Mitch gripped his gun tight and stared hard at the rocks above; it was dark, so dark! He couldn't make out anything no matter how wide he stretched his eyes.

"No!" Mitch snapped and raised the rifle up pointing at the rocks. "I'm not running!" he said shakily and fired off a round in the dark. It the flash of the shot he saw the eye shine of half a dozen figures and fear penetrated him.

Second ducked as the rocks to his right exploded from the shot. He showed his teeth and let out a cry before leaping down the rocky tumble of boulder and sprang for the mouse holding the gun.

Bo whipped Cotton around. The darkness was everywhere, movement was lost and he had to rely on his hearing. "Mitch!" he fired two shot, hoping to scare off the attacker, unable to see.

"What's going on!" Sam leapt down the ledge with Scott on his shoulders. First Tail notched an arrow. "An attack!" he snarled, letting it fly.

Mitch was thrown to the ground by what he could only assume was a Jumper attack; he thrashed backwards and slammed the butt of the gun into Second's jaw. Second grabbed him by the scruff and hurled the smaller mouse into one of the rocks. Mitch winced and slid to the ground but stumbled upright and pointed the gun at the oncoming Jumper.

"Second!" Scott gasped and without thinking, jumped from the ledge beside Sam straight down, landing on the mouse's back and flattening him to the ground as the shot rang out.

Second gasped and stumbled to the side, clutching a clipped arm but had no time to nurse the wound as Bo charged from behind.

Pip flew down and cut in front of the quail, halting in its path and bared his teeth with a screech, causing Cotton to shriek and stumble backwards, feathers ruffled out in terror.

Sam and First Tail leapt down to the ground as Scott wrestled fiercely with the mouse he'd jumped, managing to kick the rifle away as they rolled in the dust.

First Tail loosed an arrow the exact moment Bo flung himself from the saddle. There was a gasp and grunt of pain behind Bo as Charlie rode out of the grass on his own quail and took the arrow, toppling backwards off his saddle to the ground.

"CHARLIE!" Bo shouted and scrambled to him as June and Jared appeared behind him, guns drawn and ready.

Mitch kicked up, launching his attacker free, in the dark he couldn't tell much, but his attacker was smaller than the first!

Scott landed hard the same moment he heard a familiar voice shout 'Charlie!'

"Bo!?" Scott gasped and looked up at the mouse he had been attacking the saw heard a fierce squawk from a quail and saw their inky silhouettes against the sky. "STOP!" he shouted.

Mitch froze. "Scott?" he breathed just as he was tackled to the ground by Sam.

"Mitch!" Scott gasped. No! It couldn't be! "No! NO! SAM NO!" Scott charged and bowled Sam away and stood in the middle of the fighting and chaos. "STOP IT! STOP!" he shouted as loud as he could with hands raised for both sides.

Sam jumped up; bewildered Scott had interfered and raised his hands. "Hold it!" he shouted to First and Second, shouting once more in their native language.

"Stop!" June shouted to Jared and the others.

There was a tense pause, broken only by pained gasps and heavy breathing.

Scott was trembling all over. He looked over and could make out a form getting up on the ground and rushed over, skidding to a halt next to him. "Mitch?" he breathed.

"Scott!" Mitch could hardly believe it, in the dark he could barely see, but this was Scott in front of him! "Scott!" he scrambled up and wrapped him in a tight embrace, crushing his little brother close. Scott was shocked then hugged him back tightly in return.

"What is going on!" First Tail snarled as he shielded Second Tail, arrow at the ready but pointed towards the ground.

"Wait, Mitch…" Pip looked up at Sam. "Sam! Its Scott's brother!"

"You're *alive*!" Mitch's voice was hoarse as he clutched Scott's face, he could barely believe it. He was alive. Alive and safe!

"You are too! I thought you… I thought you were…" Scott couldn't even finish as they both got to their feet.

"I… I…" Scott whirled to the other. "No! Its ok! They're friends!" he turned and bolted to First Tail. "First, it's my brother! He's alive!" Scott couldn't help but grin as he said it.

"Friends!? They *hurt* Second!"

"*They* hurt Charlie!" Jared called from the back.

"Charlie?" Scott frowned and rushed towards the others, Mitch following close.

Bo was sitting in the grass, shaky and numb, helping Charlie sit up. The arrow had pierced him straight through near his shoulder and Scott could seeing the point protruding through his vest in the back.

"Charlie…" Bo's voice was shaking so hard he didn't seem to notice anyone else around him. "Charlie it-it's gonna be ok."

Charlie winced, jaw clenched tight, he nodded stiffly up at Bo, trying to reassure him as much as himself.

Sam and the other Yàkin approached cautiously.

"Stay back!" June warned them nervously, raising her rifle halfway.

"Who's she?" Scott frowned at the stranger.

"She's June, she's with us." Mitch assured him.

"Well they're First Tail, Second Tail, Sam and Pip and they're with *me*." Scott said defensively up at her. "Put that gun down before you start something again!"

June scowled at him and pointed the barrel at the ground, but still gripped it tight.

Sam looked down at the injured dormouse then stashed his arrow and bow, crouching close.

"He's lucky you missed your mark, Firsty." Sam looked over his shoulder at the grim-faced cliff guard.

"If he were lucky he wouldn't have gotten hit in the first place!" Jared snapped scathingly.

"You fired at us first!" First Tail pointed accusingly.

"Stop it!" Pip and Scott both snapped at once.

"Charlie's hurt, he needs... he needs a doctor." Scott said nervously.

"Then he's a goner. Unless you can make one appear." Jared huffed grimly.

"Shut up!" Bo snapped, close to hysterics. "He's not a goner!" he looked down, wincing at the amount of pain showing on his silent friend's face.

"Wait! We know a doctor." Pip perked up. "Dr. Baranov, Sonya's father. He could help him."

"What? You want to bring in a whole troop of settlers into the village! Are you *mad*!" First Tail exclaimed. "Owl Fear will butcher them!"

"We have to do something." Sam retorted more calmly. "Come on." He stood up. "Pip, go tell Sonya and her father what happened. We'll be there as soon as we can."

Pip nodded and took flight, showering them all in a small cloud of dust.

"Can he ride?" June asked Bo, who took a moment to register the question.

"Charlie, you think you can ride?" he asked weakly.

Charlie breathed out slow then nodded. With Bo's help, he was able to get up on his feet, but he was still shaky. With Bo and Sam's help they were able to get him into Cotton's saddle, Bo rode with him to help keep him upright.

Mitch turned to Scott. "Where are we going?" he murmured.

"Skytown." Scott beamed at him. "Its *real* Mitch."

Sam watched Mitch help Scott up into Charlie's saddle for the ride and folded his arms slightly before turning back to First and Second, who was wrapping his arm with a scrap torn from Firsty's sleeve. "Come on." He murmured.

Back at Sol Diablo's camp, word had already spread about the traitor skink and the arrow. They had heard the gun shots from the others as well, some wanted to rush over and investigate, other wanted to turn tail and flee. No one was approaching the Gila himself, who was sitting moodily before a lantern, cleaning his massive pistol.

Delgado stepped into the light and tossed the yellow stoned necklace on the ground in front of him.

"So the rumors are true." The Gila smirked. "Rudy was a turnscale."

"I suppose so." Delgado frowned. "There are Jumpers in those cliffs. I think we found them, but they're armed and have the uphill advantage, as well as the cover of night." He folded his arms expectantly.

"Well, what are you waitin' for." Grunted the Gila, his dark eyes narrowed under pebble-scaled brows.

"I held my end of the bargain." Delgado frowned. "I brought you here. I suppose I can take my leave now."

"You suppose all the wrong things." Sol Diablo sneered, showing curved, white teeth. "I'm not finished with you yet."

Delgado glared at him, fists tightening. He should have known the Gila's words were just a carrot dangling in front of him. "Then what else do I have to do." He growled angrily through clenched teeth.

"At the moment, get out of my sight. Go back to the cliffs, find the city and come back. Bring those two with you again." He gestured to Spike and Stubs where they were sitting beside a large boulder, still shaken from the ambush.

Delgado glared at him. A suicide mission or so it seemed. He snorted and settled his hat more firmly on his head. "Very well." He growled and turned to leave.

"Oh, Delgado." The Gila's voice made him half-turn in annoyance.

"A little something for your trouble, for being a good little lizard." He tossed the opal necklace back to him and Delgado caught it. He stifled a scathing remark and stashed the opal in his vest before stalking off to find his quail once more.

51

Scott knew the Yàkin were uneasy about bringing settlers directly into the village but his worry for Charlie steeled him as they made the nerve-wracking crossing of the rock archway to the plateau. He was relieved to see the black shapes of the Skytown cacti against the moon the higher they went, and at the top, familiar faces were waiting for them. Carol and Sonya were waiting with Pip and Dr. Baranov, who carried a small lantern.

"I know we're supposed to have no lights but he needs it to work." Sonya explained apologetically. "It sounded serious so we wanted to meet you here so he wouldn't have to travel as far." She looked up seeing Charlie, half slumped foreword, looking like he was about to pass out in the saddle, Bo was holding him upright, leaning back so that the protruding spine of the arrow didn't prick him in the chest.

Working quickly, Dr. Baranov was able to remove the arrow, but Charlie was still in a lot of pain despite the half-bottle of whisky they had given him to dull it.

Dr. Baranov mumbled something to Bo and he arched a brow in confusion.

"He says he's surprised he hasn't heard him say much of anything." Sonya handed her father his scissors to cut the gauzy bandage strips he was using.

"Oh, Charlie hasn't spoken much since he was a kid." Bo murmured shakily. "He's always like this." He watched the doctor patch him up the best he could before helping him redress with his shirt and vest, his left arm in a sling around his neck made from the same material as the Yàkin's clothing.

"Is he going to be ok?" Bo asked worriedly, seeing Charlie on the verge of passing out again.

"He needs rest." Sonya looked up from dressing Second's bullet graze on his forearm. "You lot could stay with us." She offered.

"I think before we offer them any sort of refuge we need to let the elders know they're here." First Tail said from the back where he was leaning, arms-crossed against a boulder.

"I agree." Sam grunted beside him.

"I'll talk to them." Scott nodded and looked at Mitch, who was watching him with pride.

Sam frowned and looked at the ground. "Fine, let's go then."

"I'll go with you." Mitch said. "If it's alright."

"You should stay here." Sam grunted. "You'll just cause trouble."

Mitch frowned up at the Jumper and Scott arched a brow before coming between them. "Maybe Mitch should come, to represent them."

"Scott's right, Sam, the elders would want to see him I think." Second nodded towards them as inspected Sonya's work on his arm.

Sam rolled his eyes and started walking. Scott glanced at Pip and shrugged before following with Mitch while the others went with the Baranov's towards their cactus home. Pip cleared his throat. "Scott, wait."

Scott turned to see Pip push the arrow he had taken from the fallen lizard forward for him to see.

"Scott I recognized the skink down there, after the fight, he's one of them."

"What? Are you sure?" Scott murmured nervously.

"Scott, they're *here*." Pip shook his head gravely.

Below the cliffs once more, Delgado rode on the very edge of the shadow accompanied by Spike and Stubs, who were too nervous to utter a sound for once. Delgado was glad for their silence but still took extra caution the closer they got to the rocks. Finally they reached the base to the far left from where Rudy had been killed. Delgado was going to try and avoid that area, but he wasn't naïve enough to believe they wouldn't run into more Jumpers on other parts of the cliffs.

Delgado dismounted and signaled for the others to do the same.

"The birds won't make the climb." Delgado secured his gun belt more securely around his middle and looked up the monumental rock they had to scour.

Spikes winced. "You want us to leave 'em here and go… up there?"

"Yes." Delgado hissed impatiently. "Unless you'd rather try to climb up there in the saddle and let your floundering bird alert every Jumper in the area! You'll look like a cactus yourself with all those spines stinking out of you."

Stubs looked at Spikes and dismounted but Spike stayed in the saddle. "Wh-what if I stay and watch the birds?"

Delgado glared at Spikes but would have rather have him down here than sniveling in his shadow up the side of the canyon. "Fine, stay here alone, get climbing Stubs." Delgado shoved the other unwilling lizard towards the rocks before starting to scale them himself.

They made good time getting to the top of the canyon for as slow as they went. Delgado kept one hand on his gun handle and walked cautiously across the open ground on the summit until he realized the rock edge dropped down to the river far below, and across the river a large plateau. He flattened himself to the ground and Stubs followed suit as they wriggled to the edge of the rock and looked out through the shadows at the plateau.

"What's that thing?" Stubs whispered in a grunt.

"Just part of the canyon but… hold up." Delgado squinted. "I thought I saw something." He stretched his neck and stared hard down at the spot on the edge of the plateau in silence until he saw it again. A pin-prick of light in the night. A lantern.

"We found 'em, go tell Sol Diablo." Delgado grunted to Stubs as he pushed himself up to his knees and looked along the river for a way across. "There's a stone bridge over there. He'll have to take it to get across to the plateau."

"Why you tellin' me to tell him?" Stubs frowned.

"Cause I'm staying up here, now get." Delgado shoved him towards the way they had climbed up. Stubs flopped over then snorted and crawled away, eager to get away from the canyon once more.

Delgado settled his back against the nearest boulder in shadow and tilted the brim of his hat down. He was tired and done with running up and down and all around this canyon for the Gila. He was calling it a night. He rested his hand on his knife hilt and went to sleep.

52

Scott was puzzled by Sam's behavior as they walked across the plateau to the Crest. Mitch walked close beside him, looking around at the saguaros and the scattering of Yàkin that had emerged for a better look at them.

Scott had nearly forgotten about getting up to the Crest when Sam whistled for the ropes to be lowered. "Hold on really tight Mitch." Scott warned.

"Hold on... what?" Mitch stepped onto the rope loop with Sam and Scott and gripped the ropes hard. "They pulling us up? That doesn't seem very-" before Mitch could say 'safe' Sam had jerked the rope twice and they were launched upwards. Mitch cried out and clung to the rope as it zipped up through the arms of the Crest until they reached the deck and were pulled in by the attendants.

"That was *horrible*!" Mitch stumbled shakily off the rope onto the deck. Scott followed him and rested a hand of his shoulder. "I know, I hated it too..." he trailed seeing a line of elders already waiting for them. Pip was on the deck with the arrow and talking to Wind's Howl but they all went quiet when Scott stepped closer to them with Mitch and Sam. "Wind's Howl, we need to talk-"

"You failed to mention the settlers, bat!" Owl Fear snarled at Pip, who quailed back slightly but tried to straighten up.

"I was gettin' to that, but I thought they wanted to tell you themselves." Pip scuttled back to Scott looking nervous. "I was just bringing then the arrow and tell them about the liza— "

"Who is this." Wind's Howl was frowning at Mitch, who stepped closer to Scott protectively.

"Wind's Howl this, this is my brother. He was at the base of the cliffs outside—"

"Your brother is *dead*! Or that another lie!" One elder snapped, Owl Fear pushed through and stalked closer to Scott. "You left the village! You left the canyon! After everything we said!"

Scott looked worriedly at the elders and stepped back. "We were looking after Pip we weren't leaving!"

"He signaled his settler friends in here!" Owl Fear told the others. "His brother lives! You brought settlers into our midst!" Owl Fear whirled to Sam then took her staff and thrust the end into Scott's chest, knocking him down and pinning him to the ground.

"Hey!" Mitch lunged forward but one of the rope attendants grabbed his shoulders and held him back.

"Let him go!" Mitch thrashed.

"Mitch i-it's ok." Scott said nervously, rubbing the back of his head as he looked up at Owl Fear's furious face "Owl Fear, I'm sorry, I didn't mean to do anything wrong! We didn't know my brother was out there, I swear, I thought he was dead. We went to get the arrow and we heard shots."

"Who is *we*, who else was with you!" Wind's Howl demanded, looking at Sam.

Sam winced and sighed. "First and Second led us to the body, the mice were down there when we got there and we surprised each other. Second got shot and we got one of the mice with an arrow. We had to bring them back to get help after we realized it was Scott's brother."

"That was not your right." Wind's Howl shook his head. "How many mice are in the village now?" Wind's Howl massaged his throbbing temple with his hands.

"Just five." Scott gasped from under Owl Fears staff digging into his chest. "Plus me."

"Let him up, *please*!" Pip winced, looking to Owl Fear and Wind's Howl. "Sam *say* something!" Pip turned to their friend.

"Like what." Sam frowned at him. "We're all in trouble."

"We won't be any trouble! All we want to do is go home and never come back to this place again!" Mitch wriggled in the arms of his restrainer.

Sam looked at him in surprise then down at Scott.

"We should not let them leave, they know too much, they have seen too much and know where we are." Owl Fear bared her teeth.

"Owl Fear, keeping them here would be wrong. They do not belong here." Wind's Howl shook his head. "We will let them go, if they promise us they will never tell a soul where Skytown is, and they must never return."

"Never?" Pip looked surprised.

"We promise." Mitch said promptly. "We'll even leave at first light. You won't ever have to worry about us again. Just let my brother go, and we'll be gone."

Owl Fear glared at him. "I do not believe in settler promises." She removed the end of her staff and hobbled back to the others. "But I want them gone. The sooner the better."

Mitch was released and he hurriedly went to help his brother up. "Come on Scott," he grumbled. "Let's get out of here."

Scott looked up at him then back at Wind's Howl who was staring at him expectantly. "Your word, Scott Thorn. If we let you go, you must never tell anyone about us, and you may never return."

Scott looked at Sam desperately then back at his brother. He had no choice. He nodded weakly. "I promise…" He looked up as the elders started to leave. "Wait, Wind's Howl." He raised his hand.

The elder turned and blinked at him to go on.

"What about the lizards? The Gila? They're looking for the village. What are we going to do?"

"We will keep hidden, our fate is not your concern anymore." Wind's Howl turned and walked away, leaving Scott feeling horribly deflated and helpless.

"Are you happy now?" Sam frowned at Scott, and turned away, walking towards the ropes, he stepped onto a loop and started his descent without them.

After a frightful solo descent from the Crest, Mitch and Scott were able to catch up to Sam on the way back to the Baranov's cactus.

"Sam, I had no choice." Scott puffed as he reached his side. "I had to promise them, they might have hurt my brother."

Sam snorted. "You just want to get out of here as fast as you can." He quickened his pace so Scott was practically jogging to keep up with his massive strides.

"What are you talking about? You knew I wanted to go and you said you'd help! I can't just stay here forever! I have a home to get back to! But all that aside, I think you're missing the point! The Gila is coming! And your elders aren't going to do anything about it! If he finds this place it could be a disaster!"

Sam stormed up the stairs inside the Baranov cactus keeping his back to them.

"What's going on?" Mitch caught up, frowning in concern. "Why's he so angry with you?"

"Hell if I know." Scott frowned and dashed up the stairs after him.

Upstairs in the shorter cactus much of the inner chamber had been hollowed out to create a snug room that served as a living space below and a bedroom up a ladder notched into the wall above. Down below, Charlie was sound asleep on Dr. Baranov's cot, left arm in a sling across his bandaged chest and shoulder. Bo sat on the edge of the cot near his feet talking animatedly to Second Tail, sitting in a chair at the tiny wooden table with First Tail standing beside him, as if keeping guard over his brother against any potential hostility. Jared was standing cautiously by the doorway, trying not to make eye-contact with anyone. June and Sonya were sitting on the floor with Carol, talking quietly as Dr. Baranov sat in his chair, smoking his pipe. A breeze blew in from the open window hole that led out to the little skydeck outside where Pip was hanging and listening to them all.

Sam stormed into the room, causing heads to turn as Scott followed in his wake.

"Sam! What is wrong with you! We need to think about what we're going to do about the Gila!"

Sam whirled so fast, Scott ran into him and stumbled back. "What do you care what happens to us! You're leaving! Go back to your own kind!"

"*Sam*!" Pip scolded and dropped down from the doorway to enter the room. "Have you lost your senses!"

Scott flinched, stung by Sam's words. The look in his eyes was so similar to the hate he'd seen in Owl Fear's, and he couldn't look away.

"I care a lot!" he retorted. "Why shouldn't I care!"

"Your brother's alive. Go home. You don't need us anymore and we don't need you." Sam towered over him.

"That's enough!" Mitch stormed forward protectively, tail raised assertively as he stared up at the outraged Jumper. "Come on Scott, let's get ready." Mitch grumbled.

"Wait, you're leaving? But Scott! The Gila!" Pip scuttled over.

"I know." Scott said tensely. "I have to leave, Pip. I promised the elders, it was the only way."

"So you were just going to vanish?" Second blinked in confusion. "Come morning, just leave?"

"This isn't how I wanted *anyone* to find out! I didn't even know we were leaving until we spoke with the elders minutes ago, I'm sorry!" Scott kneaded his brows. Everything felt like it was crashing around him. Sam had turned on him, the Gila could be on the Yàkin's doorstep and he felt like he was being stretched from his brother at one end and by his worry for the Yàkin and his friends at the other.

"We have to go, I'm sorry it's so sudden." Mitch rested his hand on Scott's shoulder. "We have a long journey to go. Scott needs his rest."

First Tail sighed heavily. "I suppose I should be relieved we'll be rid of you all soon."

"Firsty." Second frowned at him. "You can't mean that."

"I said *should* be." First Tail helped him up. "But they need their rest, and you need yours. Let them be. We'll escort them out of the canyon in the morning." First Tail turned to Carol. "You should head back home too." He advised.

Carol sighed, knowing First Tail wouldn't want her staying where there were so many settlers, no matter how friendly they claimed to be. She stood and cast a sympathetic look to Scott before following the others out the door.

Scott watched them go and looked to Sam. "Are you going to even talk to me!" He narrowed his eyes.

"I have nothing left to say." Sam frowned. "Have a safe journey." He turned and walked briskly out the doorway after the others.

"Prickly crowd." Bo arched a brow, watching them leave. "Been living in cacti too long."

"They're upset!" Sonya looked sharply at Bo. "You boys should get some rest, it'll be sunrise in a few short hours." She turned to Scott and deflated slightly. "I wish you didn't have to go so soon."

"Me neither…" Scott mumbled as she climbed up to the second level. When Mitch went to check on Charlie he walked past the others out onto the skydeck. Down below he could hear the fading voices of Sam and the others, arguing in Yàkin language below. He sat down; letting his feet hang over the edge he cradled his head in his hands.

"I don't know what's gotten into him." Pip appeared beside him, his ears angled towards the voices long out of Scott's hearing range. "I'll try to talk to him Scott, I'm certain it's not you he's so angry with."

"I don't know what to do anymore, Pip…" Scott admitted weakly. "These past few days, I would have given anything for Mitch to appear out of the blue and take me home… take me out of the nightmare we've all been trapped in." he crossed his legs and propped his chin on his fist. "But here in Skytown… I feel safer than I have all week. I'm worried Pip, I really am, that the Gila might find this place. If he does, he'll kill them all. Owl Fear was right to hate me coming here. We've led that monster right to them."

Pip's ears angled back. "You can't go thinkin' that. We're lucky to be alive, I ought to know. Even if he did track us here, I think the Yàkin won't go down so easily. You've seen 'em! Sam, First and Second? They're tough as the desert itself, Scott."

"The Yàkin don't want to fight." Scott pointed out worriedly. "They just want to live in peace."

"Sometimes you must fight to protect your peace, Scott. And I have a feeling, if they're pushed to protect it, they will fight."

"Scott?" Mitch appeared in the doorway. "Come on, get some sleep."

Scott sighed and bowed his head. "Pip you have to promise me that you will try and keep everyone on the alert if the Gila comes after I'm gone. Keep Sam safe, and Carol, Sonya, everyone. Sam would have done the same for us." Scott turned to head inside.

Pip looked up and nodded somberly. "'Til the end." He promised as Scott reluctantly turned and went inside. The long-eared bat returned his focus to the shadows of the village. He couldn't let it end like this. He wouldn't let it.

53

A cruel, satisfied smiled revealed Sol Diablo's curved teeth as he snapped the reins of his roadrunner onward. The budding sunrise streaked the gray dawn horizon with shots of red and gold. His scout's words had improved his mood greatly, and now, Stubs was leading him back towards the section of the canyon where Spikes remained, nervous but watchful.

Sol Diablo's mind twisted from vengeful thoughts of slaughtering his runaway captives for the destruction of his mines and the death of Morgan to the riches that surrounded the Skytown legend. Jumpers were the most gifted in opal mining, and he planned to exploit that gift down to the last glittering rock.

Behind the Gila, his posse followed in tense silence. Some were eager for the blood that was surely about to be spilled, others were barely containing their nervousness at the thought of facing the savage wild mice that plagued their campfire tales and saloon talk. No matter what the feeling, the cutthroat band rode onward to the cliff, armed to the teeth, and ready to cut down any living thing in their path.

Up on the cliffs, Delgado stirred from his much-needed rest in the rock crevice. Sunrise was here. He winced and stretched tired limbs before making sure it was safe to leave the shelter of the crevice. He rubbed his arms; he would be more comfortable when the sun came up a little higher. He flattened himself down to the ground to looked down over the edge of the canyon towards the plateau where he had seen the light. From this vantage point, the canyon wall was higher than the plateau, allowing Delgado to look down at the dozens of monstrous saguaros. Nothing too out of the ordinary at first, but as the light of dawn strengthened; the cacti seemed to bear more detail even to Delgado's naked eye; ropes and wooden platforms? It didn't take Delgado long to realize that the cacti were all connected in an elaborate village, and he couldn't help but feel impressed but all the craftsmanship that must have been involved to build it that way.

"Skytown." He muttered, remembering long ago, a name he had once heard in passing, describing the hidden city of the Jumpers: a city in the air, the last stronghold of the wild mice.

Well, it certainly was no magical floating city, but it was still awe worthy enough to take Delgado aback for a moment. He couldn't see any individual Jumpers on the ground for the brush and scrub tree branches blocking his view around the village, but he would wager there being a fair few of them living there. Vaguely he wondered if they would outnumber the Gila's forces, and if that would hinder Sol Diablo's decision to invade, if those were his plans.

Delgado wouldn't have to hold onto the question long, because moments later he heard scuffling behind him and as he turned and drew his gun he saw it was only Stubs, leading Sol Diablo and a small ragtag bunch up onto the rock face. He holstered his piece and frowned at the Gila when he saw his face did not look pleased at the sight of him.

"You didn' come back down last night." He growled.

"Sent word back instead, figured I'd keep watch up here, make sure no one ambushed you come morning light." Delgado snorted. The lie was bought by Sol Diablo, who grunted back and shouldered past him to crouch and peer over the edge. Internally, Delgado relished the thought of an ambush of Jumpers turning the Gila into an arrow-bristled pin cushion.

"Would ya just look at it, look at the size of it!" Sol Diablo's dark eyes glittered like those of a tarantula taking in its victim. "Heh, mighty fine place to hide, if I don't say so myself. Though I don't reckon they thought they'd ever be found. They're in a bowl, boys. We could take 'em out from up here, smoke 'em out like wasps, only way I see out is that bridge of rock over there, we can just pick 'em off until they surrender. Before the week's out, fella's, this village will be ours."

Delgado huffed slightly. "*Wasps sting*." he muttered before turning around to face him. "You think they will give in so easily?" he arched a scaly golden brow-stripe. "You've obviously forgotten what happened the first time settlers tried to wipe them off the face of the earth."

"Settlers used farm guns and pitchforks. And, while I find those effective, Delgado, I came with something a little more heavy duty." The Gild turned and beckoned one of his rats over. The rat unslung a bag from his shoulder and set it down with a thud. Flipping open the top Delgado saw the familiar brown cylindrical bundles.

"Dynamite." Sol Diablo sneered. "Brought the whole lot from the mines, every saddlebag is packed with enough to level a jailhouse, bricks, mortar and steel bars. Let's see how their prickly cactus stand to that." Sol Diablo stood and walked towards the edge on the other side to check the rest of his posse. "I'll need three good-sized sling shots that can haul a bundle this size from this cliff top to those cactus down there. And I'll pay the first group to fashion them up *triple* their current wages." Sol Diablo chuckled darkly as his forces scattered to find material to build such devices.

Delgado frowned as he watched the Gila. He didn't think this plan was very well thought out, then again, he already though the Gila might be a touch mad. The next few hours would prove how mad he really was.

Scott couldn't believe he had been able to fall asleep, but sure enough his brother was waking him with a gentle shake on the shoulder.

"Come on Scott, let's get going." he murmured and went back to wake up June who was asleep on the floor across the room.

"I want to get out of here as soon as possible, these Jumpers give me the creeps." Jared wrinkled his nose, looking like he hadn't slept a wink. "I think we're lucky we weren't scalped in our sleep, or had our tails cut off..."

Scott frowned as he stood and straightened himself out. "Shut up, Jared." He grumbled. He took slight pleasure in the annoyed surprise on Jared's face but the feeling was short lived as he turned and walked out onto the skydeck, rubbing his eyes awake. Pip wasn't there anymore; he wasn't sure where his friend would be. He thought about Sam and a lump of sadness settled in his gut. Sam had been his guardian, a protector, a brother. Most of all he had been a friend that Scott knew would stop at nothing to reach his goal. Had he really lost that Sam? Was this new Sam so bitterly against him leaving that he was willing to throw away everything they had gone through? Turn their friendship into the same hate for settlers that he had seen on the faces of so many Yàkin? Scott couldn't bear to remember Sam like that. He heard footsteps behind him and saw Bo walking out onto the deck, bushing off something in his hands.

"Found this on the trail, well, Charlie found it. And it's a lucky thing he did, we thought we'd lost you for good, kid." Bo ruffled his headfur and set his hat back on his head.

Scott tilted the brim back, looking up. "You found it!" he smiled, then his smile faded. "Where did you find it?"

"That canyon about a day's journey back, where we first saw that nasty crowd of lizards. Charlie found it in the river at the bottom, then we picked up your trail and were able to track and guess our way here." Bo smiled. "I'm glad we found you safe and sound, Scott. Wouldn't be the same back on the ranch without you." Bo clapped his shoulder and Scott winced, rubbing the area he'd patted. The shot wound from Delgado was healing but still tender.

"I'm fine." Scott assured him. "Go on I'll, I'll be there in a minute." He nodded. Bo turned and went back inside and Scott looked out towards the rest of the village, already starting to liven up, he could see the fishers heading to the paths that lead to the river below. Tunnelers were coming out of the ground and switching shifts, and Scott could hear the youngsters playing on one of the larger skydecks further up the cactus platforms. He just watched the village quietly for a while and let his mind still. It wasn't so different from Redcliff, really. If he closed his eyes, it was almost the same. Different voices belonging to different people, but the premise was the same. He blinked them open feeling a tap on his shoulder and he turned with a jump to see Sonya.

"Your brothers and the others went down to the quail, they told you to come down as soon as you could." Sonya pressed a bag into his hands. "For the trip, it's enough food to last you two or three days I should think." She smiled weakly at him. "I wish we didn't have to see you go so soon."

"Thanks, Sonya." Scott smiled weakly. "I'll miss you. I think I'll miss this entire place. I just wish I could have seen a little more of it."

"Maybe someday you could come back?" Sonya asked hopefully.

Scott didn't have the heart to tell her that wouldn't be an option again. "Maybe." He murmured. He turned and headed back inside towards the stairs.

Pip was up in Sam's cactus room, hanging from the ceiling and staring impatiently at the dark door hole that led through the center of the cactus. He had heard the steps leading up and had heard them pause before their maker came into view.

"I know you're there, Sam, so you better just get up here and deal with me before I come down those stairs after you." Pip scolded, dropping to the floor with a messy flutter.

A frowning Sam appeared and stalked past him. "What do you want, Pip."

"Perhaps an explanation for your wretched behavior last night for a start!" Pip turned to follow him with his eyes. "I looked everywhere for you last night! I couldn't find you! I got worried! Scott's leaving any minute aren't you going to at least tell him goodbye?"

Sam sighed heavily. "Leave it be Pip, it's better he goes." Sam went over to his water skin and poured some into a clay bowl to splash and clean his whiskers. "His kind doesn't belong out here."

"You've had a thorn in your side ever since Scott found his brother last night! I thought you of all creatures would be happy for him!"

"I *am* happy for him!" Sam snorted. "You don't understand, Pip." He set the jug down, brushing water from his whiskers. "Scott has his brother, he's going home. He doesn't need us anymore."

"Scott cares about what happens to us after he's gone, he cares what happens to you, to the Yàkin, to this whole place! A place that flat out told him they don't trust him and they never want to see him again. He still cares, Sam, and you know it. You won't find that kind of devotion from just anyone." Pip flattened his ears when Sam didn't turn around, barely acknowledging him at all with the slightest flick of his tufted tail. Pip let out a heavy breath. "I can't force you to be anythin' but yourself, but I can't believe you're just going to let it end like this. Let your friendship be all for naught."

Sam looked over his shoulder and glared at him. "Settlers and Jumpers don't mix, Pip. Its better Scott knows that and stays away, where he's safe, then get hurt trying to stay here." He looked away, glare softening. "It's for everyone's own good."

Pip snorted. "You go on and believe that then. I'm going to go bid my farewells to him then, and perhaps if things tend to stay this way around here, you won't have to worry about my shadow hangin' around either." He turned and flew out the window before Sam could object.

Mitch cinched the saddle strap tight and patted Bowie's side. "I got your quail ready, June." He came over to check on her where she was sitting on a flat slab of rock while Sonya was re-wrapping her leg for the last time.

"Just chew on these if the pain starts up again, it'll help reduce the swelling." Sonya handed he some dried bundles of what looked like slivered root bits. "They're bitter and tangy but believe me, they help."

"Thanks again, Sonya, you're a talented doctor." June beamed at the younger doe as she got to her feet with a wince, taking hold of the forked stick she was using as a crutch.

"Does can't be doctors." Jared muttered under his breath.

"Better doctor than you'll ever be." Bo shouldered him back with a huff. "You ready to ride, Charlie?" Bo watched as Charlie beckoned his mount to crouch low so he could get into the saddle. The dormouse looked over his good shoulder and nodded before turning his attention to Sonya and her father and tipping his hat in modest thanks for their help.

"Hope you weren't going to leave without saying goodbye!" Carol called, bounding over slightly out of breath, a gaggle of young Yàkin swarmed behind her.

"Wow, look at those guns." One whispered, at the mention of guns the lot of them crowded shyly behind Carol.

Bo smiled and titled his hat up. "These? Oh don't worry, fellas, these aren't meant for you."

"Are guns better than arrows?" one inquisitive young doe stepped out from behind Carol.

"Depends on who's shooting them, and their aim!" Second Tail grinned, crossing the long cactus shadow with First Tail to see them off. "Stick to your bows, Murmur." He ruffled her headfur and looked over at Scott. "We came to see you out of the canyon, make sure you don't fall off the edge like last time." He winked teasingly.

"Scott give you a hard time?" Bo stepped up into his saddle and patted Cotton's neck feathers.

"Only a whole lot." Second Tail grinned and folded his arms.

"Not true." Scott smirked, feeling he was going to miss the cliff sentries, even First Tail.

First Tail sighed. "Well, you weren't what I expected of a settler. I suppose that's a good thing."

"Uh, thanks?" Scott said uncertainly.

"Sorry to cut goodbyes short but we need to get a move on to cover as much ground as we can before dark, and we still need to take breaks with Bowie's foot acting up." Mitch stepped up into the stirrup.

"We can't leave yet!" Scott looked to his brother. "I haven't seen Pip or Sam, I have to say goodbye."

"I'm here!" Pip fluttered down, causing the quail to snort and spook slightly. "Wouldn't let you leave without sayin' good luck." Pip scuttled forward and wrapped Scott in a one-winged, leathery embrace. "But I won't say 'goodbye', because I promise this won't be the last we see of each other, I'll fly to Redcliff and check up on you time to time, I will."

Scott beamed at the thought. "I'd like that." He looked up towards Sam's cactus and Pip followed his line of sight. "Is he coming, Pip?"

"I tried, Scott, he's stubborn as a stone." Pip's ears set back. "I'm sorry."

"I'm so angry with him." Carol frowned. "He was going to help you get home, I don't understand why he's taking it so hard now."

"It's ok." Scott said, making her turn in surprise. "I don't blame him. Tell him I said goodbye?" he asked Carol.

"I will." She promised, stooping on one knee to hug him properly. "Stay safe, little one, don't be getting yourself into any more trouble." She smiled teasingly.

Scott nodded and turned to Mitch, who was already up in the saddle and reaching down to help pull him up on the back.

Scott clambered up and looked down at Pip with a swallow. His friend nodded back in silent promise as First and Second Tail started to lead the small posse away out of the village and towards the trail to the bridge.

"Goodbye, Skytown…" Scott looked over his shoulder one last time before facing forward again.

"What was that?" Mitch asked.

"Nothing." Scott shook his head as they crossed the rock bridge once more.

"Have a safe journey." Second Tail smiled to the group at they reached the outer trail that led down the side of the canyon. "Just please, try not to share this with others."

"Our lips are sealed, and Charlie won't say anything either." Bo chided as Charlie rolled his eyes good-naturedly.

"Hope that shoulder heals." First Tail nodded to Charlie gently. "Rest it up."

Charlie nodded to him as Second flung his arm around his brother playfully. "That's Firsty for 'I'm sorry I shot you.'"

Charlie grinned and nodded sincerely.

"That's Charlie for 'You're forgiven.'" Bo winked.

"Goodbye, Scott." Second Tail sighed. "It was good to meet you."

"Bye fellas, I won't forget you, I promise." Scott swallowed hard and leaned back as they began their descent. Before long they had reached the ground and were heading off towards the hills, leaving Skytown behind them.

54

Atop the bluffs, Sol Diablo squinted beneath the shade of his hat seeing mounted quail cross the narrow stone bridge in the distance. He snorted and turned back to the others. Mice were no longer his concern. His prize was before him; the legendary Skytown itself. He went to check the progress of the giant slingshots. He smirked as he came upon the two most successful looking contraptions fashioned from supplies the others had brought with them.

"Impressive enough to look at. But will it work?" The Gila plucked at taught elastic material connected to the pocket, made from the sole of someone's boot.

"She should work just fine!" The collared lizard grunted out from around a grass blade clamped in his teeth. "Would you like to test it, sir?"

"Fine then." Sol Diablo reached down to the piles of dynamite bundles beside the slingshot. "About time to send 'em a message I suppose." The Gila took a drag on his cigar stump then used it to light the fuse with a hiss and a spark.

Sam bounded out of the entrance tunnel to his cactus home and leapt down to the ground, but by the time he reached the bridge he knew he was too late. Scott and the others would be on the other side of the canyon by now, maybe even to the hills. He sighed out and turned away into the shade of the closest saguaro and started to walk back towards the heart of the village, his tufted tail leaving a slight trail as it dragged in the dust.

Pip was up on one of the circle skydeck platforms with a dozen or so other Yàkin that were laying out fish and fruit to dry for the day. He was helping himself to a roasted cricket when Sam climbed up to his level and paused when he saw him.

"He's gone… I was going to…" Sam looked down guiltily.

"I'm sorry." Pip sighed, setting his food down. "They waited as long as they could."

Sam said nothing and trudged over, sitting cross-legged across from Pip and his food. Pip glanced down then nudged the cricket towards him. "It doesn't have to be forever." Pip tried to assure him.

Sam picked up the cricket and looked up at Pip just as an explosion several saguaros away sent earth and dust flying. Sam jumped to his feet and Pip flapped up into the air, hovering to see.

"That was dynamite!" Pip called down. "But that can't… no…" Pip landed back beside Sam as two more loud bangs hit, sending dust clouding the village area below out of sight. "Sam! It's *them*!"

Sam turned and looked at Pip, eyes stretched wide in fright. "Go to the Crest! Tell the elders what's going on!" Sam shouted urgently over another explosion that blew up a smaller prickly pear cactus near the edge of the village, sending chucks of cactus flesh and needles spraying in every direction. Screams sounded from across the village as panicked Jumpers ran for cover or bolted up into their cactus holes. Others were running towards the danger, screaming the names of loved ones.

Pip nodded and leapt from the platform, winging his way through the ropes and cactus arms towards the great crested saguaro.

"Well, looky there. Works just fine!" Sol Diablo laughed hoarsely from the cliff top. "Hold yer fire!" he barked at the lizards manning the two slingshots.

Pip flew over the heads of the rope attendants on the Crest platform, the two were gaping down at the billowing dust in a panic, as he landed the elders poured from the doorway and huddled in frightened groups. Everyone was talking, screaming, hysterical. Pip was shunted to the side as they all bustled about, he had to tune out their scared voices to try and locate Wind's Howl. He finally found him alongside Owl Fear, pushing their way to the front of the platform to see what was going on.

"Winds' Howl!" Pip called as someone stepped on his wing. "Ack! Excuse me!" Pip flapped out his wings to clear a path before scuttling over to them both. "Wind's Howl! Owl Fear! We're under attack! It's the Gila! The lizards we told you about!"

Owl Fear spun around to face him with surprising speed for someone her age. "YOU!" she seethed, her voice and body shook in quiet rage. "YOU! You lead them here! You lead them to US!" She raised her staff to bring it down on Pip's head but Wind's Howl caught her arm.

"Pip is *not* the one attacking us!" he told her firmly. "We must do something!"

"Yes!" Pip flinched back as Owl Fear stepped aggressively towards him. "We're surrounded along the top of that bluff to the East! What are you orders?" Pip asked then his ears perked. "Wait!" he turned around and angled his ears towards the bluffs. "He's calling us…" he narrowed his emerald green eyes.

"Attention, Jumpers!" Sol Diablo cupped his scaly hands around his mouth as he called down to the frenzied village. The dust clouds were thinning and Sol Diablo's form stood dark against the bright sky. "I am Sol Diablo! The Great Gila!" He straightened up. "Quite a find this was! Any other critter'd have marched in and killed the lot of you on sight! I have a proposition!"

Pip curled his lip back, showing his teeth as he relayed the Gila's message in a mutter to the hushed elders.

"You lot can all live to see another day, if you throw down all your opal stones on the other side o' that bridge! And then I'm gonna need a few diggers to take us to your mines! If not, I'm afraid it's my job to finish what the settlers started! I'll blow Skytown sky-high!"

Winds' Howl looked grimly up at the ridge. "If it spares our people's lives. We must obey. With those things exploding all around us lives could be lost." He looked to Owl Fear.

"That horrid demon!" Pip hissed and looked back to the elders. "You can't trust him! He's lyin', he won't let anyone live, he'll take everythin' he's wants until there's nothin' left, and when there's nothin' left he'll have no use for any of you!" Pip turned his ear back towards the Gila's call:

"You have ten minutes to give your answer! Or we start bringing you to the ground!"

Wind's Howl looked behind them at the frightened, angry elders. "We must fight." He murmured, he was met with silence at first, followed by shouts.

"If we give him what he wants he will go!"

"But he could come back!"

"We must leave…"

"We outnumber them! We should fight!"

"We cannot risk the lives of our fellow Yàkin!"

"There won't BE any Yàkin left if you *don t* fight!" Pip spread his wings with a leathery snap. "The Gila is not like the Yàkin people! He has no honor, his word means nothin'! You can either give up and wait to be destroyed, or drive him back and save yourselves! Defend your home! It's *yours*!" Pip looked to Owl Fear. "You can't be driven off again. You can't let them destroy you all once and for all. You must show him he has no power over you. I know you don't want to, but you *must* fight!"

Owl Fear pursed her lips and closed her eyes. She banged the butt of her staff on the platform. "Very well." Her dark eyes squinted open. "Tell that filthy creature he has come to the wrong place, to think we will so easily give into his demands." She turned to the two rope attendants. "Ready the scouts, the guards, the fishers, the sentries and warriors! Ready all the able Yàkin to stand and fight! Get everyone who cannot underground and out of sight!"

Pip watched them nod and bound away across the bridges or down the ropes before he turned and dropped off the skydeck into the air. He raised himself up over the cactus until he saw the Gila and his lizards lined up along the ridge across the divide but he dare not fly any closer. "Oi! Gila! The Yàkin will not surrender to you!" he belted out.

"Have it yer way! And be the first to die!" The Gila drew his huge pistol and aimed it at the bat, but before he could squeeze the trigger an arrow hissed through the air and stuck clean through the Gila's forearm. "AUGH!" Sol Diablo stumbled back, dropping his gun over the side of the cliff, where its distant fall ended with a splash in the river.

Pip gasped and looked over before he dove for cover to see First Tail standing on the ridge just above Sol Diablo, Second Tail behind him. First Tail had already notched another arrow and sent it thudding straight into the skull of one of the lizards manning a slingshot. The lizard fell dead as the Gila pointed at them.

"KILL THEM!" he snarled. First and Second bolted from sight as a chorus of gunshots went off. "After them!" Sol Diablo turned and saw Delgado watching the others give chase. "You!" he snarled, yanking him over by his vest. "Go after them you lazy worm!" he shoved Delgado backwards so hard that the skink fell and skidded across the stone. Delgado stood up, eyes blazing, before he turned slowly and disappeared after the others.

Sol Diablo turned to collared lizard on his left. "Follow him." He hissed. "If he tries anything, shoot him dead." He bared his curved teeth as he ripped the cactus spine arrow from his arm with only the slightest flinch.

Pip lit back down on the Crest's platform. "He's gonna come after us with everything he got, we've got to move everyone to the safest place in the canyon! Anyone who can't fight!"

"The tunnels." Winds' Howl called to the other elders. "Hurry down and tell everyone to go down and as far back as they can, if they need to, they can escape with them, the tunnels let out into the river below. The fishers have the gourd boats there, they can take them down the river to safety."

Pip's ear's snapped upright as he heard the rubbery twang of elastic in the distance. "GET DOWN!" He threw Wind's Howl and Owl Fear to the ground, covering them with his wings as a bundle of dynamite hit an arm of the Crest above them and exploded, bits of cactus and needles shot in all directions and dynamite bits rained down from above. Pip had felt the sting and when he raised his head from and shook the cactus rubble from his ears he gasped shock to see two cactus spines sticking into the membrane of his wing, He tried to raise his wing but his eyes widened in horror to see the spine had pierced straight through his wing membrane and were driven deep into Wind's Howl's ribs.

"Get off!" Owl Fear thrashed weakly out from under Pip's other wing. She turned and saw Winds' face pulled tight in pain.

"I'm pinned to him!" Pip winced. "You have to pull the spine free!" he gasped. Owl Fear just stared at her grandson, face shocked. "Owl Fear!" Pip called. "Someone help Winds' Howl!" he shouted to the other elders, pulling themselves out of the debris and hurrying over to help. They pulled the spines free and Pip stumbled back, looking at the tiny holes in his wing. He hissed in pain and looked at Owl Fear as she tried to help the others bring Winds' Howl into the Crest to help him.

"Owl Fear! What do you want the others to do?" Pip hobbled after her. Owl Fear turned rigidly to him, face blank for a moment. "Whatever it takes." She gasped out before hurrying after the others. "Do not let them get in here!" Pip nodded and stretched his wings. Thankfully, his flying wasn't affected.

Pip flew low against the ground across the village, avoiding the bustle of Yàkin racing in all directions. Many had retrieved bows, quivers and spears and were rushing towards the eastern cliff edge to try and pick off the lizards on the rim, while others rushed towards the winding path off the plateau to man the bridge in case any tried to come across into the village. Pip even saw a small group of terrified Yàkin children crouched under a sage bush, clutching their tiny bows and stone knives close. "Get underground!" Pip called out to them as he followed the defenders out of the main village.

Pip spotted Sam rushing down the path towards the bridge loaded down with a full quiver of cactus spine arrows across his back; his face and clothes were hastily smudged in red clay to keep him hidden.

"Sam!" Pip panted, landed in the brush beside him and who he just realized was Carol beside him. "Winds' Howl was hit from the blast, he's hurt."

"What are the orders from the elders?" Sam notched an arrow to his bowstring as another double round of explosives went off. One hit the plateau and sent rock crumbling and flying every which way, the other hit the side of a saguaro and blew a chunk out of it to their right.

Pip looked to the bridge. "Just don't let them cross. Keep them out. That's all we can do!" Pip flinched at another explosion from above, followed by screams. "We can't reach most of 'em with the arrows from the plateau! They have the advantage of height and those boulders up there are like parapets to hide behind! We need to take out whatever they're usin' to chuck the dynamite out here! I can't get close enough to that ridge without bein' gunned down though…"

"Anyone outside the village?" Carol asked breathlessly a blast sounded in the air from a stick that blew up before it reached its mark, scattering the plateau face with bits of debris.

"First and Second!" Sam stiffened, hearing gun shots followed by the sight of First Tail and Second Tail diving behind a spur of rock near the bridge on the other side, pinned down under fire, pursued by five other lizards, including one Pip and Sam instantly recognized by his brilliant blue tail.

"They'll never make it across. It's too open." Pip murmured. He shut his eyes tight, flinching from the sound of guns going off on the other side of the bridge. First and Second were stuck. No one could get out to the cliffs where the blasts were being sent from. The only ones already on that side may already be too far gone… but it was the only idea he had.

"We need Scott, I'll go fetch him. He's already on the other side, he could dismantle those—"

"NO!" Sam snapped, turning sharply to Pip. "Scott's *safe* out there! I can only hope he keeps riding far away from here! Don't you *dare* bring him back!" Sam shouted as dynamite hits the rocks nearby, spraying them with gravel bits.

Pip flinched and shook off the rubble. "I'm sorry." He shook his head and flapped up into the air as Sam made a grab to stop him.

"Pip, no!" Sam reached but his friend was already flying across the divide. Sam jumped up with Carol, sending arrows hissing towards the lizard posse on the rocks to give the bat some cover as Pip sailed over the cliff top and out of sight. Sam dove back to the cover of the rocks and grass when the shooting returned and looked grimly at Carol. If Scott came back, he could be killed, and they didn't think of something quickly, they would be too.

55

Scott twisted in the saddle behind his brother and looked back through the trees hearing another distant sound. It sounded horribly like explosions. "Mitch I'm telling you, it's not thunder!"

"Scott I'm sure it's nothing." Bo said, riding up alongside him. "You're probably just hearing things and thinking it's the worst after these last few days."

Scott tried to settle down again but he was too tense. When he heard another booming sound in the distance he grabbed his brother's shoulders. "That's not thunder!" he protested. "That's the sound of dynamite! I know it!"

Mitch pulled Cali up short. "Scott how would dynamite end up out here?" he shook his head. "You're just a little shell shocked." he perked his ears hearing another boom. "Ok, well, I believe that's not thunder now…"

"We have to turn around! I have to go back! That's gotta be him!" Scott slid off the saddle and clambered up onto a large, craggy stump to try and see beyond the hills.

"Who's him?" June asked. "Those lizards?"

"Yes!" Scott pushed his hands through his headfur, knocking his hat off without realizing it. His brother slid off Cali's back and stooped to pick it up.

"Scott I'm sure they're fine. Besides, we aren't allowed to go back. You promised, so did I, they'd probably skewer us if we returned." He dusted off his hat and climbed up beside him. "We have to get home."

"Mitch, they're in trouble! I just… I have to go back!" Scott grabbed his hat back.

Mitch frowned. "Scott I already lost you once, I'm not bringing you back there, I'm sorry! I can't lose you again."

Scott bristled but before he could answer he heard another voice calling his name and he looked up in time to see a bat flying haphazardly fast towards their patch of trees and brush.

"Pip? PIP! Over here!" Scott cupped his hand around his whiskers and called out to him. Pip heard from a distance and dropped lower, landing with a thud against the side of the stump, he stumbled up onto it, panting raggedly.

"Th-thought you were… long… long gone!" Pip gasped out as Scott rushed over and helped him up.

"Pip what's wrong? What's going on?" Scott demanded.

"They're here!" Pip's eyes were desperate. "They've surrounded the bridge! They've been lobbin' explosives from the mines at the plateau! Wind's Howl is hurt badly, First and Second are pinned down. Sol Diablo's demanded the Yàkin surrender, or he's gonna blow the place to rubble!"

Scott felt like his stomach had been turned to ice, his whiskers trembled at the thought. "Sam? Carol and the others??" he blurted out.

"They're safe for now! They were when I left at least! Scott, they're pressin' in on the bridge it may already be too late! We need to disable the catapults or whatever they're usin' to send that dynamite into the village. I can't get close enough and there's too many guns!"

"Hold on!" Mitch frowned, stalking over. "You came to drag my little brother into a warzone! I won't have it! I'm sorry but Scott's safe out here!" Mitch rested a hand on his brother's shoulder. "It's my responsibility to keep him safe and bring him home!"

"No!" Scott shrugged out from under Mitch's hand. "Mitch, we have to help them! They're my friends!"

"They told us we weren't allowed to return!" June pointed out as she and the others rode up to the base of the craggy stump.

"I'm sorry but no! I won't let you!" Mitch clenched his fists. "I'm not bringing you back there to die!"

"You don't have to." Scott frowned levelly. "I'll go back myself!" He turned and looked at Pip, who turned sideways and nodded quickly. Scott ducked under Mitch's snatching arms and clambered onto the bat's back. Pip launched into the air, wings pumping hard with the extra weight.

"Scott NO!" Mitch stumbled after them and looked up.

"I'm sorry, Mitch." Scott gritted his teeth. "I have to!" he nodded as Pip winged away and headed across the hills and brush once more, flying low.

Mitch stumbled off the stump and ran a short ways but his brother was long gone already. His heart hammered in his chest. "We have to go after him!"

June rode up next to him and Bowie churred worriedly in Mitch's ear. "Mitch, the Jumpers are Scott's friends, they need help. If anything he owes them, and so do we."

"I know." Mitch said shakily. "I know! I just... I *can t* let him get himself killed!"

"He won't, we'll be there." Bo rode up and Charlie followed him with a grim nod. "We'll join the fight together."

"What?? No!" Jared backed his quail away from the others; his amber-brown eyes stretched wide with fear. "Run after Scott? Into the fight are you mad? Those wild mice will kill us for returning if the lizards don't gut-shoot the lot of us first! I... I can't." he looked down fearfully, breath hitched slightly. "I can't do it."

Mitch sighed, Jared was terrified, he couldn't blame him when his own gut was thrashing around inside him, trying to break free. "I won't ask you to. Jared, ride back. If anything happens to us... well, Pa deserves to know."

Jared looked down at him from his mount, malice gone from his face; he glanced at each of them, riding off most likely to their deaths. He looked at Mitch and nodded quietly. "I'll... I'll tell him everything." he promised.

"Then get going, ride as far away from this place as you can." Mitch clambered back into Cali's saddle and turned to ride off.

"Take care, Jare-Bear." Bo tipped his hat grimly and Charlie nodded as well.

"Mitch—" Jared started as Mitch was about to spur off. "Good luck."

Mitch nodded and snapped the reins. "Go Cali!" his hen chirped and took off out of the shade of the woods and out into the blazing heat of the midday sun. Mitch rode hard and fast, Scott may already be there, it may already be too late, but he'd still fight. He owed the Jumpers, the Yàkin, for saving his brother's life. It was time to return the favor.

56

The ride was rough on both Scott and Pip. Scott was jostled by Pip's frantically pumping wings and had to wrap both arms around his neck to keep from being buffeted off down to the ground rushing beneath them. If Scott were any bigger Pip couldn't have managed, even now his was breathing ragged and his flight pattern was sloppy as he barely stayed above the brush-line.

The sun was pushing past the box canyon, shining in their eyes before they reached the base.

"Where were the shots coming from?" Scott called to Pip who nearly bucked him off in shock.

"Land sake's Scott! My ears are *right* there!" he panted back. He flicked his left ear forward. "From that way!"

Scott saw the area Pip had gestured to. Cleaved sections of canyon wall riddled with natural stone columns. The lizards must have found easy ground for scaling the walls without alerting the sentries.

"Let's land off to the side." Scott spoke lower as they hit the shade of the canyon.

"Land. Right." Pip panted as the thought occurred to him.

The landing was rough; Pip skidded into the dust and flipped ears over tail-flap, sending Scott sprawling into the gravel.

Scott stood and brushed off his pants, admiring two torn knees holes with equally skinned up knees underneath. He beckoned Pip into the grass and the two crept along the canyon base towards the area the lizards had used.

"Why are we starting down here?" Pip whispered, shuddering as he heard the blasts up above.

"Quail couldn't've climbed up the way they went, they must be down here." Scott pulled the grass apart and saw he was right. A huge covey of quail was gathered at the base of the rocks. Scott scanned them and saw their saddlebags were bulging.

"Get back!" Pip hissed, both ducked seeing a collared lizard dash over to one quail and unclip its saddlebag. The lizard brought the bag to the base and passed it off to another who scaled the wall with it slung over his shoulder.

"The quail are carrying the charges." Scott murmured. "We have to get rid of the quail to cut off the supply!"

"There's two lizards guardin' 'em and they keep coming down to fetch it, how're you gonna get rid of them then?"

Scott frowned and looked at the bat to answer when a loud, angry squawk made them peer out to see one of the lizards leap back from where Sol Diablo's roadrunner mount was tethered.

"Damn bird!" The lizard seethed. "See if you get fed again while we're here!" he stormed back to the other lizard.

Scott looked at Pip then to the Roadrunner and swallowed. "I have an idea."

"I already don't like this idea." Pip frowned. "What are you— "

"Just stay down, Pip, whatever happens," Scott scurried out of the grass towards the rocks near the roadrunner.

"I hate this plan…" Pip breathed and flattened himself to the ground, ears thrumming with a hundred heartbeats of the creatures around him, but none were as rapid as Scott's.

The roadrunner towered over the quail, nearly five times their size with a cruel, pointed beak and heavy, curved talons. The Gila was too large for a normal quail, and the roadrunner was too massive for any other creature to control. Every instinct told Scott to flee from this predator, despite its bound beak harness.

The roadrunner faced away from Scott, pecking gravel between its toes, making throaty grumbling sounds of annoyance, it was tied firmly to a spur of rock away from the other birds to prevent any rebellious hunting. Scott knew unleashing the roadrunner could cause a panic and drive the quail in all directions. Without the quail with their loaded packs, the Gila would run out of ammunition to lob at the village from above. Scott prayed he knew what he was doing.

Unfortunately, Scott was staring so intently at the roadrunner, worrying about alerting it that he missed his footing as he stepped up on the clay slab that he tripped and fell forward, catching himself on his hands. The roadrunner raised its head, translucent lid flickering and crest raising as Scott rolled behind a rock and pressed himself flat to the ground, heart smashing around his chest. He didn't dare look up until he heard the sound the roadrunner pecking at its talons again. He slid out from the rock and saw the reins tied around the spur of rock just above the roadrunner's head. With a jolt, he realized he'd have to climb on top of the rocks to reach it; he'd be in view of the bird and the lizards if they looked over. He was having second thoughts about the plan altogether when a new blast sounded overhead. They would be running out of explosives and coming back for more soon. It was now or never.

Scott climbed up the rock as quietly as he could and reached for the reins, he grabbed ahold of them just as the roadrunner whipped its head up and turned on him, crest raised in surprise. It made a muffled squawk through its bound beak and lunged for him, Scott ripped at the reins tied to the rock, falling in the process down at bird's feet. He scrambled up as the roadrunner stabbed down at him, only just missing him. Scott yanked at the loop of the reins and untethered the massive bird, then realized he was trapped, the bird kicked out at him, catching his vest on his talons and pulled him down. Scott had the breath slammed out of him and rolled to avoid the murderous beak, scurrying under a narrow cleft of rock but the shelter was shallow and he couldn't press back any further than he was.

Pip stiffened in his hiding spot, the roadrunner was grunting and making so much noise that the lizards had been alerted and were hurrying over. "Scott... C'mon get out of there!" he whispered urgently.

The roadrunner scraped at the cleft and jabbed its bound beak in after Scott, who flailed and kicked to drive it back. He heard the lizard's shouting as they rushed over and yelped as and beak lunged towards him. He froze for a moment in panic, he heard the boots scraping the stones as they lizards were nearly upon them. He thrust out his hands and grabbed the leather strap that was keeping the Runner's beak closed; with a mighty yank backwards he pulled the strap off just as the lizards jumped down beside them. Scott pressed back as the bird withdrew its head and screeched at the lizards. Scott saw two sets of boots from under the rock, one set ran off as another was lifted off the ground screaming. The roadrunner bashed the screeching lizard to death against the rock Scott was hiding under and gulped it down before taking off after the other with a screech.

Scott stayed frozen under the cleft, mortified until he heard wing beats and Pip landed on his rock.

"Scott?? *Scott!*" he whisper-called as Scott pushed himself out from under the rock shakily.

"I-I'm here!" he panted; Pip nearly tackled him with an embrace.

"Don't *ever* do that plan again!" He jabbed his vest with his thumb claw then peered over the rock to where the roadrunner was chasing the second lizard though the covey, scattering the quail in every direction.

"That should buy us some time." Scott scrambled over the rocks and saw a Gambel's quail tugged at his reins where he was tied near the cliff wall.

"C'mon!" Scott hurried over to the quail and patted its wing to calm it. "Help get those saddle bags!"

"What for?? I thought the whole point was to send the dynamite *away* from the canyons! Scott we need to get to the slingshots before those lizards take the bridge!" Pip said exasperatedly as Scott caught the reins of a passing quail, relieved it of its saddlebags and slapped it off again.

"Pip! They can't cross the bridge if it isn't there!" Scott panted, loading up the new bags on the Gambel's saddle.

Pip stared at him blankly. "We're goin' to need a lot more saddle bags…"

57

Mitch urged Cali to run faster as they reached the foot of the canyon where they had left that morning. There was no sign of Scott or Pip at all and he was starting to panic.

"Maybe they're already inside the village!" Bo called, looking up at the difficult climb ahead of them.

"Then let's hurry." Mitch snapped his reins and Cali stumbled up the first ledge and paused, unsure where to jump next. Bo and Cotton breezed past them.

"Follow me! Cotton's got a sixth sense for these sort of trails!" The black-and-white ranch hand spurred ahead and the others filed behind him as they made their way up the secret switchbacks.

An earth-trembling boom from over the canyon made the quail chitter nervously and Mitch knew Scott had been right. This was dynamite, the lizards had attacked it seemed almost the moment they had left that morning.

When they finally reached the top June found them the tunnel that led down to the bridge and took the lead.

"We're almost the—look out!" she pulled sharply on her reins and Bowie squawked to a halt as they almost slammed into First Tail and Second tail when they dove inside the tunnel. First Tail shouted something in *Yàkin* and looked at them in confusion. "What are you doing here!" he growled

"We're looking for Scott!" Mitch slid off the saddle and rushed over to them. "He came back to help you when he heard the explosions!"

"We haven't seen him!" Second panted. "But we're pinned down! We can't cross the bridge back to the village and there's a whole troop of lizards breathing down on us! We just dove in here for cover— Firsty!" Second shouted as a lizard leapt into the tunnel mouth from above. First Tail spun and thudded an arrow between his eyes, followed by a kick from Second that sent the body catapulting from the entrance into the dust.

Bo slid off Cotton and pulled out both his guns from their holsters. "How many out there?"

"I don't know." Second shook his head. "We heard them and tried to take out those slings but we couldn't get close enough. There's dozens though." Second refused to take his eyes off the entrance of the tunnel, fingers tightly curled around his spear.

"We have to keep them off the bridge." First Tail said grimly. "If they get across the village could be slaughtered. Our elders have refused to surrender again. We have to fight them off or die." He pulled out another arrow and nocked it.

"Let us help you." Mitch pulled his long gun from the saddle holster and crossed over. "Maybe we could buy you some cover across the bridge."

"This isn't your fight." First Tail frowned. "What are you expecting to gain by us winning?"

"I don't want to gain anything but my brother's safety, and he's come back to fight alongside you, you're his friends, that makes you my friends. I'll fight beside you, if you'll have me."

"All of us." June added. "Trust us First Tail, you need more friends than enemies."

First Tail looked sour but Second Tail clapped his shoulder and murmured something to him low in *Yàkin*. Finally First Tail looked up. "Fine, I trust you, don't make me regret it." He looked towards the entryway. "Now we have to figure a way to keep them off the bridge!"

Outside the tunnel, Delgado flattened himself against the rock face and started to reload his six shooters slowly.

"Pick up the pace!" the collared lizard hissed in his ear.

"They're stuck in that hole, they aren't coming out anytime soon. I have no hurry." Delgado frowned at him. "Unless you want to volunteer yourself to follow in Davis's footsteps go jump down there and try and get them out yourself. We all know well that worked out."

The collared lizard fumed and turned away from the remaining two posse members. "You know, I've had enough of your lip!" he pulled a rifle from another lizard's hand and pointed it at Delgado. "So why don't you get down there yourself!"

"I didn't know you wanted to die so badly today." Delgado's eyes slitted and he rested his hand on his gun as if he were going to draw it before he grabbed the barrel of the rifle and yanked it forward, pulling the larger lizard off balance. He kicked the collared lizard's backside and sent him falling down the rocks right into the mouth of the tunnel. BANG! A shot from the tunnel made the lizard fall still. Delgado arched a scaly brow. They had guns? They hadn't had guns when they chased them in there!

"You killed Chuck!" two lizards turned on Delgado.

"Are you blind! He was shot from down there!" Delgado pointed angrily.

"Was no—" the lizard yelped and fell back with an arrow in his chest, down below the Jumpers had burst out of the tunnel accompanied by the same mice Delgado had seen on the trail!

"Fall back!" Delgado ordered the remaining lizard.

"I ain't takin' order from y—" the other lizard fell to a shot in the leg from the black-and-white mouse's gun and an arrow grazed Delgado's side. The five-lined skink leapt back then turned and scaled the rock wall for a quick escape and the wounded lizard limped off, shouting for help.

"All clear up there?" First called to Second as his brother bounded up to check.

"For now but more are coming!" Second bounded back. "We need to move!"

"Should we just run across the bridge then?" Bo asked.

"No! We have to defend it on this side too or they could just charge through to the other side!" First Tail planted himself in front of the bridge entrance. "We have to hold them here! We need more Yàkin!"

"First Tail!" a voice from above caught them all off guard as Pip flew down. "Thank heavens you're both alive!" he turned and saw Mitch and the others and his joy faltered. "Er, yes, hello—"

"Where's my brother!" Mitch demanded.

"I'm right behind you!" Scott rode through the tunnel on top of a fully loaded down Gambel's quail. "Quick! Help me get these saddle bags off!" Scott slid off the bird and started pulling down the swollen pouches.

"Scott! What are you, what's in those?" Mitch ran over and opened a bag. "Dynamite?"

"Uh huh!" Scott pulled down another bag and Second rushed over and helped pull down the rest. "There's enough here to blow up Redcliff itself!" he dusted off his hands. He turned to First Tail. "First Tail! We need to destroy the bridge! I know it's important but if the get across— "

"Great!" Second Tail grinned. "First Tail they'll never get across without the bridge! We control the water below and they can't cross the divide without it! Its brilliant!"

"It's dangerous!" Mitch pointed out. "How are you going to blow up this entire bridge?"

"He doesn't have to blow it all! Just enough!" Pip interjected. "We'll blow it from both sides!"

"How do we get across again if we do blow up both sides?" June protested.

"Easy! You all cross to that side and I'll blow it from here and fly across again!" Pip gestured with his wing to the bridge. There was a loud BANG and Pip fell hard, clutching his shoulder. "Augh! Get down!" he gasped out. "They're back!"

Sol Diablo stomped down the rock path cocking his shot gun as his posse ran ahead. "And where's Delgado?" He grunted to the wounded lizard who had fetched him.

"He bolted sir! Like a coward…"

Sol Diablo snorted. "I'll deal with him myself. Kill the others, boys! Take that bridge!"

58

"Pip! Scott shouted as they all dove for cover. Pip was still stuck out in the open! And one stray shot into that pile of saddlebags could botch the whole plan! Scott was practically tackled to the ground behind a boulder by Mitch while June took cover just inside the tunnel so she could try and pick off the lizards around the corner.

Second Tail dashed over and snatched up Pip, "You've got to get across now!" He bounded inside the tunnel with Bo and Charlie over to June.

"That's not the plan!" June shot a lizard in the tail and he cried out, running back into cover.

"Plans change!" Second set Pip up on a quail. "Firsty and I will cover you, just get into the village, we'll just have to blow it from this side!"

"How will you get back??" Bo grabbed his wrist.

"We will figure something out just go! Take Scott and Mitch out there too!" Second turned to go but June pressed her rifle into his hand.

"Use this!" she blinked worriedly at him. "I'll see you on the other side!"

Second Tail nodded grimly and jumped outside beside First Tail and held up the gun, shooting at the lizards with June's too-small-of-a rifle.

"What's going on over there?" Carol asked Sam. "Hey! I see quail! Sam they're coming over the bridge!" Carol jumped up in the grasses. "Cover the quail coming in!" she repeated the shout in *Yàkin* and sent arrows sailing over the rider's heads into the rocks on the other side.

Sam bolted from cover to intercept Bo's quail when he saw Pip slung over it like the kill of a hunt. "Pip!" he picked him up and set him in the shade. "Pip!" he shook his good shoulder.

"I'm ok." Pip winced. "Ugh, the plan! No!" Pip looked across the bridge as Charlie raced across after Bo, followed by June.

First Tail spotted the Gila and trained an arrow on his heart then a gunshot sounded and he loosed it off course, killing the lizard to the Gila's right. First Tail fell back clutching his arm as blood seeped between his fingers then yelped as another shot clipped his leg.

"Firsty!" Second jumped in front of his brother and threw the empty rifle aside. He grabbed up First Tail's bow and pulled an arrow from the ground, sending it into the crowded nook the posse was hiding in.

"First Tail!" Scott pulled up on his reins as Mitch started across. "Mitch wait!" Scott pulled himself around on the bridge and raced back to the two sentries just as Second took a bullet to the side and yelped, dropping down behind their rock shield.

"Second!" First Tail gasped seeing him hit.

"First! Second! Come with us!" Mitch rode back with Scott.

"We have to hold this side!" First Tail grimaced and shook his head.

"Take my brother." Second pushed First Tail towards them.

"Second? No! You're hurt worse than I am! Take him!" First Tail demanded.

Second winced. "I'll hold this side, Firsty. You can still make it." He seized his brother's hand. "Live for both of us." He yanked First Tail's quiver off his shoulder and slung it over his own.

"What! NO!" First Tail ducked as a bullet cracked off a rock near their heads.

Second Tail stumbled upright and grabbed the kicking First Tail, slinging him over Mitch's quail. "Go!" Second slapped the bird's wing and sent the frightened hen running across the bridge.

"Run Scott!" Second stood and loosed more arrows into the posse, yelping as another shot hit him in the leg.

Scott's bird fought to flee but Scott knew Second couldn't hold them all by himself! He looked to the dynamite. If Second fell there would be no one to set it off… "Hold them, Second! I'll take care of the bridge!" Scott leapt off his bird and ran to the bridge, grabbing the bags and shaking their contents across the top of the stone bridge.

"Go back!" First Tail thrashed off Mitch's quail on the other side and crashed to the ground. Carol rushed to his aid. "Second is over there!" First's eyes were wide as he stared across the divide, watching his brother stumble as he was hit again. "SECOND!"

Mitch twisted around. "Where's… SCOTT!"

Sam looked up to see Scott on the far side of the bridge laying out bundles. "What's he…" he froze. "He'll never make it across! Scott no!"

The Gila hissed angrily at his frightened posse as they crowded back. "You're gonna take all day about it! It's just one Jumper! Kill it!"

"He's not going down!" a horned lizard stammered.

"And why have the explosives stopped falling!" Sol Diablo glared at the cliffs then saw another lizard running over to them.

"Sir! Something's happened to the covey guards! And the quail are scattered! We have no ammo and that roadrunner of yours is running amok!"

"WHAT!" The Gila snarled before grabbing the unlucky lizard and hurling him, screaming, over the cliff in frustration. "Get out of the way! I'm killing that rat myself!" Sol Diablo barreled down the rocky ledge down towards Second Tail.

"Light it and run, Scott!" Second shouted over his shoulder as Scott emptied the last bundle.

Scott's heart hammered as he searched his pockets. "I have no matches!" he shouted, grabbing at his vest. "Second! Look out!" he pointed as Sol Diablo crashed down in front of the Jumper. Second stumbled back and shot an arrow into the Gila's chest but this just enraged the thick-hided lizard further. He swatted Second with a massive backhand, throwing him to the ground and knocking his bow aside. Second pulled two arrows from his quiver as the Gila stormed over and he stabbed them both through the roof of his boot into his foot. The Gila howled and jumped back to rip out the spines as Second rolled and grabbed ahold of his spear, squaring off with a wince as he stood in front of the bridge.

Scott almost let himself get distracted by the fight and snapped himself out of his. Fire! He needed matches!

"Scott!" Second shouted, digging into his ragged pant pocket and throwing him a pouch. Scott dove and caught it as Second went back to fending off the massive Gila. He shook the pouch into his hands, two rocks fell into his palm. Fire starters! He scrambled to the explosives and struck the rocks together near the fuse lines.

"Come on!" he begged. "Hurry!" he struck the rocks with a flash of sparks several time until finally the fuse lines held a tiny glow, then it died. He needed tinder! He heard a gasp and turned to see the Gila had thrown Second down and had him crushed under his massive boot. Second struggled to move but he was stuck fast. Scott was out of time. He jumped up and looked around. He spotted his brother across the divide. "MITCH!" he cupped his hands around his mouth. "SHOOT IT!"

"What!" The Gila looked up and spotted Scott on the bridge, then he saw the dynamite. "NO!"

First Tail saw his brother trapped and heard Scott's cries. "Shoot the dynamite! Shoot it now!" he shouted at the mice.

Mitch held up his rifle and swallowed hard before squeezing the trigger.

Scott dove behind the rocks but the explosion still threw him down hard. It also blasted half the lizard posse off the ledge into the river far below. The blast threw the Gila back and sent up so much dust that Scott couldn't see the rocks in front of him. He heard the thunderous splashes far below, chunks of the enormous stone bridge falling away. He coughed and struggled to rise to his feet and look over the rocks.

Second groaned and stumbled to his hands and looked towards the bridge, all he saw was dust, but as it started to clear he saw a gap that no lizard could ever clear. He grinned and looked around when a huge scaly hand grabbed him from behind and hauled him off the ground. The Gila bellowed in rage looking at the destroyed bridge then glared at Second Tail as he thrashed weakly in his grip.

"You'll pay for *that* with your miserable life!" The Gila snarled. Second slammed his spear into the Gila's thigh and the Gila roared before grabbing the Jumper in his venomous jaws, shaking him like a rag doll and throwing him into the rocks. He stood, heaving in rage before turning to his posse, only a fraction of them were still standing. "Move out! Find another way across!" he snarled, ripping the spear from his leg with a wince and snapping it in two over his knee. He trudged through the dust after his forces.

"Second Tail!" Scott breathed, jumping over the rocks and rushing towards the Jumper's broken body. He rolled him over, coughing in the dust. Second winced and looked up at him, the huge circular bite mark was crushed around his belly and chest, the fur was matted and red with blood.

"Scott." He breathed. "We did it." He winced.

"No, no it's not over! Scott shrugged out of his vest and pressed it against his wounds even though he could see the venom affecting Second already, hitching his breath, taking him down from the inside. He was dying.

"Scott. You came back for us." Second's voice was fading. "Thank you… keep protecting us. My brother… your brother." He winced hard, tears showing in his eyes. "You should go. Go on, you have to stop them."

Scott felt like there were flames and claws in his throat. He grabbed Second's hand, feeling him squeeze back in return.

"I won't leave you." He promised. "I'll stay with you just hold on, Second!"

Second smiled weakly at him then his eyes flickered and closed, his body went still.

Scott stared at him in disbelief. "No… no… no." he felt Second's hand go slack in his and he hugged the Jumper close, doubling over him in grief.

59

Across the divide, the dust was starting to settle. First Tail hobbled out onto the remaining part of the bridge with Carol as a support. "SECOND!" he called. "SECOND! ANSWER!" he squinted seeing the dust fall away, he saw Scott kneeling above something. "Second?" he breathed. Sam and Mitch ran up beside them as Scott looked their way across the divide and slowly shook his head.

"No." Firsty's eyes welled. "No… NO!" he fell to his knees. "NO! Second! No!" Carol dropped to her knee beside him and wrapped her arms around him, her own tears smudging her red face paint.

Sam shook his head in disbelief then saw the gap between the two bridge halves. He could get Scott across with a rope. "Scott!" he called. "Just stay there! I'll get you across!"

Scott barely heard Sam as he rested Second Tail's head down gently and stood up. He looked at his hands and wiped his blood off on his chaps. He looked across the divide and saw First Tail, he could hear his cries from around the stone walls. He swallowed the burning lump in his throat and looked down seeing the spear the Gila had snapped. The Gila. Up until this moment Scott didn't think there was a creature on earth he could hate more than his kidnapper, Delgado, but that hate was a dull annoyance compared to the rage that coursed through him now. The Gila was behind it all. The Yàkin disappearances, the death of Sam's mother, his abduction, his brother's near-death, and now Second Tail. Scott had been trying to get away from him this whole time but now he knew he couldn't do that anymore. He couldn't just run from the Gila and expect him to stop all this wickedness. To stop the deaths he had to stop the Gila himself. He opened his eyes, and turned to the snapped spear and rushed over, grabbing the tipped end, just his size now. He whistled and the Gambel's quail ran over from the tunnel.

"What is he doing?" June asked Mitch, who came up to her side and squinted seeing Scott mount up and start riding down the trail after the Gila. "Scott! No!" his eyes bulged. "He's gonna get himself killed!"

Sam looked up from where he had been getting rope from Charlie and saw him ride off. "Scott!" he threw the rope aside and slung his bow around his shoulder. "Move!" he told June and Mitch as he ran to the edge of the bridge and checked the gap between the half arch and the other side. He turned and ran back towards the village.

"Sam! You'll never make that!" Pip shouted. It was almost as long at the jump he failed when he and Scott fell into the river!

"Then I'll die trying!" Sam called and sprinted down the path and sprang off the bridge, sailing into the air.

Sol Diablo reached the top of the rise where the slings had been stationed and looked around in shock, the place was deserted, even the little fire they had been using to light the dynamite bundles was starting to smoke out. "Where are those cowards!" he seethed. An explosion immediately behind him sent half his remaining posse into the river with a screech.

"They quit." Delgado called down, standing on the rock above Sol Diablo's head. "And so do I." He glared down at the remaining five posse members as if daring them to make a move.

"Kill him!" Sol Diablo snarled, Delgado withdrew from sight amidst the chorus of gunfire.

"NO! No you idiots! I'll kill him myself! Get out of my way! Get out of my sight!" he bared his teeth and stumbled up the path after the skink. Delgado cut across the open and took three shots to the posse, winging two and making them withdraw.

"Should we help??" A horned lizard asked.

"Let 'em kill each other for all I care! I'm getting out of here!" a whiptail turned and ran down the rocks, followed by another.

Sol Diablo pulled his second huge Gila-sized pistol from its holster and shot into the brush after Delgado.

"I'LL REAM YOU DRY!" he bellowed, stomping into the thick, dry grass. He pushed through the twigs but they kept snapping back in his face. Furious, he stomped out and grabbed a fistful of smoldering fire wood. "I'll burn you out you yellow-streaked mite!" he blew onto the embers and tossed them into the grass. "I'll burn this whole place around you!" he threw chunks of smoking wood into the grass all around the cliff edge.

Delgado watched him from his hiding place. The Gila was slipping; his loss of the bridge and his crew was making him angry and reckless. It could be used to his advantage but he had to be careful. Already the grasses to his left and right were crackling to life; the flames crawled through the grass, sending up black smoke. The dry vegetation was as good as paper against the fire. Delgado slunk closer to the rocks for cover as the flames started to circle back, closing them both into a ring.

"COME OUT AND FIGHT YOU WORM!" Sol Diablo shot into the brush twice more when he heard a quail snort and saw a mouse ride up above him on the rocks.

"Look who's here." Sol Diablo sneered, spinning the chamber of his pistol agitatedly. "Looking for me?" he fired a shot and it whistled past Scott's face but Scott kicked at his bird and the quail leapt off the rock straight onto the Gila himself, bowling him down, scratching and pecking. The Gila roared and bodily threw the bird off but Scott was on his back, clinging tight and stabbing at him with Second's spear tip.

"And I found you!" he shouted, holding on as the Gila tried to reach around and pull him off. He slipped and the Gila grabbed his ankle, holding him upside down in front of his face.

"I don't need guns!" He hissed, throwing his pistol aside. "To bite you in half!" A hissing sound filled the air and an arrow slammed into the Gila's shoulder, making him screech and drop the mouse.

Scott landed hard and scuffled backwards, looking up he saw a hazy Jumper shape through the smoke.

"Run Scott!" Sam jumped down in front of him, shrieking a Yàkin war cry. He sent two more arrows into the angry lizard's chest but the Gila was just too massive to go down.

"Sam! Look out!" Scott stumbled to his feet seeing Delgado slither out of hiding.

Sam turned and trained an arrow on the skink but the Gila reached out and slashed him aside with a heavily clawed hand. Sam was swept off his feet and fell hard, rolling towards the edge.

"Sam!" Scott dove forward and slid on his stomach in the dust and grabbed Sam's sleeve as his lower half plunged over the side. Sam grabbed at the ground and held on, kicking at the rock face to try and climb up.

The Gila sneered and stomped over, grabbing up the spear tip. "Looking for this!" he raised it to slam it between Scott's shoulders when he went ridged and cried out, he spun to reveal Delgado clinging to his back, his knife buried to the hilt in the back of his neck. The Gila stumbled and fell to the edge, flailing for balance. Delgado sprang off his back onto solid ground but the Gila screamed in rage and grabbed his brilliant blue tail jerking him off his feet as he plunged over the edge. Delgado went over and grabbed onto the tangle of roots from the burning brush above and fought to hold on as the heavy Gila scrabbled at the rocks below, a tight grip on his tail.

"If I go down! I'm taking you with me!" the Gila's eyes burned with rage, reflecting the flames that crackled above them.

Delgado's claws were scraping from the strain of holding them both up. "Not *all* of me!" he gasped out and gave his body a sharp wrench.

The Gila's mouth gaped as he fell backwards into space, screaming and shaking Delgado's wriggling severed tail in his hand as he fell down the canyon and landing with a sickly thud on the river rocks below.

Scott stared wide-eyed over the ledge and saw Delgado climbing up. "Hold on Sam!" he gasped and struggled up, he rushed over and grabbed the Gila's huge pistol and tried to heave it with both hands. Delgado climbed back over the edge and dusted himself off before hearing a grunt and a click as Scott managed to cock the hammer back on the gun.

"Get back!" he demanded, arms and legs shaking from holding up a gun the size of a cannon compared to himself.

Delgado panted and looked over the edge then back and Scott. He made no move to draw his guns, and seemed mildly impressed that a mouse could even lift a gun that size. He raised his head and gave Scott a small nod, tipping his hat.

"Scott!" Sam strained, still dangling over the edge. Scott looked over at Sam but when he looked up again Delgado was gone. He looked around but the skink had just… disappeared. He dropped the gun and ran over to Sam, pulling him up and over the edge.

"You're hurt." Scott coughed through the smoke, seeing the claw marks that had shredded Sam's shirt with the Gila swiped him.

"I'm fine." Sam winced. "Come on, this fire's spreading, we gotta get out of here." Sam coughed hard into his arm as the smoke grew thicker, the flames were now too high for a Jumper to clear, and Sam was in no shape to attempt either.

Scott looked around and saw the Gambel's quail still crouched by the rocks looking frightened and singed.

"Come on!" Scott helped Sam up and they hobbled over to the bird.

"Help me get this saddle off!" Scott tugged at the straps.

"Don't you need it to ride? Scott this bird'll never get through these flames just leave it!" Sam coughed as he pulled the saddle off and Scott started taking apart the wingstrap harness.

"We're not going through the fire!" Scott coughed hoarsely, feeling dizzy. He yelped as a floating bit of grass ember landed on his shoulder. "We're going over the edge!" he pointed towards the cliff and down at Skytown itself.

"You're crazy!" Sam hacked out.

"I know!" Scott wretched and grabbed onto the fussy bird as it ruffled its ragged, un-trimmed wings. "But bandits don't groom their quail regularly enough! It can fly!" he pointed at its long, scruffy feathers.

"I don't think it's a good idea!" Sam jumped to avoid a burst of flame that singed his tail tuft. He yelped and stamped it out with his foot.

"You got a better plan!?" Scott gestured to the flames around them and Sam winced before helping Scott on the bird's back and he clambered on behind him.

"Hold on!" Scott snapped the reins and urged the bird towards the edge but the frightened quail just danced along the edge.

"Move! Come on! Fly, bird! *Fly*!" Scott pushed his legs around the bird's wings and wrapped them around its neck. "FLY!" he shouted just as the flames rose behind them in a blazing gust. The quail shrieked and exploded over the edge of the cliff with furious flapping wings and singed feathers.

"How do you control this thing!" Sam grabbed Scott's shirt as he slipped off the back. "I'm falling off!"

"Hold on tight! I'm trying to land!" Scott and the bird shot towards Skytown in an uncontrolled, smoking descent.

"Watch out for the cactus!" Sam shouted as the quail nearly flew headfirst into a prickly arm. The bird squawked and veered left, spinning down towards the ground.

"The ropes!" Scott shouted but the quail flew right into them and flipped upside down, falling towards the ground doubly fast.

"LOOK OUT!" Sam and Scott shouted at the Yàkin gathered below as the ground rushed to meet them. Then everything went black.

60

Scott wasn't sure how much time had passed since the crash. He vaguely remembered being woken by thunderstorms once or twice, but never long enough to wake completely, and both times it had been at night, the same night? Two different nights? He couldn't tell. But today he finally felt a stir to wake. He winced and sat up, he was inside the Baranov's cactus, asleep on one of the little floor cots and dressed in hide clothing, Yàkin clothing. He looked to the side and saw his brother asleep in a chair with June next to him, slumped against one another for support. Both looked utterly exhausted. Scott rubbed his pounding head heard voices down the steps that led to the village. He pushed the blankets off his bunk and tip-toed past his brother and June. They looked like they could use the rest. He made his way downstairs and walked headlong into Bo.

"Hey! You're awake!" Bo grinned and wrapped him up in an embrace, lifting him off the steps.

"Oomf! Nice to see you too?" Scott gasped as he was set down, he grinned as Charlie slapped Bo's shoulder with the back of his good hand and gestured pointedly at Scott.

"What? I *was* being gentle with him! I'm just happy to see him! So are you so don't keep trying to suppress it, mister." Bo smirked.

Charlie sighed then nodded to Scott and gave him a pat on his shoulder.

"I'm glad you're both ok... how long was I out?" Scott asked.

"About four days." Bo shrugged. "I gotta tell you, seeing you and Sam coming flying out of the sky on a flaming quail. Well! Let's just say that was some legendary stuff right there!"

"The quail was on fire??" Scott startled. "I… I didn't know. No wonder it couldn't rudder, is… is the bird—?" he winced. The bird wasn't his but he'd grown a little attached to it after all this.

"It's alright, a little scuffed up, a dinged wing, nothing a couple of good quail ranchers couldn't solve."

"I'll let you know when I find some." Scott teased then his face blanched. "Sam! Where is he? Is he alright??" Scott felt his heart start hammering painfully.

"Hold your quail! He's ok." Bo grinned. "Come on outside." He gestured him out into the sun and Scott swallowed before following him into the light.

All around the village was in various states of repair, but the Yàkin were smiling and working hard to patch holes in cactus walls or rebuild platforms.

"Forgot you'd been out so long, there's someone here I know wants to see you." Bo lead Scott over to the lower market platform and climbed up a crudely made ladder. "They made this for us." Bo smirked. "They were laughing the whole time, like it's the most hilarious thing in the world that we can't jump!"

Scott tried to look past Bo. "Where are we going? Who wanted to see me?" Scott figured the elders would be furious with him for returning… let alone blowing up their bridge. What was going on?

"You'll see." Bo helped him up onto the platform. "Hey Buck! Sir! He's awake!"

"Buck??" Scott's jaw dropped. "My *Pa's* here??" he saw him across the platform, clear as day! Talking to Wind's Howl of all critters! Buck turned and looked over and his expression changed. Buck ran over to his son paused just in front of him.

"You're awake…"

"I… I yeah I—" Scott's air was cut off as his father embraced him. "I thought I lost you, twice." He growled weakly into Scott's shoulder. "You're safe…" he let go.

"I…" Scott was too stunned to form proper words. "I- you… how did you *find* me??" he blustered.

"I've been on your trail since Dennis at the post told me what happened. I got lost for a ways, Ran into some stuffy sheriff in a dollhouse town, then three days ago I ran into some trashy mice at an ol' dump of a joint. They thought they'd be funny with me so after I cleaned a few of their clocks they pointed me in the right direction. Then two days back who should I run into, but Jared." He pointed across the platform where Jared was sitting and eating some roast cricket by himself. The dark ranch hand stood and crossed over to Buck's side.

"Jared told me everything and led me here." Buck smirked. "So of course I return to here you've been through some hellish ordeal and nearly got yourself killed! They weren't sure you'd ever wake up!"

Scott winced. "Yeah… sorry." He looked down.

"Why?" Buck smirked. "When I'm so proud of you."

Scott looked up and blinked in surprise, he saw Wind's Howl appear at Buck's shoulder and beam down at him, his arm in a sling. "And he's not the only one. The Yàkin are blessed to have you and your friends as our allies."

Scott smiled weakly. "I…" he trailed then yelped as something shoved him from behind playfully.

"Coulda woken me up you know!" Mitch grinned at him, giving him a firm hug. "I wake and you're just gone? Way to give me a heart attack! Though these days that seems to be your profession."

"Calm down, he's been out of it for a while." June pushed Mitch's shoulder. "And he's probably starving."

"More thirsty than anything." Scott admitted.

"Here." Bo handed him a water skin and with a pained jolt, Scott recognized it was Second Tail's. His death bit into him anew when he took hold of it, the smile faded from his face. "Where's First Tail?" he asked quietly.

Wind's Howl sighed. "He and the other Yàkin who lost loved ones in the attack held their ceremonies two days ago. He's been sitting vigil on our side of the bridge for some time now. You can find him there."

Scott swallowed hard and took a guilty sip from the water skin.

Mitch frowned in concern. "Scott, his death wasn't your fault. I know it ended terribly, but Second Tail knew exactly what he was doing."

"Pa?" Scott looked up. "I'll be back, I just have to talk to him."

Scott wanted to find Sam and Pip more than anything, but he couldn't run from First Tail forever. First Tail had given Scott and the other settlers his trust and minutes later his brother was killed. He wouldn't blame the battle-scarred sentry if he hated him.

He spotted First Tail sitting at the entrance to the broken bridge, staring out over the divide with a cloak draped around him. His ragged ear perked when Scott neared.

"First Tail?" he spoke quietly. When he didn't respond he stepped gingerly closer to him, and saw his sunken eyes were staring wistfully out into the void. Scott sat down beside him. "First Tail... about Second's death. I never wanted it to happen. I just... I just wish I could have done something! I was right there and I just—"

"Stop." First Tail held up his hand and looked over. "I don't blame you for my brother's death." He said quietly. "Second Tail knew I would have stayed behind too, he wanted me to live, so he sent me away. He didn't want to see more deaths of those he cared about."

"But still." Scott rubbed his eyes. "I should have done something... you... *trusted* us to help, and I let you down."

"I never said that." First Tail shook his head. "I will never forgive the Gila for killing my brother." His dull eyes flashed with fire. "But you? I don't blame you, because ...it's not your fault. And Second saw the good in you before I did. You could have come back to safety after the dust cleared. We could have holed up in here and waited out the Gila for months. But you didn't do that, you went after him Scott. You went to stop him. I misjudged you, but Second saw who you were right away." First Tail looked down at his palm at the green opal hoop earring that Second used to wear in his ear. He winced and closed his fingers around it tightly.

Scott swallowed the lump in his throat; he couldn't believe that First Tail didn't hate him. He looked over at his ruffled headfur and sunken eyes. "Are you ok?" he asked gently.

First Tail closed his eyes and for a moment there was only the shush of the river far below and the wind against the canyon rock. "No." he said at long last. "But I will be." He stood up and picked up a forked stick he was using as a crutch for his injured leg. He reached over and rested a hand briefly on Scott's shoulder, then turned and limped back towards the village.

That night, Skytown threw a magnificent feast up on the lower platform. The fishers had caught and smoked a huge fish over a spit and the gatherers made a great pot of stew, spicy and red with beans, wild onions, peppers and corn. There were little loaves of seed bread everywhere and all the Yàkin kept asking Scott and Sam to retell the tale the Gila's death so often that pretty soon the children were interrupting and telling the story themselves. Scott never told the part about Delgado's final nod, or his disappearance, as far as he knew Delgado jumped over the edge into the river, he'd never have survived that fall, or the fire.

Sam and the Yàkin also pestered Buck and Mitch and the other ranch hands to tell their harrowing journey over and over. They especially loved when June knocked out all the bandits by herself and when Mitch killed the roadrunner. Eventually, the wine and partying caused them all to get drowsy and the festivities ended just before sunrise, even if some of the younger Yàkin continued to bounce through the village in a hyper craze, their facial fur stained with juice and sticky with honey-sweets.

The next day was bittersweet. Buck decided they had been gone from home long enough, and although Alice's health was improving when they had returned from Monty, he still didn't want to leave her all alone.

Scott brushed the mud and dust off his Gambel's quail with a smooth feather brush, smirking when the quail churred happily. "Guess your last owner didn't brush you down a lot." He teased.

"You come up with a decent name for that Gambel's yet or are you going to keep calling him 'Bird?'" Mitch asked as he cinched Cali's saddle bags on tight, they bulged with seed bread, dried fish, cactus fruit and other goodies the Yàkin were giving them for the journey home.

"Well I offered my suggestion." Sam walked over and ruffled the bird's headfeathers.

"Yeah, and I thought it was corny." Scott grinned.

"What was it?" Mitch asked.

"*Smoky.*" Scott and Sam said in unison.

"Smoky's perfect!" Mitch laughed. "Especially from his singed-feathers smell." He snorted.

"Hey! I clipped out all the singed ones." Scott rolled his eyes. "Ok fine, Smoky it is." He laughed As Smoky ruffled his feathers and a puff of ash clouded the area.

"Sure you clipped them all." Mitch teased. "I'll show you how to do it better when we get home."

"I wish you didn't have to go." Sonya and Carol walked over. "We know it's not forever though."

"Exactly, I'll visit and Pa's already said if you came to our ranch he'd keep you safe." Scott encouraged.

Carol looked wary. "Maybe we'll meet in between."

"Sure." Scott agreed. "Come to see us off?" he asked Sonya.

"Almost, Pip and Owl Fear are down at the Painted Wall, they have a surprise for you, Bo, Charlie, Mr. Buck and June are down there already."

"A surprise?" Scott left Smoky with Cali and headed after the ladies down the path to the painted wall.

"Ooh just wait!" Pip hobbled over with his bandaged wing. "It's not quite ready!"

"It's fine!" Owl Fear snorted. "That bat is a perfectionist. He can see it as its being painted!" Owl Fear called from the rocks.

Scott gasped as he came in. "Hey! Sam that's... that us!" he pointed to the wall. "You documented our whole journey?" He saw the painting of Morgan, the tunnels, the fall into the river, the meeting at the Crest, the goodbye and return.

"Is that?" he pointed to a bird made of flames with lines of smoke trailing off its feathers. Atop its back were a small dark mouse and a white painted Jumper. "That us!"

"And Smoky!" Sonya laughed.

"Smoky? Fitting." Owl Fear climbed down with Wind's Howl and Carol's help.

"For what?" Scott asked.

"For this, because you have shown yourself a true friend to the Yàkin people, Scott Thorn and Pip Jarlath O'Ryan, The elders and I have decided to make you an honorary Yàkin yourself." She smiled wryly. "As you may have been told by Sam, a Yàkin's name is determined by an event that occurs the day they were born. Your name, occurs, on the day you returned." She pulled a little cloth bundle from the satchel and unfolded it to reveal a circle of orange-yellow flecked opal. "To your Yàkin family, you name has been declared Smoke Rider.

Owl Fear nodded and turned to Buck and the others. "I hope you all have a safe journey home, Quiet One." She passed Charlie, "Chatter Mouth." She smirked to Bo, June snorted beside him. "Bright Eyes." She passed June to Mitch, "Stone Will." She looked to Jared who looked away guiltily. He didn't help fight, he didn't think he would get Yàkin recognition, but to his surprise she paused by him. "And Dark Cloud."

Carol and Sonya passed them each their own opal stones and stepped back.

"You are now all, honorary citizens of Skytown. Please, protect our home as if it were your own, and don't tell our whereabouts to others."

"We won't." Scott nodded. "We promise."

It was a bit tricky to cross the make-shift bridge between the two arches with the quail but with enough ropes and planks they made a decent bridge for them to hurry across.

"Pip, we never heard your name." Scott asked as they waited on the far side of the bridge.

"Oh, they gave it to me already." Pip grinned a pointy-toothed smile. "You were out cold."

"Well? What is it?" Scott pressed.

"Trusted Wings." He said proudly, thumbing a tiny green opal bead around his neck. "I'm relieved it wasn't Moon Ears!" he laughed with Scott as the last quail crossed.

"You have a safe journey home." Carol hugged Scott tight. "You come back and see us soon!"

"I will, I promise." Scott let go as the others said their goodbyes. He was wrapped up in Pip's free wing and he grinned, hugging the bat back. "Keep an eye on everyone, and fly over to Redcliff as soon as you can!" he grinned. "My Pa left some directions for you to follow with the Baranov's."

"You can bet I will!" Pip let go. "I'll miss you though."

"I'll miss you too." Scott spotted Sam back by the bridge and crossed over.

"Hard to believe you're leaving again." Sam smiled weakly.

"Yeah, but at least it's on good terms this time." Scott nodded. "And I'll come back. You couldn't keep me away from here." He gestured to the village across the divide.

"Yeah." Sam looked down a moment. "Scott, about before, I never meant to say that before you left-"

"I get it, it's ok." Scott shook his head. "You were upset."

"I didn't want you to go." Sam finished. "You're like a brother to me, and when your own brother came back it felt like he was stealing you away, and you'd never want to come back." Sam admitted.

Scott grinned. "Sam, you'll always be my brother too." He held out his hand. "And I'll always come back for you."

Sam smiled and shook his hand, then pulled him up on the rock so they could embrace properly.

Scott let go and stepped back, clambering up into Smoky's saddle.

"Ready to go?" Buck grunted to them.

"Ready as I'll ever be." Scott nodded.

"Let's go home." June smiled at Mitch.

"Yeah." Scott tugged his hat more securely down on his head. "Home." He gave Skytown one last look then nudged Smoky down the ridge after the others. Ready to begin the journey back to the Thorn Ranch.

Christine Ridgway has been drawing pictures and writing stories since she could hold a pencil. She loves stories about animals and enjoys watching westerns with her dad. Ten years ago, she combined her love of animals and westerns into a sketch on a scrap of paper of a cowboy mouse and a lizard, and she has been building and expanding the world of Skytown ever since.

Christine lives in the beautiful Pacific Northwest and enjoys spending time outdoors skiing, hiking, and climbing up old fire watch towers. Indoors, she's an author and a digital artist who works on comics and illustrations both in traditional and digital medias.

Examples of Christine's art can be found at christineridgway.carbonmade.com

CPSIA information can be obtained
at www.ICGtesting.com
Printed in the USA
BVHW041729060821
613849BV00017B/465